I0694704

Songs of War

Songs of War
A Dance of Darkness

Skye Westdijk

First published in 2019 by Libra Confictura

ISBN: 978-9-08-300710-6

Printed and bound by Ingramspark

Cover made by Cakamura Designs

3d print

So that all our dreams may come true.

The Great Sea
The Maw
Cisla Imen
White Spine
Anndar
Temple of Light
Academy of Nirs Imali
Telryn
The Kiran
The Plains
The Dawn
Irs Ia
Emerald Woods
Arqa
Mir Mithan
Silver Temple
The Watched Seas
The Asal
Murra
Ravens Pass
Xisk
Distrum
Rindun
Scorching Marshes
The High Seat
Frostrin
Uanor
Mir Ahak
Frostpeak
The Moving Desert
The Vein
Cold Bay
Ehura
Brach Ku
Durgash
Sars
The Vein
Green Hills
Brahkar
Red Mountains
Shagar
Fragar's Bay
Dead Strait
Acus
Rudn nu
Dark Bay
Soul Perils

Prologue

Blood had never been so dark.

Blood of light, drawn by shadows.

It dripped from skin and stone, no longer kept by flesh and veins. From the tips of her fingers it fell to the ground, joining the blood of her children, who lay scattered across the throne room. White creatures, children of light, last of their kind, who had given their lives to protect their creator. Yet it had not been enough.

The floor was a shadowed crimson that hid the white marble below. The light of the rising sun reflected on it, casting a scarlet rainbow upon the lifeless faces.

Above them towered the throne, the Lady of Light seated upon it, her empty eyes watching the abyss forever.

Only moments ago, she had realized she had failed her people as she watched the shadows crawl into the room, ending the lives of her children.

Only moments ago, she had surrendered to death once again.

Only moments ago, her last breath had left her lips. Now she sat on her throne like a statue, her crown circling on the ground, catching the light that fell through the high windows and radiating it in a dazzling display before it finally stopped moving and the sound faded, so only the sound of dripping blood was left.

Only she had seen the eyes of her murderer, only she had known who would come from the depths of the shadows.

Chapter 1
Naka

A tiny snowflake slowly drifted down through the cold and icy air and landed peacefully in a sea of crimson. The empty eyes of the dead stared at it as it melted away in the warmth of the blood, while black leather boots lightly stepped through it.

"Please, I beg you, I will never speak of this, I will run and never come back. I promise! I promise!" one man cried with a trembling voice. He sat on his knees between his fallen brothers and sisters, all covered in blood. The figure stopped in front of him and remained silent before it softly said, "Don't beg, it makes you weak."

As soon as the man looked up to see the face his throat was slit by her spear, and he fell to the ground, joining the other corpses. The figure took off her hood and revealed the face of a woman, an Ilunari. Her eyes a bright violet, hair as black as a raven's feathers falling down to her knees, her skin as pale as the snow around her. It couldn't be said how old she was, she looked like she had just matured but Ilunari were blessed with eternal youth so it was easy to be deceived.

She looked around, trying to find her bag that she had dropped when she was attacked. Earlier that day she had gone to a nearby trading village, Grun'Udul, to trade the few things she collected during her hunts that week. It wasn't much and perhaps she was better off keeping it for herself but she liked to eat something other than her everyday boar and winterroot. Spring was around the corner anyway so life would return to the woods as soon as the snow had fully melted.

Silence surrounded her, the snow absorbing any sound, as she searched for her bag and walked home. She knew she would have to come back to this place to burn the corpses, she didn't want to draw any predators this close to her home. After a few moments she found her bag, covered in snow and blood, and walked back home.

Her thoughts ran wild, she had heard rumors in the village that could change everything. Traders had spoken of the death of Varne, the king of the Shadow Lands, and of his son Xere, who was crowned the new king on the same day. King Egil, ruler of the Shining Lands had sent word out to all the races of the Shining

Lands that this would change the course of the war. Now that a new king sat upon the Throne of Darkness, Egìl would gather their forces and launch a new attack to finally bring an end to the War of Shattered Light. He had comforted his people with the promise that they were far stronger and more experienced than this boy king, seemingly forgetting that Xere was older than the war itself, an Ilunari born centuries before the war started, and thus had walked this world far longer than Egìl. Egìl claimed to have been granted immortality until he had avenged Nuana, Guardian of Light. He had been the one to find her corpse after she was murdered, ascending from human king to King of the Shining Lands within a moment. The Shining Lands had rallied behind him, sending their armies toward the border, just in time to receive the armies of the Shadow Lands. For years it had been a bloodbath, the war had been back and forth, taking a toll on both Lands, but eventually it settled. War became occasional battles to defend the border and was more of a tension between the Lands than anything, but now with king Varne dead the War of Shattered Light would bloom again.

A cold and towering wall stood before her. With her hand on the stone she walked along the rock, found the entrance and slipped inside. Almost immediately she came back outside, now without the bag, angry at herself for not immediately cleaning up the bodies.

Night had fallen over the dark, winter woods and she took a different path than the one she took on the way home, wary of any danger that might have lurked in the shadows. Her steps were quick and silent, like the wind and shadows of the forest. When she arrived at the bloodbath, she crouched toward some half-dead bushes on the side. Crows were flocking around the bodies and some lunar moths fluttered above the blood. She always loved those moths, they fascinated her in some way. They were rare and lived only in these forests. Their wings were a pale white, almost glowing in the darkness of night. They looked stunningly beautiful yet lived by drinking the blood of the dead. One never saw them anywhere but near fresh blood. She did not see any signs of danger and sighed when she realized the task ahead. She was tired but it had to be done. There were ten bodies which meant a big pile of wood. Not too far away a tree had fallen down during the harsh winter. It would be perfect to build a pile so she brought its wood to the bodies. It was heavy work but she didn't stop until she had built a pyre with the trees and bushes. She had built a little staircase to be able to lift the bodies upon the pyre. After looting the bodies, she removed their armor to sell or salvage and hid everything useful in a nearby bush. When she searched the young man who had begged her for mercy she found a letter. It was sealed with the royal seal of the Shadow Lands so she assumed it was sent by King Xere. The seal was an eight-pointed star within a woven circle made out of black wax. She put it away quickly and removed his armor. After she had put all the bodies on a pile and lit the pyre, she watched the flames. The fire grew and grew, consuming the flesh of the dead as it spread the horrid stench of burning flesh. With a sigh her hand reached into her coat and found the letter. She stared at the seal a little while, doubting if she would break it, not sure if she wanted to know what it said. A quick snap and the seal was broken. She could still throw it in the fire, never read it, be done with it. But something inside of her had hope, hope that she would finally be done hiding, waiting until she could complete the task she was given so long ago. She closed her eyes and sighed as she took a deep breath, readying herself to read the letter. The crackling of the fire was the only thing that broke the silence as she read it.

Dear Naka,
Come back to the Shadow Lands.
He is dead, but I assume you have already heard the news. I now sit upon the Throne of Darkness and I am no longer subject to his ways. We are preparing for war, gathering whatever forces we have left to fight what I hope to be the final battle. The Shadow Lands need you now more than ever, I need you. It is no secret that you were send away all those years ago and that you will hide from the world until you complete the task that was given you, I simply ask you to hide here, in the Dark Palace. Perhaps we can mend the bond that was broken so long ago. I am afraid of this war, and I can see the people are too. We stand no chance against the full force of the Light; however, you might be able to turn the tides and save this world from destruction. The people here no longer hate you and they will no longer hunt you as they once did, I promise this to you. I assume you will read this letter after you killed my people, but you don't need their help to get to me.

Hopefully you will come back to me and give me a chance to make the Shadow Lands your home once again.

King Xere,
Ruler of the Shadow Lands and King of Darkness.

Her face was as cold as the air surrounding her. A lonely tear ran down her cheek and fell in the snow, frozen before it hit the ground. She stared into the fire for a while, dreaming of what her life could be, before throwing the letter into it. The flames quickly devoured the paper, leaving nothing but ashes.

The words haunted her thoughts as memories from her past emerged. She had never let any of these feelings take control but right now they had taken over.

The night had taken all the warmth of the day and she knew she had to go back. If she didn't the cold or some creature would take her soon enough.

Back inside the cave she started a fire to chase the cold away and cook some food. She roasted some of the boar she had hunted last week and as soon as the fat started sizzling her stomach cried out for something to eat. She ate quickly, knowing she wasn't done for today and sleep had to wait a little longer, no matter how tired she was. After she finished, she walked to the back of the cave. The light of the fire could barely reach back here. She sat down right at the border where shadow battled light and cut her hand with her spear. Blood dripped down on the stone and the world around her shifted.

The cave fell apart in darkness and an endless field covered in twilight emerged from that darkness, Elebok, the realm of Passage. It was filled with flowing grass, little blue and white flowers and countless stepping-stones leading to trees, lakes and past the horizon. It was eerily beautiful for a place that guided the dead into the afterlife. The fields went as far as her eyes could see until it seemed like there was no end to the ocean of green, blue and white. Naka pushed herself up and grabbed her spear. In front of her walked a young boy, a human. He carefully moved from one stone to another, walking the same path Naka needed to walk. The stones lead to a silver-leafed tree towering in the distance. She followed the boy, watching him jump from stone to stone, not paying mind to anything around him. She felt sorry for him. He probably had no clue where he was and where he was going, he had probably even forgotten how he got here, forgotten that he had died.

They had almost reached the silver-leafed tree. It was quite impressive, reaching high into the clouded skies above. Its blood-red roots rose above them, surrounding them with the gnarled wood. Naka's spear was made from the same wood as the tree, although it was more polished so it was more vibrantly crimson. The trunk was so thick and high that there could be an entire city inside and there would still be space left and it was covered in delicate leaves the size of a hand, which seemed forged of starlight. Naka glanced at the leaves and sighed, she was tired and had absolutely no desire to be here but it was necessary. The boy disappeared in the crowd of others who now joined this branching path, that was like a river that grew as small streams merged themselves with it. As they got closer to the trunk the stones were bigger and formed more of a road instead of a path of stepping-stones. The path was now filled with people of every race from both the Shining Lands as well as the Shadow Lands. In death they were all equal, no matter where one was born or who one may have served. The tip of her spear glowed brighter now. It had been glowing since she took her first soul with it, but now, she only saw it glow if a new soul had been taken.

Finally, she reached the base of the tree. A male figure turned around, wearing a long, hooded robe of pure white. The hood revealed only his thin lips and his chin, his muscles twisted underneath the robe as he moved.

"Naka, I see you have come to visit us again. You have brought Nárymm, of course." His voice was deep and calm.

She just nodded and kept silent.

"I am glad that you come to deliver these souls so soon. They don't deserve to wander that world like that. How many have you brought this time?" he continued.

Naka simply kneeled and handed over her spear as she said, "Master Irion."

The Master took it and observed it for a while. "One even begged for mercy you could have shown." Naka remained kneeling and silent while he spoke, she knew she was to be judged for every soul she took and someday she would need to pay the price. The spear now floated between his hands, slowly spinning around as small swirls of light flowed out of its tip, into the bark of the tree, pulsating through it, into the leaves. The glow faded from the spear and the Master handed it back to her. She nodded as she took the spear in her hands, thanking him. A feeling of safety came over her, even though nobody would harm her here she liked to have a weapon to defend herself. The Master continued while his gaze moved to the distance, overlooking the paths around the tree.

"Someone from your past passed through here, but I take it you have heard that already," he said and Naka's face turned to stone.

"Yes," she simply replied.

The Master seemed to look closely at her, completely seeing through everything. Naka felt naked and exposed, she knew nothing could be hidden from him. That was something she learned the hard way. After a while he turned away, seeming to have noticed she had no desire to speak of this.

"Thank you, Master. I have no further business here so I will go back now," she said firmly.

The Master turned around and opened his mouth but as he began his sentence a loud thunder echoed across the fields. Strong winds blew across the grass, the earth shook and the skies appeared to burn. All the souls stopped and looked at the sky, wailing and screaming in confusion. Naka had no idea what was happening, she had never seen this before. The Master too looked up as what seemed to be a star fell from the sky and landed between the roots of the tree. They ran toward it, the sea of people moving apart as they pushed through. Between the roots of the tree lay a large circular stone with engravings on its edge, symbols that she hadn't seen in a long time, symbols as old as the world. The roots were untouched by the impact of the fallen star. In the middle of the stone flew the star, a silver wisp, bright and the size of Naka. It looked like the swirls that had left Nárymm but much, much stronger.

Naka could feel its power vibrating in her soul and body, embedding a feeling of nakedness and vulnerability inside of her. It was as if it knew everything, not just about her but about *everything*.

Men and women in white robes like the Master's gathered at the edge of the stone and in the surrounding roots. The Master slowly stepped into the circle and kneeled in front of the silver wisp. After a long silence he stood up and stepped away. With a raised voice he addressed the surrounding men and women, his voice echoed between the roots.

"Follow the roots and find any wandering souls. We cannot have any mayhem here no matter what. I'll take care of this." They all nodded and disappeared one by one until only Naka, the Master and the silver wisp were left.

"It wishes to speak with you, Naka. Leave Nárymm with me."

She handed the Master the spear once more and he stepped away from the stone circle. Naka moved closer to the edge of the circle but hesitated to step in it. She could feel the power, beckoning, drawing her in, almost calling for her as it lured her in. Nothing happened when she stepped into it. Then a voice, more beautiful than anything she had ever experienced filled her mind.

Her eyes were tied to the silver wisp as it spoke, which nearly blinded her but somehow it didn't trouble her.

"Naka, there is no need to fear me. I know everything about you, I saw the moment you were born and I have seen the moment you will die. Long ago you received a task and it is time you complete that task. Find me and we will set it in motion. Perhaps you can lay down your burden once and for all."

A single image flashed through her mind. A tree of dark wood, rising high from a massive lake of silver water, its leaves a pale grey and green. A tree she had hoped to never see again.

"You know where to go, you know who to find. They will let you enter and lead you to where you need to be, I will make sure of it. Now go, there can be no more waiting, the time has come for you to play your part."

Naka was thrown back to the edge of the stone circle as the wisp disappeared with a flash of light. The skies roared once more before they became calm again.

The Master helped her back on her feet.

"I, I don't understand," Naka said. "Who was that? How did it know?"

The Master sat down on the roots of the tree, gesturing to a spot beside him.

"Come sit with me Naka. I cannot tell you who it was, for at this moment, nobody knows for sure. Did it tell you it was time?"

Naka nodded, lost in thought, wondering how he could know about her task.

"Then it is happening sooner than I expected." Master Irion fell silent for a moment before he stood up and handed her Nárymm. "I hoped you would have more time but it seems you will have visitors in a few moments. You should hurry or you will return here sooner than you would like, and this time not voluntarily." Naka grabbed her spear and bolted for the path. But before she jumped over the thick roots, she turned around. "Thank you, Master Irion," she said.

She ran as fast as she could to the end of the path, which was crowded with both normal and white robed people. Several had strayed from the paths and were screaming and sobbing in the sea of grass. She could see the end of the path and jumped for it.

Her body was thrown into the cave and she growled as she stood up. "Great," she said, dusting herself off. She started to grab the necessary things, food, water, clothes. There wasn't much of value besides Nárymm and her life so it was easy for her to leave it all behind. The image still flashed through her mind, she would have to go to the Dan'um, to the heart of the Emerald Woods, east of the Scorching Marshes. It would be a long journey but maybe it would be her last.

Suddenly she stopped. Voices were speaking near the entrance of the cave. They had found her. Lights shifted and she suddenly realized she had been gone for the entire night. Somehow she always forgot time was different in other realms. She couldn't escape when they were at the entrance. She cursed softly. How could she have been so stupid to hide somewhere with just one entrance? Yes, it was hard to find, but it was only a matter of time before someone worked it out. She pushed herself into a crack in the wall and hoped they would walk past her. The crack was near the entrance so she figured that once they had entered, she could run outside and maybe would live long enough to escape. As they entered Naka held her breath, she tried to push herself further into the crack while observing the people who entered. They wore armor she did not recognise at all. It was all black except for a circle of white dots on the left shoulder. Most of them were human except for two Kir'in, with their typical long, black hair, emerald eyes and long fangs, and a Laretu, his skin like red clay and four ram-like horns that were polished and clad in iron spikes. Only the Laretu would be a challenge to outrun but she trusted her own skills enough, she might even win the fight against the group but she didn't want to take the chance.

"Find her," the only woman said. She was human and emitted a certain dominance. Her face was cold and thin, hardened by endless war and discipline. Her black hair bound in a tight ponytail, she was missing one eye and instead there was a black gem in her socket that seemed to see everything. Naka recognized the woman as one of the secret commanders of Egìl, it had been Naka who had taken out her eye the last time they hunted her. The others started to search through the cave very thoroughly, turning everything inside out. The woman stood in front of the entrance, just beside the crack where Naka hid, and observed everything with a watchful eye. Adrenaline rushed through Naka's veins, one chance was all she had and if she failed, they would take her or kill her. Either way, she would not have it. She could run outside and toward the south, she would go toward the river Asal. If they followed her she could lose them there, it was tricky to cross the river, but luckily, she had figured it out last year. Even if they didn't chase her, she would go that way, she could end her tracks there and continue to Murra, the Laretu capital. She would need supplies after all for her journey. The woman now moved further into the cave, out of Naka's sight. This could be the only chance she would get, it would be a matter of time until they found her. She clenched her fist around Nárymm and took a deep breath. She slowly moved toward the edge of the crack and looked around the corner. They were in the back of the cave, searching through the last things. She bolted to the exit as fast as she could, hoping they were too late to notice. But as she reached the exit, she could hear the woman shout behind her. The morning sun blinded her but she ran into the woods. Her path led through the shadows, knowing that the sun was melting the snow and turning the soil into mud which would slow her down significantly. As an Ilunari her steps barely dented the snow, leaving almost no tracks. Behind her she could hear somebody falling, probably after getting their feet stuck in the soggy mud. But there was no time to enjoy his stupidity. The sharp sound of a bow releasing an arrow cut through the morning air and Naka started zigzagging between the trees. More arrows appeared in trees around her. This was not the first chase she had been in but this one was different, these people were trained to do nothing but hunting down their prey, and they were good at it. Naka jumped over a fallen tree, knowing she was close to the river. Its roars could be heard already. She realized she was not supposed to hear it already. Too soon. It was spring.

"By the Guardians," she whispered. After the letter from King Xere her thoughts had been all over the place, and now she had forgotten that during spring the river grew wider, almost tripled in size, especially after such a harsh winter like this one. She had no idea if she would survive crossing it now. The path she needed to take was dangerous at normal times, now it would almost be suicidal to cross it. She knew where to place her feet, the river was almost as deep as normal, it mainly grew wider in spring. The waters would be rougher and dangerously cold. An arrow skimmed her arm and she pushed her legs to run faster. If she could be there a little sooner, she would have more time to cross. She couldn't dodge the arrows when crossing, so she needed as much as a head start as possible. Only a few footsteps could be heard behind her, somehow she felt like the woman was right behind her but she had no time to look back. Naka reached the Asal, immediately searching for the stones, which started almost two meters into the swollen river. The currents dragged at her feet as she waded into the icy water, the cold shocking her muscles. Her whole body resisted but she pushed it further into the wet cold. With difficulty she reached the first stone and climbed on top of it. She was dripping wet all the way up to her waist and it took her a lot of effort not to start shivering. The other stones lay just below the surface but could be seen all the way to the other side. There were a lot of stones but one could only cross the river if they stepped on the *right* stones. The others either moved or were too slippery, and if someone stepped on them the waters would embrace them, their corpse would be lost to the waters forever. She had crossed half the river when her hunters appeared at the edge of the forest. Most of them immediately followed her and tried to get to the first stones but only one made it out of the water. The woman remained at the edge, her black eye piercing across the river. The last man carefully picked the stones he stood on. Naka had not stopped and was almost at the other side now. She heard the man scream when he fell into the cold embrace of the Asal, leaving only the woman to hunt her. Naka stood on the last stone, ready to leap to the bank of the river when a fiery pain cut through her right leg. Her feet slipped as she jumped and within moments, she was submerged in the icy waters. Her hands could barely grab the roots of a tree to prevent her from being dragged down the stream. When she climbed out of the river, she saw the handle of a dagger sticking out of her leg, on the other side the tip came out of her leg again. She looked up. From across the river the woman looked at her with an emotionless face before she disappeared back into the forest. Naka crawled into the woods, leaving the knife in until she could properly take care of it. She ripped a piece of cloth from her shirt and wringed it to get the water out. After that she took off her leather gloves and put one between her teeth. She took a deep breath and quickly pulled out the knife. She cursed at the sharp pain and the blood pouring out of the wound. She had to be quick now. She bound the cloth carefully around her wound biting down on the glove hard enough to puncture the leather. Her breathing was heavy as she let herself fall on the moss behind her. The sun was rising high above her and she closed her eyes, steadying her breath. She would have to get moving, she had no desire to be found by her hunters anytime soon and Murra was only hours away. She had just scrambled to her feet when a young, female voice behind her spoke.

"There you are."

Chapter 2
Rynn

The yellowed pages of the book fluttered as Rynn flipped through them one last time. He closed the book softly and shut his eyes, savoring the last words of his favorite story. It was one of the few stories where a human was the hero, one of the few stories that didn't treat humans like a weak race. The warm, silent library was his favorite place to be at the Academy of Nirs Imak. Nobody ever came in this part and this allowed him to be completely alone, away from the noise and people. When he opened his eyes, he found himself amazed once again at the beauty of the library. The ceiling reached almost as high as the Cathedrals of Air in Cysta Imen, the Ilunari capital city. The dark wood and old gold made a beautiful combination filling the roof with a warm and dark appearance that radiated to the lowest parts. The light coming through the enormous windows fell on the countless tiny motes of dust and made it seem like the room was filled with small orbs of golden light.

Rynn stood up and moved past the high shelves that came down from the ceiling. The endless amount of knowledge, the countless old books, all the mysteries, he had read through all the books he could get his hands on. He smiled, remembering the potions he brewed so he could stay awake all those nights. He reached the gap in the shelf where he took out the book and put it back. Satisfied with the completely filled bookshelf he decided to roam the halls a little more. Books of all sizes, on almost every topic known to the world. They were all here. He could spend an eternity in this knowledge but somehow he always ended up in front of the same painting. It was a painting of the first human king, king Narallu. Rynn liked the painting because he and the king looked alike, both a dark skin, black, curly hair and eyes with all the colors of the forest floor. Rynn always stared at the painting when he was nervous, so it was only natural that he lingered here as long as he could on this day. This afternoon the Games of Nirs Imak would begin. He really didn't look forward to it. It was not that Rynn was afraid of ending on a low rank, which was completely fine. The Games were not about competition but about showing your skills. They were a way to determine your role in the society of Telryn, the city of magic. There was no winning or losing, so no pressure there. Besides, he was the best of every class and excelled in every school of magic and was therefore excused from the classes to study in the library. The professors could not teach him anything anymore, but the library could. No, his fear did not come from the possibility of failure. It came from the fact that almost every mage would be watching him perform his magic, and judge him on it. The thought alone made him uneasy. After the Games and the ceremony, he would leave for home. He hadn't been home in eight years, he missed his father and sister, Sëah. He was already looking forward to living with his family again. Even though it would be weird, it would be the first time he would be home again after the death of his mother. She had been murdered alongside many others, the day Rynn left for the Academy. It had been a day many lost their loved ones. Blood had flowed through the streets of Anndar as assassins from the Shadow Lands slit the throats of every person who believed in Nuana's return. Rynn couldn't help but cry as the memory resurfaced, and wiped the tears from his face. He hadn't spoken with his father but luckily his sister had sent him letters every now and then, letting him know how it was going with their father and how she had taken it upon herself to teach the street children of Anndar, just like Rynn had done.

The golden light had slowly turned to the fiery color of an early sunset. He had little time left to get to the main courtyard where the games would begin.

The courtyard was already crowded with people. People from all races of the Shining Lands lived here although they were mainly Ilunari and Surr'um. He knew there were only three humans, him being one of them. One was a cook without magical abilities, and the other one was a teacher of green magic who tended the Garden of Birds. Rynn moved toward the other students, grabbing some food along the way. Professor Ira, a tall, beautiful Surr'um, stood in the middle of the courtyard and beckoned the students to stand in front of her. Her velvety voice could be heard in the entire courtyard.

"Students of Nirs Imak, it is my honor to start the Games with the complex and honorable school of restoration and healing. But before we start, I must remind you that this is not a competition. Breaking the rules will result in immediate disqualification and banishment from both the Academy as well as Telryn. To remind you of the rules, all magic must be yours and using magic from any other source is forbidden. Hurting anyone outside of the school of combat is forbidden, losing control of your magic will result in a lower rank. Multiple offenses will result in banishment from Telryn and its society. Lastly I want to remind you that the Games of Nirs Imak are not actual games but a way for the council of Telryn to determine where you best fit in this society. As many of you know, the city of Telryn is a loyal ally to King Egil so expect to serve in his army before you come to live in Telryn.

Now, let us honor the great Nirs Imak, High Guardian of magic and knowledge, founder of this Academy. Today we will heal those who have returned from battle, as a thanks for their service to the Throne of Light. There is a great variety of injuries. Some have gone blind, others have simple scratches. We will start with the easiest injuries and work our way up to see how capable you are. If any problems occur, I will be here to assist. Best of luck, students."

The crowd applauded and some raised their hands to the skies, praising Nirs Imak. From the other side of the courtyard the group of those in need of healing came toward them. Some limped but most could still walk. They stopped before the students and formed several groups. Each group had a different degree of injuries, ranking from scratches and bruises to missing limbs and deformities. Every student had to heal one person from every group in front of Professor Ira and the city council of Telryn until they found injuries that they couldn't heal anymore. Rynn knew he would be last for the council was already aware of his potential, they simply needed to follow the rules and let him perform in the Games first. He could see the council sitting across the courtyard, three Ilunari, known to be the wisest and most powerful in Telryn. If he didn't leave for home it would be very likely that Rynn would become the fourth member of the council, the first human counselor in centuries.

The Games were beginning and the first student was a shy girl who quickly worked her way through the injuries, Rynn hadn't seen her before but then again, he barely knew anybody at the Academy. Eventually she walked toward a boy barely of age whose face was filled with scars. She put her hands on his scars with a look of confidence as a soft, white glow filled her hands. It only lasted a couple of seconds but when she was finished almost his entire face was free of scars, she bowed as a sign that she was finished. The boy thanked her, clearly happy with the result as he felt his own face and escorted her to the buffet under the crowd's applause. Student after student healed their person, everybody using a magic of different difficulty. Some struggled with a single cut and others healed a broken leg with ease. The professor and the council treated them all the same, they knew that everyone tried their very best.

This went on until an Ilunari boy named Biran chose to heal a man who had a deep cut over his chest. Biran was known to brag and bully so the professor was already inching toward him as he started the healing, keeping a close eye so the man wouldn't get hurt even more. Biran had only just begun his healing when he bragged to his friends that it was just a flesh wound and he would 'heal it quicker than they could find a date'. Suddenly the man started to shake heavily and foamed at the mouth, screaming out in pain. Professor Ira ran toward the two and pushed Biran away, who's face had turned red, but it was hard to tell if it came from embarrassment or anger. The professor started to whisper in High Speech, the ancient tongue of the High Immortals, a tongue Rynn didn't speak, in a desperate attempt to heal the poor man. His veins were so thick they looked like they could burst at any time and Rynn took a step forward but stopped. The entire crowd was looking at the man and Professor Ira. Biran had run off and was nowhere to be seen and the professor was still chanting but trembled, her eyes assessing the wound that didn't seem to improve at all. Rynn couldn't stand it. He ran toward the professor and the man, kneeled on the other side of the body and looked the professor in the eye.

"I can do this professor, trust me."

She looked him in the eyes for only a moment, the usual brightness had gone from her eyes and they were now filled with despair and exhaustion. She lifted her hands from the body and revealed a wound he did not expect. The wound had turned as black as night and it started to spread in the man's veins, dark blood crawling under his skin. It became awfully silent as the man stopped screaming, he was nearing death. Rynn knew he had to cleanse the wound first and then use more powerful healing magic than the professor had used. Cleansing was the easy part, the blackness was drawn out of the wound within seconds, then the healing began. Usually, Rynn would channel energy into the wound to let the body heal it, but with a wound this big it could kill Rynn, so he had to find another way. The only other way he could use was to weave flesh and skin back together and then restore the veins and muscle underneath, it would be tricky but the other option was death, either for the man or for Rynn. So, he began, pulling and twisting the flesh of the man to close the wound, it wasn't pretty and would leave a serious scar, but the man would live. Veins slithered beneath the skin like snakes as Rynn tried to find their proper places, the man's face showed how excruciatingly painful it was but he made no sound. Rynn had barely finished when professor Ira pulled him back from the man.

"Careful, Rynn," she whispered, unable to take her eyes of the twisted scar on the man's chest. It was awfully ugly, nearly horrifying even, it looked like someone had burned his chest time and time again. As soon as Rynn stepped away he noticed how tired he was, his legs swaying beneath him and his mind turning around before his vision went dark, not even feeling his body hitting the floor.

He woke up in his own room, tired and sore but overall feeling good. The Academy was quiet, awfully quiet, not that he complained about it but he just wasn't used to it. Golden light of the early morning sun fell through his high windows. He realized he was still dressed in the same clothes he had worn at the... the Games! He started changing into new clothes when suddenly a sharp pain pierced his mind, an imaginary needle stabbing his thoughts, raging through his memories. It felt like an eternity before the pain eased and his mind started to settle down. Once it did, he realized there was a hand on his forehead and he quickly looked up. He stared into eyes filled with mists, swirling around and ever changing. Their depth drew him in, guiding him deeper and deeper into the silver mists. Lost within them he heard a voice calling for him. Rynn could not hear the words, it sounded as if it spoke through a thick layer of glass or water. Then the mists suddenly faded from his mind, throwing him back into his own thoughts, though he could feel the mist still circling around his mind. The eyes belonged to a girl his age. Hair a flaming auburn surrounding a face so beautiful it stole his breath away. Her skin untouched and radiant, faint markings on it as if her skin was made of wood.

"I don't know what exactly you are looking at now, but I do think it is considered polite to answer when someone asks you a question. Are you alright?" Her voice was soft like a summer breeze and Rynn's tongue had decided to imitate the dry desert sands. "Y… y… yes," he stuttered with a hoarse voice. He could not think of any other words and realized his mouth was still open. He closed it abruptly, making a loud clacking noise. The girl giggled and lifted her head.

Rynn shot to his feet, almost collapsing again. The girl smiled and held her hand out. "Are you still okay?" she asked giggling.

"Yeah I'm good. All good over here," Rynn quickly responded, making weird gestures with his hands until he realized it looked really stupid.

"Sorry you had to see that." He wished deeply that the earth would just split open and take him to prevent him from making an even bigger fool of himself, if that was even possible. Her smile faded as she turned her head in his general direction.

"Don't be sorry, I would have loved to see it but I have never seen anything, and never will." He understood immediately and hoped the earth would split even more.

"You are blind."

The girl nodded. "Come," she said. Not a single person was present in the halls as they walked toward the Eastern Gardens in total silence. Even in the gardens there was no escape from the seemingly eternal silence. The girl breathed in deeply and closed her eyes as soon as the sunlight hit her face. She bathed in the warmth and really seemed to enjoy the touch of the light. Rynn noticed she was barefoot as she stepped onto the fresh grass and moved gracefully through the trees toward the side of a pond surrounded by willows. She sat down and did not move so he sat down beside her. Light reflected on the small ripples in the water, the wind rustled the leaves of the trees walling the world outside. He could sit here forever in silence, with or without the girl, although he liked her presence, even though they had met only minutes ago.

"I am Yira by the way." Her voice did not break the enchantment but blended completely with the surroundings. A soft summer breeze in the beauty of spring.

"I am Rynn," he responded. His mind had settled and acted normal again and he took a breath to apologize but before he could speak, she stopped him.

"There's no need for that. Many people don't notice my blindness at first, I've become used to it. Before you offer to heal it, I have to tell you that this can't be healed. The Abariimm decided it was to be a part of me since I was born without sight. I don't think I would even want to see the world through my eyes anymore. After all these years I have grown used to it, learned to see the world in a different way, a way beyond sight." Rynn had listened carefully and observed every line of her face. He had indeed thought to heal her for a moment but when she mentioned the Abariimm he was quite stunned. The Abariimm were beings of legend, the first creations ever, judges of the worlds and if she had seen them, received their judgement then she was a High Immortal. A true High Immortal, a divine being of incredible power, sitting right beside him. They lingered in silence for a few moments before she continued.

"I do think you should get ready to continue in the Games. They stopped them because of you and forbade anyone to come in these parts of the Academy," Yira said. Rynn was surprised that he actually did not care at all if he participated in the Games or if they had stopped because of him. He really wanted to know more about her but she stood up before he could ask her why she was at the Academy at all she had already gotten to her feet and started going back. He followed her at a small distance but he could not find her after he moved through the trees, he was confused as to how a blind girl could disappear so quickly. A bird started to sing his song in the grand oak tree near the pond and others joined him, only seconds later professor Ira appeared in the doorway.

"Rynn, you're awake. Are you alright?" He nodded gently, still looking around for Yira. "Good, good. The others are concerned and the Council is desperate to see more of your magic. We do really need to complete the Games before anything else, time is running out. King Egìl wants new mages for his army, he is preparing for a final invasion to conquer the Shadow Lands. I think you would serve the Shining Lands well." Her voice was calm but Rynn could distinguish a sudden haste in her tone. He followed her inside toward the great hall, ready to continue the Games. It needed to be done, he knew that, and when they were, he would go home.

The following days were weird, everything revolved around Rynn and he nearly cracked under the pressure. No matter who performed magic, all eyes were set on Rynn, showering him with attention. He only came out for the games and fled to either the library or his room to spend the remaining time in peace and silence. The Games continued as planned in the standard order of magic schools, meaning enchanting was next. They had to enchant a weapon and a piece of jewelry, both to aid their wielder in battle. Many enchanted the sword to ignite itself when desired and the jewelry to either endure heavy pain or heal wounds quickly. Rynn, however, enchanted the sword to freeze the blood of those it wounded. For jewelry he picked a ring casting a spell on it that would guide the hand holding the weapon or shield to defend the wielder from any attacks. He was praised for his creativity and skill, even receiving a smile from one of the judges.

Conjuration followed and they had to endure a long speech from the Council about how conjuration was to be taken seriously and that they had to apply the most important rule of conjuration. *Do not conjure what you cannot banish,* the words still echoed in Rynn's mind. There was a great variety of beings. Some simply conjured a cat, dog or another pet while others conjured monstrous creatures that seemed to come straight from a nightmare. Rynn really loved conjuration for it had been the first magic he learned and had conjured all kind of creatures to entertain the orphans in Anndar. At some point he was known for it and Rynn had used those creatures to announce that he was going to give lessons. With this memory in mind he would try his very best. He had read once about a being as beautiful as the dawn, with wings of pure light that was tall and elegant, robed in shining silk. The image formed in his mind and he wove energies together, giving it life and form to make it real. It stood amongst the creatures of nightmare like a lonely star, all eyes focused upon it until the very moment Rynn banished it again. That was the last school for the day, and tomorrow was a day of rest. Rynn locked himself in his room and slept all day, only to wake a few times to hurry to the kitchens to grab some food and secretly search for Yira, but she was nowhere to be found. Tomorrow would be the final day of the Games and the last schools, being Illusion, Transformation and Combat, would be tested. He really did not look forward to Combat at all. He had to enter a makeshift arena with somebody of equal level and duel until one of them was defeated. There would be a spell on the arena that prevented death by magic, but not injury, meaning defeat was to injure the other so much that they couldn't go on. That would be the last test, and after all their wounds had been healed there would be a great feast where they would be approached by one of the council members to receive options for their service in Telryn or to be recruited for the war. Everybody was guaranteed of a place and free to choose from their options, they had been assured by the Council many times.

When evening fell, Rynn suddenly woke up from a dream about Yira, or so he thought, she had been dancing in the mists, singing songs that sounded as old as the world. He went out to look for her but could not find her anywhere in the Academy and immediately regretted his search. Students were all over the halls and gardens, celebrating their day off and boasting to younger students about what positions they would be offered by the Council. But every time Rynn was noticed they fell silent and stared at him as he walked by, only to start whispering as soon as he had passed. He could hear their whispers echo through the halls, like wind through leaves. His dreams that night were strange, Yira was there most of the time, leading him along paths that went through fire and forests, leading to seas and over mountains, only to end up surrounded by swirling mists.

At first light the games started again, Transformation. They were put in a single row across the courtyard, facing the Council. In front of them they placed orbs of perfectly round and ordinary grey stone. Then the Council started calling out materials, starting with different kinds of stone and crystal, then followed the metals, wood and lastly bone. Transformation was one of the most difficult schools, everyone could learn the basics but only a few could go past the metals, so few that it was almost considered a separate ability to be able to do Transformation. Rynn could turn his orb into wood but when they asked them to transform it into bone he failed. He wasn't mad at himself, it was the best he could do and he was very happy with it.

Illusion was next and ended up actually being really fun. They had to become invisible at one point and somebody started a water fight. Water sprayed everywhere and people started bending water from the fountain to suddenly drop on the head of unsuspecting victims. Water spouts were summoned and the courtyard nearly turned into a lake during the fight until the Council put an end to it by evaporating all the water all of the sudden. Everyone was to get themselves cleaned up and ready for Combat.

Most with their hair still dripping wet entered the arena in the Southern gardens, and one by one they came out exhausted and injured. One victor after another claimed the applause as their reward and walked back with their combat partner. Rynn had to battle against Biran, the boy who failed in Healing and would have killed a man if it wasn't for Rynn. Rynn was aware of the skills of his opponent, it was the only school of magic that Biran was his equal in. He was a bully and very good in finding weaknesses. Rynn had stronger magic than Biran but simply didn't know anything about people. Every seat in the arena had been filled with students, professors and citizens of Telryn alike. The battle consisted of firing spell after spell, each one more violent than the one before. From fire to lightning to pure telekinesis, yet both of them managed to defend themselves. It went on for quite a while, Biran throwing fireballs and lightning bolts and Rynn waving them off like it was nothing. After a while Rynn realized his body couldn't sustain the long fight. Most magic used the body as fuel, muscles and fat or even skin and hair, and Rynn didn't have a lot of fuel to burn, yet Biran was tall and muscular and could go on for much longer. Rynn needed to end the battle before he exhausted himself. He had to somehow escape Biran's vision, confuse him so Rynn could strike him back. He quickly remembered a clone spell he had found in the library a few days ago which would create a bunch of copies of Rynn. Within the blink of an eye he had cast it, filling the arena with copies of himself that ran around and fired fake spells at Biran, who was suddenly very confused. Biran roared, unleashing flames of incredible size and power in a massive burst, destroying the clones with this pure havoc and destruction. Now the fire came for Rynn, roaring waves, ready to turn him into ashes.

Chapter 3
Inza

The forest was quiet and warm now that spring was returning after the cold winter, and Inza loved it. She ran around on her bare feet like nothing could harm her, knowing nothing here would.

"Kaell! Come on, grumpy old man. Enjoy our freedom."

Her laugh bounced between the trees and filled the forest with happiness. Kaell just shook his head and continued packing the few belongings they carried on their journey. They had camped in this spot that night, the scent of a campfire and roasted meat still hung in the air. Kaell didn't respond to her so she decided to jump on his back and ruffled her hands through his hair, messing it up as bad as she could until he smiled.

"Aha, there it is! See, you can smile, not sure if you should do it again, though."

Her voice reduced to only a whisper, "You might look happy for once."

She laughed and ran away as he tried to catch her. He grabbed her and flung her over his shoulder while she struggled to get loose. Inza punched his back but Kaell simply walked around with her on his shoulder, acting like nothing weird was going on. Eventually, he dropped her on the grass, leaving her there as he fixed his hair.

"Still think I am an old man?" he asked jokingly.

"Duh," Inza answered before she walked into the forest again, a big smile on her face.

She looked back and saw that Kaell had already finished packing their things. They were going north, toward the Ravens Pass. It was a way to get to the Plains where only a few people passed through. From there they would travel east, toward the Dan'um forests. Three weeks ago they had received a message from a banned Kelsul, a Kurr elder, that she had found different tribes of Kurr and different kinds of shifters as well. Inza had been filled with joy after that message and wanted to leave for the Dan'um forests almost right away, but her father would not hear any of it. The Kelsul that sent the message had been banned fourteen years ago for saying Kaell had been born with the Bond. The Bond was a unique connection between Kurr and animal where their mind and soul became so deeply connected that they couldn't live without each other. All Kurr were born with a gift of sorts but the magic only became permanent around the age of seven, until that time one was given a fake Mark, a symbol to show which gift you possessed. When Kaell turned seven he was sent into the woods alone to form the Bond and receive his Mark afterwards. Outsiders called this ritual dangerous, and they were right about that. They said that the feeling of the Bond being formed was so overwhelming that you didn't feel anything but that connection. So, following tradition Kaell went into the forest alone on his seventh birthday. After a week he still hadn't returned so Inza went into the forest and found him near death underneath a tree, no animal in sight. She had taken him home and didn't understand why nobody made an effort to help him. Their Kelsul had declared him Markless and banished him from Kurr lands. Their mother had pleaded for Kaell to stay, she was highly respected and managed to convince the Kelsul eventually. So, Kaell was allowed to stay in their village but every single person treated him like he had no value. Even their father treated Kaell like an outsider instead of his own son, especially after the death of their mother.

When Kaell heard the message from the banned Kelsul, Inza had seen the hope in his eyes, hope that maybe there was a chance for him to still get a Mark, to finally be treated like a normal person. Inza had convinced her dad to let her travel to the Dan'um and take Kaell with her. Her father had allowed it, and so they took off.

She didn't really like being away from all the people of her village, even though she adored nature so much more. Still, meeting people was fun. She loved how everyone had a different story to tell, especially if they came from different villages. She ran further north until she reached a sudden drop. It was deep enough to provide a view across the entire forest ahead of them. A little bit in the distance there was a wide scar in the leafy ocean. That was where Ravens Pass was. A solid two days of travelling, on foot. Inza sat down and let the morning sun hit her fair skin. A soft breeze danced through her short, brown hair, she loved that feeling. She used to have incredibly long hair that reached her ankles and was adored by most, but now they often disapproved of this length. Yes, her long hair had been beautiful, but she didn't like it. Whenever she was running through the woods it got in her face or got stuck behind branches. She remembered how she went into the woods like any other day and cut it all off with a dull knife. It had looked awful. When Kaell found her he had quickly fixed it, turned it into the beautiful shoulder length hair that she had now, although he did tease her with it for a very long time. He had always been good at fixing hair and clothes. When their mother died Inza was the only female in her home. She tried to fill the role of a woman in the household and she tried to learn those skills but she simply did not have the patience. So Kaell learned them, he had an incredible amount of patience and appeared to have a knack for the tasks of the home. He came out of the woods with both his bag and his large bow hanging on his back.

"Milady," he grinningly said as he mockingly bowed before her. Inza couldn't hold her laughter, he looked so ridiculous when he did that. His humor made her forget all those serious thoughts as quick as they came. They went toward the west to get around the drop and move further north. For a while they walked in silence but Inza's mind was never at rest.

"Kaell?" she carefully asked. He simply replied with a 'hmm'. Approval to continue granted. "Do you think they can truly help us? The Dan'um I mean." He stopped and gently grabbed her shoulder. He brushed his brown hair out of his face and looked her in the eyes. His fiery orange eyes were a color similar to her own eyes.

He took a deep breath. "The Dan'um woods are a sanctuary for shifters and Kurr and everything else that has a connection to nature. They hold answers to all of our questions. My problem cannot be solved but they can teach you to become the greatest shifter that has ever lived. They can even teach you how to control your healing magic. Father said they can even teach you the language of the earth itself." His gentle voice soothed her mind. Before any doubts could return, he gestured at the road ahead of them.

"Now get those feet moving or we will never reach Ravens Pass." With the doubt gone her mind had room for a new desire, shifting. With big eyes and her sweetest voice she asked him. "Can I please shift into something? I'll be careful, I swear. Please, please." She knew he couldn't resist her now. He knew how much it hurt her when she couldn't shift every now and then. She hadn't shifted since they left home. Another sigh, and a nod. That was enough for her. She was so excited to shift that she didn't know into what. Flying? Running? Maybe swimming? Definitely flying, the weather was too good not to fly. A raven would be fun, maybe make Kaell laugh too. She untied her necklace and handed it to Kaell, it had been their mother's necklace, the only thing left of her besides memories. It was made from silver leaves that wrapped around a glowing gem. Their mother had found the gem during Starfall, a day before Inza was born, and their father had asked the best smith to forge a necklace out of it as a gift for their mother. Nobody knew what kind of gem it was or how it got to these woods but one thing was certain, it was the most beautiful gem Inza had ever seen. When their mother died their father had given the necklace to Inza, a gift so her mother would always be with her. Kaell took the necklace, he remembered their mother much better, he was older when she had died. Inza smiled at him and he smiled back, no words were needed here. She shifted into a raven, cawing at her brother and flapping her wings to get used to them.

"Ravens Pass, clever." He smiled as she flew away. She felt sorry for leaving him alone, but that guilt faded very quickly as she soared through the skies over the green canopy, filled with newly grown leaves. Ravens Pass was approaching much quicker now. She steered away from it. Their father had warned her not to reveal her gifts to anyone outside of their village, King Egil had sent word that all Kurr fit for battle were to report in Anndar, to join the army as they prepared to strike the Shadow Lands. He had taken many of their people already, often by force, especially those with gifts like shifting and powers of healing and nature, and Inza had all of those abilities. The Kurr people knew about her powers, she was the daughter of a chieftain, there was no way they could keep it a secret. But Ravens Pass was used by other races as well, like the Laretu and the humans. Shifters were easily separated from regular animals because their eyes remained the same, Kurr eyes being a fiery orange made it easy to be discovered. But that wouldn't be a problem until they reached the pass, until then she would enjoy the heat of the sun warming her feathers.

It was nearly evening when she decided to find Kaell. He wasn't hard to find for her. Somehow, they could always find each other, animal instinct they called it. He was already starting to set up a camp, a little bit earlier than she expected. She landed and shifted back into her human form. Every day she was grateful for learning how to shift without needing to worry about her clothes, it had taken her some time to master it but once she had, it had been absolutely amazing. As an animal she had no problem with running around without clothes, it didn't feel like being naked, however as a Kurr, it was quite awkward to not wear clothes out in the open.

"I'm almost finished with the camp and will go find us some food soon, unless you already ate?" His head turned toward her but she shook her head as he handed her necklace back. Exhausted and hungry she curled up near the starting fire, relishing it's warmth and light. Sleep came as soon as she closed her eyes.

She dreamed of having shifted into a wolf, grey and young. Her hunt for food was lonely for there was no pack around her but she was used to it, she didn't want a pack. A deer walked past, not noticing her and she leaped. Her fangs closed around its neck. A perfect kill. The deer only struggled for a short moment. She raised her blood-covered snout to the bright, red moon above her and let her howl echo through the mountains.

"Inza!"

Her eyes opened wide and she touched her mouth, searching for blood but not finding any. She looked around and found Kaell at the other side of the fire, roasting two rabbits over the fire.

"What is it? Is the food ready?" she asked with a cracking voice. How long had she even been asleep? Naps after shifting always felt like she woke up years later in some distant future. Kaell grinned and shook his head.

"At least you have your priorities straight. No, I woke you up because you were howling like mad, you wildling. I hope nobody has heard us, wolves aren't supposed to be this far south."

"Sorry," she apologized with a smile, she knew she would need to start being more careful. If she didn't shift maybe she wouldn't have dreams like these anymore.

As he took the rabbits off the fire, he almost dropped both in the fire and as he tried to save them, he flung his arms around, trying to find balance, Inza had an incredibly hard time keeping her face straight. Tears already filled her eyes as she could barely control herself. Kaell still didn't notice any of it and continued preparing their food. When he looked up, Inza pulled her face straight as fast as she could. He stood up and handed her rabbit to her, she couldn't hold back a wide smile as she took her food and he returned a foolish grin at her. Then, he turned around and tripped over his own feet, planting his face in the grass. Inza could simply not hold it any longer and bursted out in laughter. Tears were streaming down her face and she fell backward kicking her legs into the air. His laughter joined hers when he realized she had seen everything as he lay on the ground. Inza's stomach ached and she could barely breathe. When she could breathe again, she sat up straight and wiped the tears of her face. It was incredibly hard for her to not look at Kaell, if she would she would burst out in laughter again. It had been a sort of a tradition to pull pranks on each other and they had been going for a while, although Kaell was clumsy enough that Inza didn't need to do much, he was perfectly capable of making a fool of himself without her help. It all started when she had pulled her first successful prank on him. She had hidden herself underneath some laundry and waited patiently until he walked in to do the laundry. Their father had some people over from other tribes and were discussing something in the room next to where she was. When he walked in, she had waited a little more so he was settled and didn't pay attention anymore, and then, she had shifted into the ugliest cat she could imagine and jumped him. His scream was so high that she thought he would break all the glass. She had shifted back immediately and rolled on the floor, laughing and crying.

Today, however, she had no need to make a fool of him because he had done the job for her. With a big smile she devoured the rabbit and watched Kaell do the same. Not a single piece of meat remained on the bones and even the bones were gnawed on, Inza just couldn't resist the urge. Her brother was not as careful picking the bones clean and as soon as Inza noticed she grabbed them and cleaned them. His laughter made her look up. He gestured around his mouth and pointed to her. She felt, and found fat and oil covering basically her entire jaw. She quickly licked it off and threw the bones at him.

"Idiot," she called out.

"We should get some sleep. I want to walk a long way tomorrow so that we can reach Ravens Pass the day after."

She nodded and curled up in the soft grass near the fire. Her brother prepared his sleeping sack but she fell asleep before he finished.

Again, she walked her dreams as a wolf under the night skies. She was in woods she had never been in before. However, the strange thing was that she felt as if she had walked between those trees for a long time. There was no moon, no stars and Inza ran until she stood in front of a large rock. One side was broken and crumbled while the other was smooth still. On the edge stood another wolf with fur black as night. Eyes of burning orange, like hot coals among the black ashes. The wolf howled to the full moon and looked down on Inza before turning around and disappearing behind the edge. Inza ran as fast as she could trying to catch up with the other wolf. She would love to meet another shifter, even if it was in a dream. She had only met one before, a young boy from a small village to the north, who was capable of shifting into a hare. Her wandering mind focused as she spotted the wolf at the edge of the forest. It disappeared in the shadows of the forest where not even the night could enter. Inza followed carefully, not knowing what hid within the forest. Sound did not even fade away, it was just removed from existence leaving behind a silence where the sound of blood rushing in your veins ruled your mind. Her paws led her now, following the deep, primal instinct within her that seemed to know the way.

The trees were old, she could feel their eyes following her every move. They felt violent, powerful and angry. She used to connect with the trees at home, listen to their tales, but these trees were dark and felt... bad. Their whispers were of death and hate, corruption and pain. She couldn't even understand most of it, their tongue was older than anything she had ever heard. There was no sign of the other shifter, or any life for that matter. Her paws carried her through mist and over thick roots. Under branches carrying the shadows that once were leaves.

The endless sea of trees stopped and revealed an open space lined with trees that seemed as ancient as the world itself. They rose like pillars along a path, leading to a throne the size of a small hill. On it sat a creature cloaked in shadows and twilight for the red light of the moon was still absent. He was dressed in black, ragged cloth that revealed his, well it wasn't exactly skin. His skin was made of bark and wood, as if he was made of the trees that surrounded him. On top of this wooden body a face was hidden in shadows, only revealing two stars of dawn that appeared to be his eyes. Two enormous horns grew from the side of his head, they were more intricate than anything Inza knew or could even imagine. They weren't exactly horns nor antlers but something in between, sticking out from his head like bone branches heavy with moss. The shifter she had followed now sat beside the throne. Others appeared at the edge of the enormous pillar-like trees but seemed to not enter what could be deemed the 'hall' between the trees. Inza felt the power radiating from the creature and knew she needed to show respect. This wasn't a normal dream, if it was a dream at all. A whisper filled the air as the creature spoke. His voice was deep and rustling, like a strong wind through the leaves. Inza didn't understand the words but she could feel them. They forced her to transform back into her human form. Another whisper and her clothes were ripped from her body by the wind of his voice. She fell to her knees and covered herself as she curled up on the ground. His gaze went straight through her, there was nothing she could hide from him, she was exposed but somehow, she felt free. Whispers carried by wind filled the woods again and the creature gestured slowly to the shifter beside the throne. The wolf transformed into a woman with long pale hair and pointed ears. She reminded Inza of how the Kurr of more ancient times were described in the stories. Her eyes glowed the same orange color as the creature on the throne and her lips did not move as she spoke. She stood between the throne and Inza as her voice filled Inza's mind.

"Let neither light nor darkness blind you. They will fight to restore the balance that was lost, but it is a wound that needs to be healed, not a war to be won," was all she had to say. Inza looked up from the ground and opened her mouth, not being able to create any sound. She had so many questions. Who was this creature? Where was she? What did the warning mean? The hushed whispers of the creature's voice filled the air once more and Inza looked into the dawning light of the woman's eyes as she gently kneeled and caressed Inza's cheeks. The world around her slowly fell apart as their eyes closed and their lips touched.

Sound returned, the chirping of birds and rustling of the leaves was almost deafening after the heavy silence in her dream. She wasn't sure if she was awake but as she opened her eyes to greet the light of early dawn, she spotted her brother. Still confused she stretched the tiredness out of her limbs as she greeted him. He responded with a simple nod over his shoulder as he took some bread out of his bag and broke it in half. Inza noticed his gloomy face. His eyes avoided hers as he gave her one half of the bread. She knew of only one thing that could destroy his mood overnight. Kaell had nightmares about losing their mother. She had been taken away by king Egil's men to fight in the army because of her gift of healing. Kaell had been with her when they took her, unable to stop the men. When the same men came weeks later to bring her corpse home Kaell had disappeared for days, blaming himself for her death. He came back, covered in blood, and with a new bow. Nobody ever spoke of it again and even Kaell acted like it never happened. In the years that followed Inza noticed how much Kaell longed to leave the Kurr, how he hardened when he wasn't with her. She was glad he could finally get a break from all the hatred of his own people.

Now they were here, only a day of travel away from Ravens Pass and Inza already found it hard to understand the trees here, their language was so different from the ones at home. She was determined to learn all she could from the other shifters, perhaps they could teach her new forms to shift in, animals that didn't live near their home.

And she would ask them about this strange dream. If it was a dream at all. It felt different, stronger. More like a vision. She wondered if she should tell Kaell. Right now would be the wrong time. He would listen and try to understand but she would only burden him with more questions. Maybe when they reached Ravens Pass.

Kaell threw dirt and gravel over the fire to make sure they wouldn't burn the forest down before they left. As he stood up, he caught Inza's eyes and quickly put on his leather jacket. He made weird faces while doing it and Inza giggled a bit before she ran off into the woods, toward Ravens Pass.

She did not notice the bloody stain on his side underneath the jacket nor the scratches on his now covered arms, neither did she realize that his weird faces were a way to hide the pain that ran through his entire body.

Chapter 4
Naka/Raven

Naka shot right up, alarmed by the unexpected voice. The voice came from a Laretu girl, just of age. She towered above Naka, her face was bright and split in two by a white smile. Her skin had the color of the red clay from which they make pottery, pierced by white scars that looked like lightning, her eyes the color of ash and a dark golden braid hanging over her right shoulder. She had four large, ram-like horns, bigger than a usual Laretu, and despite her young age they were already worn from battle with scratches all over them. As she stepped closer, Naka crawled back, biting her teeth not to scream out in pain.

"Easy there, I am not here to hurt you. I heard you screaming as I walked back home from hunting, and searched for you."

Naka's face was as cold as ice as she attempted to hide her pain. She felt a tree in her back, stopping her from moving further away.

"My mother is good with herbs and knows how to take care of your wound. Please, just let us take care of the wound and give you a proper meal. We won't bite, I promise."

Naka didn't like it but her wound needed to be taken care of and a hot meal was something she could really use right now.

"Fine," she muttered.

"I'm Etaín, by the way," the Laretu said as she picked Naka up with ease and set off into the woods.

The woods were different in these parts of the mountains, even though they were just across the river. They felt warmer, welcoming even. Naka couldn't keep up with where they were going, mainly because she fainted a couple of times. The pain in her leg was unbearable, but she didn't show it at any point, she refused to. It seemed as if they had finally reached their destination after a few hours of walking. Before them stood a large house made from stone and wood. Further down the road Naka could see the outer houses of a city which she hoped was Murra already.

Laughter rose from the house and Naka feared they had gone to some kind of inn. Etaín kicked open the door and the laughter was silenced immediately. Five men and a single woman looked at them before the woman ran off and the men cleared the table. The woman and Etaín exchanged looks and Naka was put on the table.

"Hold her still, I need to clean the wound and stitch it. We need to be quick, she has already lost a lot of blood." Her voice was steady and calm which eased Naka, the woman knew what she was doing. Icy water poured over her leg and salt burned in the wound. Cold stings of metal pierced her skin over and over, a needle followed by a thin black thread, sowing her skin back together. The woman was silent except for when she needed something and Naka was surprised by the delicate work she did with a needle that was tiny, compared to her. Naka didn't scream, didn't flinch, she had felt worse, much worse.

"Almost done," the woman whispered with a kind smile to calm Naka. One of the men returned from outside with some plants. He handed them over to the woman who started mixing them together with some other things Naka couldn't see. She returned to the wound with a paste that looked like some animal had thrown up.

"I hope I don't have to eat that," Naka said, nodding at the paste. The woman smiled and shook her head before she took a handful and massaged it onto the stitches. She had only just touched the stitches when the slow moving agony filled Naka's leg again. It felt as if her blood had turned to ice and her muscles felt as steel, cold and hard. When she removed her hands, the paste started to overtake the pain. A soothing and warm wave washed over her leg, chasing away the pain, numbing her muscles. Etaín lifted Naka up again and moved her upstairs, into a room with a bed at least twice the size of Naka. Naka could barely keep her eyes open and was trying to determine if she was safe as she clutched onto Nárymm.

"What is your name, dear?" the woman asked. Her kind voice let her know she was in good hands. They couldn't know her real name, but she couldn't think of a fake one, so she translated her name into common tongue.

"Raven," she whispered before the darkness of sleep came to take her away on journeys she would possibly never remember.

Feverish dreams ruled her sleep. Dreams filled with countless enemies whose eyes Naka had shut hundreds of years ago. She fought and fought, defeating them all once more until only one was left.

King Varne.

Suddenly she was chained to the darkness, unable to move as he struck her with a whip. Every time the whip cracked and tore open her skin his words echoed through her mind.

"This will make you stronger. You can never show weakness, you can never feel pain. I will make sure you will never feel pain, I will make you perfect."

She hated his voice, hated what he had done to her. Yet she thanked him, because of him she had already felt the greatest pains, thanks to him she was stronger.

"Accept your darkness within, and the world is at your feet."

His whip cracked once again and she looked into his lilac eyes before she woke up.

She did not recognize the room she woke up in so she kept her breath steady. Light was soft and grey as it shone through the window above her. Looking around carefully, she could see there was nobody in the room. Deep brown walls surrounded her and the room was filled with weapons, Nárymm among them, and armor but, surprisingly, also with dresses and jewelry, clearly made for a Laretu. Naka remembered what had happened and threw the bed open and saw her leg. There was a new bandage on there, it was clean still and when she touched it, she didn't feel any pain. When she carefully undid the bandage, she saw that the stitches had been taken out and her skin had closed up, it was still a fresh scar but it was closed. She noticed someone had taken off her clothes except for her underclothes. Her outfit was on a table next to her bed, nicely folded and cleaned, and her cape hung on the backside of the door. Naka carefully stood up, wiggling her toes and moving her leg around, noticing she barely felt any pain anymore. She put on her clothes and saw her knives on the table as well, perfectly cleaned and sharpened even. What must they think, a wounded girl with this many knives and a spear, lost in the forest? She would leave quickly, before anyone came looking for her, before they realized who she truly was. They had been kind and she wouldn't want them to get hurt because of her, they had been kind to her and she didn't want them to pay the price for that. Naka knew what happened to those who sheltered a traitor of the Shining Lands, it was nothing good.

As soon as she opened the door she was greeted with the sweet, thick smell of eggs and bacon. Her stomach rioted, demanding she go down and eat all she could find. She knew she couldn't sneak out, and she did still need to eat. After contemplating all her options, she decided to go downstairs, eat and leave right after, never to return. First, she had to go erase the tracks and then she could go south to Murra. At the bottom of the stairs, Etaín stood up and helped her down the stairs, not that Naka needed the help. They walked to the table where the delicious food was presented. There was roasted chicken and beef, fresh bread, baked eggs and bacon, roasted nuts and even some fresh berries. Her stomach growled even louder and the whole family started laughing. She was put at one end of the table facing who she thought to be the mother on the other end. Etaín clearly resembled her mother, having the same hair and horns although the mother's eyes were golden brown instead of ashen grey. Several scars crossed her face, pale like lightning against their reddish skin.

"Goodmorning dear, you must be hungry, so eat as much as you like, you can use some good food it looks like. We are going to go to the training fields so the children can spar with some friends." Naka already filled up her plate as the mother spoke. "I believe we haven't even introduced ourselves yet, how rude of us. My name is Mira, mother, and head of this family. This is Urdin, my husband." She nodded at the older man. His hair was a dark brown, he was the only one, the others all had golden hair like their mother. A large scar crossed the left side of his face, just like Mira, souvenirs of the War of Shattered Light, Naka figured. Laretu were known to be great warriors and both men and women fought in their armies. Both were to be feared on the battlefield and it wasn't uncommon that they found love there. The father smiled when Naka realized she had been staring at his face.

"I know this face is pleasant to look at, don't worry," he spoke in his deep voice. Laughter rose immediately, preventing Naka from apologizing. The four sons directly imitated the father in an overly dramatic way, striking mocking poses every second until they saw their mother's gaze. She nodded at the boy on her left, "This is Kaav, the oldest, although he doesn't always act like it. Next to him Uyr and Entu, our personal troublemakers. Across the table Etaín, who you've already met, and Eor, our youngest and somehow wisest." The four brothers looked very much like each other. All golden blond hair, all ashen grey eyes and large horns, although everyone had different piercings in their horns. Kaav's hair had been cut on the sides of his head, the rest of his hair ended just above his shoulders, the usual hair of Laretu warriors. Uyr and Entu's hair was wild and seemingly untameable but somehow looked like it was supposed to be that way. Only Eor's hair was short and looked like he actually took care of it regularly. Etaín wore her long braid again, a look that suited her. Naka smiled for a moment and introduced herself as Raven once more.

"An unusual name for an Ilunari, but a lovely name nonetheless. What brings you to these parts, Raven?" the mother asked. It was clear that she was the head of the house, surely the father had a say, but her word was law.

Naka was not planning on telling them a lot about herself. She took a large bite from the roasted meat in front of her. It was best that people knew as little as they could about her. She had to come up with something while she chewed her food, avoiding the curious looks of the table. She swallowed her food. "I'm from Cysta Imen, originally, but started travelling the world after the death of my parents, I'm quite good with my spear so I make myself useful protecting others in these times of war." Naka was satisfied with that story, it would cover why she carried these weapons and it was an easy story to keep up. They all seemed excited and eager to know more, but Naka just shoved more food on her plate and ate it very slowly to avoid talking.

"An Ilunari mercenary, that's pretty amazing if you ask me. You must have countless good stories to tell. I can only imagine all the places you have seen, the battles you have fought. I suppose I found you after some bandits chased you down?" Etaín burst out. Naka nodded as an answer, she wasn't exactly wrong.

"You know you are welcome to stay as long as you like, there is enough space. And it's nice to have an extra girl in this house filled with little boys." When she said that she looked at her brothers, who immediately imitated her dramatically.

"Well, we will bombard you with questions another time, dear. Right now, we should get to the training fields, you guys need all the practice you can get before you get to the frontlines," Mira laughed and got up.

"Actually, I should leave. The longer I stay the more danger you are in," Naka said. The others looked at each other before Mira came to Naka and took her hand.

"You have been unconscious for four days. On the first day a woman came to our door, Human, one eye of onyx, hair as black as that eye. She claimed to be one of King Egìl's commanders, looking for an Ilunari fugitive. Little did she know that Laretu are one of the most loyal races to King Egìl, so we know all the commanders, we know the official armor. We know she wasn't who she said she was, so we told her that we saw an Ilunari run north. She left immediately. Now we know she was actually a bandit, although she did look the part so it didn't take much guessing." Mira paused for a moment and smiled. "If you still want to leave then I understand and we will give you some food for the road, but you are welcome to stay a few days to recover properly. I'm sure Etaín would love to have another girl around." The words were kind and honest and Naka felt bad for the family, she knew the woman actually was one of the highest commanders of King Egìl, and Naka was actually a fugitive. She just smiled and thanked Mira, she figured she could stay a few days, the threat had passed and Naka needed a little time to get herself together before she travelled all the way to the Dan'um forests in the east.

The sound of steel on steel echoed through the air, long before they arrived at the training fields. The fields were actually just large fields, no stone paths or court, just grass, mud, dirt and rocks. Dazzling patterns of light moved around on the grounds as the sun hit the moving blades. Laretus clashing, their feet digging into the dirt, sweat pearling on their reddish skin.

Etaín and her brothers were greeted by the ones not focused on their combat. Two of them looked identical to each other. Green eyes, black hair, tall and muscular, around Etaíns age. Naka could clearly see they were twins as even their movements were similar. Naka placed Nárymm against the stone she sat down on besides Mira. Etaín and her brothers were now fighting too. Eor challenged Entu while Uyr dueled Kaav and Etaín went up against both of the twins. The mother followed her gaze.

"She can defeat any of them. Her brothers faced her a couple of times before they acknowledged she was the best amongst them even though Kaav was a challenge for her. Now she is training with the twins. They wish to fight as one so they become an even greater challenge when together. She could probably still win this with ease if she wanted to, but she is going easy on them, for now." The smile on her face was one of pure pride. Naka observed the twins more closely now. Their movements were almost in harmony yet they did not communicate in any way, but she knew better. Twins had a special bond, a bond that could improve both of them in many ways. Naka looked at Nárymm, the desire for a friendly fight itched in her limbs as she stood up. Mira looked at her with slight concern in her eyes, probably because she didn't want to see Naka's wound rip open after it had just healed.

After a quick inspection of the wound she nodded, giving Naka the permission she had waited for. Most of the fighters paused their combat to watch her. Her long black hair hung loose and reached her knees, her black leather outfit contrasted with the light brown armor of the others. Eor, the youngest, stepped forward and bowed to her.

"I will duel you. I am not the best warrior of our family but I hope I can be a challenge to you nevertheless. You know our rules?" he asked.

"Do repeat them for me once, it has been a while since I fought according to Laretu rules," Naka answered.

"Alright. Since this is a friendly duel killing is forbidden and will be punished by death. The fight will end as soon as one is defeated, defeat being surrender or when you cannot fight anymore. Any weapon is allowed, except for ranged weapons and magic, otherwise you are completely free to fight however you like," he said. Naka nodded that she understood.

Both bowed to each other and Eor drew his sword. The other Laretu warriors had gathered around them, eager to watch this duel. She didn't feel any pressure, neither did Eor. Losing was nothing to be ashamed of. '*Defeat is the best teacher, if you can survive the lesson.*' was the motto of most Laretu warmasters, and this wasn't a fight to the death. Eor stepped forward and Naka immediately lashed out with Nárymm, hitting his ankle and knocking him off of his feet. She pointed her spear at his neck, stating her victory. Everyone burst out in cheers and applause, Eor's face showed his surprise and he still appeared to be processing the fight. Naka couldn't help but laugh a little, people often underestimated her, not knowing the centuries of training she had had. The rush of combat, however short, felt amazing. No killing, no death, just dueling. She helped Eor up and bowed once again.

Kaav stepped forward now. "I challenge you. It would be an honor to fight against someone who defeated a Laretu within seconds. I do warn you, I have fought in the army for the past two years, so, I will be more of a challenge than my brother." Naka simply nodded again and bowed. She knew she had to be more careful, he was properly trained and part of the army. This would be a proper fight, acting on mistakes each fighter made. She had to observe his movement, find his weaknesses. She wasn't afraid to make any mistakes herself, her training had been cruel and awful but it had made her strong, very strong and nearly perfect.

Kaav wielded dual axes, quite unusual, but it only meant a challenge. He dashed forward only to step back as quickly. Naka remained calm and started circling around him. Their eyes were locked on eachother, both knowing that the eyes were the key to defeating your opponent. They often reflected the intentions of the other and revealed their next move before they could act. Suddenly, he came at her with his axes spinning in his hands, but Naka was prepared and dashed to the side. He turned and swung his axe sideways at her. She hooked Nárymm behind his axe and pulled him closer. His body was close to hers. She could feel his breath above her, deep and steady, his warmth radiating on her. He was stronger than she was, but relied on this. She had to utilize the fact that she was quicker and smaller to get him off balance. Their eyes met over the blades of their weapons and Naka smiled. Naka suddenly turned, holding Nárymm with both hands and pushed quickly against his chest. He tried to balance himself by placing his foot a little behind him, breaking his stance for only a moment, but a moment was enough. She grabbed Nárymm tightly and pulled it out of the axes and hit Kaav on his chin. He stumbled backwards and Naka finished it off by placing her foot right behind his, flooring him. Kaav moaned and grabbed his chin. "That's what they call a challenge!" he exclaimed before he burst out laughing, the crowd following him with joy as they applauded them.

The following days she spent training on the fields whenever she could, she had noticed she was a little rusty and there was no real threat for now. She enjoyed the friendliness of the duels even though none of them were a serious challenge so far, she didn't blame them. They were great warriors, there was no doubt about that, she had just been trained in very unique ways, and was much older than any Laretu, than most mortals really.

Everyday, Etaín bombarded her with more questions and everyday the lie Naka told her became more elaborate. Naka didn't like to lie to Etaín, she didn't deserve to be lied to, so she shaped the stories around cores of truth. In her life she had seen many places and fought many battles, she had hidden all over the world, and so she twisted those memories into stories about who she was.

One day, about a week later, Naka had just won a duel against the twins when Etaín grabbed her arm. "We have a surprise for you," she whispered excitedly as she pulled Naka away from the training fields and back home.

They reached the house and Etaín dashed inside, Naka following her with curiosity. It had been many, many centuries since someone had had a surprise for her that didn't involve trying to kill her. Etaín was describing the battle between the twins and Naka to her mother as if Naka was the Guardian of Battle herself. Her mother laughed and beckoned them to follow her.

"Right, the surprise! Raven, you're going to love this!" Etaín exclaimed. In the back of the house there was a large room with a single table and some large closets. Etaín's mother smiled but was interrupted before she could say anything. Etaín's enthusiasm was so intense that Naka was afraid she would explode of pure joy.

"Okay, so tonight there is a ball, well, more of a feast, hosted by Warmaster Kruvv in the Great Hall in Murra to celebrate the Laretu victory against the Kurr like, forever ago, I'm not sure why we still celebrate that actually, but I won't say no to a feast, and we were invited but we want you to come as well. My mother made a dress for you. She went to the market a few days ago to get fabric for your dress. We kind of guessed your measurements but they can be changed of course. We can braid your hair and make you look pretty and just help you forget about your worries for tonight," Etaín rambled on with big eyes filled with excitement. This was not what Naka expected when she heard the word surprise. She had no words to explain how incredibly touched she was that someone had done something so kind for her, so she simply nodded yes.

"YES! Okay close your eyes so we can make you pretty and then you can see the final results." And so, she did.

After a long while of trying her very best not to open her eyes Naka was finally allowed to look in the mirror. The dress looked like the twilight sky was draped around her body. It glimmered like starlight was woven into the fabric itself. The dress followed her body perfectly and revealed her pale shoulders and neck, her perfectly straight hair falling down her back like a black waterfall. Naka felt like she could gaze at the dress forever, get lost in it's deep black and blue color. She had not looked this beautiful in so long, she didn't even remember when it was. The dress dragged over the ground as she moved around, making a soft, rustling sound as the silk grazed over the wood. Etaín and her mother were busy getting dressed themselves while Naka admired herself. It wasn't the first time she wore something like this and even though looking like royalty made her feel confident it also reminded her of her past but she tried to shake the unhappy feeling. Etaín's dress flowed over her body like liquid silver. It showed a completely different side of her. A single white flower was braided into her hair, matching the color of the scars. Her mother wore a dress the purple of the nightshade flower, and she hid a knife on the side of her leg which couldn't be seen at all even though the dress was quite tight. It was fitting that Mira wore the color of a nightshade, Naka thought. Beautiful, but very deadly.

"Thank you," was all Naka could say to them before she choked up. They smiled and simply nodded as Mira took them each on a different arm.

"I really don't want to leave my spear behind, it is very important to me," Naka mumbled.

"I understand that. That is why I have it stored in the carriage that will take us to the ball, just as your belongings. Just in case. We have our own weapons with us as well. What would a Laretu be without their weapon? They are usually put in the weapon chamber upon entry but you can access it at any time. It is just not custom to wear a weapon in a stranger's house, it is a sign of distrust, so you best not mention the knife under my dress," Mira said, giving Naka a motherly smile. A heavy weight lifted off Naka's heart. Nárymm was there if she needed it. The men of the family were nowhere to be seen.

"Where are the men, if I may ask?"

Etaín giggled. "We did not want to make you feel uncomfortable and send them to change at the home of Wur and Wush, the twins from the training fields today. And my mother doesn't like their fooling around and complaining about waiting." Her mother gave her a funny face as reply. "My best guess is that they are at the ball already, complaining about our late arrival and wreaking havoc on the buffet." Her mother snorted in agreement.

"Come," she said.

In front of the house was a beautiful carriage made out of a dark wood. Four horses were there to pull it. All of them were the exact color of the wood. Their manes were braided with silver bands and white flowers like the one in Etaín's hair. Naka could feel the presence of Nárymm and it eased her mind.

"My ladies," the coachman said as he opened the door for them. Naka sat beside the window, gazing outside, hoping to see some of the surroundings. She hadn't been in Murra for a very long time, only in Grun'Udul every now and then. Etaín was already calming down a little as she discussed with her mother who was coming to the ball. Her mother wanted her to find a partner because almost all her brothers were married or soon to be. Kaav and Uyr were married but their wives lived at seperate homes until Kaav and Uyr had built their own houses, Entu was to marry this summer and Eor was just a romantic who did not want to settle yet. Etaín stated that she liked her freedom and changed the subject to something that didn't interest Naka. She gazed out of the window and let her thoughts loose until they had arrived at a large caste. Well, it was more like a pretty stronghold, with high walls and towers surrounding the massive rock-like building from which music, laughter and chattering emerged.

"Time to socialize," Etaín teased as they stepped through the oaken doors, into the warm hall.

Chapter 5
Rynn

The raging flames approached with immense speed. Roaring and hissing they scorched everything they touched. Rynn faced his oncoming defeat with confidence, hands raised at the flames. He couldn't think of a spell that would help him here, so he let his heart do what was right. Rynn knew there was an enchantment that was supposed to save them from death and yet he feared for his life for he did not trust the strength of that enchantment to save him from a power this great.

As the ocean of fire hit his hands a shockwave went through his body. The flames twisted and turned before his hands before they wrapped around his dark brown skin and disappeared beneath it. His veins glowed as if they were filled with molten stone and iron. The glow flowed through every vein, moving further across his arms toward his chest. It crawled over his neck moving underneath his robes and into his face, where they met his eyes. His normal brownish green eyes suddenly became the essence of fire itself, bright and orange, flickering like flames.

He clenched his teeth, it hurt as the fire filled him, he felt it eating away at his own energy, felt it settling in his heart and soul. There was no control for Rynn, fire had taken over, burning a way into him. A final roar escaped from the flames as they faded into his veins. The entire arena fell silent. Where the flames first roared there now was an ocean of silence and tension.

Rynn lowered his hands, pure power in his veins, a feeling of might within him. He was afraid to open his mouth, afraid to lose this feeling, but he knew his body couldn't hold this energy much longer. With all his power he tried to hold it, giving the fire a place in his heart where it would never leave, where he could always use it. But there was simply too much his body couldn't hold at this moment so he forced the energy down into the ground. The ground around him flashed as a fiery essence whirled around his feet, the crowd gasped and shielded their eyes.

When Rynn opened his eyes, he was blinded by the sparkling effect of light breaking on twisted glass. The floor of the arena was normally filled with mainly sand, and all of it had turned into a sea of crystal clear-glass that reflected the sunlight and shattered it into countless colors. People gasped and started shouting, pushing themselves to the edge of the arena to get a better look at what had happened. A thud crossed the arena, Biran. He had fallen on the floor, probably of pure exhaustion, he had thrown all he had into this spell, and Rynn had simply absorbed all of it. Rynn respected the boy, it had been a spell of incredible strength that had made Rynn felt like his magic was no match. Rynn wanted to run to Biran and see what he could do for him but could barely move his body. His veins still glowed, but now looked like embers on a campfire. He could still feel the rush in his body and tried to contain it. The professors would inspect him and attempt to draw any excess energy out of his body. But that was not what he wanted. He could use this energy, he could change the world, give the weak and broken a chance, maybe even end the war. He hid this fire deep within himself where he could feel its presence all the time but the professors would not find it, not with their abilities.

Biran had been lifted up and was brought to the Academy for healing and recovery. People started to come Rynn's way but he turned around and stumbled out of the arena through another exit. He had no intention of speaking to people, he would go to Professor Ira for a short inspection so they would not suspect anything but after that he would leave before the feast would begin.

Packing his belongings for his journey only took a few moments, he didn't have much besides a few clothes, the letters from his sister and some books he had taken from the library. He lifted his robes and inspected his body. Black scars marked his skin everywhere, every scar a single vein. He released a tiny flame from his heart and watched his scars light up like they were filled with lava. In the mirror he could see his eyes had turned into the same fiery orange as his veins, only now did he notice that most of his black, curly hair had burned off, leaving him with very short curls that barely covered his scalp.

"What is happening to me?" Rynn whispered to himself as he looked at his own eyes. Never had anybody absorbed magic like that, no book mentioned it. It wasn't just the fire that he took in, he felt all his magic was more powerful, as if he had taken all of Biran's magic. Rynn prayed to Nirs Imak that it wasn't true, that Biran still had his magic, but nobody answered. He pushed the fire out of his veins and fixed his robes. He would try to find Yira and say goodbye. When he walked out of his chamber, he ran into one of the headmasters, Headmaster Kavur. Headmaster Kavur was a Laretu, towering above him like a mountain, tall and strong, with horns that were engraved with words of protection and other small enchantments.

"Come," was the only thing he said to Rynn before he turned around and walked away. Without hesitation Rynn followed. He figured that he should not raise any suspicion about leaving, not now. He would get more attention than usual because of his performance in the arena and it would already be difficult to leave unseen at all. The headmaster led him toward the eastern wing, where Healing and Protection was practiced. Professor Ira was already sitting in a separate room and Headmaster Kavur pushed him inside and closed the door. In every corner stood a Surr'um, he had never seen their faces before in the Academy but they all looked similar to the professor. Professor Ira told him to remove his robes and lay down on the stone table in the middle of the room. The stone felt as if ice was pressed against his skin, it was an effort to relax and the fire within him made an attempt to heat the table but failed to do so. Rynn hoped they wouldn't find that very fire and he attempted to build a barrier around it so that they wouldn't be able to reach it. Surr'um were known to be exceptionally good at breaking minds and barriers within them. This was probably the reason that he was inspected by five of them. Each grabbed one of his limbs and pushed it onto the frozen stone. Rynn struggled for a moment but their grip was too strong. Professor Ira strapped him down with stone chains just as cold as the stone he lay upon, so cold they seemed to drain his energy. The stone chains looked ancient, filled with symbols Rynn didn't know and ice seemed to move across the stone, as if it was alive. His dark skin was covered with white frost where the chains touched, patterns of white swirling across his wrists and ankles. He didn't understand, it was a simple inspection. At least, it was supposed to be. Professor Ira leaned over him and looked him in the eye. "They are just precautions. We can be quite rough when searching through your mind and soul. If you take down all your barriers, we can search without doing any harm, because we will break down any wall we find." She looked up for a moment, inspecting the motionless faces of the Surr'um around her before she looked him in the eye again.

"The inspection has been ordered by the High Council. You have taken in enormous amounts of energy and power and lived. This was considered impossible, for humans at least. They are, after all, the weaker race." Rynn realized he had surrendered to her soothing voice and fought back. The chains seemed to be a lot more than just cold. They had slowed down his magic, suppressed it in a way. He checked his barriers, trying to fight against her voice. Almost every single one was torn down or crumbling. Professor Ira laid her hands on his temples and he could feel her presence rampaging through his mind. He focused on the barriers around his fire and memories of his family. Nothing happened. He gave attention to the thoughts that had been crossing his mind. Who was she really? Professor Ira would never call humans the weaker race, she knew what he could do. But before he could consider her motives the Surr'um opened their eyes.

Agony.

Pure agony and torture shot through his body and mind and soul. His back curved further than his spine could bend. His bones and flesh twisted inside his body as they raged through his mind. Their energy wove into his own as the Surr'um wreaked havoc within his mind and soul. They found his lonely hours in the library and went through it with extreme caution, examining everything he had read and seen. His dreams, desires and wishes. They were about to find his barriers when his mind was suddenly filled with a silver mist. Thick swirls separated the Surr'um from each other, and clouded his own mind. He could reach only one memory.

"Yira." She appeared in his mind's eye a moment before he heard the doors of the room slam open. The Surr'um turned their heads as the girl stood in the doorway, a sword in each hand. Yira ran toward the first Surr'um, and pushed both swords through the slender body. The Surr'um collapsed as the other four stumbled back, their faces filled with fear. Yira jumped on the stone table and cut Rynn's chains with one swing of her swords. His fire burned again and chased away the cold. She grabbed the stone chains and threw them onto the seemingly paralyzed Surr'um. They screamed as they were thrown against the floor. Professor Ira's eyes turned an icy blue, just like the others. Their skin cracked and fell off like old paint, revealing skin like the night sky. Their blonde hair turned into strings of tarnished steel, beaten and worn.

"Quickly now," Yira whispered. Rynn followed her.

"What were they? What happened to Professor Ira?" Rynn asked but Yira did not turn around.

"Those are Shar'um, Surr'um tainted by shadows, skinshifters, illusionists and a real pain in the ass. If your Professor Ira was ever a real person, then she is dead."

"Why are you saving me? Isn't everyone at the Academy in danger?" Rynn exclaimed with heavy breaths.

"Because it seems we need you specifically to bring back the Lady of Light."

Rynn was speechless as Yira dragged him through the halls.

"Get them, now!" the Surr'um, or whatever they were, were running after them. The face of the Professor was still partially covered in cracked skin, only revealing one half of what lay beneath. Screams now echoed through the empty halls, the screams of children. They had just left the East wing and stood in the Great Hall leading to the front doors. Yira ran toward them and Rynn followed. From both sides, tall creatures with skin as night appeared, each holding a sword of icy blue steel. They turned toward them, blocking the great wooden doors that meant their escape. Yira hesitated but Rynn stepped forward, his eyes filled with fire.

"Don't, it's what they want." Yira put her hand on his arm. His fire eased down and retreated deep within his soul. Her hand felt extremely comforting on his skin, soothing his anger. Yira's head shot toward the doors. She sheathed her swords and put her hands on Rynn's ears. All sound disappeared from the world yet his eyes had enough to see. The high windows that were filled with glass of every color exploded in a cascade of broken light and rainbows and shattered again on the marble floor. Blood dripped from the ears of the Shar'um and fell among the shimmering fragments of light. The walls cracked, tears running through the stone, shaking the core of the Academy. Yira took her hands off his ears and stepped toward the great doors. She turned around. Her eyes filled with mist caught the shattered rainbows, her long auburn hair danced around her in perfect harmony. She was more beautiful than anything Rynn had ever seen. Her lips moved but he could not hear a sound. She turned around again, moving toward the doors when she turned her head to the left. Rynn followed her eyes and only now noticed a girl with the same auburn hair. She looked exactly like Yira only she had braided her hair in such a way that it revealed her ears. They were slightly pointed. A thin layer of crystal was intricately spun over them, it seemed to be as fragile and delicate as a spider's web. She looked toward Rynn. The other girl's eyes were bright and green, unlike Yira's. Their gaze moved toward the right. Another girl with the same auburn hair and eyes of green stood there. Her lips were pierced by seven rings of moonstone. They went through both her upper as well as her lower lip, sealing her mouth. Yira looked back at him and gestured to follow. His hearing suddenly returned to him. Screams still echoed through the halls, breaking the enchanting beauty of the light in the shattered glass. Both the other girls passed them. They both wielded dual swords that looked very much like Yira's. The blades were the same strange, red metal but the hilt was unique for each pair of swords, each one having a different gem. Yira had already walked outside of the doors onto the great square in front of the Academy. Rynn quickly walked past the dead creatures, careful not to stand in their grey blood. The bright evening sun hit his face as he walked onto the square, forcing him to close his eyes for a moment. Yira stood at the edge of the square where the forest began and gestured him to hurry there. He rushed toward her as she disappeared between the trees. It was hard following her but she knew exactly where they were going. Finally, they stopped. There was nothing special there, no reason to stop.

"He can't walk there," she mumbled to the empty air in front of her. She directed herself to him.

"Do you know how to teleport?" He knew how it worked but had never done it before, and teleportation could only be done if the caster had been there before.

"Yes, I know how to do it, I've just never done it before," he replied.

She nodded and was silent for a moment. "I will guide you, you just do your thing and I will send you to the right place. You will be safe there." She stepped away from him and mumbled again. Rynn could barely understand a word. She was talking about 'Finding her' and 'helping her' or something. He had no clue, but he trusted her for some reason.

"Okay, let's do this. You use your magic and I will guide it."

She kept silent as he tried to remember how it worked. Most of it existed of focussing on the destination and seeing it as if you were already there. But anything else was still hard to come by. His mind had faced enough, a torture inspection and after that his entire mind had been clouded, not exactly the best circumstances. An image flashed through his mind. Some sort of building, it looked like a temple of some sort. Deserted and ancient. It was built in the side of a mountain, high enough that there were thick blankets of snow. A big circular hole was cut out at the edge furthest from the entrance. Three large pillars rose from the edge of the circle. He focused on the spot right before the entrance and made himself ready to teleport. When he was ready, he reached for Yira but she stepped away from him.

"I need to stay here," was all she said before she pushed his mind.

His feet hit the cold, hard grey stone. The snowy wind cut his bare skin as if it was an icy knife. He damned himself for forgetting his robes, but he rushed his fire through his veins, lighting up his eyes and the scars that marked his entire body. Immediately he felt warm, so he decided he could keep it in his veins until he was somewhere warmer. He looked across the open space toward the large hole near the edge. Beyond that was a stunning view. He could see the river Dawn flowing through the sea of green. He could even see the human capital, Anndar, far to his right. He hadn't been there since he left for the Academy all those years ago. Seeing the white city was strange, the beauty of it contrasting with his last memory of it. His rage fueled his fire and his veins glowed brighter as he thought of that day. The sun descended past the upper ridge and blinded Rynn for a moment. He decided to go inside of the temple and find a place to sleep, and hopefully something to eat. After casting one last look across the edge toward the south-east, where the Academy lay, he went inside. As he stepped through the entrance he was hit with a wall of warmth. He pushed the fire out of his veins for it was not needed anymore. Once his eyes had taken the time to adjust to the darkness inside, he looked around. He stood in a large circular room, across it, two staircases hugged around a pillar that supported the ceiling. It was engraved with all kinds of intricate symbols that seemed ancient and secret. He had never seen any alphabet alike it, although it did resemble the letters from High

Speech. *Perhaps a dialect*, Rynn thought, he had never bothered to learn the languages, everyone spoke common tongue anyway nowadays. Small holes were carved out of the walls of the chamber, almost every single one filled with a dusty orb of some pale crystal. Besides stones and strange engravings there were no signs of life. On one hand it made him wonder, why would anyone build a place this far away from everything? On the other hand, he adored it. Finally, a place where he could be truly alone. Who would live here? This place was so deserted, not even a fool would consider living here. He decided to investigate the back of the room where the stairs came together. The stairs were slippery. It seemed as if they had been walked thousands of times. At the top of the stairs he stood before two large stone doors.

"Damnit. Is everything made of this stupid stone around here?" he muttered to himself. He pushed hard, and fell through them as the doors slammed open with a loud bang. They moved extremely easily and required little effort to open. Rynn cursed as he pushed himself up. He was slightly pissed off. First he had been tortured by some strange people from a race he did not know. Then he had to run for his life and discovered there were two girls who looked exactly like Yira and then, Yira had just bailed on him and pushed him here to this strange place somewhere in the mountains. He knew that Yira probably had a good reason to send him here, and she would probably show up as soon as she was done at the Academy, he just hoped she would bring food and explain all of this to him. It wasn't that he was mad at her, he was just really confused about all of this.

Now he was in a room, circular again, that presented seven passages. He sighed.

Suddenly his mind was filled with a sweet and soft voice. "*The middle one,*" it whispered. Rynn hesitated, it was too simple.

"*It's too obvious so nobody goes there, hidden in plain sight,*" the voice whispered again. That actually made sense to him. He stepped into the dark tunnel and opened his palm, focussing his fire to his hand pushing it outside his veins. A small flame burned within his hand, it wasn't steady but it provided light. Only the veins around his hand glowed this time. Every time he used the fire he felt more comfortable with it, more in control. His steps were quick and certain, knowing he could defend himself, he was a powerful mage and in possession of this new fire. He might even be the most powerful mortal mage alive. Somehow he liked the sound of it but knew it was wrong to do so and pushed the thought away. He reached the end of the tunnel and drew the fire back into his heart. The room was lit by some white light without a source, or at least, not one he could find. On the walls were engravings once more. This time there were more than words. He touched the deep marks in the stone, they were old but made with exceptional precision. Lines formed countless images, most still perfectly intact. They told the story of how the War of Shattered Light had begun, the story of Lady Nuana's murder. The Guardian of Light, Nuana, had been slaughtered inside her Palace in the city of Anndar along with all of her children, the Nuans. Her palace stood there long before the humans settled in this world, and she chose to help them. Humans were considered weak and irrelevant in the beginning, short lifespan, weak bodies, unsuitable for combat and very unskilled in magic. Lady Nuana gave the humans her land to settle on after the Surr'um and Laretu had waged war with them for many years and nearly brought the human race to extinction. It was because of this land that humans became the success they were today. The story said that it was a human who found her, Egíl Tallren, the King of the Humans, who was given immortality until he had avenged Nuana's murder. However, some books said it was the ancestor of the present king, both bearing the same name. Nevertheless, humans lost their protector. The engravings, however, showed some strange engraving next to Lady Nuana's corpse. Somehow it resembled a bird in Rynn's eyes but he knew it was supposed to portray Lady Megana, Lady Nuana's sister and High Immortal of Darkness. It was Lady Megana who murdered her own sister and then tried to take over the Shining Lands, every story said the same. She had even murdered every last Nuan so there would be no trace of the Light left, no creation of Lady Nuana to fight back.

The events after her death were even engraved. After the murder followed great sorrow, a land torn apart by grief. The first attack from the Shadow Lands came the day after Lady Nuana was buried, starting the still ongoing war that kept tearing the Lands apart.

It took the Shining Lands decades to drive the forces of the Shadow Lands out of their borders, after they did, Lady Megana simply disappeared without a trace. There was no mention of her anymore in any part of history, not in these engravings nor in any book out there. She was never seen anymore, only alive in memories. Most thought she was dead, that she could not live without her sister or the guilt of killing her. Most High Immortals disappeared from the world, at least for a while. Rynn had read that once they were everywhere, doing the task they were appointed to do by the Abariimm. The final part of the engraving was a large eye, with in the center a gem. Around it was a writing in common tongue.

"In the Vault will be found, the return of the Light. But only Light and Darkness can open the doors."

Rynn had never heard of this prophecy, he didn't even know which vault they were talking about. He did his best to plant the image in his mind, maybe he could find a book on it somewhere and figure out what it was all about.

At the end of the engraving stood another pair of stone doors. On them there was a final engraving, it showed Lady Nuana being reborn, her light shining across the entire door, behind her stood one figure that was barely visible. Before he could push the doors open, they swung open by themselves. Bright blue light hit him and his hand rose to shield his eyes from it. Something called him, he could feel it in his bones. The light slowly faded as he stepped inside the room. It was another circular room, smaller than the ones before. The light had faded almost completely and Rynn could see a large crystal orb in the back of the room. He moved toward it but hesitated when he saw what was inside. It couldn't be. He rubbed his eyes and walked around the orb, inspecting it for glamours or anything alike, but he could not find any. The orb now only glowed faintly. What was inside existed only in the old tomes of the Library, in stories that were not remembered. Inside of this orb there was something that hadn't been seen since the beginning of the War of Shattered Light, the last of its kind.

It was a Nuan, and she was alive.

Chapter 6
Etaín

Etaín, her mother, and Raven walked into the warm hallway where they were greeted by one of the servants. He led them toward the weapons room where he made sure they left their weapons behind. From the corner of her eye Etaín noticed Raven hesitating to put down her spear. It appeared she couldn't find the right spot for it but eventually she put it right next to the door. In the meantime, Etaín and her mother had both put their weapons with those of her brothers and father.

As her mother was announced Etaín gently squeezed Raven's hand and gave her a smile. Raven looked into Etaín's eyes and gave a soft smile. She was glad she met Raven, she hoped they could be close friends someday, because Etaín somehow felt very comfortable around Raven in a way she hadn't felt before. Raven looked away and pulled her hand away as well, leaving Etaín with a slightly numb feeling.

It was now her turn to be announced. As she stepped through the doors the large ballroom revealed itself to her, now in hushed whispers as her mother walked down the stairs before her. "Etaín of house Mirdar," echoed through the halls followed by the usual applause. Oh, how she dreamed to one day be announced by her deeds, to be more than just a member of her house. There were not enough stairs to properly daydream about her future titles. She followed her mother through the crowd toward her brothers and father. Etaín knew people considered her to be beautiful but seeing her mother in this dress walking with such strength in each step, seemingly invincible, it made her feel like a shadow of her mother's beauty. Nevertheless, she kept her head high and back straight, smiling at all the faces still in awe of her mother's beauty. All the eyes looked away from her and toward the doors when the servant's voice echoed through the halls announcing Raven as "Raven of Cysta Imen," stirring the crowd by announcing herself without a house but with a place which was very unusual for Laretu customs. Raven was Ilunari though, so perhaps it was common for her to do it this way. Etaín turned around as quickly as her dress allowed so she could watch Raven's entrance and the stunned looks on the faces in the crowd. The Laretu were warriors and traders and many had fought side by side with the other races of the Shining Lands yet, Ilunari were a rare sight. They often kept to themselves, rarely leaving the floating isles of Iri'iun. Even the few Laretu who had seen an Ilunari looked at Raven with awe, after all, Ilunari were considered the most beautiful people, and Raven certainly was living proof as to why people said that. Raven appeared on top of the stairs. Her dress flowed over the steps like a river of night, the fabric shimmering just as bright as the heavenly stars. Every move held such grace, elegance and a slight hint of power that she could have been a queen for all they knew. The fact that Raven was much smaller than the Laretu seemed to fall away, her presence was so powerful that her size meant nothing. People stepped aside as she moved through the crowd, ignoring all the staring eyes and taking position at Etaín's side after greeting Etaín's father and brothers. The entire room was staring in silence until her mother laughed, "Well then! Let the music play!"

It didn't take long for the noise to return to the room, consisting mainly of conversations about the 'Ilunari woman.' Eor immediately started telling their father about Raven's most recent victory against the twins, giving Raven not a single moment of rest. Etaín already knew that she had to save Raven from her brother's attempts to impress her before she went mad. Uyr and Entu were already back at the buffet eating like it was their last day. Kaav was out of sight, probably with his wife or people from his warband. Etaín saw her mother chatting with a father and his son and she just knew her mother would come over in a bit, wanting to introduce her to some nice people and she'd be stuck with them for the entire night thanks to one of her mother's attempts to find her a suitable partner. First of all, she didn't want to get married and settle down, not yet at least. Second of all, she wanted someone who could stand their ground in a fight, and every guy in this room had already tasted their defeat by Etaín's hand. The thought of having a partner who she didn't meet in battle felt weird and if she didn't have a challenge fighting him it was a no go.

She walked past the buffet, admiring all the roasted meat, they had roasted a direboar big enough to feed everyone at the ball and stuffed it with nuts and mushrooms. There was a whole array of fish and even some blue crabs that lived in the far north of the mountains, Etaín grabbed a piece of the direboar and quickly moved out of her mother's sight.

Etaín knew most of the people there, the house of Mirdar was well known thanks to Etaín's parents. Their deeds at the front had earned the respect of many Laretu and so they had been invited to ball after ball, they had come to befriend many houses, especially after they learned of Etaín. There weren't many Laretu daughters around these parts, so Etaín had become really popular really quick. Lost in thought she bumped into a tall woman and Etaín had to take a step back to find her balance. The woman was taller than her, making Etaín look up to see her face. No horns, pale skin tone, eyes as red as blood without pupils and flowing black hair, her face covered in a web of scars, yet stunningly beautiful. Her red dress cascaded onto the cold marble floor. Her dress was made from countless, tiny scales of metal, softly ringing as the woman walked. Etaín started to apologize to her, still somewhat surprised by her appearance, but the woman smiled and walked past her. Etaín was speechless, the smile the woman gave her had revealed her teeth, filed into sharp points. Something was wrong, she knew it. She turned around to find the woman walking toward Raven.

Suddenly she remembered. Her mother had told stories of the High Immortals who turned against Lady Nuana, the Guardian of Light. She remembered them because they scared her, especially one of them, Lady Shyvna, a Guardian of Battle. Eyes filled with blood and teeth like daggers. A beautiful woman covered in webs of scars.

"No way," Etaín whispered to herself. The woman held out her hands before her, and a sword began to appear out of thin air, as if she summoned it. There was no doubt left, this was Lady Shyvna, and she was out for blood. Etaín charged toward the woman as fast as she could in her horrid dress. She hit the Guardian in the back with full force, planting her horns into her flesh and knocking her down. The woman screeched as she fell to the floor, flying a small distance away from Raven and Etaín. Raven's eyes met Etaín's, they both knew what they needed, weapons. Raven dashed through the crowd, pushing everybody who stood in her path aside, and Etaín followed. They had just reached the weapons room when they heard shouts of battle coming from the ballroom. Raven had already cut off the bottom of the dress with a knife. Etaín followed her lead and grabbed her axe from the rack to cut off the bottom of her dress. They were barely finished when Etaín's father rushed into the weapons room.

"You need to get to safety. Your mother has taken the woman's weapons, but new ones appeared out of thin air. Mira struck her several times, but it seems that woman cannot be harmed by us. You need to go." His tone was serious and hard as stone, yet a hint of fear showed in his eyes. Raven stepped forward with her spear in her hand.

"There are not many weapons that can harm Shyvna, but Nárymm can." she said, nodding at her spear.

Urdin's eyes widened, "Shyvna? You mean the High Immortal? It cannot be… There is no point in fighting her. Only another High Immortal can kill her." He moved aside as Raven stepped past him.

"Yes, that's Shyvna, but trust me when I say she can be defeated. After I am done with her she will regret coming here." The silver tip of Raven's spear glowed in the light of the hallway and Etaín's father nodded. He quickly grabbed a longsword and nodded once more. Raven threw the doors open and Etaín's blood froze in her veins. It was a horrible scene. A true bloodbath. Corpses all around the whirlwind of blades that was Shyvna. Her vicious grin revealing her filed teeth, her blades killing almost everyone who came at her. It was the 'almost' that made Etaín proud to be of House Mirdar. Her mother faced the High Immortal with pride and strength. Armed with blades just like her opponent she dueled the High Immortal of Battle itself. Her dress was ripped and stained with blood but Etaín could not tell whose it was. Raven walked toward the battle. Every move was serene, there was no wrath, she was completely in control of her emotion as every step took her closer to the Guardian. Etaín looked toward her mother and was just in time to see the Guardian send her flying into the wall. Etaín yelled out of rage and dashed down the stairs, hearing her father do the same. The Guardian already stood over her mother, ready to take her life. There was no way she would make it in time, and neither would her father or Raven. Blinded by rage she stormed toward her mother. Suddenly Raven stood behind the Guardian and her spear slashed Shyvna's back. The Guardian cried out and turned around, leaving Etaín's mother alone. Raven and Shyvna engaged into an intense duel without screams or shouts, just the sound of steel on steel and steel in flesh.

"Mom!" Etaín yelled. One of her horns was broken and her face and body bloody and bruised, her nose was bleeding and there were several cuts across her face, but she was alive. Her mother looked up to her and then nodded toward the duel.

"Go help her. This isn't a fight she needs to take alone."

Etaín carefully kissed her mother's forehead before she grabbed her axe and ran toward Raven. She felt her rage, Guardian or not she would tear Shyvna apart.

With a loud roar she charged into battle once again. The Guardian did not even look at her as she lashed out with her sword at Etaín. Etaín ducked and barely dodged the sharp blade. Etaín knew she was not capable of harming the Guardian with her axe but she could give Raven an opportunity. Her axe was heavy but she gathered all her strength, lifted it above her head and hurled it at Shyvna. The axe just missed the Guardian's back and buried itself into the dark wooden wall. The Guardian twisted toward Etaín.

"How dare you throw a weapon at me, you *Karnar*?" Shyvna hissed and pushed Raven away from her, knocking her down.

"Stay," the Guardian snarled at Raven, "We're not done yet." One step and Shyvna stood beside Etaín swinging her swords at Etaín, who had no defenses left. Etaín was ready for her death, it would be a glorious one. She would be proud to die this way, fighting a Guardian herself.

But today was not that day.

Etaín's father pushed Etaín out of the way and lifted his longsword with both hands in an attempt to block the dark blades. As the blades hit the longsword it shattered like glass, the shards flying past his face and cutting his skin. The dark blades of the Guardian fell unhindered, planting themselves into his chest. Shyvna pulled them out quickly and laughed, flashing her sharp teeth. Scarlet rivers flowed from the two deep wounds across his chest. Deep enough to cut the floor below him. His lifeless body hit the floor, his empty eyes staring into the nothingness. Etaín was proud, seeing her father dead hurt but the pride of how he died was much stronger than sorrow, his death was glorious and she would make sure the world would know, but first, she had a High Immortal to kill.

Shyvna's wail cut through the air as Raven's spear slashed her face from her cheek to her eyebrow, gouging her left eye. The Guardian stumbled back, blinded and screaming, lashing out to the air, not seeing where her enemies were. The remaining Laretu quickly came to their aid, pulling Etaín away from the still screaming Guardian. Raven wasn't done with Shyvna yet and jumped up, ready to slam her spear into Shyvna's neck, her eyes two pools of shadows. Right before the spear hit Shyvna, she stepped aside and Raven's spear hit the ground, sending a shockwave of shadows across the room. Raven looked up at the High Immortal and was already dashing at her, ready to plant her spear in Shyvna's chest but Shyvna disappeared and Nárymm instead hit the wall, sending a crack through the stone all the way to the ceiling.

Etaín's brothers had gathered around their mother and were helping her out of the building. Etaín barely noticed being dragged out of the halls into the fresh air of the night. The cold brought her back to reality and she looked around for her mother. She was standing again, leaning on Kaav's shoulder. Unable to speak and with tears in her eyes Etaín hugged her mother, trying not to hurt her. Her mother took her head in her palms and wiped the tears from Etaín's cheeks. "His death was honorable, he gave his life so you could live. We survived this and it will make us stronger. Your father will now get his well-deserved rest in the Whispering Halls while he watches over us as we defeat our enemies," her gentle voice soothed her pain. Etaín knew her mother was right. Their father died in the most honorable way he could and she should be thankful for it. All that was left to do was make him proud.

As she turned around to look for Raven, she spotted her walking away from the crowd. Etaín only needed a few quick steps to catch up with her. She walked beside Raven who didn't even look at her. After a few more steps she stopped. Leaning on her spear she caught her breath for a moment before she spoke.

"I'm truly sorry about your father, he was a brave man." Her voice was rough, her eyes were fixed on the ground as she continued, "Shyvna came for me, and will come for me again. I will not forget the kindness you have shown me but in return I must leave so I won't get you killed. Goodbye, Etaín."

But before she could take another step Etaín had grabbed Raven's shoulder, stopping her.

"Raven, if Shyvna comes for you again, then there is no place I'd rather be than by your side. I have a fight to finish with her and if I let you go alone, I will not get any of the action myself." Etaín found it hard to keep her voice steady, but she was confident in this decision. This way she would not lose a friend and she had a better chance to avenge her father. She could travel the world and return home, knowing that Shyvna would never harm anyone again.

"You can't. I only bring death," Raven said, pulling herself loose and continuing to walk away.

Etaín would not let herself be beaten that easily, yet she ran back. Her eyes met her mother's and those of her brothers. Laretu never said goodbye, because eventually you always saw each other again, be it here or in the Whispering Halls. Instead Kaav stepped forward and handed her one of his axes. They were fine weapons that had proved their worth in many battles. It was a big gesture to gift his own weapon to another.

"You can get the other one when you return." His deep voice was steady but she knew that he would miss her, they all would, and she would miss them. As she ran back toward Raven, who hadn't stopped walking, she glanced over her shoulder one last time. No tears, no regrets, no goodbye. Their faces might have seemed emotionless but Etaín knew that it was just a mask.

She averted her eyes, finding Raven again and when she caught up with her, she ignored Raven's looks, telling her to leave her.

"Where to?" Etaín asked. After a long silence Raven answered.

"To the heart of the Dan'um forests." She seemed to want to say more but closed her mouth.

Etaín had never been past the Blood Forest, which lay only hours from here, and the idea of travelling all the way to the Dan'um forests excited her as much as it scared her. She could still go back home, but she wouldn't, she had a goal and she needed to rise above her nerves, perhaps she would earn a title or two during the journey so she could come home with pride. The red canopy of the Blood Forest stretched out before them, a lonely road leading through the trees all the way into Ravens Pass, Etaín scanned the edge of the mountains to the South, that was Kurr territory. Laretu and Kurr weren't at war anymore, and hadn't been for a long time, but the stories of their ruthlessness were still told among the Laretu. Etaín didn't fear them, nor hated them, but couldn't help but stay on guard. She had seen the Kurr slaves that the Northern clans held, those Kurr were cruel and filled with anger, not something to take lightly, Etaín just hoped the free Kurr were more peaceful, well she hoped not to bump into any. Etaín was amazed by the forest, with its white barks and ruby leaves casting shadows that colored the forest floor in all shades of red.

They had been walking for over two days now. They had reached the Blood Forest the night after the ball and passed through most of it during the next two days. It wasn't hard to find their way as long as they stayed on the road, they wouldn't find many animals here either, especially not predators. Those lived deeper into the forest, but even though no predators meant safety, the lack of animals also meant little food. Raven had managed to hunt down some rabbits and find some edible roots and berries but it didn't even begin to fill Etaín's belly. *We should have packed some food from the ball*, was all she could think to herself every time her stomach growled, but she didn't complain out loud, Raven did her very best to find any food there was. Raven was preparing the food while Etaín got the fire starting and she felt questions burning in her mind.

"Raven?" she carefully asked.

"Yeah."

"Why are we going to the heart of the Dan'um forest?"

"Because apparently that's the place I need to go," she answered almost immediately, as if she knew Etaín had wanted to ask that.

"Okay. And is there a reason that the Guardian of Battle is trying to kill you?" Etaín wasn't sure she wanted to know the answer.

"Yes," was all Raven answered.

"Yes, what?" Etaín frowned, not understanding the sudden harshness.

"Yes, she has a reason. It's a stupid one but it is a reason." Raven noticed Etaín's face and softened a little bit. "Look, there are a lot of people out there who hate me, for who I am and for what I've done, then there are the people who are desperate to find me because of what I can do, and then there are the few people who do not know me. You are one of those people, and I want you to know me for who I am now, not for my past, because I like having you around,

Etaín." Etaín was slightly shocked by Raven suddenly opening up, she didn't expect it at all and wasn't sure what to say. She felt flattered that Raven said she liked having Etaín around, it was a mutual feeling, and Etaín could live with not knowing Raven's past, she had a feeling she would learn it anyway when the time was right. Etaín gave a simple nod as response that she had understood but then smiled.

"Okay, so, what is your favorite color then?" Etaín asked, confusing Raven. "You said you wanted me to know you for who you are now. This is me getting to know you. I'll go first, my favorite color is probably purple," she said, and Raven smiled.

"Fair enough. I don't really have a favorite color I think, but if I had to pick one, it would be blue, blue like the morning skies," she answered, seriousness fading from her voice. Etaín fired question after question, she was curious who Raven was and she enjoyed learning more about her. They kept on talking, Etaín telling stories about her youth and about her family, legendary tales of her people fighting incredible monsters and going to war. She hoped that if she herself opened up, that Raven would do the same, but she just listened and laughed at her stories. Etaín was too afraid to ask what Raven really was, she had seen Raven's eyes at the ball and Etaín knew Raven wasn't just a mercenary nor a normal Ilunari, they didn't fight High Immortals like Raven did. The next day they walked while Etaín kept telling stories, before they realized it the stars had chased the sunlight over the horizon and Etaín and Raven left the ruby leaves and pale barks behind and traded them for the towering walls of grey stone of Ravens Pass. In the distance they spotted an orange light, a campfire, and their joy disappeared, making way for cautiousness as they got closer to the light.

Chapter 7
Rynn

A real Nuan, it couldn't be. They were murdered in the War of Shattered Light. Hunted down by the Guardian of Darkness, Megana. This girl, well woman, must be the last one of her race. The Nuan reminded Rynn of his mother. She was devoted to the Guardian of Light, Nuana, and often told stories about Nuana, about how she created the Nuans and how she protected the Human race in their time of need. Nuana watched over the Humans after they were almost driven to extinction by the other races, it was that story that had made Rynn's mother so devoted to the Guardian of Light.

To stand before a Nuan himself, the last legacy of the Guardian of Light, if only his mother could see it. He heard the orb calling to him, hushed whispers clouded his mind, making his fire flow into his veins and his hand reach for the surface. As he laid his hand upon the orb it started to pulsate, like a heartbeat. He couldn't think, had no control over his own mind and body. The pulses became stronger and cracks started to appear in the previously flawless orb. With every pulse the surface cracked more and more. The sounds of breaking glass echoed through the stone halls, bouncing between empty hallways and the round walls of the room. Rynn stepped back and pushed himself to the wall, shielding his face with his arms feeling shards cut his bare chest as the orb exploded violently, sending shards flying everywhere.

He lowered his arms and looked upon the Nuan lying among countless shards, completely naked and unharmed. Legend told that the Nuan were truly beautiful creatures, and this Nuan was living proof. Her skin was a milky white, her eyes as pale as the winter sun. She was tall and thin, almost fragile like the first flowers in spring, her hair the color of freshly fallen snow. The Nuan seemed too weak to stand up but no matter how much Rynn wanted to help her, he could not move, his mind wrapped in clouds and his body not for him to control. The Nuan struggled to get up, falling down several times while Rynn watched her in silence. Once the Nuan stood before him, she observed him with her white eyes. He broke from the grasp and let his own eyes glide over her body. Her skin was almost translucent. Spun like silk over her bones and flesh. His eyes roamed over her small breasts, further down her untouched skin, following the flow of her stomach, her hips, inner thighs, even her ankles and all the way back. Scouting the hills and ridges of her lips and cheeks he found her eyes gazing into his soul. Exposing his heart and mind to her as she roamed his mind like he had roamed her skin. He had no desire to block any thought, she could read him as much as she liked, and so she did.

"Do you surrender yourself to me, Rynn of Anndar? Are your mind and body mine to control for as long as I need them to be?" a voice whispered in his mind, the same voice that guided him through the temple.

It could have been seconds, minutes, hours, even days, Rynn had lost all of his senses as the Nuan read him. When she finally turned away from him she left his soul weak and trembling, exposed to her every whim. Rynn looked down and noticed that his fire still flowed in his veins, pulling it back immediately. The Nuan was walking out of the room as a whisper filled his mind,

"Come."

There was no need to doubt it, it was the voice of the Nuan. Rynn trusted her completely, a creature of the light could not have any cruel intentions.

Her movements were graceful and soft, the cold stone upon her naked skin did not seem to bother her at all. Rynn followed her through the halls all the way back to the first hall at the entrance. As they entered the first hall the Nuan put her hand on the engraved pillar, her fingers following every ridge and carving as she walked down the stairs. The orbs in the wall seemed to light up whenever the Nuan passed them, filling the room with a faded green light, as if the sun shone through emeralds.

"What are they?" Rynn asked.

"They are my kin," she whispered in his mind. *"Their essence, waiting to be reborn, waiting for the next Lady of Light to rise. To give them life again, to end their suffering."*

The room was much bigger than Rynn initially thought, there were rows upon rows of holes in the walls. Many were filled with orbs, softly pulsating.

Whispers filled his mind, answering his thoughts. She was still in his mind but he did not care, not that there was anything he could do against it.

"Once we were many, teaching the ways of Light and protecting those who followed those ways. After Lady Nuana was killed, assassins came for us, shadows so dark not even the light could banish them. So many died, so many suffered, so many lost their way as the darkness smothered the light." Rynn could hear the pain in her voice and yet she showed none of it on her face. Suddenly she turned her head, as if she had heard something and moved toward the entrance of the temple and outside of it, Rynn followed without thinking. The Nuan lifted her chin and seemed to wait. Rynn felt something in his mind, something else besides the Nuan. He couldn't tell what it was but it felt strangely familiar.

Mist.

Engulfing, thick, silver mist.

Yira.

He blinked and Yira stood in front of him, both the girls from the Academy at her sides. As soon as she appeared Rynn felt as if heavy chains fell from him. His mind was no longer filled with mist even though it circled his mind still. He noticed that his memories were a bit vague after the moment he freed the Nuan. He had willingly surrendered to the Nuan but only now realized how quickly she had rooted herself in his mind. Nuans were masters of mind working according to the books, but their beauty took breathtaking to a whole new level. He felt his cheeks burning and forced his eyes to the ground as he now remembered his eyes roaming the Nuan. Yira and the Nuan had not moved since, they seemed disconnected from the world around them. Rynn's best guess was that they were having a conversation since the Nuan seemed to communicate through ways of the mind.

The stare-down only lasted a couple of breaths longer before Yira suddenly broke the silence with an annoyed "It's settled then." Yira turned her gaze to Rynn, widening her eyes as a sign of her irritation.

"It seems you were the right one. This is Ara-Ashin, the last Nuan in this realm and thus the only one who can restore the Lady of Light. Which is also the reason she was protected by her brothers and sisters of the First Generation, who sacrificed themselves to put Ara-Ashin between realms, being the orb you probably found her in. Me and my sisters were tasked to protect her and find the one to save her. We chose you to save her because of your magic and because of your mother, who received the blessing of Nuana when she was young. That's a short explanation of the story."

Yira walked past him and went inside the temple again, her sisters following her closely.

Rynn sighed and followed again, it seemed to be the only thing he did since the Games, following. Behind him Ara-Ashin followed them as well.

"You will need to go to Xisq, capital of the Kir'in," Yira continued. "The city was built to safeguard the most precious and powerful relics there are, hence the name, which means vault. You must find something called the Heart of Light in order to make Ara-Ashin the new Guardian, if she is indeed the chosen one." She paused for a moment, seeming unsure of her next words, "A prophecy foretold that the Vault is the place where the new Lady of Light will be chosen, but to do so we first need the Heart of Light."

Wrynn remembered the engravings he saw before he found Ara-Ashin, and the prophecy about the Vault.

"You mean you don't have the Heart yet?" the Nuan exclaimed. It was strange hearing her voice cut the air. It still echoed in Rynn's mind yet it trembled the very air around him.

"Wouldn't expect anything else from you and your sisters. You weren't there to protect Nuana, nor did you care when my people were slaughtered like pigs. Sometimes I wonder if you remember your duty as High Immortals, or if you just go around speaking of prophecies and losing valuable artifacts that could save the world," the Nuan spit the words out, not even trying to hide her fury. Deep down Rynn felt her fury as well, his fire burned in his heart, his eyes revealing the flames. Yira's sisters looked toward him, making him realize what was happening so he pulled his fire back into his heart.

Ara-Ashin and Yira seemed to have fallen back into their telepathic arguing until Yira suddenly called out. "Fine," and threw her hands in the air. "Go ahead and travel to Xisq yourselves, open the Vault, retrieve the Heart, become Lady of Light, but listen very closely to me Nuan. If you ever try to lecture us again on our duty as High Immortals I will show you how mortal you yourself are. The whole world thinks your kind is extinct anyway and it would be our pleasure to make that belief a reality." Yira spit some words in High Speech that sounded anything but kind before she continued. "You will stand out too much, even in Xisq, assassins are everywhere and besides that, both of you are barely dressed. Rynn, our precious Nuan wants to use your powers to teleport to Xisq and by the looks of it you'll need to use magic to make her appear more common."

"Where will we get the clothes?" Rynn asked. He feared he knew the answer, that they would have to steal them.

"Where do you think?" Yira replied. Rynn nodded, stealing it was. He didn't like it at all, it was wrong but did they really have another choice? His clothes were still in the Academy and he figured that after all this time there was not much to be expected of the clothes in the temple, if there even were any. Ara-Ashin seemed very comfortable walking around without any clothes and it wouldn't surprise Rynn if they all used to walk around like this. He found his eyes roaming her body again and quickly turned his eyes toward the floor.

"Well then, I don't want to stand around forever, I have a Heart to find and a world to save," the Nuan spoke aloud as she gave Yira and her sisters a look filled with hatred. She grabbed Rynn's arm as the silver mists took control of his mind again.

Soft, green grass tickled his bare feet.

A warm breeze caressing his face and torso, filled with the scent of spices, flowers and filth.

Rynn opened his eyes. They stood in a field just outside of Xisq, a city with its own beauty. Buildings made out of stone and steel creeped up the hillside, creating a maze of alleys and marketplaces. Behind the rooftops they could see countless masts and sails of the ships that lay in Xisq's harbor. The higher up the hillside they looked the more extravagant the buildings became. Green marble and glass woven through the grey stone of the buildings. On top of the hill stood a palace, overlooking everything else. Its high walls and towers surrounding the pale green palace, the home of the Empress.

As he was admiring the view, he heard a sigh coming from behind him, Ara-Ashin. Rynn turned around quickly and found her looking at him with one white eyebrow raised and her arms crossed.

"Sorry," he responded, "something more common, yes. Erm, I think it would be best if you were human, something like me. We could pass as friends or maybe even lovers?" He blushed at the thought but her eyes filled with disgust.

"Human is about the exact opposite of a Nuan," Ara-Ashin began, disgust woven into every word, "Nuans were created to mirror perfection in the eyes of a Guardian, to be a perfect image of light and purity. I doubt anyone even remembers why humans were created, I would want to forget a past like that, however I can assure you it wasn't anything close to perfection. This one time, however, it seems to me that it is the best option to appear human, so we don't stand out as a duo."

Rynn heard her disgust but desperately hoped she didn't mean it, she was probably just hurt about the fact that she had to change her appearance when she looked so flawless. He was quite sad himself that he could no longer awe at her beauty.

Rynn had already started a spell to change her appearance when he realized something they had learned about glamours in the Academy. It was difficult to keep a glamour up on something that was constantly moving, luckily Rynn had found a solution to it, a simple enchantment that constantly refreshed the glamour on whoever wore the enchanted object. This meant he would need an object, the only thing he could think of was a ring his little sister had given him just before he left for the Academy. It looked expensive but it was nothing more than engraved iron, kept free from rust by a simple enchantment. He sat down to enchant the ring with a glamour so that Ara would look like his little sister when she would be older. It took him a while to get all the details right but when he looked up, he found Ara standing in front of him holding a bunch of clothes.

"I got tired of watching you mumble to a ring so I got some clothes. I grabbed the ugliest ones so it wouldn't look out of place on a human." She threw a shirt at him that was barely big enough and a brown cloak as she dressed herself. For herself she had grabbed a plain, grey dress, some old leather boots and the same brown cloak. Rynn handed her the ring and after she put it on Rynn had to take a step back. She looked exactly like his sister, but grown up. The same rich brown skin color and the same brownish green of the forest floor in her eyes. Her hair was long, black and curly and embraced her face like clouds. Rynn felt a strange sense of pride as he looked at his sisters image. He knew it was still the Nuan underneath the glamour but it didn't change the feeling.

"I truly feel violated. Let's find the Vault, get the Heart and go right back to the temple," Ara-Ashin said, investigating her new body. Rynn's pride was ripped away but somehow, he couldn't find it in himself to blame the Nuan. Nuans were after all made to be perfect, she had said so herself.

Rynn wondered if she knew where the Vault was. According to legend only the High Immortals used to know until they created the Nameless Order and tasked them with protecting the Vault, but this order was long gone and only remembered by the old books in dusty libraries.

Rynn had been to Xisq before, with his father to trade their goods. He was very little back then but he did remember being very impressed and somewhat scared by the big and crowded city. Rynn came from the human capital of Anndar and even though Anndar was much bigger, Xisq was stuffed with people and market stalls. They joined the crowds on the main road going into Xisq, they blended easily into the busy stream of people as they went through the massive gates.

Entering the city, they were greeted by a flood of shouts and scents. The streets were more like rivers of people, trying to get through the countless market stalls that stood seemingly random through the street. Rynn remembered that his father once told him that there was nothing you could not find in Xisq, except maybe personal space. From live animals to pottery to glass figurines to weapons, everything was here. The sun rarely touched the ground as it was blocked out by people and roofs and tables. The air was filled with so many scents of so many different things that it made your head dizzy and your eyes water, laying heavy on your lungs. Merchants were shouting in order to draw you to their stalls, yelling their prices and complimenting you to earn your favor. Rynn quickly thought of protecting his possessions but realized he had none, that made it easy to not be robbed. He pulled the hood of his cloak over his head and gestured Ara to do the same. She rolled her eyes at him but followed his lead anyway. He figured they should be as unrecognizable as possible because she would not be recognized in her normal form but Rynn would, perhaps the same people who were after him at the Academy were here. He had almost forgotten about it. So much had happened, he found a Nuan, probably the last one and he was now in Xisq to find the Heart of Light, whatever that was. He hadn't read anything about it in books as far he remembered nor had he heard about it in the history or mythology classes.

Ara leaned toward him. "I can't read minds since we passed the gates for some reason. It seems we need to ask around for the Heart," she whispered. Rynn hadn't even considered her mind reading an option to find the Heart.

"At one point you might need to explain what this Heart is exactly. I have absolutely no idea as to what it is," Rynn began, but she only sighed and looked through the streets as if she would find it in the middle of the street. He found it a bit rude but let it go. Keeping his eyes open for any signs of danger he followed Ara as they hopped from one merchant to another and asked them 'what they knew about a heart.' Most merchants tried to sell them hearts of live animals and one even went so far that they slaughtered a chicken in front of them and pulled out its still beating heart. Others told them about love potions or small statues of a heart. When they asked about a different heart, a one of a kind heart, the merchants suddenly grew silent and either changed the subject or told them off. They had even gone to parts of the market in dark alleys far away from the main road but received the same treatment and were even offered some of their wares to leave them alone. They realized they wouldn't learn anything from the merchants so they decided to go back to the main road and maybe even move toward the higher parts of the city in hopes of the people being more trustworthy.

Just as they reached the main road somebody ran into Ara, almost making her fall onto the street. Rynn looked around but it was too crowded to see who it was so he looked back at Ara. His heart skipped a beat. The glamour was gone, her original form was visible for everybody to see. He pulled her hood down as far as he could and dragged her toward the side of the road. She struggled in his grip but didn't fight him off. Rynn prayed to the High Immortals that nobody had seen her, it would draw attention to them and most certainly attract the assassins that both Ara-Ashin and Yira had spoken about. Rynn checked Ara's hand and as he suspected her ring was gone, his ring, the gift from his little sister.

"What are you doing? Have you gone completely mad?" Ara hissed to him. Rynn held up her hand in front of her face but she went on. "Yeah, that's my hand. What about it?"

"Your hand is white again," he said as he pushed it down again. Her aggression disappeared as she realized what that meant.

"Can you put a new glamour up?" she asked but Rynn already shook his head, "Great. Well, we have to hide, stay away from the crowds. If I'm dead the Heart will be lost forever, only a Nuan, only I can retrieve the Heart and become the Lady of Light."

Rynn looked around but there was no way they could hide anywhere. People were everywhere, some already looked their way and he was certain that they had already been spotted by several people. He just hoped that none of them was an assassin.

"It's probably best if we go back toward the black market. It's less crowded and there are more places to hide, I suppose. Just keep your head down and your hands under your cloak, that way you will be the least visible," Rynn told her as he guided her through the crowded streets.

The further they got away from the main road the less crowded it became but Rynn also imagined that they would be more vulnerable to attacks if an assassin had spotted them. Rynn stopped in an empty side alley far away from the main road to catch his breath.

"Why are we stopping?" Ara asked but as soon as she looked at Rynn she knew. He was panting with his hands on his knees, sweat pearling on his forehead.

"Humans." She sighed, shaking her head.

A low chuckle came from the shadows, "Yeah, they're not the strongest race." Further down in the alley stood a figure cloaked by the shadows, leaning against the wall. His pearly white fangs caught the light as he smirked. A Kir'in, great. Kir'in were known to be assassins when they weren't traders, and this one didn't look like a trader at all. The figure stepped away from the walls, casting off only a small part of the shadows. His eyes were a bright emerald green, hiding behind locks of black hair. A scar cut through his lips near the right corner of his mouth and continued all the way up to his eye. Rynn stood upright again, fire in his eyes and ready to use it but more people appeared on both sides of the alley. There was no way they could get away unnoticed.

"Ah, the boy who turns his eyes to flames. I know some people who would pay a royal amount of gold for you," he said with a voice as sweet as honey. His gaze shifted to Ara who looked him in the eyes defiantly. He threw her hood back.

"If I am not mistaken you are a Nuan, and here I was, thinking they were extinct. You learn something new every day it seems." His smirk turned into a full out smile, "Today is my lucky day. You are just what we need, and if not, I could sell you for enough money to buy the world." He lifted her chin as if he was admiring his greatest prize.

"Let's take you home," was the last thing they heard as they were knocked out and taken away.

Chapter 8
Kaell

Kaell clutched the hilt of his knife tight enough to turn his knuckles white. He stood beside Inza, who was shivering in her sleep. All kinds of animals had surrounded him, boars, foxes, crows and even a mountain lion. Kaell was already out of arrows, they now stuck in several boars who had run off. It was a challenge not to kill the animals, just hurt them enough to make them flee. A fox leapt at Kaell and he was barely quick enough to step aside and slash its leg, making it limp back into the shadows. The crows circled around him, blocking his view of the other animals.

Suddenly, the mountain lion burst through the black flock, its claws and teeth aiming for his throat. Kaell dropped his knife and grabbed the jaws of the beast with his hands, preventing them from locking around his throat. The mountain lion dug his claws into Kaell's chest and Kaell forced himself to keep quiet as not to wake Inza. It took all of his strength to keep the animal off of him and he knew he couldn't keep up for much longer. Just when the teeth scraped his throat the mountain lion suddenly withdrew its claws and moved away from Kaell. Inza's nightmare was over and the animals disappeared as fast as they had come. Kaell sighed and stayed down for a little more, desperately needing to catch his breath before he went to tend to his wounds. Slowly, he got up and started binding his chest with some of the bandages from his bag. It didn't take him long, he had done it many times before. He threw away his torn and bloodied shirt and put on a new one. After he was done, he pulled new arrows out of his bag and filled his quiver, washed the blood of the bow and attempted to get the blood stains out of his jacket, but wasn't successful so he put it in his bag. He was glad he was prepared for nights like this by bringing new shirts and extra bandages. When he was finally done he sat down beside the campfire and breathed deeply, trying to suppress the pain in his chest, constantly checking if the blood came through the bandages.

Kaell had been really glad when they reached Ravens Pass and made camp, he didn't expect the animals to come all the way into the pass. He had expected to see other troubles, mainly Laretu travelers because here, they were no longer in Kurr homelands but on the border of Laretu and Kurr lands. He really hoped they wouldn't run into a Laretu; they were fierce warriors, out for blood and he wasn't sure he could fight one off right now.

Suddenly he was ripped from his train of thought by Inza, who slept beside him. She snored quite loudly and it made Kaell smile. He really hoped this night wouldn't be a repeat of last night. Inza was gifted with shifting and healing, the two most precious gifts of their race, but with it came a curse. Whenever she had nightmares the life around them tried to protect her from everything but herself, meaning that animals and plants attacked anything that came near her. Nightmares didn't happen that often but when they did Kaell was always close. Everybody made a vow not to tell her. Their father feared she would feel burdened and suffer under the knowledge that she was a danger to the people around her whenever she was afraid. The curse was the real reason behind their journey to the Dan'um, so that he could find a cure. As of late her nightmares became more intense and more animals came everytime she had one. Their village didn't notice at first but the last month the people started to notice and even though they could hide it from Inza for now, their father feared it wouldn't be long until Inza found out or the village got too much trouble because of it. So, they left for the Dan'um woods, keeping the village safe and Inza as well. The only problem was that all the animals could now focus on attacking Kaell instead of a village and have him fight for his life every time his sister had a bad dream, but he would gladly do so. He decided to check on the wounds on his chest. They were already healing, for once, he was really glad to be Kurr. They were known to heal quicker than any other races, probably because of their close connection to the nature around them. It would only take another day until it was completely healed.

The sound of steps echoing through the pass made him shoot upright. He couldn't hear how many people, everything echoed in the pass. They did come from the Laretu side of the pass. He grabbed his bow and arrows, ready to shoot if needed. He doubted that it would scare them off but it was better to be prepared.

Kaell waited silently beside the fire. As the steps came closer, he could hear two separate steps, one light and barely audible, the other the quite opposite, as if a two-legged bull was walking there. It took them forever to enter the light of the campfire, but Kaell waited, with a drawn arrow aimed at the sounds.

They stepped into the light and he saw a Laretu.

"Stop right there." Kaell's voice was soft but it didn't remove the serious tone. "Take another step and this arrow will end between your eyes, Laretu." They stopped and Kaell took a good look. The Laretu was a girl about Inza's age, tall, large horns. Her skin was already filled with pale scars that looked like lightning against her reddish skin. Her eyes were an ashy grey but instead of the usual bloodlust they were wary, but thankful. Another girl stood beside her but she was no Laretu, she was much smaller and pale as snow, pointed ears and bright violet eyes. Kaell wasn't sure what an Ilunari was doing here but her eyes were cold and distant, ready to kill.

"What is your business here?" Kaell asked, "And speak the truth."

"We simply ask to sit at your fire, Kurr. Food too, if you can share it, we have nothing left. You have my word, blood will not be spilled tonight," the Laretu answered. Her voice was soft and kind, something he didn't expect but she had given her word, a vow a Laretu would not break. He hoped.

"You can sit down and I will share some food." He lowered his bow, "I do ask you to be quiet since my sister is asleep." Both of them nodded in agreement. Both sat down by the fire and he handed them some bread and received an honest 'thank you' from both. Kaell sat down besides Inza again.

"So, where are you headed?" he decided to ask. The Laretu looked at the Ilunari, who seemed unsure as to tell him.

"The Dan'um forests, eventually," she answered, her tone was defensive and cold, her eyes locking with Kaell's as she spoke. He wouldn't tell them they were going there too. There was no way he would travel together with a Laretu, he wouldn't risk it, no matter how kind she seemed to be, the stories existed for a reason.

"Well, you can travel with us until the end of the Pass, there, our ways must part. I think you can see why, Laretu." The Laretu simply nodded and continued to eat her bread.

The crackling of the fire was the only thing that broke through the tense silence. Kaell tossed his bloody bandage into the flames, it spread the most horrible smell.

"I'll take the watch," he said.

"I needed my sleep anyway," the Laretu replied.

Kaell didn't care to ask her name, he wouldn't use it. The other girl, however, still had his interest. He had never seen an Ilunari, only heard stories about them. How their beauty was beyond compare and their cities filled with light and elegance. He knew they were the people of the air and their royal bloodline descended from the Master of Air himself. Now that he had seen one, he understood that people called them the most beautiful, the Ilunari was very pretty even though you could see the marks of rough times on her face.

"Is there a reason your eyes are glued to me?" Her sharp voice cut through his thoughts and he realized he had been staring right at her.

Her violet eyes now held him in their grasp as he muffled some sounds that didn't resemble words in the slightest.

"I, uhm. Sorry. It's just that I have never seen one of your kind."

"Yeah, well now you have so get over it, we're not that special."

Kaell wondered how somebody could sound so cold, like her heart had been replaced with black ice, cold enough to freeze air that she breathed.

The night was long, dark and silent. Kaell spent his time sharpening his arrows and gazing into the dark, while the Ilunari stared into the fire, her face as cold as her voice and her violet eyes reflecting the orange flames. Sometimes Kaell looked at her, wondering what her story was, wanting to ask for her name but never having the courage for it. Inza slept deep, softly snoring every now and then, he was glad she wasn't restless. If she had one of those nightmares now there was no way they could hide her secret from the other two. In this pass there was no way any creature would enter willingly, it was common knowledge even though nobody knew why.

The Laretu seemed restless in her sleep, she was turning constantly and Kaell kept a close eye on her. You never knew when a Laretu would thirst for blood. He noticed the Ilunari did the same, she probably also knew what they could be capable of, but she seemed like she could defend herself though, why else would she carry a spear that deadly.

Morning finally came and as the sun pushed the veil of night over the horizon Kaell thanked the High Immortals that they could move on and reach the end of the pass today. Not a single word had been spoken except for the couple of times the Laretu had cried out calling her father in her sleep. Even now she sobbed, her soft crying echoing between the stone walls of the pass. Inza shot upright, grabbing his hand. He saw her eyes passing over the strangers, yet she asked nothing but simply tucked her necklace underneath her shirt. She trusted his judgement blindly, but she remained wary.

Inza stood up and moved around the fire toward the Laretu, Kaell grabbed hold of his bow.

"Why do you cry?" Inza asked. Her voice was calm and soft, like always.

The Laretu did not answer nor move so Inza sat down beside her.

Wiping the tears off her face she looked at Inza, the same wariness showing in her eyes.

"My father was murdered by that bastard Guardian Shyvna, and even though his death was glorious I can't get the image of his lifeless body out of my mind."

Kaell didn't see that one coming and let out a shocked 'oh' drawing the attention to him so he averted his eyes to the ground.

"I am sorry," Inza continued, steady as if it didn't shock her, "I'm sure he was a good man and a great father, who died bravely fighting for those he loved."

The Laretu seemed unsure of what to say but through her tears broke a smile.

"Yes, he was, and he did."

Inza suddenly hugged the Laretu who was both surprised and glad.

"My name is Inza by the way."

"Etaín. It's an honor, Inza."

Inza walked back again to Kaell and looked him in the eyes, he saw the fear and nerves falling off of her. He was so proud of her, it was reckless but brave, so he gave her a smile to show his pride.

"We should get moving if we want to leave the pass before nightfall." The Ilunari's voice was still sharp but less cold somehow. She was right though, and Kaell packed their belongings. Inza helped him, seeing a chance to exchange a few words.

"I'm sorry but I couldn't see her cry on her own like that."

He nodded, she knew he understood. "It is always good to keep enemies close."

"She is not an enemy, Kaell."

"Time will tell."

"They can't all be bad, and by the way, that war was more than a hundred years ago, you act like you were there with those judgements, you're not *that* old," she said teasingly. He stuck out his tongue and she smiled. There was truth in her words but he would still keep an eye on both of them in case they stopped being friendly.

"Let's go, we got a long, straight walk ahead of us," he said.

Etaín softly chuckled before she followed them, Kaell looked at her but was cut off when the Ilunari walked past and whispered something in a language he didn't know, it didn't sound nice.

He was starting to be more annoyed by the Ilunari girl than the Laretu. She wouldn't give her name nor anything else and the fact that she didn't show emotion somehow bothered him quite a bit. Kaell decided he would walk behind them all so he could watch both the Ilunari and the Laretu.

Up in front was Inza who was excited to see something new. She saw the great raven statues first. They were carved into the walls of stone, watching travelers with their stone eyes. The ravens reached all the way up to the top of the pass, where tree roots wrapped around their heads. It seemed strange to think that they were carved by hand. Each raven was identical to the others except for the cracks and broken parts. The pass was completely straight and almost seemed more like an ancient cathedral than a pass, silence seemed fitting and even Inza walked with a slower pace while she was enchanted by the rows and rows of ravens that towered above her. Every raven was several hundreds of meters wide and Kaell figured that even the Laretu must feel small here, they were much taller than any of the races but compared to these ravens everybody looked small. Every once in a while, Inza fell back to walk next to him and he noticed she didn't like having two strangers between them, especially not with the Ilunari girl, cold as the stone that surrounded them.

"How old do you think they are?" asked Inza as she nodded at the ravens.

"Far older than anything we know, at least. Didn't the Kelsul teach you anything about this?"

The Kelsul were the elders of the tribes, the source of their knowledge and the people who made sure that knowledge was passed on to the newer generations since the Kurr didn't write books.

"They didn't teach me anything beside the Kurr ways and the Shifting Path, the trees told me tales but never about Ravens Pass."

Kaell wasn't surprised. He respected the Kelsul and they were very wise but just like many Kurr, they had never left their homeland and their knowledge came from the Kelsul before them or from the few travelers that passed through their lands. It wasn't like he knew more about the world but he travelled further than any Kurr he knew and now he and his sister would be the first Kurr to leave their homeland freely since the War of Shattered Light. Maybe one day, when they were old and grey, they would tell the stories of the world to the children.

"You truly are isolated from the world, aren't you?" the Ilunari girl scoffed.

"Well your people only learn from the books in your libraries," Kaell shot back.

Her eyes shot to him, holding him in their icy grip. "They are not my people."

They all stopped, Inza hiding behind him and Etaín looking from one to another.

"Well..." the Laretu started, "Now that that's clear maybe we can move on and perhaps you can tell us the story of Ravens Pass, Raven?"

Raven. So that was her name. It seemed strange that such an elegant people would name their child Raven.

"No thank you, why don't you tell them? Your people know the story too don't they?"

Even toward Etaín her voice didn't show any emotion.

"They do. I do. See this as a thank you." She nodded toward Inza, who blushed a little. "As long as we keep moving because I can't wait to get out of this stone prison, I don't like it a single bit."

They all started walking again, Raven in front whilst Etaín kept close to Inza.

Kaell couldn't hide his smile, Etaín felt vulnerable, he could tell. The idea of a vulnerable Laretu was quite funny to him.

"The legends of Ravens Pass are old, far older than my own people," she began her story. "It is said that it existed long before the Guardians and even the Elders. Once there was a majestic temple dedicated to the Ancient Elyon, Lord of the Night Sky, where now the Blood Forest grows. It was built from the most precious obsidian stone, one that glowed with a dark blue when light hit it. Everything was open yet not a single ray of sunlight could reach within the temple. Through the obsidian flowed veins of pure starlight from which the stars itself were created by Elyon, as a gift to his mortal lover making him the Lord of Stars. In return the Lord of Stars gave him these ravens for their wedding, two hundred ravens carved into the mountain pass. One for each of the years it took Elyon to make the Pass."

Inza was basically stuck to Etaín and completely engaged in the story.

"Oh, please tell me the story of Elyon and his lover," Inza begged. "Please, it sounds like a good story."

"Alright then," Etaín laughed "It's not like I have anything better to do. So, Elyon was an Ancient, the Lord of the Night Sky, living in his temple secluded from the world. But he grew lonely being all by himself so first he created ravens from the darkness of the night itself to keep him company and serve him. It took away his loneliness for a while but it didn't take long for him to grow lonely again. Every day he would wander the mountains that surrounded his home. And one day he saw a hunter, camping at the bottom of the mountains. It made him curious, no mortals ever came close to the mountains, so he took the form of a raven and flew down to investigate. The hunter was a beautiful mortal with a pure heart, an Ilunari, actually, for not many other races had been created yet. Elyon watched him from a distance before he returned to his temple at dusk. The next day he couldn't help but fly to the hunter, watching him hunt and gather his food, never getting close enough for the hunter to see him.

As the days passed Elyon slowly fell in love with this man, he took away that lonely feeling that had haunted him for so long. Yet he couldn't find the courage to show himself and tell the man about it. One day he returned right before sunrise in the form of a raven to look at the hunter as he slept. He had never been this close and it made him happy, so happy that he grew careless, so careless that he woke the hunter up who immediately grabbed his knife in an attempt to kill the raven. But right before he could stab the disguised Ancient, Elyon threw off his raven form, revealing himself to the hunter. The poor man was shocked as Elyon explained who he was. After all the confusion was gone, they spent the entire day together as Elyon told the hunter stories of the world and the hunter took him hunting. Ylendar, the hunter, asked him if Elyon would join him again tomorrow, so he wouldn't feel so alone. Of course Elyon promised he would, glad that he had finally spoken to Ylendar. That night Elyon crafted the stars one by one, from the light that flowed through his temple as a gift for the mortal.

The days went on and they kept meeting and talking until one evening, Elyon gave the stars to the man he had grown to love, and together they placed them in the sky. That night, Elyon was not in the sky but besides his lover.

Now that they confessed their love to each other, Elyon was determined to get his lover to live with him. Unfortunately, the mountains stood between his temple and his lover and without flight, nobody could cross the mountains. So he started to carve the mountain, for two hundred nights he carved until he had cut through the entire mountain range, allowing his lover to cross the mountains and join him at his side in Elyon's temple. The following night they married and Elyon made sure Ylendar became the Lord of Stars, making him a High Immortal. This way they could rule the night sky together for all eternity, never having to be alone again.

Ylendar used his newly given strength to carve two hundred ravens into the side of the pass, one for each night they had worked to be together. But that night Lord Malon came down from the skies, the Lord of the Moon had grown jealous of the stars because he was no longer the only light in the nightly skies. Two hundred nights his rage had grown and now that the pass cut through the mountains, he could come to the Lord of the Night in his temple.

So, that night when the moon was out of the sky he came, blinded by rage and jealousy, and murdered Elyon. Drenching the soil with the Immortal blood. With that same blood dripping from his hands Malon left again, satisfied with his revenge. Elyon was dead by the time Ylendar could take his lover in his arms. All night he wept over his murdered lover and as his tears fell so did the stars emptying the night sky until nothing but black, empty darkness roofed the world.

That night he sang the song of the Night for the first time, holding back dawn until the moon would rise again ten days later. He buried his lover on the tenth night, in the middle of the forest, where now the Scarlet Willow grows and just before dawn arrived, he used his tears to enchant the ravens in the pass to be eternal watchers of the pass, so that nobody could ever visit his lover with evil intentions and do him harm. Every ten years he comes down from the skies again, to visit his lover when the moon is gone, and takes the stars with him."

Etaín took a deep breath and let her eyes glide over the ravens on either side. "And that's what we call Starfall nowadays."

Her story was finished and Kaell almost applauded her. It was a beautiful story and she had done a great job telling it. However, Inza's curiosity seemed to only have grown with every word.

"He made this pass for his lover? That is so romantic," she sighed, "I hope that someday I will find love like that." Etaín laughed and looked at the ravens.

"Me too, Kurr, me too." Inza fired question after question at the Laretu, who tried to answer each of them as well as she could. Kaell smiled at the two, his sister might have been right after all, they weren't all bad.

The end of the pass was only a couple hours walking away so he let his mind wander as he listened to the questions and answers, imagining the entire story in his head. It made the last part of the trip seem much shorter than it was and he figured that there was no need to part ways immediately after they were out of the pass. Inza seemed to like the Laretu girl, he had to admit he did as well, so maybe they could even travel to the Dan'um together. It would make the trip more enjoyable and then there was no chance for any awkward situations if they would meet each other on the way there for there weren't that many different ways to get to the Dan'um forests from here. The Ilunari also seemed to know how to get to their destination for some reason, and if she would keep quiet along the way she wouldn't ruin the mood.

They came close to the end of the pass and the Ilunari decided to camp there instead of outside of the pass, easier to keep watch, she said.

Kaell agreed. As they set up camp, he decided he would ask them tomorrow if they could travel together. If Inza had more nightmares along the way, he could hide it as a random animal attack.

The Laretu and Ilunari offered to keep watch this time so Kaell could get some sleep, so he did, although it was brief. He dreamed of the story Etaín had told that day, and slept peacefully for the first time in a long, long time.

Chapter 9
Naka/Raven

Naka was incredibly grateful to leave Ravens Pass behind, they were too vulnerable there for her liking, absolutely no place to hide. Besides that, it meant she was getting closer to going her own path again. Etaín had taken a liking for the Kurr it seemed and Naka hoped that by the time they reached Distrum they would be friends, that Etaín would travel with the Kurr so that Naka could go to the Dan'um on her own. It wasn't that she didn't like Etaín, it was actually nice to have some company after all those lonely years. It was just that because Naka cared for Etaín that she needed to leave her behind, nothing good would come to anyone who got close to Naka.

She had absolutely no problem leaving the Kurr behind, the girl was innocent and pure but simply too energetic for Naka, her brother, however, managed to annoy Naka with his questioning eyes and gloomy silence. Kurr were never her favorite people, always secluding themselves, not knowing anything of the world outside of their forests, they ignored the world and so Naka thought the world should ignore them as well.

After an hour they set foot outside of the pass, where the grey, solid stone ended as suddenly as the green forest began. Spring had reached these sides of the mountains much earlier. Flowers in all sorts of colors and shades bloomed in the fresh grass. The chirping of birds danced on the soft breeze that caressed the newly budded leaves on the trees. Sunlight dripped on the ground, lighting up the dust in the air, creating small specks of gold and yellow all around them. To the east, Naka could already see the Plains, the large sea of grass that parted the Shining Lands right through the middle, all the way into the Shadow Lands. The Plains lay much lower than where they were standing now, surrounding this forest with cliffs, except for one side which was about two days of walking to the south. The further you got to the south, the lower the forest descended until it was on the same level as the Plains that hugged it.

The road to Distrum was made out of large stones and curled its way along the edge of the forest, it was easy to travel on and smoothed down by the countless merchants that used this route.

Those merchants were the reason the Kir'in built Distrum on this road, which then became a large trading post, even though it had seen its best days. Nowadays, it was considered to be more of a mercenary outpost or a place of luxurious living, depending on which side of the road you were.

"I know we have left the pass now," the Kurr boy started, "but I wanted to say that, if you want, we can travel together, maybe the entire way even. You see, my sister and I are also headed to the Dan'um forests so our paths will cross again anyway."

He sounded so insecure as he spoke, Naka could tell they hadn't seen much of life yet, they were but children compared to her.

Etaín was the first to react. "I'd actually like it if we could travel together, I never figured Kurr would be nice to be around, and I prefer a larger company for a travel this long."

Naka didn't expect anything else of Etaín, she was glad that she would travel with them, that way the Laretu wouldn't see it as leaving when she chose to travel alone.

"Raven, what about you?" Etaín asked.

"I will travel with you until Distrum, there I must go my own way," she tried to sound as cold as she could. "It's better that way."

Naka turned her back to them, to avoid Etaín's disappointed looks.

"We should start walking again, Distrum is still two days away," she said as she started moving down the road.

They could hear the city before it could be seen. Sounds of vendors shouting their prices and people chatting drifted through the wind. Two days of forest sounds and life stories had made Naka yearn for the sound of a city. One more curve and they would see the gates of Distrum. One more curve and she could travel alone again. She had never liked company much and even though she didn't mind Etaín it would be better this way. Nobody would be in danger because of her and she wouldn't have to watch over the others.

They crossed that final curve and now faced the gates of Distrum, the split city.

It was more of a fortress than a city to be fair. The walls were thick enough to sustain a full on siege, the towers high enough to see anything from far away and shoot it down. Like a river, the road ran through the middle, splitting the city in two with an island in its middle. The island being the guards keep.

Naka noticed the Kurr girl falling silent as she gazed upon the massive walls, she had probably never seen a proper building. The Kurr lived in wooden homes that resembled large huts more than houses, it worked but it was primitive compared to structures such as this.

This city was considered a Laretu jewel, it was practically impossible to take the city from the outside. Armies could only attack from one side due to the impenetrable forest and the cliffs on the sides, and the road on the other side went straight on for quite a while, so any hostile armies would be spotted in time. Not to mention the double gates and walls on the inside to repel any attackers. A tactical masterpiece indeed.

They stepped through the gates now and Naka observed the inner road as well as she could. Guards every meter on the keep's walls and every couple meters on the inner walls, every tower manned, all Laretu of course. No getting out unseen. So, she had to stay low, not draw any attention. It was likely that there were spies here, spies that were desperate to find her. She made sure Nárymm was still safely secured on her back, there was no way she could ever lose that spear, not even if they killed her.

"Which gate do we go through now?" she could hear the Kurr boy ask.

Naka chuckled, "The one that looks like the place where you can afford something."

"This city is so big," the Kurr girl said, you could still hear the awe in her voice. Poor thing, she had probably never left home and now she was travelling to the Dan'um all the way across the world, Naka knew what that was like.

Passing the gate, the sounds of merchants turned into a wall of noise and smell, especially sweat and ale. It was a Laretu city but the merchants were all Kir'in and their main wares here were three things, food, ale and weapons. Many Laretu came here to sell their skills in battle, ever since the war, hoping for eventual recruitment into the army. It made them decent money and their lust for battle was quenched, so, no downsides really. They got their food fairly quickly, thanks to the coins Kaell had in his pocket, one vendor gave them enough food to last them at least a week. Naka would only take her part, she could hunt and avoid going to another city, that way she could reach the Dan'um faster so she wouldn't have to deal with the others once there. All she had to do was to find the silver wisp, whatever or whoever that was, and then she could move on before the others even crossed the Dan'um borders. The thought of leaving right away crossed her mind but, before it could take shape the city bell rippled across the city, leaving utter silence and confusion. It was only used in times of war but since it only sounded once, it seemed strange that it was now.

"The guards, they are leaving post," she heard somebody murmur.

"Yeah, king Egìl ordered all the cities to replace their guards with soldiers from the army, because of the war and everything," someone else explained.

Naka looked up. The guards actually were leaving their posts, laying down their weapons with faces of defeat. It was painful to see Laretu humiliated like this. The guards barely left their posts as troops dressed in white, silver and gold took their posts upon the walls, troops that were a mix of all races. King Egìl's men.

Now she had to lay low. She grabbed a piece of fabric from a nearby stall as the owner's gaze was fixed upon the walls, and wrapped it around her face. It was pointless really; her eyes would give her away as Ilunari and there really weren't that many outside of Iri'un. Naka knew Egìl's troops were trained to question every Ilunari, Naka's actions in the past had single handedly caused them to do so. They didn't understand why she had killed the people that she did, they just hated her for it. It took but seconds for the streets to fill with similar guards. They flowed through the streets, taking post on every corner, pushing aside anybody who stood in their path. Behind them followed a man on a horse with shining armor and a wide golden cloak. His hazel eyes glancing over every face as he spoke his words. He had a handsome face with full, brown hair that was pushed back, only one small scar ran across his chin but otherwise his skin was flawlessly perfect.

"By command of King Egìl, Ruler of the Shining Lands, these troops will now guard this city. The former guards have served well but will now be trained under my sister's command in Anndar to serve in the King's army." His voice was harsh and bored and tainted with war but nevertheless he took the time to speak his words, his eyes still roaming every face.

"What a disgrace," Etaín mumbled, it was, but Naka didn't really care for it, she just had to get out of here without drawing attention to herself. As she was looking around, searching the best escape route her eyes met those of a guard across the street. It only lasted seconds but she knew she had to move now. She turned around to tell the others to run.

"Ilunari!" she heard the guard yell.

"We've got to move, now," she snarled at the others, it was their choice if they wanted to come but if they slowed her down, she would leave them behind. Behind her the crowd became restless and guards pushed their way through the confused people. Naka tried to move between the people as much as possible, slipping into the first alley she saw. A loud horn sounded but she didn't look back, the gates were the only way out now and she had to get there quickly. Her initial counting of the guards was pretty pointless after the sudden switch, but she was pretty sure she could fight her way out and move into the forests, no sane person would follow her there.

"Raven," she heard the Kurr boy say behind her, "they are closing the gates, we won't make it in time." He tried to sound calm but she knew his heart rushed as much as hers. At least he finally did something useful, she praised Kurr ears, even she couldn't fight her way through closed gates.

"Let's keep moving anyway, we're easy to find when we stand still," Etaín urged.

"No shit," she responded angrily. But there was only so much city to hide in.

They ran around another corner, into another alley, empty and dark and Naka looked around. All three had kept up but the Kurr girl's eyes were filled with fear and she clung to her brother with heavy breaths. She couldn't leave them behind now so, she stopped in the alley.

"Stay in the shadows and find your breath." Her own voice was calm still and cold as always, this wasn't the first time she had to run, nor was it the first time she had gotten herself locked in a city.

"There isn't much to run to and they will comb through the city so we might need to fight our way out."

"I might be able to provide you with what you so desperately need, darling," chuckled a voice. Even though he stood in the light, shadows seemed to linger on his body. His smirk revealing his pearly white fangs.

"Get to the point, Kir'in," Naka growled.

"Easy there sweetheart, it's not like that is usual among your own kind." He spoke his words like honey, slow and sweet, "My point is, that I can offer you a way out of this… sticky situation."

"I take it your generous offer needs something in return?"

"I see you are familiar with the concept of trading, delightful," the Kir'in said, rubbing his hands together.

"The guards are closing in, we should hurry," the Kurr boy softly spoke.

"Very well, this is my price," the Kir'in said, eyeing the Kurr boy. "Tell me your name, Kurr, and stay for dinner, then I will hide you from those guards."

Kaell fell silent and Naka sighed, "His name is Kaell and we'll stay for your dinner if we must, now get on with it."

"Oh no, sweetheart, I want to hear it from him." The Kir'in brushed Kaell's cheek and the Kurr's face flushed a bright red

"Just say your name, have you lost your tongue?" Naka hissed to Kaell.

"It… It's Kaell, and we'll stay for dinner." his voice was almost breaking. The fool was so charmed he seemed to forget a whole city was hunting them.

"Marvelous, a pleasure to meet you Kaell."

Behind the Kir'in the wall swung open, revealing a small room with stairs leading down.

"After you," he said as he bowed like they were nobility.

Naka dreamed of the day she could get that confident smirk off his face. She descended the stairs and entered a large stone room, she didn't trust this Kir'in but it seemed like a better option than facing the guards. A large fire burned in the center, making shadows dance around it and making the rough edges on the walls seem like mountain ridges. Between those ridges were gaps of darkness that seemed to be tunnels. The Kir'in moved around the fire and the shadows seemed to embrace his body wherever he moved. In the light of the flames his emerald eyes looked like a forest on fire.

"So, what is an Ilunari's business so far into the world, travelling with both Kurr and Laretu?"

"My own, that's what it is. You hid us and we paid your price so we just owe you dinner, that's it." Her voice had that usual ice to it. She had gained it over the years of trusting nobody but herself and she wasn't planning on losing it because it kept people away so well.

Etaín sighed, clearly annoyed. "Maybe, you have forgotten that the city is on lockdown, Raven. They know we haven't left the city so hiding won't do the trick." The Laretu turned her head toward the Kir'in, "What do you want in return for getting us out of this city? I assume you can at least? You Kir'in rogues always seem to have your ways."

His smirk now almost split his face in two.

"I'm flattered, rogue is a very nice change from the usual names they give us. But yes, we do have our ways but, they are our ways, not yours. And you don't have anything of that value as far as I can see. I mean I think the guard commander would pay a royal amount if I turned the Ilunari in." He paused. "But where's the fun in that. So, tell me, what can you offer in return for my services dears?"

"We could not kill you," Naka offered. He was a fool for being all alone here, trying to suck them dry. She had barely spoken the words or in every tunnel appeared at least one person, quickly outnumbering them.

"Valuable, but I'll take my chances. Any other offers? I mean, I really do enjoy your company but, I'm a busy man so you best speak quickly before I turn you in, as boring as that would be."

Inza stepped from behind her brother.

"We will be in your debt if you help us because we have nothing to offer you right now, sorry," her voice trembled with every word. Naka was actually surprised by her courage to speak right now, that was the last thing she would've expected.

"A favor? I don't really do favors darling, I can't buy anything with them, I can't even put them on display." The Kir'in shook his head and chuckled as he turned away from them, "Does anybody know if they pay for all four of them or just the Ilunari?" he asked his people in the shadows.

"They only seek the Ilunari, milord," one whispered back.

"Then I guess we'll sell the others as slaves in Xisq, except for maybe the boy, I like that one."

A human girl appeared in one of the hallways, she could be no older than twelve. Her face beautiful and pure with pink lips and rosy cheeks but her eyes made the fire seem dim. It wasn't hatred that burned in her hazel eyes, it was more of a determination. Naka would recognise that look anywhere, for she had lived with it for many, many years. The girl had shaved her head completely bald and missed her left arm. She wore all black, blending in with the darkness around her and Naka could already see several knives hanging on her belt but suspected there were more, hidden away in the armor.

"Maybe they can be of use, Aergo. We still need a distraction." Her voice had that same icy edge Naka had, but somehow her voice was much sweeter.

"Oh yes! How could I have forgotten? This is why I like you so much Lily." He rubbed her head and bowed down to kiss it.

"Well then, I know something you can do to repay my, let's say, kindness." He turned around again, his face still split by his eternal smirk. "Back in Xisq, there is something that I need done. Unfortunately, our faces are known so I cannot send any of my people, let alone go myself. But here you are, four fresh, new faces with at least some skill in battle it seems. Or at least a dire wish to get out of here." He paced around the fire "Same thing really. So, will you pay that price my dears or should we take you back into the streets of Distrum?"

"Xisq is still weeks away from here, if you could get us out of the city, we would have to travel off-road and even then, be careful. And there is no way I will travel with you all the way to Xisq so you will have to do better here." Naka would rather die fighting every city guard in Distrum than be a prisoner of some Kir'in thief.

"First of all, ouch." Aergo placed his hand over his heart and made a sad face, "You really think little of me, don't you?"

Naka simply nodded, there was no use in acting sweet if he was willing to hand her to Egil's men for coin.

"I thought so, that's okay, you're not alone sweetheart. Second of all, Xisq is a couple of weeks, on foot. We Blackfangs, however, have better and much quicker means of transport. But you'll see that as soon as you accept my offer. Lastly, you wouldn't be my prisoners, as long as you do what you're told. Now that that's out of the way, what do you say?"

"We'll take it," Kaell stated, he turned to Naka and lowered his voice. "Raven, there is no way we can get out of this city alive, and you may have a death wish but I certainly don't and me and my sister need to get where we're going. So, we're taking his offer." His words were confident now and it seemed he would not accept her disagreement if she would give any.

"Take us to Xisq, we'll do what you want us to do but we're gone after that," she confirmed.

"First, you still owe me dinner, and then we will discuss how you will pay me back for heroically rescuing you," the Kir'in said, winking at Kaell.

He turned around and gestured to follow him, so they did. Naka expected they would need to kill someone when he said 'take care of' but in all honesty she didn't really care. She despised the thought of killing for him but she needed to get to the Dan'um, and if he could really take them there as quick as he said he could, she'd make that trade. If he betrayed her, she could always kill him after all. The tunnels were dark, but not dark enough to be blind inside the cold stone. Her hands grazed across the rough stone and she felt drops of warmth where the edges had cut her skin. *No touching the walls*, she thought to herself.

They passed through several chambers with more tunnels and stairs, each similar to the one before, there was no way they could find their way back but she hoped she didn't need to find the way on her own here. A couple of chambers later they entered a chamber with only one tunnel and one staircase leading down. The staircase was surprisingly smooth and Naka had to be careful not to slip and fall down the stairs.

The further down they went, the more noise they could hear. Steel on steel, and steel on wood, the hollow sound of arrows hitting a wooden target. Soft laughter emerged every once in a while, but was easily overshadowed by a woman shouting. Finally, Naka stepped off the last step. They now stood in a massive, round hall. Some tables were scattered on the left, with several people drinking and talking while on the right people were fighting in drawn circles or firing arrows at targets on the wall. In the middle was an unusual bonfire with smokeless flames, casting its dancing shadows upon the stone. Across the bonfire were two massive wooden doors covered in wrought iron. They looked as if they were taken from some old castle and Naka was seriously curious on how they got them here. The walls and ceiling had the same sharp ridges like every other chamber they had come through.

"Milord," the woman who was training the recruits said with a voice of steel. Her face was as worn as the doors across the room. Scars and wrinkles painted her mahogany skin but her icy blue eyes were still bright and young. Every corner of her face was sharp as the tips of her ears, and seemed that it could cut through steel itself. Her ash-grey hair was tightly tied back and her pose was strong and fierce. Her thin lips formed a soft smile as the Kir'in nodded at her.

She was miraculously beautiful and Naka suspected she was a half-blood with her Dan'um ears and skin and Kir'in eyes.

"How are our recruits?" he asked in his honey sweet voice.

"They need to control their emotions more but they are ready to be Shadows soon. I suspect we can send them to Kir Narahmm within a month."

"Good, we may need them more than we expect."

"Are those new recruits, sir?" she asked, nodding in their direction.

"Stop with the titles, dear, I have told you so many times and yet you still won't. They are no recruits, unless they change their mind of course." He looked at them, opening his arms as a welcoming gesture but received no reaction whatsoever. "No? Sad, you're missing out darlings. No, we have a deal, them and I. So, we're going to Xisq where they can be of use to me."

"I see."

"Would you mind joining me there, I believe we have some people who owe us answers," the Kir'in said to the woman, who simply nodded in return.

The heavy doors sighed in their hinges as the Kir'in pushed them open. Behind it lay a large chamber that held nothing but two pillars. The inscriptions were unfamiliar to Naka and seemed to slowly move across the stone in the flickering light of the flames.

The doors sighed again as they closed, holding back all the light and filling the room with a heavy darkness.

"Welcome to Xisq, the original one, my darlings," his voice like honey said as the older woman opened the doors.

Behind those doors was not the large hall they stood in before, not even close. In front of them lay a massive, underground city, or the remains of one. Roofs and peaks and walls rose up to the ceiling of solid stone. They overlooked a large open space that resembled a town square from a crumbled tower. Right outside the doors the other walls had fallen away, just like the balcony, which was little more than a couple of rocks. The city went as far as they could see with a main street running from each side of the main square and streets and alleys branching from that one again. There was life everywhere they looked, people moving through the streets, even stalls and markets dotted through the city. In most places the roof was hidden in clouds of darkness because the sea-green light of the streets couldn't reach that far. The light came from clusters of crystals, dotted across the city like stars, growing from the buildings themselves. Naka was ripped out of her astonishment by his voice, dripping with sweetness.

"Here we are, out of Distrum. It's time to fulfill your end of the deal."

"Just get on with it and tell us what we need to do, Kir'in," Naka sighed, she couldn't hear his honey coated words any longer.

"Don't be such a drag, dear." He smiled at her with amusement in his eyes. "I just need you to burn down the city."

Chapter 10
Ara-Ashin

There was absolutely no way of knowing how long they had been here. Out of the windows she could see nothing but darkness and stone and the only light they had came from the clusters of crystals that dotted the walls around them. Ara looked between the bars of her prison door to check on the human who was locked across the hall. She didn't expect it to be any different than the last time, and she was right again. He was still asleep, he had been since she had woken up after they were knocked out in the streets of Xisq. Humans were truly weak. How could he even hold so much power in his human heart? He should have been consumed by it right away.

As long as he got her back to the temple after she got back the Heart, she didn't care what happened to him anymore. She did have to find a new way to get him to do whatever she asked, her grip on his mind was weaker since they entered the city but she would find a way, his mind was weak after all so she wouldn't need her powers to charm him.

The lock of her prison caught her eye, it was a simple lock, made from iron, so she rattled it, hoping to maybe break it but it was stronger than it looked. Ara wondered what the Vault would look like and how she would open it. The Nuan were never given a key of any kind, they weren't the keepers of the Vault after all.

Doubt gnawed at her mind. She didn't have the key to the most well secured door in all worlds, there was no way she could open them. The Vault didn't care that she was Nuan, a sacred creation of the Light. She would need to find someone who could help her, or even find a clue somewhere, perhaps she would find some in her birthplace, that was, after all, the origin of light, so it would surely hold some kind of clue about the Heart.

The first Nuans were created in another realm, the realm of Light, home of Nuana herself. After Nuana's death a few Nuans fled to this realm, hoping to find safety from the shadows there.

Ara knew how to cross into this realm even though it would be different than she remembered. Focus didn't come as easy as always. The cold from the floor seeped into her body and her head still hurt from the hit she took in the streets. It wasn't optimal but she had no choice right now. Little by little, she managed to pull herself into the Realm of Light.

Light tickled her face. The bright, white light seeped through her eyelashes and she smiled.

Oh, how she had missed this place, her true home. This is where the first light was created, crafted carefully from the tethers of Virmannan, the ancestral body that was everything and nothing at once, woven and folded and torn apart only to weave it again and again.

Ara opened her eyes, letting the light wash into her eyes. It was purer than any light could ever be and only Nuans were not blinded by it for they were crafted from it. She was sitting on a round slab of white marble in the middle of the water. This realm was formed as an island, floating in nothing. Water filled its surface for the largest part and paths of white marble stepping stones curled around the central temple.

Almost dancing, she jumped from one stone to the next, enjoying the world from which she had been gone for so long. Scattered across the water were lilies, with petals that glowed like the light of dawn. Among them grew large trees with roots that curled into each other. Their trunks and branches made from a purplish crystal and their leaves dripping with starlight.

She looked toward the horizon, where the water fell from the edge into the depths of light. It was there, where she had spent the most time, gazing into nothing, thinking about their ways. She had never questioned them, she knew they were right, it was just that she was always trying to follow them better and understand them more.

The stones guided her gaze toward the temple. Its roof rose high into the air, higher than any peak she knew. It was made from the same white marble as the stone she stood on. Its simple, but yet elegant style was what Nuana preferred and she had used the same style for her palace in the mortal realm, which would later become the center of Anndar.

Ara entered through the large archway the stones had led her to, she sighed in relief as a feeling of rest and peace embraced her. The archway led to the central hall, a large circular room where light fell through the enormous windows filled with stained glass that reached up to the rooftop itself, like six leaves of a closed lily, waiting for dawn. The colorful light fell upon the magnificent crystal structure in the middle of the room. It told the story of how the first light was crafted. The clear crystal was entwined and braided together in the most breathtaking way, catching all the colors of the light that fell through the windows and putting them back together to cast patterns of pure, white light onto the walls that surrounded them. Ara could look at it for days on end. Losing herself in the beauty of the light.

"No Nuan could ever ignore its beauty, could they?" a familiar voice echoed between the light.

"No, we could never, not that we would ever want to," Ara responded, her voice echoing, just like his.

"That's true," the voice chuckled, "I know you haven't come to admire our home, sister, but I am afraid I cannot give you the answer you seek."

"Then I will take the answers you can give, for I cannot ask more of my brother."

He stepped out from behind the crystal statue, he was one of the very first Nuans. A soft glow came off of his entire body, his eyes nothing more than orbs of light. The original Nuan were created in this realm from the First Light by Nuana herself. They were bound to this realm and to the Light more than Ara and her generation were. It was impossible for the first Nuans to leave their realm of creation in any way, however, Ara's generation could cross over however and whenever they wanted before Nuana was murdered and with her a part of their powers.

"You are still easily lost in thought, I see, Ara-Ashin. It has always been a weakness of your generation that we have to accept." He spoke without moving his lips but here physical and mental voices were equal and hard to separate.

Ara forced a smile in response, she knew it was her weakness. The reason they had it was because Nuana had taken the humans under her protection shortly before she created the last generation of Nuans. Ara wasn't allowed to despise humans, she was taught to respect her creator's choice and to admire her for taking care of such a weak and broken race. She did, however, blame the human race for allowing Nuana to die. After all it was the humans that had allowed to let the enemy slip through and murder their protector, and if all that wasn't enough a human king now sat on her throne as if they could ever replace her.

"Sorry brother. Forgive me for my weakness, I struggle with it every day. I also must admit that I have forgotten your name since I last visited this realm." She bowed to him as she spoke this. She knew she wasn't allowed to show disrespect to the first generation and she couldn't risk banishment now that she needed their knowledge.

"You are forgiven. Our Lady made you dwell alongside a lesser race for far too long." He paused, looking deep into her eyes. "My name is Marin-Ishana, I didn't expect you to forget one of your masters this quickly, Ashin." His voice was as harsh and clear as the light he was forged from but now she remembered. He had indeed been a master, he had taught her the way of sight but she was never gifted nor truly interested enough in it. The Light had always shown her what she needed and she needed nothing more than that. She knew he had not really forgiven her for he was still calling her Ashin. It meant 'untaught' and was given to the students who had yet to pass their first challenge. Ara never passed her challenge, not that she ever started it. When the time was right and she was allowed to start it Nuana was murdered and their priorities shifted. Not long thereafter all Nuans but Ara were murdered as well, besides the original ones it seemed. This all was more important to her than the challenge, so an Ashin she was.

She slightly bowed to the Nuan and tried to hide her hollow smile.

"Now, sister, I might not give you the answer you seek but I can show you where to find it. Follow me," he said, turning away. Ara followed him through the arch underneath one of the enormous windows. It was much darker here. The bright light couldn't fully reach here it seemed, it wasn't blocked it was more as if it respectfully waited outside the arc. Ara's eyes were aimed at the floor, watching the cloak of the Nuan flow and swirl across the stone with every step he took. She felt even more unworthy, being dressed in these simple human clothes. Especially because the area beyond the arcs was always forbidden for anyone not of the first generation. As children they told each other rumors of what lay here, from portals to weapons. Anything their young minds could come up with.

"The floor will not give you the answer and neither will my cloak, Ashin." His whispers echoed between the stone like a soft breeze.

She pulled her gaze away from the flowing white and carefully looked around. There was no way she would look like a child in front of one of the masters, she was better than that. The hall seemed only a couple of meters long and yet it took them many more steps than the eye had guessed. On the wall at the end of the hall was a large silver circle, softly glowing in a silver light. It was big enough to step through. She would've used the word 'mirror' but at second glance it would be wrong for a mirror reflects and this showed not the hall in which they stood but instead flashes of a forest. The forest was green like emeralds and dense enough to be a wall, in the middle, a massive tree with greyish green leaves and a dark bark rose above the canopy.

"Where is that?" she heard herself ask.

"It is where you will find your answer. We know much, sister, but we cannot know all. However, there is someone who might know the answer to your question and this forest is the most likely place where you will find him. Or her. We don't know that yet." His voice seemed to ripple the image, as if this mirror, which it was not, reacted to his voice like a living being.

"Thank you, brother, but there are many forests, all dense and green. Where would I begin?"

The original Nuan looked at Ara sideways, clearly disappointed.

"It is the home of queen Serielye, the heart of the Dan'um forest, Ashin." He paused again, softly humming before he continued. "You have become weak and lost much of what was taught to you. There is no teacher to show the ways again and there is none who can complete this task but you on that realm. It is against our tradition but there is no other way so I have no other choice." His eyes met hers briefly before he walked away from the mirror that was not a mirror. "I will train you, Ashin."

To say that she was rusty was an understatement. The Ishana's training focused on every aspect of their former training at the same time. Meditation, combat and their powers all had to be proven in what they called '*Kannpa Aïna*', the Trial of Roots. They had been on it for a while now and the Ishana wasn't impressed with her. Her greatest strength was her meditation, she had a stable mind and could easily be in this realm and Allaea at the same time. Powers were something she hadn't received any training in yet so it was something they put aside. Ara and her trainer had been in combat for the past hour or so and Ara had been defeated too many times already.

As they danced among the roots of the largest tree in the realm they fought, he with his chakrams and she without a weapon. Her feet had trouble finding balance on the crystal bark and she stumbled from one to the other, hoping she would not fall down or even in the water below. The Ishana almost floated across the roots as he spun and ducked. His movements were quick and elegant and light, his cloak like a river of white, flowing around the roots as he moved. Every strike was meant to kill, stopping as it touched her skin, leaving a cut as a reminder of her defeat. Drops of blood dripped from the many cuts, marking her skin with creeks of red, so dark it was almost black. Her breathing was getting heavy now and her muscles hurt with every move but she would not surrender, she would fight until she achieved victory or died trying.

Her foot slipped on the smooth crystal as she tried to step on another root, she tried to grasp another root but could not take hold of it. The air was knocked out of her lungs as she hit the cold water below. Her now heavy clothes pulled her down and she slowly sank into the abyssal depths. Ara started to panic as she couldn't see Marin-Ishana above her. He had to save her even if it was against the rules of Kannpa Aïna, she was the last Nuan with the ability to walk Allaea and therefore the last chance of rebirth for Nuana. If she died, all that would be lost, balance would be gone for a very long time, if not forever and their Lady of Light would never live again.

As her eyes frantically searched the surface of the water for any sign of rescue, she spotted something from the corner of her eye. At first it was only a white spot that grew larger as it rose from the depths below her, but soon she saw it was a serpent-like creature. Black as deep as the bottomless depths from which it came with a spot as white as her own skin between its eyes. Its fins were the same black as the rest of its body and flowed through the water like the cloak of the Ishana. Ara locked eyes with its cloudy white eyes that lay like beads between his scales. Lost in its beauty the world around her faded as it spiraled around her until its head was at the height of her own. The creature was massive, its head the size of a longboat, its body so long that it disappeared into the depths. Ara wouldn't be surprised if it was long enough to encircle the island but she had absolutely no fear as the world around her went dark and she passed out.

Ara awoke coughing and with a heavy pain in her lungs. Every cough brought water from her lungs and she rolled over to her side. The water in her ears and nose poured out and more water flowed out of her lungs now, allowing her to take a deep breath as she looked around. She lay upon the stepping stones near the temple door. At the edge stood Marin-Ishana, his back facing her as he gazed across the water of the island.

"You're alive after all, Ashin. You failed the Kannpa Aïna and should have died but it seems you are too important to die in the eyes of the Master. I will not train you anymore, nor will any Nuan master. You will be given chakrams fit for an Ishana by the Master's order and are to leave immediately and not return until our Lady has returned."

He paused and looked at the sky. He seemed tense and quickly turned around. "You must leave, now. Shadows are here."

He put his hand on her forehead and she was thrown back into the prison cell. She started shivering as she was still soaked and the prison cell was much colder than the realm of light.

"Ara," she heard Rynn whisper. "Ara?" Great, the human. Almost had she forgotten about him, at least he was awake now. Maybe he could just teleport them out and she could find the key in that forest.

"What is it, mage?" she hissed back at him.

"What were you doing? And why are you so wet now? What happened?"

She could barely see him in the shadows of his cell.

"I went to my people for answers but only got useless clues followed by a training that I was too weak to complete." There was no way he could miss the annoyance in her voice.

"Maybe I can help with those clues. I have read every book in the Academy so maybe it can be of use." Ara looked up and saw a spark of hope in his eyes. She smiled, either she had still grip on his mind or he was too stupid to notice her disgust of humans.

"I highly doubt it, mage, unless you know where to find some queen named Serielye, apparently she is in the heart of the Dan'um forest or something."

Rynn went silent for a moment and Ara scoffed, just like she thought.

"Queen Serielye has been the Dan'um ruler since the beginning of time, she was old before this world was born, and the heart of the Dan'um forest would be Irs Ia, the Dan'um capital deep within the Eastern forests. But I figure you know all this as well, since it's common knowledge and all?"

Ara felt a warm rage in her heart. If it was common knowledge how was it that she didn't know it, kind of ruined the meaning of the word common. An insult was what it was, humans knowing more than Nuans.

"Of course I know." It was wrong to lie but he wouldn't notice so it didn't matter. "I simply expected it to be more difficult to find the answer."

"Well if there is something hidden in that forest that you need to find it will be a lot of things but simple is not one of them, Ara." His voice was soft, and guilt seeped through it. So now he felt guilty, great. She truly didn't understand how humans dealt with all these emotions all the time.

"What is so important that we need queen Serielye to help us find it anyway?" he asked.

She rolled her eyes at him and turned away, pushing her hair back to dry.

"The key to the Vault," she eventually sighed. "I suppose this queen either knows it or that she can give us some directions at least."

"So, we came here to open the Vault but you don't have the key, and you only just realized that. Would it not have been wiser to..."

"Yes. It would," she hissed back at him, cutting him off.

Rynn's mouth shut abruptly and he slid into the corner softly mumbling in the darkness.

"Why don't you just use your magic to teleport us to those forests, then we can get on with this."

"I can't," he whispered as he avoided her eyes.

"What do you mean you can't? You could teleport us to Xisq as well so why can't you just teleport us out of this horrid prison?"

"Yira guided my power. I never learned teleportation, humans aren't supposed to be capable of having enough energy to teleport."

A mage as powerful as him and he couldn't even teleport himself without the help of those damned sisters. At least they were useful for something then, since they failed to protect the Heart like they should have.

"Are you capable of summoning your fire on your own?" She could barely see him nod across the hall. "Well maybe it's an idea to melt the lock so we can get out of here?"

"Yes. I mean, I could try." Hope now mixed in with his voice. '*Finally,*' Ara thought.

His eyes lit up like burning coals in the darkness, she could see the fire seep into his veins and followed it toward his fingers where a small fire started to burn. It grew almost white as he focused it onto the lock.

"You won't find anything reacts to magic here anymore, boy." A voice of steel echoed through the hall.

Rynn stopped his fire and drew it back into his body as soon as he heard the voice. Both of them looked toward the doorway. In the doorway stood an older woman, battle and time painted her mahogany skin with scars and wrinkles. Her hair was grey like ash and tied back tightly so nothing blocked her icy blue eyes.

"At least, nothing under the control of Nirs Imak. He burned this city long ago and his fires consumed all that they could. All that is here now is immune to magic. Now, let us talk for a bit, shall we?" She started to pace through the hallway between them.

"We have no desire to talk to any of you. There is nothing we can offer you so let us go," Ara sneered at her.

"My lord seems to disagree with you there. Both you and the mage have great value, be it very different ones. There are people who would pay a handsome amount of gold for you, my boy. But the value of you, Nuan, is far more complex than gold." The woman locked eyes with Ara as she squatted in front of her cell.

"You being soaked and covered in cuts raises the question how you got to be like that. We most certainly didn't do this to you. However, legends always speak of how Nuans were such masters at meditation, so I guess that is all the explanation I need.

"I hope you learned something useful or you might end up as a slave with a purpose you can certainly guess. Many would pay mountains of gold for the last Nuan. So, let us see how much you are worth, sweetheart." A smile broke through like a crack in a frozen river, "What do you know of the Vault, Nuan?"

Chapter 11
Etaín

"You want us to do what now?" Etaín exclaimed. "You can't possibly think we will do your dirty work, Kir'in."

There was no way he was serious. It would kill countless people who had nothing to do with this.

"Well you haven't even heard the details dear. It seems better than the alternative though. We can only guess the horrible things they would do to the pretty Ilunari here and trust me, they will. For you however, slavery seems to be quite unpleasant. Do you know what they do to Larety slaves? No? Well, usually, they cut off your horns and put a chain around your neck and then they let you do all kinds of heavy lifting." The Kir'in's words dripped through his teeth, feeding the rage Etaín felt inside her.

Raven put her hand on Etaín's arm, soothing her anger a little. "Then tell us the details. A city of stone and steel and glass doesn't burn easily."

Etaín couldn't believe it, Raven wanted to burn down a city as payment for some strange shadow portal.

"You would burn a city because he put us through some portal?" She looked Raven in her eyes. "I'd rather have died fighting my way out of Distrum."

The Kir'in started to laugh and walked toward what was left of the balcony. "A city of stone, steel and glass doesn't burn at all, my darlings. No, I was kidding when I said you need to burn the city, that would take away most of my business and we can't have that, can we now?" He turned back around again and looked Etaín in her eyes before he continued. "I need you to pretend to be an officer of King Egìl who has come to check the guard." He turned toward Kaell and Raven. "And I need you to kill certain guards when they come back to their post." He shrugged his shoulders when he said that, as if it meant nothing to him.

Etaín wanted to ask him how he even thought this was better but Raven was quicker.

"How exactly did you picture this? Etaín can't just pass as an official of Egìl. The killing is not a problem here but why not just kill those guards without all the fuss?"

Not the question Etaín expected. She had no idea killing innocents came so easily to Raven, especially because it was the wish of some thief.

"Excellent questions, my dear. But none of your concern, all you need to do is accept my offer, or not and face the other fate. Either way, I'll gain from it so I don't really care."

"What about my sister, Kir'in? You will not hurt her, or I swear it by the High Immortals you will regret it." Kaell's voice was fierce enough to send shivers down Etaín's spine, she truly believed him as his orange eyes seemed to burn like fire.

"No harm will come to her, handsome. She will stay at my side and under Lily's protection. I have no plan for her, she is more of a reassurance that you return from your little trip, and this way she will keep her innocence which we all value so much, am I right?" The Kir'in's voice was still as sweet as honey but everyone could tell he was serious now. Kaell didn't seem to accept this promise until Inza stepped in front of him and hugged him.

"I'll be fine, Kaell. If it's really needed, I can still defend myself." Her words lessened the fire in his eyes and seemed to ease his anger.

"Fine, we're in," Kaell said in a low voice, clearly not approving of it all. Raven and Etaín simply nodded after looking at each other. Etaín had taken a liking to Inza in the past few days. The Kurr girl was so pure and full of wonder, it was hard not to like her. Etaín would not hold Kaell back if anyone hurt his sister, and she believed that if anyone did, he would destroy the entire world for her.

"Well then, now that that's settled, I believe you still owe me dinner. We can discuss the plans during a meal, I presume."

The food was truly amazing, Etaín hadn't been away from home for that long but she already missed proper food more than ever. She had stuffed her plate with everything she could find on the table, and eaten it all with great pleasure. For once, she couldn't care less that maybe it was all stolen simply because her stomach started crying out as soon as she smelled the meat. The others were less enthusiastic about the food and Kaell barely ate anything. All night he had been keeping an eye on their host who seemed to enjoy the attention and gladly returned the stare. In the meantime, the

Kir'in and Lily had explained the plan. The older woman with mahogany skin disappeared after they left the portal.

They made the plan seem quite easy and it seemed like everything had been planned for a very long time. Etaín would be dressed in the armor of an official general of King Egil who had lost it to a deal with the Kir'in or something. Lily would forge a letter saying that Etaín was there to inspect all the guards. For Raven and Kaell it was simpler, they would get some black leather armor and were to sneak into the halls between the guard posts of the Keepers Guard, that were apparently underground, right next to the city they were staying in now. As soon as those guards returned from the inspection, they would take them out and come right back. Etaín would simply do the fake inspection and as soon as she was finished move toward the lower levels of Xisq where people would wait for her and reunite her with the group. After that they were free to go. Nothing difficult, at least that's what their host had said, Etaín doubted it would be as simple as that. Lying had never been something she was good at but she figured that if she acted like her old battle master she might be able to pass as a general of some sort. She figured that would do and practiced her tone as she walked through the city after dinner. The city was quite beautiful and seemed almost unreal. When they stepped out of the portal, they could see that the city lay underneath the ground but now that Etaín walked through the streets alone, looking up from time to time, it was almost like she walked underneath a starry night sky. Crystals were dotted across the roof of the cave, imitating stars and creating their own constellations. In the dim light of the crystals Etaín saw strange markings on a lot of buildings, remnants of what could only have been magic, very powerful magic. Yet every building stood tall and nearly every house seemed to be lived in. Etaín had walked quite a bit and now heard water streaming. When she got there, she saw a small river that had carved its way through buildings and streets, small clusters of crystals grew on the sides, covered in glowing moss, children were laughing and playing in the water. They didn't stop when they saw Etaín but some women came toward her, probably some of the mothers.

"Greetings, Laretu." said one of the women, a Kir'in with sapphire eyes and soft, green hair. "What brings you here?"

"I was just walking around the city before I went to bed, but I didn't expect to find a river here." Etaín laughed with surprise, she was quite stunned to find such a lovely place in a city she expected to be filled with thieves and murderers.

"Yes, it's truly a sanctuary. Lord Aergo has given us a safe place in these times of war, and we will be forever indebted to him. Are you a refugee too, my dear? You don't look like you are one of the Blackfangs, but looks can be deceiving of course," the woman said, looking around the place with a grateful look on her face.

"Euhm, no, me and my friends have a sort of deal with Aergo. I suppose that is him at least, he never introduced himself." The woman gave her a questioning look.

"Black hair, emerald eyes, large scar across his face, honey-sweet voice?" Etaín continued.

"Ah, yes. That's Lord Aergo," the woman responded before she shouted something at one of the children who was climbing one of the walls of the cave. Etain only now noticed the massive waterfall that came straight from the ceiling and formed the start of the river at which she stood. Several pillars rose up around the waterfall, supporting the ceiling there, on one of them stood a small house, hidden in shadows and water. It looked much newer than the houses in the city that Etaín had seen so far, what was most unique about it was that there were no windows in it, nor was there a way up the pillar to reach the house.

"Ah yes, that's the one place we are not allowed to go to in this city, so don't let your curiosity grow too much." the woman laughed. "My name is Kerdanna, by the way, I'm one of the many refugees here, as you might have guessed."

"Etaín, pleasure to meet you," Etaín said, bowing to the woman. "If you don't mind me asking, what is this place? I never heard of a secret city underneath Xisq."

"That's because it is only talked about in forgotten legends, written down in dusty tomes. This city is the original Xisq, although it burned down in the Second Era because the then ruling Emperor rejected Lord Nirs Imak's request to build his Academy here. Lord Nirs Imak then buried the remnants deep within the earth and forced the remaining Kir'in to flee to other places, which is why we have more cities than Xisq nowadays. After many, many years the Kir'in came back to this place in the Fourth Era and built their city, having forgotten Xisq. Eventually, somebody discovered that this was the old location of Xisq and they named their new city Xisq in honor of the old city, even though nobody could find the ruins. It turned out that this location was amazing for trade, especially when a few thousand years later the humans arrived and eventually settled in Anndar, where they used the river Dawn to trade, thus making Xisq one of the richest cities. It wasn't until a thousand years ago that Aergo's grandfather, Bluse, discovered these underground ruins of this once great city and used it to house his band of thieves, just as his son, being Aergo's father. It wasn't until Aergo was in charge that refugees were welcome here, finally finding sanctuary in this world torn with war. He saved us." Tears started to fill the woman's eyes, tears of pain, of things lost, yet her face showed she was strong and she wouldn't give in to that sadness. One of the children came running up to them, giggling and with red cheeks.

"Miss?" he asked, patiently waiting for Etaín to respond, who crouched down as far as she could because the boy barely reached above her knee.

"What is it, child?" she asked the boy, who started to glow immediately.

"Euhm, what are you?" he shyly asked, to which Etaín could only laugh.

"Mhati, that's very rude of you. Apologize to the lady right away," Kerdanna exclaimed, her expression apologizing to Etaín who didn't mind it at all and actually couldn't stop laughing.

"Don't worry about it, I get it. My kin aren't exactly a common sight in these parts." She turned to Mhati. "I am a Laretu, my people live in the mountains far to the east."

"Awesome, can I touch your horns? They look so nice," the boy now shamelessly asked while the other children started to gather around them as well. As she bowed her head, the children started touching her horns and some even touched the scars on her face and arms. Two girls started to braid her hair, putting small flowers in them that they found in the moss, and when they were done all of the children wanted to sit on her shoulders, cheering as they sat meters high above the ground. Even Kerdanna gave in to the joy and sat upon Etaín's shoulders before she urged the children to go home because it was getting late. Etaín had no clue how she knew it was late but did start to feel tired as well and decided to go home herself to finally get some rest after this long day.

However, she didn't get much rest as nightmares haunted her sleep. Images of her father's corpse flashing before her eyes as she dreamt that she was fighting Shyvna herself, and losing.

A hand on her shoulder woke her up and, still lost in the nightmare, she punched at the person's throat. A boy stumbled backwards and fell to the ground, grabbing his throat. After a few shallow breaths he passed out against the wall and Etaín sighed and let herself fall back into bed.

The boy was lucky she didn't have a weapon underneath her pillow, he would've passed out for good then. Etaín spent another moment thinking about her father and was grateful for his sacrifice, she hoped he was proud of her. Now, she had to get ready, today they would pay their debt and move on from this den of thieves, and refugees, who had changed her view of Aergo.

As she tried to put the armor on, she cursed whoever designed it. There were belts and straps everywhere and she realized the boy wasn't just sent to wake her up. Etaín closed her eyes and grunted out of irritation. The door opened and Raven appeared. She glanced over the boy and smiled.

"They sent you one as well I see. Mine met the same fate, poor things." Her voice wasn't as cold as usual but actually reminded Etaín of Raven before the ball. It was nice to hear some warmth in her voice again. "Now, I heard you moan across the street so I'd figured I come and look."

"I'm glad you did. This damned armor was designed by some madman, and I can't get it on properly."

Raven smiled at her and seemed to be amused by the look of Etaín being defeated by some straps and belts.

"A warrior defeated by her armor, that's a rare sight. Let me see if I can save you here."

Raven started to fiddle with the straps and belts as Etaín waited patiently.

"Raven?" she eventually asked.

"Hmmm."

"Do you think we're doing the right thing here? You know, doing his bidding?"

"Those guards don't deserve to die but I have to get to the Dan'um and this is the only way he will let us go so, I don't think we have a choice."

"What do the Dan'um have that's so important?"

Raven fell silent for a moment.

"Your armor is all done." She sighed. "Answers, maybe a future, but in all honesty I'm not completely sure. Someone very wise told me it was very important and I trust his judgement. I hope you can understand that."

Etaín nodded, she could understand that.

"Oh wait, before we go," said Etaín. Raven looked her in the eyes and for a moment, Etaín lost her train of thought as she was struck by the bright violet.

"Euhm, well. Laretu generals always wear warpaints of some sort on missions and stuff. Do you think I need that as well?"

"I'm not an expert but I don't think there are enough Laretu generals outside of the Western Mountains for other people to know. So, the choice is yours."

"Well it's kinda like a battle isn't it?" Etaín chuckled, "So I would prefer it but…"

"Then let's get some paint for it, I think it will make you more believable. Are you planning on using this?" Raven pointed at a metal can with water across the room, Etaín shook her head and Raven grabbed it and splashed it in the face of the boy that was still unconscious against the wall. He awoke gasping for air and got on his feet as quickly as he could when he saw both girls standing in front of him.

"Dear boy, get us some paint, will you?" Raven said, trying her best to give the boy a smile.

"There you are." Aergo's voice echoed through the room. "I thought you'd never come. May I say, you look like a true general, darling."

They were gathered in a large room that appeared to be an old throne room of some sort. The throne itself was made of white marble and was broken, the entire back had crumbled away, but it didn't stop Aergo from sitting on it. The rest of the room was made from the same white marble and reached quite high. Some of the windows were still intact and were filled with stained glass portraying several men and women wearing fancy clothes and a crown, the same one in every picture. Probably the past Emperors and Empresses of the Kir'in. A lot of the pillars still stood tall in their effort to hold up the stone roof. All of them were covered with carvings of leaves and water in such detail that it looked like they could come alive at any moment, if they were not made from marble. Only a few of the pillars had crystal clusters on them, barely lighting the room and casting soft shadows that turned into utter darkness behind the throne.

The Kir'in stood up from his throne and gestured at a group of five people to his side. They were all dressed in white armor somewhat similar to Etaín's.

"These lovely people will act as your escorts. Lily figured that it would be strange if a lone general appeared in the name of King Egìl, so she rounded up some folks for you. They are to stay out of your way and follow your orders when necessary but also to make sure that you do not tell our little plan to anyone. If you do, both you and your innocent friend here will feel the consequences." He smiled at Inza as he said those last words and Kaell tensed up immediately, throwing a warning look at both Etaín and the Kir'in.

Etaín nodded, she agreed it would seem strange if she arrived all by herself. The thought of telling the plan to anyone hadn't even crossed her mind but with this warning she would watch her words even more carefully.

The bald girl named Lily handed her a sealed letter.

"From this moment you are General Murana, one of the king's war masters. You are here to inspect the military force in Xisq, especially the guards. A horse will be waiting outside of the gates. Just ride up the main road toward the Palace and demand to see Lord Vorin in the name of King Egìl. It's best to act as emotionless and serious as possible, that seems to be the way most generals are. Especially ask to see the Keeper's guard, by the way, those are the guards we need gone." The girl's voice was so young and it was weird to hear that frost in her voice, she must have been through a lot. Before Lily walked away, she turned around and nodded at Etaín's face. "I like the warpaint."

Etaín smiled at the girl, but was unsure if Lily saw it. She realized she had to ride a horse, and she most certainly could not. Laretu never rode horses, they could walk further than horses without stopping so they didn't need them.

"Euhm well, about the horse…" Etaín started.

"Please don't tell me you can't ride a horse," Aergo sighed, he looked up and mumbled something mean that Etaín couldn't quite hear.

"Aergo, it's fine. Then she doesn't ride the horse. They'll believe it anyway, Egìl is doing lots of check-ups lately," Lily said to him, obviously not worried about it.

"Why would he do that?" Etaín asked, but before the girl could react Raven was already answering.

"He is preparing to attack the Shadow Lands now that King Varne is dead. Egìl thinks Varne's son won't stand a chance, that he'll fall quicker than his father." All the warmth that was in her voice earlier today was gone, both from her words and her eyes. The girl simply nodded once and went to stand behind Aergo.

"You should get going, now that the day is still young, dear general," said Aergo.

Escorted by the five people she walked toward the doors, already changing her posture and pulling up the facade to the best of her ability.

The underground city was truly a maze and if it wasn't for her escort, she would have been so helplessly lost that she probably would have died without ever seeing the sun again, regardless of the exploration she had done yesterday. It took them a full hour until they emerged from some hidden cave outside of the walls and Etaín was blinded by the bright sunlight that grazed her face. They waited until somebody confirmed the road was safe so they could get on it unseen. Two of her escorts walked a couple of steps in front of her while the other three formed a V-shape behind her. In her head Etaín kept on repeating her fake name and had to watch every move trying to copy her old battle master. She was glad they popped up so far from the walls, it gave her enough time to get the hang of everything by the time they reached the gates. The closer they got to the gates the more noise and smells filled the air, shouting merchants and scents of so many things mixed it numbed all her senses and made her eyes tear up. When they reached the outer gates the guards on top of the walls saluted them and she noticed them straightening and grabbing their weapons tighter. Etaín realized that in order to look more legitimate she had to keep an eye on the guards and military points in the city, at least that was something she didn't have to fake.

Inside the city, the streets were flooded with people and market stalls, but as soon as they saw her and her escort the sea of people parted, making enough room for them to walk. Those who dallied or didn't see them were pushed out of the way by the two escorts who walked in front. Etaín noticed herself enjoying this power a lot and it added to her confidence. Her eyes were scanning the city walls and searched for guards. She also tried to look at many faces like she had seen the general in Distrum do, but a lot of people averted their eyes as soon as she looked in their direction. They reached the second gate without any problems and there too the guards saluted them and let them pass unhindered. Only past this gate did she see guards in the streets and there were quite a few more on the walls and beside the gate. Past the second gate the streets were far more organized and peaceful as most shops were inside buildings that were now made of a light grey marble and glass unlike the grey-stone and steel buildings of the first ring they just passed through. Here the people didn't really look at them but instead glared at them as soon as they passed. Etaín noticed that as they got closer to the last gate, there were more and more guards, she could already see them standing on top of the white marble wall that protected the most inner circle.

They were halted at the final gate.

"What is your business here, general?" the guard asked after he saluted her.

"We come to see Lord Vorin Brynai in the name of King Egil." Etaín tried to sound as serious as possible.

The guard nodded and saluted her again, gesturing the others to open the gates for them.

"We'll send word to Lord Vorin, he'll meet you in front of the guardhouse, general."

Etaín nodded and marched through the gates with her escort. This part of the city was completely different from the other parts. The buildings were made out of white marble veined with emerald, making it look like green fire as it caught the sunlight. There was a wide, open road leading to the palace on top of the hill, which looked like a crown of some sort, elegant spires, connected by high arched bridges and in the middle a large spire of glass with veins of marble and emerald woven into the glass. It shimmered in the morning sun, almost blinding your eyes if you looked at it.

Other buildings were placed in a symmetrical order around the palace, those were all made out of the same veined white marble without any glass. Etaín's escorts knew the way apparently so she just followed them. The guardhouse was a low spire, but much wider, located on the side of a large field behind the palace. In front of the steel door stood a tall Kir'in who bowed as soon as he saw Etaín and her escort arrive. The man reached to about her chest, which was quite tall for a Kir'in but still he looked fragile compared to any Laretu.

"General." He had a voice with the force of the waves yet sharp like the weapons he wielded. His long black hair was braided into four braids, one on each side of his head, falling over his shoulders, while the middle two hung loose down his back. His eyes were like the dark-blue depths of the ocean and three long scars flowed down the side of his face, disappearing under his hair.

"We were not expecting you but I am sure you were sent with good reason."

"Naturally, Lord Vorin." She gestured at one of her escorts who handed the lord the forged letter. She waited in silence as he broke the seal and carefully read it. He frowned and when he was done, he asked,

"An inspection of the guard? May I ask why the king wants this to be done? We'll cooperate of course, I am just curious, General Murana."

"I do not know the reasons behind his every decision, Lord Vorin. I simply follow the given order, although I suspect it has to do with the preparations for the attack on the Shadow Lands." Etaín herself was surprised she sounded so calm and serious, maybe it wasn't as hard as she feared.

"I guess we can never rest as long as that boy king sits on the throne of the Shadow Lands, can we?" he responded and Etaín gave him a small smile, she did agree with him on that.

"I shall summon the city guard here. In the meantime, you can inspect those at rest here, General. That way, the walls are not left unguarded, I am sure you do understand." He made a small bow to her and went inside the guardhouse for a moment. Etaín started to feel nervous again, when was the right time to ask for the Keeper's Guard? Would Raven and Kaell have enough time to slip inside? She didn't even know how they were to slip inside actually, it was never said even though she was sure there was a way for them. She just hoped it would all work out without too much trouble in the end. It didn't take the lord long to return and Etaín figured she would ask about it right away.

"My Lord, even though I am here to inspect the city guard and all that comes with it, His Majesty also had a special request," she said in a more hushed tone.

The Kir'in simply nodded in response and Etaín continued.

"He has asked that I inspect your Keeper's Guard as well, he would like to make sure that the Vault is well protected. So, if you would be so kind to summon those as well, after I am done with the city guard."

Vorin's eyes locked with hers and tried to read her for what felt like minutes. Eventually he nodded.

"If my king commands it. We do not have any replacement for those at this moment so it will have to be quick. We cannot keep it unguarded for long. I assume it won't be more than a simple inspection of equipment and perhaps a little skill, General?"

"Of course not, we wouldn't want to keep them off post for too long," Etaín assured him.

The first group of guards was lining up on the field behind them. It was a group of about a hundred guards, all Kir'in and all male.

"Unsheathe your blades for the General to inspect," commanded the Kir'in. There was no need for him to raise his voice as its sharp tones cut through the air and could be heard across the entire field. All at once they unsheathed their weapons and held it in front of them.

Etaín started to walk between the ranks, she knew that it had to be believable so she checked each blade and each guard's armor as if she was really there to inspect it. It was a boring task and it took her quite some time and she asked random guards questions about how they took care of their weapons and things like 'How long does it take before the gates are fully closed?' and 'How do you let the city know there is an enemy incoming?' and she checked all the answers with Lord Vorin who nodded with every answer. When she was finally done, he commanded them to switch with the active guard and they moved out.

As the new guards moved in, they were not as organized as the other group and Lord Vorin let his sharp voice cut through the air.

"Guards. General Murana is here to inspect you in the name of King Egil, show some respect."

Etaín could see Vorin glance upwards at her from the corner of his eye, trying to spot any reaction in her face. She, however, kept a pretty good straight face.

The same process repeated itself as she checked every guard again and asked similar questions. Some of their armor was loose and she pointed it out, making the men hastily fasten it. She understood it, it was incredibly hot to wear armor while standing still in the blazing sun all day, it felt like being cooked alive. Even her white armor started to have the same effect on her, but she had to push through. It took her much longer to check these men, they were all sloppy and tired and there was much more to inspect.

"I am done with these men, Lord Vorin," she eventually said to the Kir'in, she couldn't help but let some disappointment seep through in her voice. It wasn't like she expected much of the Kir'in force, their part in war was to make as much money as possible from it, not to fight the enemy. However, this unprepared mess of guards was quite sad. Xisq would fall quickly if they were to face a sudden attack from the Shadow Lands. She felt the need to speak her mind as the guards shuffled into the guardhouse.

"Xisq would not be able to fight off any hostile force like this, my lord. I hope you are aware of this."

"We are," he started. "You must understand, General, my people do not like war in any way, nor have we ever had any military force outside of the city guard. We have but one single task, defending the Vault. Our walls are impenetrable and we can last for weeks without outside connections. Plenty of time to allow the armies of our allies to march here and fight them off. It's an ancient vow made by the first of our people that we plan to keep."

Etaín wasn't sure as to what to say, as she disagreed with the strategy of staying alive until help came but simply nodded at him.

"Then let us look at your Keeper's Guard, Lord Vorin. I most certainly hope they are better disciplined than your city guards."

"I have trained them myself, General. They are deadlier than the Empress' most personal guards. I'm certain you will be pleased with them." He put no effort in trying to hide his pride and Etaín hoped with all of her heart that Raven was capable of killing those guards. Then she remembered Kaell's eyes when Aergo threatened Inza and all her doubt disappeared like snow in the sun.

Four men stepped onto the field, dressed in plate and leather armor, which was a dark red with markings of gold and silver. They were armed with both a large square shield and a sword. As they drew their swords Etaín had to put a lot of effort in not gasping or showing any excitement that could give her away. The blades were forged from Bleeding Steel, a metal that could be found in the Red Mountains in the Shadow Lands. The native tribes considered it sacred and outside of their culture only a very few had possession of it.

She had seen it only once, Warchief Kanu, their leader, wielded a large battle-axe made from the beautiful scarlet steel. The red and black patterns wove across the surface like waves crashing on the shore. It took a true master to forge anything from the steel and many feared its power. It was said that a cut from Bleeding Steel could create a wound from which a mortal could only recover with the help of a very powerful healer. It was rumored that Bleeding Steel, if forged right, was deadly to even High Immortals.

"The sight of it always sends shivers down my spine, General," Lord Vorin said with a soft voice. "There is some sort of power around them that we mortals could never understand."

Etaín nodded in agreement, "Yes, there certainly is."

Etaín wasn't sure if the legends were true, if they were then those weapons could turn the tide in battle. Bleeding Steel could avenge Nuana's death, even the Lady of Darkness would fear those red blades.

She went about her checkup and found these four men far better disciplined. Their armor was completely clean and their blades sharp. Their shields were also free of rust and completely undamaged. In fact, nothing was damaged. It seemed strange to her that nothing was damaged, maybe they didn't get a lot of fights down there but what about training? The only way for equipment to come undamaged out of training was when it wasn't used.

.

"When was your last training?" she asked the guards but none seemed to react to it. Their eyes remained fixed on the air behind her and none moved to speak. Etaín turned around to find Lord Vorin giving her a questionable look and even her escort gave warning looks.

"You do know that the Keeper's Guard has to go through certain, euhm, rituals, General?" the Kir'in asked with a voice dripping with suspicion. "We sacrifice their blood to Lord Beasm, a High Immortal of war, if their blood is accepted then the guards are granted sacred powers, only to be defeated by the very best. Meaning, they don't require regular training."

Etaín feared his eyes would pierce right through her act. She tried to get herself together, desperately thinking of ways to get out.

"Of course, Lord Vorin. I simply misspoke, it's a habit to ask for training, apologies." She smiled even though she was pretty sure he knew something was off. Behind the Kir'in she could see one of her escorts rolling their eyes.

"It happens to the best of us I guess," he said as he slightly bowed. "Their last training was right after the last Starfall, if you must know. They were heavily trained before they were recruited for this post. If you doubt their ability to fight, I can ask them to duel you, General. I think you'd be surprised how well a Kir'in can fight."

"I never questioned your guards, Lord Vorin," Etaín began. "However, no Laretu would ever turn down a good fight." She smiled, hoping to turn his attention away from her mistake.

Another Kir'in came running toward them and bowed deeply before Lord Vorin.

"My Lord," she said and she bowed toward Etaín. "General. The Empress invites you to her palace."

Chapter 12
Aergo

This was the closest he had ever been to completing his lifelong dream, finally he would open the Vault. He seriously hoped that Kurr boy and Ilunari girl would be capable enough to take care of the guards. None of his people were and he wouldn't go himself, they would immediately recognise him and that would be about the end of it. One of his most trusted people was already retrieving the Nuan and that mage boy. Aergo was happy they ran into both of them. Word of the mage had spread across the land quicker than the fire he kept in his veins. A rare catch he was. The Nuan however was not at all what they expected to find. Nuan were killed ages before Aergo was even born and belonged to the tales of the past.

"Aergo! You're going to be late for the party if you keep pacing around like that." It was Lily who ripped him from his thoughts. He smiled at her and kissed her head when he passed her. She sighed and raised her middle finger at him.

"That's a rude gesture for a child to make, dear." Aergo chuckled at Lily.

"If you prefer me kicking your ankles just say the word, my lord." She paused as she mockingly bowed to him.

Aergo laughed and walked out of the throne room as he fixed his sleeves. He had a soft spot for the girl. Three years ago, he had taken her in when he found her in the streets at the age of eight, covered in blood that was not her own. It didn't take him long to find out that a couple of men had been found dead alongside the road from here to Anndar. The pieces of the puzzle fell together even though he swore to never speak of it again. Lily had grown to be a strong and loyal girl over the years and Aergo would trust her with his life. He saw her checking over her shoulders if he was indeed still following her and didn't get lost in thought again.

"Such a big day and all he can do is smile at me like a dumb sheep." He heard her sigh as she shook her head.

"My lord," a steeled voice came from the shadows. It was Rysa, the commanding trainer of his Shadows, deadly assassins and master thieves. Her icy blue eyes pierced the darkness without effort. Behind her walked the Nuan and the mage boy, both chained in Baran steel chains. It blocked their magic powers nicely, they were one of the more valuable things Aergo owned. The Nuan was covered in tiny cuts and was soaking wet for some reason. He shrugged his shoulders, as long as she was alive, it was fine. Even further behind them the Kurr girl appeared. Aergo could see fear in her eyes but her face was determined.

"I see you have brought our guests, Rysa. Good, good. Then we can start the party as soon as our two other, well, friends, return." Aergo rubbed his hands together, he was ready.

The dark woman simply nodded once and moved to walk behind him on their way to the gate.

When he arrived, there was already a small crowd of people who were chattering happily and full of excitement. Many greeted Aergo as he passed them and then were occupied with the Nuan behind him. It wasn't a secret that they had captured a Nuan but not many had seen this mythical creature and even though she wore hideous clothes it could not hide the radiant beauty that held so many of their eyes. Aergo looked around but could not find the face he was looking for.

He sighed. "Where is Tuales? Without him it will be kind of hard to start the party."

"He arrives whenever he arrives, and you know it Aergo," Lily answered him with a hint of annoyance.

Aergo knew Tuales arrived when he wanted but he had hoped that this time would be different. He growled, Tuales was the one they needed to open the wall between here and the Vault. Nobody was certain what or who he was but he had some powerful magic and he always said he had served the Kir'in for a very long time. He was the one who created the portals that they used to move from city to city, and he also claimed to be able to open the Vault.

Small gasps came from his right and his eyes shot toward the sound. The Ilunari and Kurr moved through the crowd, both had the foulest smell clinging to them, he guessed the old sewers didn't smell as if they hadn't been used in centuries. Aergo spread his arms in a welcoming gesture but before he could speak the Kurr already snarled at him and went straight to his sister. The Ilunari's eyes were fixed on the Nuan and the Nuan's on her.

"Where did you find that?" the Ilunari asked. "And spare me your sweet talk this time."

"You do take the fun out of everything, don't you?" he laughed at her, she didn't seem to find it amusing in the slightest. "We found her with the human boy on the streets, if you must know."

"And I suppose you made a deal with them as well, generous as you are? Didn't you, Kir'in?" she mocked him.

Aergo put his hand over his heart as if he was hurt again. He enjoyed this Ilunari, most were bland and boring, like their dusty books at home but this one had a bite to her, a raw edge that one had to be careful of before it left them bleeding.

"My dear, no. Deals are for people I like, these two lovely people are my prisoners." He gestured at the Nuan and human.

The Ilunari didn't seem pleased with the answer but he doubted anything he said could please her.

"Where is Etaín? She should have been back by now. You best not play any games with her Kir'in. I can assure you that you will beg for death when I am done with you."

"My oh my, there is some fun in you it seems." He grinned at her. The Ilunari's eyes filled with disgust.

"I'm sure that your Laretu friend is just fine. Don't forget my people are with her as well so we both want them to return safely. You and your friends can wait here until she returns. Maybe you and the Kurr can even take a bath in the meantime. I would be glad to show you to them but right now, there is something else I need to take care of, dear."

Aergo turned to the wall in front of them and seriously hoped Tuales would show up very soon. There was only a limited amount of time and he wanted every second of it. At nightfall there would be somebody to bring down food for the guards that were now dead. Aergo was about to turn to Lily to complain about it when the crowd split. A tall man walked toward Aergo, Tuales. Tuales was as tall as a Laretu and dressed in black and crimson robes that flowed across the floor like a river of shadow and blood. The shadows clung to his body as if he moved through tar, but his eyes, one like a ruby and one like a sapphire, burned through it like strange stars in the nightly skies. His long, ghostly-white hair reached all the way to the ground and surrounded his skin that had the color of old parchment and was covered with marks in a deep red that seemed to move as the shadows caressed it. Tuales always send shivers down Aergo's spine and didn't fail this time. The mage, or whatever he was, had an aura of power and darkness around him that made Aergo feel as if Tuales could lay waste to the entire world with just a simple glance.

"We can begin now. Where is it?" Tuales' voice was as if hundreds of people whispered at the same time. Rysa pushed the Nuan forward and Tuales softly pressed his finger against her cheek. Ara clenched her teeth and started shivering, where his finger touched her skin her veins started to turn black as the shadows that licked Tuales' face. Ara started shaking heavily as shadows flowed further into her veins. Rynn started shaking softly as well, his eyes turning a burning orange. It made Aergo uncomfortable to see Tuales at work but he knew it was necessary. If it wasn't, then Tuales wouldn't be doing it. The Nuan's clothes turned to dust and she fell to the ground. As soon as her skin lost contact with Tuales' finger the black pulled out of her veins and the shaking stopped.

"She might do," he whispered as he looked down on the naked Nuan. "She has to."

"Rysa, pick her up and do whatever Tuales says, will you?" he asked the older lady. She nodded, knowing he didn't approve of Tuales' ways but also knowing that it was necessary. He seemed to know a lot more about the Vault and in all honesty, they needed his powers. Tuales and Raven locked eyes as they passed and Aergo saw the Ilunari put her hand on her still bloody spear. He also noticed that the tip of the spear had a soft glow that it did not have before.

Tuales had reached the wall and pressed his hand against it, a soft, sudden gust of wind passed through the deep cave and markings appeared on the wall. They were carvings that Aergo had only seen drawings of whenever he discussed the plans with Tuales. Crimson blood flowed through the carvings, defying gravity, it seemed to come from Tuales' own hands.

As soon as every corner and curve was filled, it drew back into his hand and the wall softly rumbled before it came apart. Like a waterfall of stone and dust, it fell into the ground revealing the large hall behind it. Honestly, large didn't even begin to cover it. Aergo had only seen the halls once but didn't remember that they were indeed this enormous. There were rows upon rows of pillars, each one engraved with softly pulsing, red-golden substances. The floor was polished marble that reflected the intricate ceiling filled with crawling statues of creatures he could not even begin to describe. Every step, every breath echoed through the halls. Even the rustling of clothes flowed through the halls as if it was a restless bird.

"We meet again, old friend," Tuales whispered before he continued softly in his many tongues, each voice speaking a different one. Aergo shivered as a chill went down his spine. The Nuan's chains rattled as Tuales dragged her across the mirroring floor by her hair, leaving behind a trail of lines of dark blood from the Nuan's wounds. Aergo tried not to feel anything for her, Tuales didn't either, so there was a good chance the poor creature wouldn't live to see the light of day again. Due to the echoes, everybody kept as quiet as possible until only the thousand voices of Tuales and the rattling of chains filled the halls. They were deafening as they grew stronger with every second and Aergo was sure he wasn't the only one to thank every High Immortal that the sound died away as soon as Tuales stopped in front of the great door of the Vault.

This too was enormous and engraved with the substance that was inside the pillars surrounding them. The markings on the door were intricate and flowed through the dark metal of the door. In the center of the door it came together to form something that resembled an eye with a pupil that was a pool of gold and red.

"Are you ready, my lord?" Tuales asked, his eyes burning with desire and a smile revealing his pearly teeth.

"I have been for a long time, my friend."

Tuales turned back to the door and pulled out a large gleaming knife stained with dark red spots and slashed it along the Nuan's throat. Rynn screamed and his veins burned brighter that any fire ever could, his eyes had turned into suns and it took several people to hold him back. Aergo seriously hoped the Baran chains would be strong enough, they were said to suppress any powers one had but this would be a test to see if the stories were true.

Tuales paid him no mind and held his hand out in front of him. Dark red blood flowed from every wound the Nuan had and gathered above the mage's hand as if it had a life of its own. It stuck to the long, black nails of the mage as it swirled above them. The Nuan's breaths grew shorter and uneven before death claimed her.

"Tuales, let her live. She is more valuable to us that way," Aergo begged him.

Without looking away or stopping Tuales answered him, his voices raw and deep now.

"I will take what I need. Her life matters not compared to the treasure inside of this damned vault, Kir'in. And I am sure I do not have to tell you how unwise it would be to stop me now."

Aergo felt his every bone trembling at the sound of Tuales' voices, a primal fear he had never felt before. He saw Lily softly trembling as well and he reached for her hand which she eagerly took hold of. Aergo's mouth was too dry to say anything anymore and he was sure his voice would be so broken that Tuales wouldn't even listen to it.

Tuales started to weave the blood through the air, his countless voices whispering words unknown to Aergo. The blood went into the pupil and embraced the golden red substances. It spread across the entire marking and wove into the gold. The Nuan was lying on the floor, paler than usual and only a few drops of blood came from the gaping wound in her throat. Tuales started to make wilder, more complicated movements as his voices grew louder. Aergo looked at the door and noticed that the dark red blood of the Nuan started to separate from the golden red in the eye. Tuales attempted to weave it together with bewildered movements but more and more started to separate until at last Tuales yelled and all the blood fell onto the floor, hiding the reflection of the ceiling.

"It cannot be! She is pure, it should have opened the door," Tuales exclaimed. Shadows slithered down his fingers and gathered in his hands. He pushed them against the door and for a moment the shadows wove into the golden red, it lasted but seconds. Then Tuales was thrown back as he exclaimed in pain.

Rynn growled at him. "If you don't use her blood then give it back to her."

"What use would it be, human? Her blood is not the key even though it was pure. It doesn't matter if she lives or not, she is of no use anymore." Tuales voices were still dark and eerie and every word still sent shivers down Aergo's spine but the human didn't seem to fear him. Aergo figured that the human was strong enough to be a serious match to Tuales.

"I know where we can find the key but they will only give it to her. That's what they say at least. Only a Nuan can hold the key to Xisq." With every word the human spoke his fire pulsed through his veins and the chains were softly moaning as if one stood on thin ice in the first days of winter.

"Then do tell me, mortal, and her life might be spared."

"The Dan'um. The key is within the Dan'um forests. That's all I know about it."

"Figures," Tuales scoffed. "They always seem to have the answers, don't they? Well then, I better get to work." He turned to Aergo, "You have a new task it seems. I will try to bring back the Keeper's Guard. I hope they didn't butcher the corpses too much, and I will put the wall back. That way we have another shot at opening this cursed door."

Aergo nodded at him. He had no doubt the mage could erase their presence here and put the Keeper's Guard back together.

Tuales moved his hands and the blood immediately reacted to do his bidding and flowed back into the Nuan's veins and with a wave of his hand her pale flesh started to move and wave itself back together as if there had never been a wound at all.

"Rysa, if you don't mind, would you help her and the human to their cells?" Aergo had to put quite some effort in keeping his voice steady. He had always known Tuales possessed gifts but to see him draw all the blood from a living creature and then weave it back in as if it was nothing put some degree of fear in Aergo's heart that he found hard to hide.

"Lord Aergo, wait for me in my tower. I will come to discuss our further plans regarding the Vault as soon as I am done here," Tuales said to him. Aergo simply nodded and gestured at everyone to go back. It was frustrating to see the Vault still closed but Aergo wasn't so sure he would pay a life to see its contents anymore, especially because he didn't know for sure what was in it after all. He felt relieved he was out of those halls even though they were beautiful. He asked Lily to show Raven and Kaell to the baths and started walking toward Tuales' tower. The tower was located near the edge of the underground city, in an almost deserted part. Nobody really fancied living near the mage and most feared him and only accepted him because Aergo did.

The tower wasn't actually a tower, it was a natural pillar that was hollowed out long before Aergo moved here. There were no crystals to light up the pillar and thus it was cloaked in deep shadows, only the dim light from within that seeped through the cracks broke the darkness. Aergo stepped through the entrance which was nothing more than an opening at the bottom. He had been here before and yet every time it felt like a new place. Shadows and light danced across the curved walls, between the hundreds of talismans and bones. Shelves filled with books, bones and blood curved around the ridges of the walls. A large staircase twisted around a central pillar in which many words were carved, each written differently than the one before, as if countless hands had written them. Dozens of candles were lit and dotted across the shelves and ridges of the walls, their flames flickering whenever the shadows brushed past them as if somebody whispered into their flames. It wasn't silent in the tower and yet Aergo could not hear any distinct sounds, it was as if voices spoke from behind a veil he could not lift.

"My lord, welcome back," Tuales said as he descended the stairs. Whenever the mage spoke with his thousand voices the voices beyond the veil echoed his words. Aergo shivered with every sound that left the mage's pale lips. He wasn't surprised to see the mage had arrived before him, Tuales possessed powers of shadows and could move from one shadow to another with ease. It was something he taught to the Blackfangs, yet nobody could master it as well as Tuales.

"I believe we have some things to discuss, old friend." Aergo's voice shivered like his spine but he could not see why he would attempt to hide the fear in his heart, the mage could see it there anyway and Aergo didn't think it wise to lie to something so powerful.

"Yes we do, my lord," Tuales said. "Someone must go and take the key from the Dan'um, if they truly have it. If not, I will have my fun with the human boy, the Nuan is yours, I have no interest in her anymore. I cannot go to the Dan'um forest anymore, so you have to go." Tuales was pacing through the room, walking from bookshelf to bookshelf as if he had lost something.

"Me?" Aergo was kind of surprised to hear it. "I was thinking about sending Lily or Rysa. I trust them with my life and they can be counted on for this."

"To send Rysa would be a very unwise move, my lord," the mage responded. "She and her mother were banished from the forest when Rysa was born so it is likely that they kill her and dump her body in their rivers. To send Lily may seem wise to you but have you considered that she has no knowledge of diplomacy? Her skills are, well, in a more deadly field than talking."

Aergo sighed, he hated the idea of leaving his people behind. To the world he sought nothing but wealth and power but these people knew he valued their company just as much.

"Fine, I will go to the Dan'um but in all honesty, I have no clue as how to get there. We don't have any shadow gates east from Xisq, and it will be horrible to go across the Marshes this time of year," Aergo said.

Tuales stopped walking around and licked his pale lips with his purple tongue. The mage fell silent and closed his eyes and as soon as he did so the whispers became louder, almost loud enough for Aergo to hear them. Soft breezes flowed through the room, as if the air itself caressed his skin and hair. Aergo started fiddling with a cord on his leather jacket, he couldn't seem to focus his eyes nor his mind on one place, instead they both shot from one thing to another.

"There is one, it was hidden long ago and even I do not like going to that place myself," Tuales whispered with only a couple of voices. It was unnerving to hear Tuales speak with so little voices, Aergo suddenly wondered if the mage even had a voice of his own.

"A place where even you don't like to go. Which place could be so unpleasant that it trembles the voice of a mage as powerful as you?" A place that made Tuales uneasy? Aergo seriously couldn't think of anything more terrifying than the mage. It would've been extremely useful to use a shadowgate to go East of the lake. It was spring and the river Dawn and the lake both flooded during this time, thus flooding the Scorching Marshes to the east of the lake. Xisq's twin city, Mayk, would be flooded as well, so no ship would be sailing east now, and the water wasn't high enough for a ship to sail through the city. He would have to go around, either south or north. South wasn't really an option for that was where the war was the most intense and Aergo most definitely didn't want to get caught up in that. North meant through the human kingdom which was perfectly doable but would take too long. Especially because they would have to avoid any towns or cities, the Nuan couldn't just be seen out in the open so close to Anndar. As soon as king Egìl found out Ara was there, he would send his best to retrieve her and they would be on the run, likely ending up in the dungeons of Anndar. With care it could be done but it was so much easier to not have to.

Tuales dropped a very heavy book on the table between them, Aergo thought the poor table would collapse under the weight of the massive thing. It was truly enormous, the size of Aergo's torso and as thick as Aergo's forearm was long. Dark, wrinkled leather was bound around the countless pages that had yellowed across the ages. The leather was marked with small holes and lines between them, drawing symbols that reminded Aergo of the markings on the Vault but these somehow felt much older. The voices were gone from the tower and the sudden silence descended on them like a thick cloud.

"What is this?" Aergo asked.

"Something your mind could not begin to understand, mortal."

Tuales carefully flipped through the pages, revealing unreadable symbols and strange drawings that held so much detail it seemed they were as alive as Aergo was. The mage stopped on a page that held a drawing of a city, large and prosperous, in faded ink. The text above it was hard to read.

"The city of Arga, the city of prosperity and first Allaean capital of the humans," Tuales said, his voices carrying pride and fear and sadness. "This is where a shadow gate east of Xisq is, right in the heart of the city."

"I have never heard of Arga. One would think a city this big would appear in many stories of the past," Aergo said.

Tuales shook his head, "The fate of this city was bad enough that nobody dared tell stories about it nor was anyone alive to tell it."

"So, it's destroyed then? Nobody alive in there?" Aergo asked.

"Nothing but nightmares."

"Then what brings the fear into your heart, Tuales?"

"There is nothing alive in there but that doesn't mean nothing there is dangerous. That city faced the true wrath of the Dan'um, the wrath of queen Serielye, what they summoned in that city is older than me, and far more powerful, something from a world lost forever."

"Does this something have a name, or do you fear it enough to not speak it?"

Tuales' eyes locked with those of Aergo and cut deep into his soul.

"He is known as the King of Embers, Lord of Nightmares, Breaker of Souls but I mainly call him brother."

Etaín was rendered speechless. The Empress of the Kir'in wanted to see her in her palace and all she was supposed to do was cause a distraction. Could she have been discovered? There was no way she could escape this city if she was. They were close to the enormous glass spire she had seen before, moving through the beautiful garden within the white marble arcs surrounding the spire.

Light cascaded on the pale flowers of the garden, blooming between the fresh grass that danced in the soft breeze of spring. The spire didn't have doors, instead there was a large opening in the glass under which the light crisscrossed in its many colors that rained down on Etaín's shoulders as she walked under it. Inside Etain could see a green marbled skeleton of the building that wrapped across the glass like vines and moss did on trees. In the middle of the room the green marble vines twisted into each other and formed a throne as they reached the white marble floor. Rivers of light were drawn across the stone and those too came together at the bottom of the throne.

On this throne sat a very tall Kir'in woman, the empress. She was dressed in the purest of silk, a shade of green as if it was made out of liquid jade. Her skin was as white as porcelain and looked equally fragile. Hair in the palest shade of green, intricately woven, flowed down her thin shoulders all the way to the floor. She wore a crown of silver and white, set with jade, emerald and diamonds, that was made with the same elegance as the arcs surrounding the spire. Her face was flawless except for a single scar that crossed her lips, like a crack in a marble statue. Her eyes were the same pale green as her hair, almond shaped, and looked at the world with a certain disapproval.

"Your majesty, I present to you general Murana, Battlemaster of King Egìl," the girl who retrieved them announced, then bowed deeply and left the room.

Etaín bowed but not nearly as deep as the girl who'd announced her, she pretended to be a general of King Egìl and those were almost as high in rank as the Empress.

"General, why is it that we received not a single word from his majesty about your visit?" The empress' voice was actually quite deep and it reminded Etaín of a river in summer.

"I do not know, your highness. I simply followed his order to inspect your guards." Etaín felt sweat pearling on her skin underneath the armor.

"Random inspections are very unusual, as you may know, general, they only occur in times of oncoming war and even then, rarely unannounced. So, I must ask, are times of war upon us again?" The empress raised her eyebrows as she waited for her answer. Etaín had to put a lot of energy in keeping her face calm and not tremble constantly. She could not keep the surprised look of off her face, however.

"Again?" she asked the empress. How could anyone be so ignorant? "It was never gone, your majesty. Ever since the Guardian Megana murdered her sister we have been at war. The only reason it is often forgotten is because King Egìl has done all he can to keep the war out of the Shining Lands. The reason for this inspection is that we are planning a serious attack and his majesty wants to know if we have the forces to perhaps strike down the Shadow Lands once and for all."

Etaín's words echoed through the spire and eventually died, leaving a still silence. The empress observed Etaín as she said all this. Her eyes revealed her disapproval of Etaín's outburst and the Empress savored the silence that fell between them for a moment.

"I see. King Egìl knows we cannot provide the military forces he seeks, that is our agreement. However, I hope the inspection went well and I invite you to eat with me, your escorts will also be provided with a proper meal." The empress' words didn't echo as much as Etaín's did, they sounded once through the room, clear as the glass surrounding them. Etaín was quite hungry, however, she always had an appetite and she suspected that the food for an empress was extremely good so there was no way she would say no to it. She did, however, remember that she was still undercover and that the empress might ask questions that she could not answer properly, though it did seem rude and perhaps suspicious to decline an invitation like this so eventually she decided to simply accept it.

"It would be an honor, your grace, to eat with you." Etaín bowed.

"Very well, walk with me then, general."

Etain nodded and the empress stood up, her silken dress rippling across the white marble like a soft, green breeze in a pale sky. They went up stairs that were nothing more than jade-colored marble vines woven into steps, thin and elegant and very frightening. Etaín was quite scared the marble would break and she would fall to the cold, hard floor. The Kir'in empress was thin and light and the marble held her with ease but Etaín was a big Laretu with lots of muscles and a love for food. Etaín didn't trust the strength of the marble enough to hold her.

"What seems to be the problem, general?" the Empress asked as she saw the Laretu hesitating at the bottom of the stairs.

"Your palace is beautiful, don't get me wrong, but for a Laretu like me, these stairs seem a little fragile, your grace."

"You truly are a people of the mountains, Laretu. These stairs carried things far heavier than you, general. Now please hurry, or leave, I do not like to be kept waiting for unnecessary reasons," the empress said as she moved up the stairs.

"Oh, and keep your head down when moving through the doorway, your horns would damage the marble."

Etaín sighed deeply as she started to ascend the stairs, trying to not look down.

"Maybe I will headbutt your doorway, your grace," she muttered under her breath. The only reason she was going to conquer these stairs was because of the food, she was already done with this dainty little empress and she just wanted to push her over or something.

She had to almost fold herself in half to fit underneath the doorway but as soon as she went through, she was greeted with an amazing assortment of smells and a table filled with so much food, she couldn't see the tablecloth underneath. The empress was sitting at the far end of the table and gestured to the only other chair in the room that was across from her at the other far end of the table. As Etaín sat down she tried to see everything on the table but there was more food than she could imagine and didn't recognise much of it.

"By Habra, Lady of Abundance, let this meal begin," announced the Empress as she touched her forehead. Etaín was surprised to see that people still worshipped the High Immortals. Laretu didn't really worship any High Immortals anymore, only when they went to war did they properly worship them. Sometimes they still called out their names in praise but it wasn't that common ever since the

War of Shattered Light began. Etaín touched her forehead as well to show praise. As she stuffed her plate with a bit of everything she could reach she noticed the Empress watching her closely, her eyes unreadable, as she herself slowly chewed on tiny bites.

"Tell me, general, how long do you plan to stay in our city," the empress asked, her eyes focused on the bit of food on her plate.

Etaín swallowed her food, "Well, I was only sent to inspect your guard and that is finished so I will take my leave as soon as we're finished, your grace."

The empress nodded slightly, "We're finished here then it seems. I do want to ask you to walk with me through the garden, to give you my answer on some of King Egìl's requests if you don't mind."

Etaín had stuffed her mouth when she saw the Empress stand up from the table. She thought it a waste to just leave all of this food, she grabbed a pear from the table as she followed the empress down those horrible stairs again. Etaín saw the empress looking over her shoulder to see if she was still following her, and gave her a wide smile. Outside they stepped into the large garden surrounding the spire and Etaín was startled to see the empress moving across gravel in her high heels.

"General, look around you as if you are admiring the garden and tell me if you can see anybody following us here." The empress' voice was hushed and she barely moved her lips as she spoke, her eyes fixed on the floor. Etaín wasn't sure what this was all about but could certainly feel the sudden tension in the air. She looked around and saw nothing out of the ordinary and shook her head.

"I don't. What is this all about, your grace?"

"I think you know Laretu, you are not a true general, at least not of Egìl. We know it. Word has already been sent to King Egìl's men and they are waiting outside of the gates to capture you."

Etaín's breath was heavy now, sweat pearled on her face as well and she felt as if she just finished training.

"Why, why are you telling me this?"

"Because I only know of one person who could have thought of this and I want to make sure that he knows that I am not as foolish as my predecessors." The empress locked eyes with Etaín and only now did Etaín see life in them. "I also know that your kind has shown incredible loyalty to the king's cause, like my own people. Both our people have given much, but without either of us the

Shining Lands will fall. We provide the money to wage war, and you the people and weapons." She was silent for a moment as she looked toward the sun in the blue sky above them. "One day, the Lady of Light will return and peace will return to our lands."

Etaín looked at the sun as well and smiled.

"Yes, she will return one day. I am still loyal to his cause, we must avenge the Lady if we ever want to know peace again. Forgive my actions today, I did not have much of a choice and I promise that someday I will make up for these lies."

The empress chuckled. "Don't ever make a promise you cannot keep, child. Now go, I may forgive your actions but Lord Vorin does not. I pray you will live to fight another day, hopefully on our side." She walked on, leaving Etaín amidst the sea of flowers.

Turning around she saw Lord Vorin standing near the entrance, keeping a close eye on Etaín as she approached him.

"Lord Vorin, my escort and I are about to leave but I need to thank you for your cooperation," she tried to say in a serious tone. She had absolutely no idea if it was appropriate but they already knew she was an imposter so it probably didn't matter anymore.

Lord Vorin responded with a crooked smile and a slight bow and gestured to the gates. Etaín's escort was already waiting there and she tried to give them a warning look even though they avoided her eyes as much as possible. After a couple of seconds, she met one of their eyes and received nothing more than a nod back.

The gate was opened and they started their journey down the main road again, through the shops and stalls all the way to the even more crowded outer ring. They couldn't see if they were followed but Etaín felt as if they were being watched. There was no way she could blend into the crowd, she was more than a full head taller than almost everyone in the streets. Etaín felt a slight tug at her arm, one of her escorts.

"Don't get scared, don't look back, just follow us," he whispered.

Before Etaín could even open her mouth to ask questions she heard a large explosion behind her and felt a blast of wind and warmth and shards of various different things hitting her back. She could barely stop herself from throwing up as she saw parts of people fly past her, limbs and blood and all kinds of things that she didn't want to look at.

The escort quickly moved into an alley and went through a door, Etaín followed them immediately, she understood that questions could be asked later.

"Hurry up, down the stairs, quickly," one said to her. They opened a carefully hidden trapdoor in the floor that opened up to a black hole with a set of stairs just like the one Etaín had seen in Distrum. She ascended the stairs as darkness wrapped around her and she had to hold the wall to not tumble down the steps. The whole way back into the underground city was just like in Distrum, countless chambers with small fires and lots of stairs and hallways carved out in the stone. As soon as they entered the city, they were greeted by a woman dressed in the purest white, she was a Dan'um with the same icy blue eyes and dark mahogany skin as the trainer, Rysa.

"Etaín, isn't it? Welcome back, I hope it all went well. I am here to escort you to the baths and provide you with new clothes." Her voice was beautiful, like a soft, summer breeze caressing the canopy of a forest. Etaín immediately felt at ease and a sudden warmth flowed into her heart. It didn't take long for them to reach the baths and lovely, warm scents of jasmine, vanilla and lavender brushed against her.

"The baths are through here, my sweet. You can undress in the first chamber and I will make sure these clothes are returned and new ones will be there when you come out of the baths," the Dan'um woman said with a soft smile. As Etaín took off the armor she noticed all the gore on the back of it. There were liquids and flesh and skin on it, and she wasn't sure if it came from people or animals but she decided she had absolutely no desire to know. She shuddered and quickly undressed until the hot steam touched her bare skin. The baths were beautiful, they were quite large and there was a beautiful mosaic across the walls, floors and ceiling. It depicted flowers, birds and other colorful animals surrounded by patterns of white and jade stones. The room was filled with a cloud of steam and scents, drawing every bit of tension out of her body, the water was nice and hot as she lowered herself into it.

Etaín sighed deeper than she ever had, this was the good life.

"What a day," she heard a familiar voice say.

"Raven?" Etaín tried to look through the steam but it was too heavy. "Raven, is that you?"

"Yeah, it's me," Raven chuckled softly, "How did you do? We expected you back a lot sooner."

"Well the empress invited me to her palace and to eat with her and then she warned me that I was discovered and, well, I think I owe her now." Etaín started to laugh nervously, this had to be the craziest day she had ever had in her life. Impersonating a general and meeting an empress. Madness, but she liked it.

"How did it go with the Vault?"

"Well, we had to wait in the sewers for the guards to walk back after their inspection before we could kill them so, we sat there for quite a while," Raven started, "After that was done, we found out Aergo has a very powerful ally and a Nuan as prisoner. We did try to open the Vault but he didn't even have the key, that still appears to be in the hands of the Dan'um if we can believe the human so, now, I guess we wait until he decides that we're going there."

"Maybe it's a strange question, but what is a Nuan? I have never heard of them." It seemed important to Raven but Etaín really didn't know.

"Nuans were the creation of Nuana, her children if you will, so called perfect beings of light. They were murdered long ago, at the start of the War of Shattered Light, and were thought to be extinct. Shadows came for them before they came for Nuana, trying to erase the Lady of Light and all her actions. It's not like anyone missed the Nuans though. Conceited and know-it-alls." Raven almost snarled the last part and Etaín nodded, not realizing Raven couldn't see that. The water moved and Etaín heard Raven get out of the baths.

"I'll go and check what the plans are, maybe you should come as well. It's time we get out of here," Raven said to her, the cold tone softly returning to her voice. Etaín caught a glimpse of Raven's back as she moved past her. Her pale skin tight on top of her muscles and bones, several soft pink scars drawn across it and a large, black tattoo across her spine, symbols and lines, weaving into each other like a web. The mist closed up and Etaín sank back into the warm waters, her heart beating hard and fast.

Chapter 14
Inza

"Do you truly think he'll let us go now?" Inza asked her brother. He looked up and smiled, but his eyes didn't smile as well.

"We have kept our word, so he has to do the same. We can leave anytime we want," he answered in a soothing voice, continuing to pack more food into their bags.

"How will we know the way to the Dan'um? We still don't have a map, father only told us to go east until we reached the forests."

"We will follow the lakeside north and move east as soon as we can, it can't be that difficult." Inza could feel his doubt, it hung in the air between them. He had never lied to her, as far as she knew, and only kept things from her when necessary but she saw no reason for him to pretend like he knew what to do.

"You could join me of course," they heard a voice say from the doorway behind them. In it was Aergo, leaning against the wall, his fangs revealed by his eternal smile. "It could save you a lot of time you know. And then I won't consider this stealing." He gestured at the food in Kaell's bag. Kaell stopped packing and turned around.

"And pay another horrible price? No thank you, we'll find our own way," her brother snarled at the Kir'in.

"I see. Well the price I had in mind wasn't going to be horrible, not in my experience. All who paid that price have found it quite, well, pleasurable really. It was simply an offer because I have no idea how you would cross the Scorching Marshes this time of year, and I wonder what would happen to Kurr as they pass through human lands. You do realize that his highness, King Egìl, hasn't seen any Kurr outside of the mountains and is desperate for your gifts?" He grabbed an apple and took a bite out of it as he locked eyes with Kaell. Inza didn't approve of the Kir'in but she had seen the fear in his eyes when the mage tried to open the Vault, and she knew that he masked a lot of his feelings, she had witnessed Kaell doing the exact same all her life.

"What do you mean about the Marshes?" Inza asked him.

"You really don't have a clue how to get there do you, sweetheart?" Aergo chuckled.

Kaell glanced at Inza before he fixed his eyes on the floor. Inza shook her head at the Kir'in and his emerald eyes revealed a hint of pity.

"The Marshes are large open fields between the lake and the Dan'um rivers. In spring the Dawn and the lake flood and drown the entire area and make it practically impossible to cross them. There is but one road that crosses them but it is only accessible in winter and early summer. I, however, have found a way to get to the edge of the forests, just like that." He snapped his fingers. "The Laretu and her Ilunari friend have already joined us."

"Kaell, if Raven and Etaín are going we really have no reason to be stubborn and go by ourselves. He seems to know what he is talking about."

"He always does," Kaell said mockingly. He looked at Inza but she really thought this was the better option. If he decided to go by himself she would completely trust his judgement but she really hoped they would join the Kir'in, even if it was just for the company of Etaín. Her brother's eyes eventually softened and he gave in.

"Fine, we'll join you."

"Magnificent. We'll leave in an hour, gather in front of the palace when you're ready to go."

They arrived last at the palace. Etaín and Raven were both dressed in fitted black leather armor and Raven leaned against her spear that didn't glow anymore, it was just silverish metal now. Across from her stood the Nuan and the human. The human still wearing his chains and Inza only now noticed the frost that had formed on his skin where the chains touched him. The Nuan was now dressed in a long, red dress that looked expensive and revealed quite a bit of her milky white skin. Her skin was still covered in small cuts and her eyes looked dull and empty. The human boy stood as close to her as possible and looked at everyone with eyes filled with fire. It was completely silent except for the crackling of the chains on the human's wrists, at least it was for a moment until Tuales suddenly stepped out of the shadows in the palace wall.

"My Lord," he said in his countless tongues. Every word ignited a fear within Inza's heart, not only because it was just straight up creepy, but mainly because she found one of the voices so familiar.

It frightened her quite a lot but when she told Kaell, he had assured her he didn't hear the same and she had tried to forget it.

"I hope you are ready because I cannot tell you what awaits you there." His voices echoed between the buildings. Aergo nodded and followed the mage up the tower to the place where they had arrived. They stepped into the room with the engraved pillar but before the mage closed the door, he looked at Aergo.

"Good luck, remember that not even the High Immortals will help you there, my Lord."

The door closed and total darkness wrapped around them. It was different this time, it felt like the darkness flowed into their lungs, taking away their breath as if they were breathing water. Shadows tugged at Inza's arms and hair and she grabbed the arm of the person next to her, not knowing who it was. As soon as the darkness had come it went away, one by one they all gasped for air as if they had been drowning. They pushed open the doors but weren't greeted by light as they expected. Instead, clouds of ash and smoke blew inside, making breathing hard again.

"What in the name of…" she heard Aergo say. Raven gripped her spear even tighter and stepped outside, leading the others out of the room as well. Inza stepped out last and sank all the way up to her ankles in the thick layer of ash on the ground. Looking around she wished they had never come here.

They stood in the middle of what used to be an enormous city. There were ruins as far as Inza could see, all covered in a layer of ash and embers. Black smudges everywhere they looked. The sky was dark and grey, clouds of dust and smoke with a dark orange light shining through them. It wasn't the dark orange of a sunset, no, this was the orange of wildfire.

Every breath was heavy with the scent of charcoal and burning flesh, Inza felt her stomach turn at the smell and had to pinch her nose. Her eyes were watering because of the sharp smell and heavy dust, the same dust went into her lungs every time she took a breath and she had to cough almost after every breath. Her body started shaking as her breath became heavier and heavier, her knees went weak and she saw the floor coming closer through her watery eyes. Before she reached the ground, she felt somebody wrapping their arms around her, it was Kaell, of course. He tore cloth from his shirt and wrapped it around her mouth, keeping the dust out of her breath.

“What is happening to her?” she heard Etaín ask faintly.

“She, just, has a hard time breathing,” Kaell said, trying to hide the fact that she was shifting as he moved more in front of her. “Just give her some space, okay?”

“Space won’t stop her shifting, idiot.” It was Raven, she appeared in Inza’s vision and placed her hands on Inza’s forehead. Her breath staggered at the cold touch of Raven’s skin.

“This is going to hurt. A lot,” the Ilunari said as she pushed her finger hard on the back of her head and top of her chest.

It felt as if snakes slithered through her spine, excruciating pain flowed through every fiber of her body. She gasped for air but couldn’t breathe at all, every muscle in her body froze and she could feel her veins filling with nothing but pain, she feared they would rip through her skin. Raven let go of her after what felt like an eternity.

“Breathe,” Raven whispered.

Air flowed into her lungs, clean but warm. The pain drew out of her body when Raven stopped touching her skin, Inza felt her body returning to normal. Nails pulled back into her body and so did spikes that had grown out of her spine. Her panic faded as she met the bright violet eyes of Raven before she turned her head away and made room for Kaell.

“Inza, are you okay?” His voice was an ocean of worry. “What happened?”

Inza couldn’t find any words, not that she could have answered his second question. She just nodded and squeezed his arm and Kaell hugged her tightly.

“Her body was shifting into everything at once, it panicked.” Raven again, she held her spear tightly and looked around worried. Her eyes were sharp and seemed to have no problem with the ash in the air. “That’s what happens when shifters come to this lifeless place, at least, most of them. Some just die.”

Inza met the eyes of the human mage, they were filled with interest, not a spark of worry to be found.

“How did you know what was happening, Raven? And how did you know what to do?” Kaell fired his questions at the girl, but she just turned her head.

"We should get out of here, quickly." She turned to Aergo, "You should've said we were going here, we could have chosen a safer route, being every other route in the world."

"This was the fastest," he responded.

Raven swept him off his feet and put her spear at his throat, "Your greed is what is going to have us all killed. This route was the slowest of them all, you idiot, I bet your bloodmage didn't tell you that." She looked at the chains on the human's wrists and shattered them with a quick strike of her spear.

"I hope you are as powerful as you look, that way we might stand a chance, but don't think about doing anything stupid." Her spear pressed softly against his dark skin, drawing a drop of blood. The mage snorted and rubbed his wrists, the fire in his eyes doused and returned to their natural brown-green.

Inza stood up with the help of her brother, she tried to wipe the dust off of her clothes but only made big smudges of ash everywhere. Aergo was facing the same problem but was more determined in his task and eventually ended up being one big smudge of ash and dirt before he finally gave up.

"I take it you know where we are then, Ilunari?" It was the Nuan, her voice was hoarse and tired but filled with distaste and hatred.

"Yes."

"Well, would you mind sharing your precious wisdom?"

"It would be pointless, we have to move." Raven turned around and started to work her way through the thick layers of ash. The others followed quickly, Inza and Kaell being last. Every once in a while, the human glanced over his shoulder and looked at her, his eyes flaring up every time he met her eyes.

"One more time and there will be an arrow in his throat." Kaell whispered after the mage looked around another time. Inza secretly hoped he would look another time but didn't want a fight at the same time, the human creeped her out. She doubted that her brother's arrow would be faster than the boy's magic. They had only walked a few steps when they heard a bloodcurdling scream echo between the broken buildings, the embers flared up brightly and ash blew through the streets.

"What was that?" Rynn asked, his veins and eyes burning as bright as when Tuales killed the Nuan.

"He knows." Raven whispered, she took up the pace, "We should really get moving now, if you ever want to leave this place."

"Was that the King of Embers?" Aergo asked, he clutched daggers in either hand.

"So, your bloodmage did tell you something about this place," Raven scoffed, "But no, if you hear him you might as well end your own life, unless you desire an eternity of pain."

Inza felt shivers going down her body and cold sweat on her skin, even in this blazing heat. If something scared Raven, what chance did they really stand? The ashy clouds grew denser in the streets and glowing cinders now filled the air as well. Hot ash started to burn Inza's skin, she didn't wear sleeves and neither did the others, she saw they were suffering the same pain except for the mage and Etaín. The human's eyes had begun burning again, his veins like lava, crawling between dark rock. Through her teary eyes Inza saw shadows move through the dust, at least she thought she did. These clouds were dense and it became more difficult to see with every passing moment. Another scream cut through the ash, closer now. Everyone had drawn their weapons now, Inza had none and neither did the Nuan. The Nuan's eyes flared up and she whispered something they could not hear as she bent over and started to push aside the ash and dust. Something glistened beneath it and she pulled two circular blades from underneath it all.

"Thank you, brother," she whispered with relief.

Inza looked at Kaell, "Do you think I should shift?" she asked him.

"Maybe not, it went wrong just a moment ago and if Raven is right you probably can't even shift." He was still worried about her but his fear was taking over now.

"Your powers don't work here, here, you are just a regular mortal," Raven said, her voice hinted with kindness, as she handed Inza a small knife. Inza took it but actually had no clue how to fight, she had done it before as several animals but that was not an option here.

Hot wind blew through the street as if the fiery skies breathed on them. Another scream echoed, so loud, so close. Soft laughter, mad and unstable, weaved into the air. Quick shadows appeared in the surrounding ash and whispers now filled the air. Inza didn't know the tongue in which the whispers spoke, it wasn't anything near the common tongue. It sounded ancient and deep, crackling like hot coals on a fire. All of them formed a circle, Inza in the middle, the others watching the veil of ash with their weapons ready.

"Just get on with it," Etaín taunted the shadows behind the veil.

"Please shut up, you have no idea what we're about to fight," Raven almost snarled at her.

"Well whatever it is, it will soon taste Laretu steel and defeat at the same time." Etaín's axe spun in her hand, with her free hand she had drawn lines across her face with the ash, marking her skin for battle.

"If you can defeat them the High Immortals themselves will raise you up to the High Seat," Raven scoffed back. It was at that moment that one shadow stopped moving, its shape only roughly visible through the thick smoke. Three bright, red flames started shining where Inza thought its head was. It stepped through the veil, into their sight.

The creature was strangely beautiful. Its body was black as the smoke that surrounded them and smooth like the scales of a fish. It was very thin, like a young tree in spring, its arms dragging through the layer of ash on the ground, ending in fingers as sharp as blades. Its face was empty and black like a polished stone, with three bright burning flames underneath each other, they were redder than blood and brighter than the sun on the smoke-black face. It didn't move at all, it just stood there, watching them. One after the other started to break the veil around them and they were surrounded and outnumbered.

"*In...di...m...aronth.*" Their whispers came slow and made Inza's muscles tighten. She shivered and felt the urge to lie down on the ground and cry, hoping they would no longer follow her.

Suddenly the veil of ash and smoke that swirled around them grew much denser and closed them in, Inza couldn't even see her own hands in it.

"Nobody move, nobody scream." It was Raven's voice that somehow cut through the dense cloud around them.

All sound had been stripped from the world, it reminded Inza of the strange forest she had entered in her dream, there too had her powers been stripped away. The smoke stayed for what seemed an eternity until it suddenly fell to the ground, and for a very short moment many faces appeared in the falling dust but it didn't last long and only the strange, polished creatures with their burning eyes remained. One stood face to face with every single one of them, close enough that they could be touched by simply puckering your lips. Inza stared into the burning red eye, unable to look anywhere else, her mind somehow felt detached, her body far beyond her reach. The creature moved his hand to her throat, sharp fingers scratching her skin, she felt weak as she could only watch its claws come closer. It burned. Inza couldn't tell if it was really hot or really cold, all she knew was that it hurt. The burning red held her eyes captive and she couldn't see what was happening to the others. She heard people moaning from pain and struggle, or at least that is what it sounded like. Inza felt whispers in her mind, burning like the hand on her throat.

"Sul…vi…m…aronth," it softly echoed through her, followed by the soft maniacal laughter that had sounded through the streets only moments before. The creature tilted its head slightly and tightened its grip on her throat. It was strange to say and Inza didn't really know why but somehow the creature seemed to smile at her. It wasn't a happy smile, more of a grin, not sweet like Aergo's but sharp, like a knife. Inza suddenly remembered the knife Raven had given her and she could feel it laying in her hand, if she could just move it. She focused all of her attention on the simple task of moving her hand a little to the front, she couldn't, even though she tried so hard.

The creature tilted its head backwards, eyes facing the black and orange sky, and screamed. It was deafening, Inza felt something dripping from her ear but couldn't reach out to feel it. Once again smoke surrounded them and blinded them from the world, the pain on her throat disappeared but still she felt as if her body and mind were separated.

The smoke fell away and again many faces appeared in the curtain of black mist. They weren't in the city anymore. Inza couldn't move her head but she could move her eyes. They were in a place that resembled a large throne room. The roof had fallen away and revealed the burning skies above them. Literal pillars of smoke and ash rose through it, swirling up from the polished, black floor that looked like a still lake, blacker than the night sky on a moonless night. In front of them was a large throne of gold and black, set with jewels of all kinds. In it sat a very large man. He was massive, with muscles as thick as chains, his skin was as black and polished as the floor upon which they stood. His face was a mask of molten gold with eyes like rubies, a crown of coal from which smoke rose above him. A bright red line ran down through the middle of his face, melting together with his ruby teeth.

In the corner of her eye Inza could see Kaell left of her and Aergo to her right. Aergo had trails in the dust on his face, trails drawn by tears.

A voice loud as roaring fire filled the halls. The smoke danced on the vibrations of the sound, Inza didn't understand any of it but did hear the word the creatures had said in the streets. *"Indimaronth."*

She had no idea what it meant but it didn't matter. Nothing moved in the room but the molten face of the King of Embers, the gold mist twisted and turned as he spoke. Raven's voice echoed through the hall as well now, speaking the same tongue as the King before them. Loud laughter came from him and he stood up, rising far above them. He was twice the size of Etaín and dressed in long robes made out of smoke.

"The mortal tongue it is. You are lucky that I know it, not all of my kind do." He went out of Inza's sight but she heard him still, soft crackling wherever he went.

"Extraordinary," he said as he passed all of them. When he passed Aergo he looked at him and caressed the Kir'in's scar with his black nail. "You will be easy, but fun." Another tear rolled down Aergo's face, carving another path through the dust on his cheek.

The King of Embers lowered himself down to meet eyes with Inza. His ruby eyes were deep and dark, and she swore she could see smoke swirling behind them.

"You are going to be difficult. I never get to work with a soul so pure and innocent. It seems your brother here did a great job shielding you from any pain." His breath smelled like burned wood. "I am sure we will find something fun in you." His golden face parted in a scarlet smile and he ran his fingers through her hair. He whispered something in the other tongue she didn't know and she heard the word the creature had called her.

Sulvimaronth.

She somehow knew that name, it felt familiar but she couldn't quite reach it. The King of Embers stood up again and moved back to the throne, paying Kaell no mind at all. He waved his hand and the black creatures came and grabbed their throats again, dragging them out of the hall, all of them except Raven, who was left with the Smoldering King in his throne room.

There was no smoke this time, instead, each one of them was dragged somewhere else. Inza was brought down several sets of stairs, spiraling down into the darkness. The heat was suffocating and she struggled to breathe properly. The scorching pain disappeared from her neck for a moment only to return, not only at her neck but also on her wrists and ankles. A flash of fire filled the room and Inza saw she was strapped on a stone table with black chains. In front of her stood a woman, her skin as black as that of the creatures with eyes as pale as ash, a golden line running down her face, blending with her lips. She held a whip made from a spinal cord and a dagger of molten iron.

"Oh, this is going to be so much fun," the woman grinned as the whip struck Inza's chest.

Nothing but screams left her, as the pain filled her veins completely.

Chapter 15
Naka/Raven

It had been quite some time since she last had a conversation in High Speech, the High Immortal tongue. She was glad the conversation was over now, it was never fun to speak with the King of Embers, all he wanted was to break your mind. He had recognized her immediately and taken Nárymm away as soon as he saw it, she didn't know where they had put it but she would tear down the city stone by stone to find it. Now she too was being dragged out of the throne room, she tried to look for any borders of light and shadow but found none on her way to wherever she was being taken. They went down spirals of stairs, screams echoing between the walls. Darkness wrapped around them and Naka felt nothing but the burning pain of the creature's hand around her throat as it dragged her further into the darkness. Screams grew softer and disappeared after a while, out of reach for her to hear it.

The darkness was denser here and Naka could smell smoke and burning flesh. Suddenly they stopped and the creature let go of her throat, dropping her into nothingness.

Naka fell, wind racing past her body as she tumbled helplessly through the air, she couldn't see anything and had no clue how far she had to fall. This would be her death; the King of Embers had warned her that this time there wouldn't be an escape and death seemed pretty inescapable.

Naka hit the ground, if it was indeed the ground. It was soft and uneven, there was a wetness to it and the sweet scent of rotting flesh. She had smelled it many times before, corpses, and old ones. Shivers went through her and she regained control of her muscles, it took a long time.

At first, she could only move her fingertips but she focused and after a while she could move her whole body again. There was no way of knowing where she was, how far she had fallen and how far she could walk. For all she knew she could stand breaths away from a wall or deeper fall or perhaps there was an endless cavern in front of her. Naka pushed herself up and felt her hands pushing in something slimy, she grunted and tried to wipe it off on her tunic but it wasn't very successful. She needed a light source of some sort, oh how useful the human boy would be here, that way she could get out of this place. Laughter rained down from far above her.

"There is no escaping from there, *Indimaronth*. But you are familiar with true darkness, aren't you? You should feel right at home." The voice of the King of Embers roared through the darkness, leaving her with a heavy silence.

"If only you knew what I have been taught, it would make you tremble," she whispered to herself. She took a deep breath, allowing the dense darkness into her lungs, and closed her eyes. Long ago she had learned to live in the darkness, how to be a part of it. The sharp smell of rot stung her nose but at least she was alive, that meant she had a chance. A soft wind blew through the dark air, it was warm, almost like breathing.

It couldn't be.

The air trembled and whistled. Naka leaned backwards and felt cold steel pass right past her nose.

One breath.

A blade through her mind.

The dance had begun.

The Dance of Darkness, a dance of both mind and body

"Most would be dead already." It was barely a whisper, High Speech again, a voice she didn't know but that sent shivers down her spine.

"I am not most," she told the darkness. Naka focused on the air around her, trying to find her attacker's energy. The air was still, a pool of darkness, wrapping around them in silence.

Another whistle of steel, another step.

"Seems this one knows the dance, not many do." A tiny tremble in this eternal black.

The attacks came quicker now, the dance moving faster. Soft flesh squishing under their feet, bones moaning as they spun over them.

"Let us see how fast shadows dance, Ilunari." The blade of Nárymm scratched her throat, "How well do you know the steps."

In the darkness they danced, blade piercing air but never skin, steel singing softly as her heartbeat drummed the rhythm. It was faster than she had ever danced even though it wasn't her first time without a weapon, she didn't need one. All she needed to do was take the steps, never fall and never ever fall out of rhythm, any other step, any other rhythm would tear her mind apart, that was the dance.

Every whistle came quicker now, the steps faster but her breath steady. The last step came and the steel sang past her eyes, Naka let her breath go and grabbed the steel with her hands. She twirled and twisted the blade, the edge cutting deep into her skin as something within her awoke, something she had forced to sleep. Memories stung her mind, memories of her first visit to Arga.

Screams, pain, pure terror, true darkness.

"Let's see how well you know the Dance of Darkness when I lead the way." Naka took the first step and immediately felt the spear pierce skin. A sharp hiss came from the darkness but Naka just danced. She had practiced the steps a thousand times and they came naturally, she ignored the power inside of her that was now awake, the power she hated, feared even. Her breath was steady and her movements fluid like the darkness itself. Power surged through her heart, she had locked it there long ago but now it flowed through her veins, binding her with the darkness around them.

Every step was followed by a hiss, a fresh wound in the skin of whoever was stupid enough to dance with her. Naka became one with the darkness, dark enough to make the darkest shadows seem bright, she breathed the darkness, and it breathed her. It disgusted her, all her life she had been nothing but her power. Now, she just hated it. The final step came and Naka thrust Nárymm, and felt no resistance as the blade went through her enemy's throat. Her attacker gurgled and she felt his dead weight pull at her spear so she pulled it back, the body joining the pile of corpses on which it stood.

"That's why you should know both parts of the dance," she whispered, her voice dark and bitter, filled with power. Nárymm softly glowed as it absorbed the soul of the fresh kill. The power still coursed through her veins, wanting to bury it deep within her heart again but needing it too much to escape from this wicked place. She focused on Nárymm, on the soul within but couldn't reach into it. The tip started to glow, its light like a star in the darkness, on the edge of the shadows a man appeared. Dressed in white, his hood only revealing his thin lips.

"Master Irion." Naka kneeled.

"It seems you still know the steps of the dance by heart, I taught you well. I am sorry to say that I cannot help you here, you must save yourself once again. Don't fear that what is deep inside of you, it is what you are," he spoke, even he couldn't hide his unease in this place. He disappeared again, the soul gone as well, taking the light away from her. In her anger her power overcame her fears, lashing out around her, drawing more and more darkness into her veins. Darkness consumed her, its hands dragging at her body, slithering into her veins, filling her lungs like water, thick and cold, only to spit her out at the entrance of the palace of Embers.

The doors to the city were right in front of her and she quickly walked to them, right before she opened them it crossed her mind. All the others were still in there and even though she wanted to go to the Dan'um as fast as she could she couldn't leave all of them behind. She sighed and circled back around.

"Yurma and Anma forsake me, why did you curse me with friends," Naka whispered, her voice dark and deep as she called upon the High Immortals of friendship, as she went back into the halls to find the others.

The only sounds in the palace were screams and wails, all of pain and fear. Naka knew what they did to their prisoners here. She had no idea where to start her search, she wanted to find Etaín first but perhaps it would be better to find the mage first, that way they stood a better chance.

"The mage it is then," she whispered to herself again.

Darkness raced out of her, flying through the halls in search of what she needed to find, every shadow obeyed her now. To find the energy of the mage would be easy, his magic would be coursing through his veins as well, he would be like a beacon here. Naka closed her eyes and indeed found him with ease, he was at the end of the hall to her right.

One with the shadows she moved past the walls, luckily not meeting one of the King's creatures. Fire blazed at the end of the hall, the stones glowed hot red in the wall. Naka grabbed her spear tighter, she didn't wait for the flames to stop burning, they couldn't harm her. Two of the black creatures and a woman with equal black skin and ashen eyes stood in the room, a whip of bones in the hand of the woman.

"*Indimaronth*," she whispered with real fear in her voice before she yelled at the two other creatures.

The two creatures screamed and lunged at her with their long claws but Nárymm had cut through their thin bodies before they reached her. The woman screamed and the mage let his fire flow out of his body once more, screaming as he did so. Naka faced the flames, who stood no chance against her darkness. A loud cracking went through the room as the woman lashed the whip at Naka, who grabbed it with ease, sending shadows down the bones who tore the skin of the woman apart, splattering her golden blood all across the room.

Naka examined the mage. There were deep cuts all across his skin, burning blood flowing from them like magma. They had bound them with black metal that moaned at his every breath. His eyes burned like suns as he looked into her own. She saw her reflection in his eyes, her eyes black like the darkness from which she had escaped, behind her swirling darkness, violent and cold. Naka slashed his chains.

"You better have some fight left in you, mage. We're going to need it now," she said to him.

Every servant of the King of Embers had heard the screams of the creatures and they would flock here. She lifted him from the stone table and walked through the door, his dragging steps behind her. Naka focused, she felt the energy of the creatures coming closer, looking past that she found all the others scattered around the palace. A hot hand grabbed her arm, the mage.

"Do you know if their visions were true?" His eyes became brown for a moment.

"They played your fears, gave them life. Like one breathes on smoldering coal to create fire, they don't have the power to show you the future, the future is in your own hands."

He nodded, pulling his hand back.

"Keep the fire in your eyes, mage. You'll need it," she said when she saw his eyes staying brown. He nodded again and his eyes turned back to burning suns.

"My name is Rynn, by the way."

"Raven." Naka replied before she moved on.

They avoided most of the creatures on their way to Etaín, who was the closest. As they came closer, they could hear a soft crying. Naka entered the room and saw Etaín weeping on the floor, at the feet of the King of Ember's servants who stood motionless in the middle of the room. Naka quickly sent Nárymm through the servants' hearts and kneeled in front of Etaín. Her hair was loose and her eyes red from crying.

"Raven?" she whispered. "Is that really you? What happened to you?"

"Yes, it's me. Come on, let's get out of here, shall we?" She tried to sound as warm as she could, ignoring the last question. It wasn't easy to feel the torture of the King of Embers, Naka was glad she could save the others so quickly. The Laretu stood up and wiped her tears from her face.

"Where is my axe? I have some things to do with these nightmares, it tried to twist the memory of my father," she said and pointed at the dead creature on the ground. Naka smiled at her. They found her axe on the other side of the room, simply laid upon a table. Etaín shook her head and grabbed it, weighing it in her hand for a moment.

Outside waited Rynn, who simply nodded at Etaín and Etaín at him.

"Who's next, Raven?" the mage asked.

"Aergo, it seems he is further down the hall." She could feel his energy there, "You'll soon have your chance to do whatever you want with those 'nightmares' Etaín," Naka said, walking down the hall.

They found Aergo in a similar room, at the feet of another nightmare.

The Kir'in was sitting in the middle of the room, several cuts on his wrists that were bleeding onto the floor. His eyes were empty and stared into the darkness of the shadows. Across the room was a dead servant, a dagger deep in its chest.

"Aergo?" Raven asked carefully. "Are you okay?"

At first Aergo didn't respond but after a moment he turned his head and forced a smile.

"I'm doing great, my dear."

"Are you really? This place brings your worst nightmares to life."

Aergo kept silent as he stood up, pulled his sleeves all the way down and fixed his hair. "Don't worry, my dear, I already took care of it. See?" he said, nodding at the dead nightmare. "It's just another day for me," he whispered hoarsely before he walked past Naka, into the hallway.

Blood was already showing through his sleeves and Naka decided to keep an eye on him, Etaín immediately shot to his side, supporting him with her arm.

"Let's move, we have three more to save," Naka said.

She walked up front, sending her darkness through any nightmare that dared block her path. Etaín and Aergo took care of any other that sneaked up on them. Suddenly a large group of them appeared in the dark hall in front of them. Naka was already spinning Nárymm but Rynn stepped out and raised his hands.

Flames burst through the hall, crashing against the creatures but when the flames disappeared, absorbed by the creatures and they started laughing. A woman with polished, black skin stepped around the corner.

"Poor mage, all he wanted was power. And power you got. We fed your fire, and it burned away all your other gifts. Turned them into ash and dust. Now, your only gift is fire, and fire cannot hurt us, to us, you are nothing but a weak human," she laughed alongside the creatures. Naka gently pushed Rynn aside again and pointed Nárymm at the woman.

"How unfortunate for you that I still have mine." The laughter died and Naka smiled. One with the darkness inside of her, she flew through the group, shadows lashing out and tearing apart anything that they could find until there was absolutely nothing left for her to kill. She looked up and looked right into the white eyes of the Nuan who was chained to the wall in front of Naka. The Nuan's eyes filled with dread and her body froze up.

"Shadowsoul," she whispered in terror.

Naka smiled. "Call me shadowsoul one more time and your species will *finally* go extinct."

The Nuan pressed her lips together but her eyes were wide.

"Ara! Are you okay?" Rynn ran past Naka and started pulling at the chains.

"I'm fine. Why are you pulling? Are you a mage or what?" she snarled back at him. Rynn immediately used his fire to melt the chains.

Poor thing, Naka thought, they had filled him with fire, burning away all his other magic, taking away who he was.

It didn't take long to free the Nuan, she was seemingly unharmed and walked behind Naka who could feel her white eyes filled with fear piercing into her back.

"Two more to go," she sighed, she felt sorry for Inza. The poor girl had already suffered a lot being stuck between shifts, Naka was happy the girl survived it, not many did.

Distant screams of agony echoed between the stone walls and Etaín grabbed her heart.

"That's Inza," the Laretu whispered with concern, "Raven, we have to hurry. I can't stand it."

Naka swung around her spear.

"Then let's go."

The screams grew louder as they went down the spiraling stairs, descending into darkness. Rynn was constantly asking Ara if she was okay and if he could do anything for her but the Nuan returned nothing but harsh comments or ignored him completely. It made Naka smile, a smile of spite, the Nuan had probably used her gifts to take control of Rynn's mind and now she couldn't stand him anymore.

Surrounded by darkness Naka struggled to keep the power in her heart under control, she hadn't been in True Darkness this long for a very long time. The Nuan started whispering the Praise of Light and Naka rolled her eyes, Nuans and their fear of darkness.

The screams were louder now and a second set mixed in. They mainly heard the screams of agony from Inza but now Naka could hear Kaell's screams as well, he kept yelling her name, threatening to kill anybody who hurt her. They came from behind a large metal door and Naka tried to slash the lock but Nárymm could only scratch the thick metal. Etaín grabbed her shoulder.

"Let me," she said with a big smile and walked to the other end of the hall before she yelled and charged at the door. She hit the metal with a deafening sound of breaking and Naka feared the Laretu had broken her every bone, but when she looked up the door lay on the ground, ripped in two and Etaín was dusting off her shoulder.

She shrugged, "Laretu, we are pretty strong," and Naka laughed at her.

"Crazy is what you are," Aergo added.

The screams had stopped for a moment and they found Kaell against the wall, his hands pushed against his ear, blood seeping between his fingers. His yellow eyes burned with vengeance and he stood up on his own, breathing heavily as the screaming continued. The sound bounced between walls, loud enough for one to drown in them. The Kurr took the lead and rushed down the hall, pushing open every door he found. Behind one they found a room filled with weapons, Ara's chakrams and Aergo's other daggers in it. Kaell's bow was there as well, or what was left of it. Large parts were scorched, and crumbled to dust upon touch. In the back of the room, however, hung bows made from the same black metal that had chained Rynn. Kaell grabbed one and strapped a full quiver around his back, pulling one out, ready to fire it.

The hall was long and dark with many doors leading to empty rooms. Naka couldn't find the exact location of Inza's energy, it was very weak and got lost between the many creatures that roamed the dark around them. The screaming suddenly died out and Kaell roared, pushing open one of the last doors. Light fell into the hallway and the first arrow flew inside. Kaell rained his arrows into the room and when Naka rushed around the corner there were already a dozen corpses on the floor. Another arrow flew through the air and a loud cracking filled the room. A woman like the one that had tortured Rynn, stood between the corpses, her spine-whip like a snake at her feet. A long golden line ran through the middle of her face, stopping at her golden lips. The arrow lay broken on the floor in front of her.

"Inza," Kaell growled. His sister lay on a stone table behind the woman, black chains around her limbs. The scarlet blood pooled on the floor below her and flowed from the countless wounds that tore up her skin. There were more wounds than skin, from cuts to lashes to tears. Her breath was ragged and shallow, it wouldn't take long for the cold hand of death to take hold of her.

"I hope you enjoyed her last moments, Kurr," the woman said with a wicked smile across her face. Kaell's muscles tightened and Naka could feel his anger in her heart. He roared again, nothing holding him back and he stormed at the woman who cracked her whip and lashed him across the chest, throwing him back. Etaín picked him up and Naka was spinning Nárymm in her hand when she was pushed aside by Kaell and Etaín held her back.

"That is his kill," the Laretu said as she looked into Naka's eyes. Naka nodded, she respected that it was indeed his, she just hoped he wouldn't die in the process. He would have to be quick so they could save Inza. Kurr healed fast, especially shifters, but they had to be in a place that was not devoid of life to do so. Kaell shot arrow after arrow, none hurting the woman, until he was struck with the whip and throw off of his feet. Suddenly Kaell grabbed Nárymm out of Naka's hands and thrust it into the woman's belly. Her golden blood dripped along the spear and Kaell twisted it, the woman wailed and screamed in agony as she desperately tried to pull the spear out of herself.

Kaell let go of Nárymm and ran to Inza who was barely breathing. Naka pulled Nárymm out of the woman and slashed the chains to free Inza. "She needs to get out of here, she might have a chance," Naka said to Kaell whose eyes were filled with tears and pain.

Etaín carefully lifted Inza from the stone under the watchful eye of Kaell. Inza's body was weak and hung in Etaín's arms like a piece of wet cloth, they really had to hurry. They ran as fast as they could toward the exit of the palace, they found nobody on their way there only the many corpses of the ones they killed before. As soon as they threw open the doors, they were greeted with the hot ash clouds of the city that wrapped around them as they ran. There was a wide, open road that went straight ahead so they followed it. A deafening roar echoed through the city.

"INDIMARONTH."

The sound raged through the streets like thunder and soon they heard howling behind them. Naka looked back to check on Etaín and Inza. Etaín ran steady and fast, Kaell at her side and Inza like a corpse in the Laretu's arms. Naka's eyes went past Etaín, toward the palace, and she immediately regretted her decision.

In the distance appeared a wall of fire, rolling through the streets like a massive, fiery wave, from it sprang figures, running toward them. In front of it rode the King of Embers, mounted upon a fiery horse. Buildings crumbled in the roaring flames, leaving nothing but dust behind. The wave moved much quicker than they could run and Naka was praying for a miracle.

"There! The gates!" Aergo shouted through his heavy breaths. He was right, they were close to the gates. That was where the King of Embers' territory ended and he could not go past it, if he could, he would have conquered this realm long ago. Naka looked back again and saw the fire much closer than the gates, the king yelling in High Speech.

"Faster," Kaell shouted at Etaín. He too had looked back and seen the approaching death. Etaín roared as loud as the flames and managed to push herself even more, flying past the others, leaving Kaell behind. Naka could feel the ground shaking beneath the thundering hooves of the King of Embers' horse and feel its dry, hot breath not far behind her. She released more power into her veins and screeched, sending shivers along her own spine. She flew like the wind toward the gates, picking up the others as she passed them. The gates shook on their foundations as Naka ran underneath them, but the fire didn't stop there. As the Nuan looked back Naka saw the reflection of fire in her eyes, fire spouting out of the gates. Rynn pushed her aside and raised his hands to the flames, his eyes determined and bright like the flames he faced.

"Stand behind me," he shouted at the others as he drove the flames toward himself. The fiery tongues roared as they hit his hands, flowing into the human's veins. His skin tore where his veins crawled, dripping liquid fire into the water at their feet, sizzling and turning solid. Rynn roared, his mouth showing the fire inside, his roar like a raging fire, from his eyes dripped fire as well, burning tears like drops of lava. The skin all the way to his eyes was torn when the flames stopped coming. In the gate stood the King of Embers who pointed his sword at Naka.

"We will meet again," he said in High Speech, his voice low and angry enough for Naka to believe it. Rynn dropped to the ground, the water steaming around him as he hit it. They looked around, they stood in enormous open plains, they were flooded and grass started peaking above the surface as it was reflected the skies, painted with the many colors of the sunrise.

Chapter 16
Rynn

Rynn didn't feel any pain, he saw his skin was torn open and fire seeped out, he only regretted it couldn't stay in his body. His every vein and muscle was filled with fire, with power, he shook all over as he tried to contain the fire within him. After several deep breaths and a lot of focus he stopped shaking and the fire stopped leaking from him, though the wounds didn't close. Instead his skin now had cracks in it under which the fire flowed like lava.

With some effort he managed to stand up again, and looked around, there was nothing but water, mirroring the skies. Not far from them moved several figures, large silhouettes with the rising sun in their back. They wrinkled the perfect reflection of the skies in the water as they moved toward them. There was nowhere to run, the waters surrounding them would eventually become too deep to walk through, and going back into the city was not an option. The King of Embers had turned around and gone back into his city of ash. Raven had seen the figures that came toward them too but didn't seem to look for a way out, instead she turned to Etaín, who had laid Inza down in the shallow water. The Kurr girl had wounds covering her entire body, they were barely bleeding anymore and her skin was almost as pale as Ara's now. Kaell's eyes were desperate and he clung to his sister, whispering in her ear as tears fell down his cheeks.

"She should be healing, shouldn't she?" Kaell whispered at Raven through his sobbing.

Raven nodded, "She should, we're out of the city. Does she usually heal quick?"

"Yes, within minutes but she has never been hurt this badly," Kaell said.

Rynn looked at the Ilunari, her eyes were violet again her skin normal. He had seen her eyes when she rescued him, and he had seen her fly through the gate. She was not just an Ilunari, he didn't know what she was but he knew Ara despised her and that meant nothing good. That spear was also something he couldn't figure out, it had glowed when she rescued him, but it glowed much more strongly now.

Raven caught him staring at her and her spear and she stepped away from him, looking toward the forest on the horizon. The figures had almost reached them and their silhouettes started to get more detail. Rynn could see people sitting on something big that almost looked like a swimming island. There were five of those 'islands' and the others started to notice them as well.

"We got company," Rynn said and Ara sighed.

"Why can't everybody just leave us alone and let us do what we need to do," she whined out loud. "Burn them so we can get on with it," she said in his mind, luring his fire out. Etaín saw the flames gathering in his hands.

"Stop it, you moron. That might be our only way out of here and the last chance Inza has left." She pointed at the silhouettes who were only a couple of meters away. They weren't swimming islands, they were large animals with a grey-greenish skin, three eyes on both sides of their head. Their long bodies ended in smooth tails that whipped on the water from time to time, Rynn could see the muscles move underneath their skin.

"*Alaere*, strangers. What are you doing here?" the man on the closest animal called out to them, he was a Surr'um. His voice was gentle and sounded a little like the wind blowing through the canopy.

"*Alaere*. We mean you no harm and need your help," Raven greeted the man as she gestured at Inza. The man jumped down into the water, sword in his hand, and walked toward Inza.

"Not all strangers it seems. Seems you're still alive, unfortunately," he whispered as he passed Raven, giving her a filthy look.

The man towered above Rynn but barely reached Etaín's shoulders. His skin was the color of oaken wood, with green hair that touched his ankles. He had eyes with the same deep brown color as Rynn but his were speckled with gold. As he spoke Rynn could see long, sharp teeth that reminded him of a hungry animal. He was now kneeling beside Inza and inspected her wounds.

"Her body is keeping her in stasis for now, she doesn't have enough strength to fully heal but we might be able to help her." The Surr'um looked at Kaell, "We don't get many Kurr here anymore, especially not Kurr like her." He gestured at the others who had also jumped off their mounts. The man glanced at the city besides them and lifted Inza from the ground.

"Let's get you out of here. *Indimaronth*, you ride with me and the Kurr, the others ride with the rest," he shouted as he climbed atop the animal again. Rynn and Ara followed a woman to her mount, the woman couldn't keep her eyes off of Rynn's wounds as he struggled to get on.

"There is food and water in the bags," she said and pointed at the bags hanging on the back of the animal. Ara didn't move at all and just stared across the water at the animal in front on which Raven sat. Rynn felt his stomach rumbling and only now realized how hungry he was, he hadn't eaten since they tried to open the Vault. The bags were filled with fresh bread, fruits and even some meat and he attacked. He ate loudly and with big bites, filling his belly until it was round and he had to lie down for a moment. The soft swinging of the animal and sounds of the water rippling made his muscles and mind come to ease and he smiled, he tried to forget what he had seen inside of the city, the horrors they had showed him, the pain he had felt. It didn't take long for his curiosity to come up, invading his calm mind.

"Lady, can I ask something?" he carefully asked the Surr'um woman. She turned around and smiled, revealing the same pointed teeth as the man.

"You already did, but go ahead, *Mar'maran*. What is it you want to know?" Her voice, too, was as if the wind rustled leaves. Her skin was dark, almost like his own, but spotted like the forest floor, her eyes were a deep emerald with a ring of gold around the iris, her dark green hair was intricately braided and laid like vines around her legs.

"What are these animals? I've never read about them in any books." He shifted a little closer to the woman, away from Ara who was still staring at Raven.

The woman chuckled. "That's because they aren't in any. We call them Oiran." She petted the neck of the animal and it softly bellowed. "They once were used in our wars but that was a long time ago, now we use them for travel, transport and heavy work we cannot do ourselves." Rynn was in awe and looked toward the other Oiran around them, his eyes stopped at the sight of Inza, pale and weak, on the one in front.

"Can you truly help her?"

The woman followed his eyes to Inza and sighed, "Her injuries are far beyond our knowledge, we as Surr'um cannot do much but pray for her. That is why you must go to the heart of the forest, find the Dan'um, they can take you to someone who can heal her."

Rynn was lost, he didn't completely understand what she meant.

"What do you mean you cannot help her? I thought you were powerful healers and all."

"We are, compared to your kind. But we are Surr'um, we do not know the more intricate ways of healing, we are useless to the Kurr girl. The Dan'um know how to heal every wound, every ailment, some even say they have mastered how to heal death itself, they can help the girl, but to find them you have to travel deep into the forests."

Rynn looked toward the forest's edge, rendered speechless. He had read every book in the Academy he could find but right now he felt like he knew nothing of the world.

The morning sun shone bright above them when Rynn first saw it, a high ridge on which the forest's edge began, guarded by enormous statues of Dan'um. Water cascaded down the ridge in several large waterfalls, joining the water surrounding them. Beyond the ridge he could see spires and trees reaching for the sky, the distant roaring of the waterfall embraced them more and more. Birds flew over their heads, dancing in the air as they sang their songs. The water grew deeper and the Oiran now walked in a line, no longer needing the guidance of their riders. Rynn noticed that the water changed color the closer they came to the waterfall. It was clear not like glass, but like a mirror of some sort. The water was silver and shimmered as the rays of sun touched its surface. He saw the Surr'um reaching down and touching the cool water, scooping it up with their hands and pouring it on their heads and faces. They laughed and cheered at each other and even the Oiran bellowed at each other.

"Welcome to our lands, strangers," the woman said, her eyes filled with joy. Rynn noticed Raven pouring water over herself and Inza and just like the others he followed her lead. He didn't trust her but she seemed to know a lot more about this world than any of them so he thought it wise to copy her.

The water was cool and refreshing on his face, it seeped into his open wounds under which the fire still burned, but as soon as the silver water touched his fire, it doused. His wounds closed up, not with skin but with a dark, carnelian crystal that still revealed the fire underneath. Rynn let his fingers slide across the smooth surface of the stone, it was warm like his skin and moved almost the same yet it was as hard as stone.

"Ara, look. My skin changed when the..." he began but was shortly cut off by Ara's look.

"Mage, I really don't care. I'm here for one thing only, unlike you, I still have a purpose on this world." she sighed, weary and annoyed. The Surr'um woman glanced over him, and Rynn could feel disapproval pouring out of her, she turned back to continue cheering to the others and poured water over herself and their Oiran.

The roaring of the waterfalls overwhelmed any other sound and the mists that came from them slowly clouded their vision. They grew so thick that he couldn't see anyone around him and he felt comforted by the swirling mists that surrounded him. A familiar feeling came over him.

Yira.

The mists reminded him of her eyes, the way he would lose himself in them and how her mists filled his mind. Even now it pushed his every thought aside, clearing his mind.

"Hey."

It was Yira. She somehow sat next to him, as real as himself. There was a soft smile around her lips, she wore a dress of a pure white, her burning, auburn hair like a smoldering river over her shoulder.

"Hi," Rynn mumbled, smiling back at her. "Are you really here or am I just dreaming?"

"No, I'm here. Wherever the mists are, I am, all you need to do is call me." Her fingers caressed the carnelian red crystal that ran through his skin.

"You hold more power than any human before now," she whispered gently, still smiling.

Rynn shook his head and averted his eyes.

"It's only fire now, I lost all my other magic in that wretched city. The things they did…" His voice cracked and a tear mixed with the drops of mist on his cheek.

"I am sorry you had to go there." She pulled her fingers away from his skin, "Only few can take your magic away, the King of Embers is not one of them. All he can do is suppress your magic by overruling it with something else, in this case it is fire, his fire. There are ways to resurface your magic and control the power within you, there might be someone amongst the Dan'um who can teach you but they need to present themselves first."

"So, I can have all my magic back?"

Yira laughed and nodded. "Yes, yes you can. Probably even more, you might become the most powerful mortal with the right guidance."

Rynn's imagination went wild. He already could do a lot with his magic and to imagine he could do everything almost blew his mind. Maybe he could bring back his mother and make his family whole again. Move to a smaller city on the countryside and no one would ever be able to harm them again. He could end this war so they could live in peace at last.

"Who can teach me?" he asked her.

"They will present themselves when the time is right, trust them."

The Oiran passed between two waterfalls and moved up out of the mists, on to a slope that was carved out in the stone behind the waterfall. They now rode behind the great waterfalls and looked out over the open wetlands that were covered in a blanket of colorful mist as the morning sun hit the droplets. The waterfalls themselves turned into grand rainbows that fell down past the moss-green rock that reached to the skies. Kaell pressed his hands against Inza's ears but Raven quickly took over and gestured him to cover his own ears. Rynn remembered how sensitive Kurr ears were, to them the waterfall was literally deafening.

"I thought I heard an annoyance." Ara gave Yira a condescending look and turned around.

Yira paid the Nuan no mind but instead followed Rynn's eyes.

"Why does she travel with you?" She nodded at Raven.

Rynn shrugged, "She has an agreement with the Kir'in I think. He got us in this position in the first place. Raven did save our lives back in Arga, but I think she is hiding something, something big."

"I'm surprised that the Surr'um allowed her to come," Yira whispered, more to herself than to Rynn.

He turned to Yira, "How is it that everywhere we go, everyone seems to know her? Why do you know her and what has she done that everyone who seems to know her somehow hates her? Even the King of Embers knew her, he had a whole conversation with her in High Speech."

They passed another waterfall and for a moment that was the only sound they heard. Rynn could already see the end of the path, beyond it he could spot a part of one of the statues they had seen earlier.

"I only know what she did, not why, but it's not up to me to tell you about her past. If you want to hear the story you should ask her yourself," Yira said, her voice as quiet as possible.

"I haven't been here since the War started," she whispered to no one in particular.

Not knowing what to say, Rynn didn't react to her. They came around the corner and had reached the top of the ridge. Beside them was a statue, a Surr'um woman carved from the same greenish rock as the cliff. Rynn could barely look on top of the foot they passed and had to lay his head all the way back to see the top of the statue.

"Welcome to our home, strangers," the Surr'um woman said, only now noticing Yira, she smiled wide. "And welcome back *Augindi*, it's been a while."

In front of them flowed a large, silver river that reflected the trees and spires that stood at its side. The trees were a bright sea of green hues, from the light emerald leaves to the dark ferns on the ground to the jade moss on the bark and roots. Light grey marble spires and buildings rose between them, ancient as the trees that surrounded them, moss and vines hanging down from almost every edge. Where there was neither river nor forest there were fields of flowers of every color one could imagine. They slowly waved in the wind, an ocean of bright sweetness, smiling at them as they passed by. In the middle of the silver water was a round platform, surrounded by pillars of white crystal that captured the sunlight in the same array of colors as the flowers that surrounded them. A cloaked figure stood on that platform, he was as tall as Etaín, short green hair on his head like grass on a summer's day.

"You are lucky today, mortals, it seems the Dan'um have found you already," the Surr'um woman said. Inza was lifted down from her Oiran when they reached the platform. Ara had jumped down and stood silently at the edge of the platform, Rynn helped Yira down, who accepted his help even though she obviously didn't need it.

Inza laid in the middle of the platform and the Dan'um was already bowing over her and went over the wounds with his hands. Rynn stepped closer to see what he was doing but stopped when he looked at him, his eyes were a bright amethyst mixed with gold and pierced right through his soul.

The Dan'um started speaking in a language Rynn barely recognised as Ili'un, the native tongue of Ilunari. Raven responded and the Dan'um sighed before he picked up Inza and stepped into the river with her, the silver water flowing into the deep gashes and cuts that crisscrossed her body.

Rynn looked to Yira, hoping she could explain what was going on. Raven and Etaín held Kaell back as the Dan'um pushed Inza under the water.

"Kaell stop, she has to be cleansed first. If you jump into the water without his permission she will die," Raven grunted at Kaell.

The silver water started flowing up onto the skin of the man, similar to how the fire went to Rynn's veins when he called for it. Bubbles and soft wailing came from the water and Kaell screamed, Etaín and Raven doing their best to restrain him. The bubbling stopped and the Dan'um stepped out of the water, not a single bit of him was wet, as if he had never stood in the water. In silence they stood, looking at the still water, around the edges of the river Surr'um had gathered and placed flowers in the river that slowly drifted to where Inza was. Kaell had fallen to his knees and was still being held by Etaín.

Suddenly the water moved and Inza surfaced as she gasped for air, she was dressed in a silken, silver dress, covered with flowers. The fabric flowing around her like the river in which she stood. Her wounds were gone, not a single scar or scratch on her skin. On her neck was an intricate mark in the same silver as the river. Her hair had grown incredibly long and reached her calves now.

As soon as she saw her brother, she ran toward him and fell into his arms, Kaell cried tears of joy and hugged her so tightly, Rynn thought he would break her bones. When he let her go the Dan'um bowed before Inza, the Surr'um at the side of the river were also bowing, much deeper than the Dan'um.

"Why do they do that?" Inza asked, hiding behind her brother.

Raven and Yira were bowing too, and Etaín, Aergo and Rynn followed their lead.

"You are an *Eobatr*, a Lifeheart," Yira said, her eyes fixed on the ground, "You are now one of the most sacred mortals to the U'um."

"Lifeheart? What does that mean?" Inza asked, her voice soft and uncertain. Kaell held her close to him, keeping a close watch on the Dan'um. He didn't trust someone with filed teeth, sharp as razors, even though he was grateful for him saving his sister.

The mist-eyed elf started talking again.

"It means your powers were granted to you by Sulvimaronth, Master of the Forest and Keeper of Life. The blood of Mirhan revealed them and blessed you." She gestured at the water surrounding them.

Inza shook her head and frowned.

"She has always had her powers, nobody gave them to her she was born this way. The only thing she didn't have was that mark and her long hair," Kaell responded but before anyone had the chance to explain it further to them the Dan'um stood up and all the others with him and gestured Inza and Kaell to follow him, talking in High Speech he lead them through the city until they had reached a large open spot filled with bright, white, lily-like flowers and fluttering butterflies in a large variety of colors. He stopped speaking and looked at Inza who didn't see it but instead was already moving through the flowers, her silver dress and fiery hair dancing in the wind while butterflies followed her wherever she went. She stopped when she saw the Dan'um looking at her, a wide smile on his face that revealed his filed teeth. Inza's eyes went wide in confusion.

"He wants to know if this is a good spot for the feast in your honor tonight," Raven called over the flowers, her voice echoing back from the surrounding trees. Inza simply nodded and the Dan'um bowed and walked back over the path, continuing to talk in High Speech. Inza came running back to Kaell, smiling from ear to ear.

"It's so beautiful out here. I feel so at home in these woods, and I kind of like this long hair, catches the wind much better," she laughed to Kaell.

"It looks beautiful on you sis, it makes you look just like mother." His voice was as gentle as he could make it. Inza didn't say anything but instead just smiled wide and hugged him tight before walking off again toward the Dan'um.

Kaell stayed at the back, he too had to admit that he felt quite at home here. Somehow the forest felt familiar, it had the same trees and flowers as the Kurr forests did, the only difference was that this forest seemed to slumber instead of sing and buzz like the forests at home. Back home there was an animal around every corner, on every branch but here he hadn't seen anything besides the Oiran, plants and the people.

They were led to a set of small buildings and Raven translated that this was where they would be staying except for Inza and Kaell. The Dan'um led them to another building made out of a white marble with crystal woven into it that resembled flowers of all kinds. The inside was more luxurious than anything they had ever seen. It was filled with all kinds of fruit and flowers, there were two large beds that were soft like clouds. Inza nested herself in one of the beds while Kaell explored a little more. In the basement he found a large bath, already filled with steaming hot water that smelled of lavender. He took off his clothes, dropping them where he stood and let himself slide into the water. The warm water embraced his body and he sighed, letting all the tension in his muscles go. He noticed this water too was silver and even the steam was the same color. It could have been minutes or hours that he laid in the warm water, his eyes closed and his mind empty, when Inza called for him from upstairs. He grabbed one of the bathrobes he saw hanging across the room and his underpants and was secretly hoping for new clothes because his old ones were scorched and dirty with ash and blood.

When he arrived in the main room, he saw Inza and a couple of Surr'um standing across from each other.

"Kaell! They came here to prepare us for the feast tonight, look at all the pretty clothes they have!" she exclaimed, pointing at several fabrics the Surr'um held in their hands. They guided Inza and Kaell to separate rooms but Kaell could still hear Inza laughing through the walls. The Surr'um with Kaell started by taking off his bathrobe and combing his short, brown hair. They then dressed him in white robes, adorned with gold and the same fiery orange as his eyes. Several pieces of golden jewelry were also given to him, a necklace made from golden leaves and ruby flowers. A bracelet woven out of two golden and one ruby string and a ring with a ruby, in which the symbol on Inza's neck was engraved.

As Kaell looked at himself he felt both beautiful and embarrassed, he felt it was too much. He had always preferred his simple leather pants and his light shirt over anything and back at home he never wore anything else. It didn't take the Surr'um long to finish getting him ready but when he stepped out Inza was not ready yet. The Surr'um waited for them in the hallway, silent and with their heads down but Kaell decided to wait up on the balcony outside of his room. The sun was hanging low and shone its golden light across the wetlands in front of them, hitting the mists of the waterfalls and turning it into clouds of gold and amber.

"You look handsome, old man." Inza stood in the doorway to the balcony.

She wore a dress of soft pink that reminded Kaell of the wild roses back at home, it flowed in the soft evening breeze, making the flowers on it dance in the wind. On her head was a crown made from the thinnest crystal flowers that caught the golden light in all its glory. Her ears were adored with a crystal similar to the crown and emphasized her pointed ears, making her almost appear Dan'um. Her arms and neck were filled with intricate drawings of flowers, leaves, butterflies and all sorts of creatures.

"You look like a High Immortal, Inza. I doubt I know the words to tell you how beautiful you are." He had barely said the words or her giggle danced in the air and her eyes shone bright like stars.

"Come on, we should get to the feast, I am so hungry, I could eat for five," she said as she locked arms with Kaell and they followed the Surr'um to the clearing. Every time they came across anyone they stopped and bowed and offered them their widest smile and some even kissed Inza's hands. All followed them to the feast and so they arrived with an entire following of people.

The clearing was filled with people who danced to the joyful music or ate from the delicious food that filled tables upon tables. Soft lights hung between the trees like the stars in the sky above them. The white flowers that grew among the grass glowed dimly, lighting up the clearing with their soft lights. It didn't take long for the Dan'um to find them, offer Inza his arm, which she took after Kaell nodded that it was okay, and lead her across the field to the tables filled with food. Kaell kept close to the edge, restless but quiet. He secretly hoped nobody would notice him and he could spend the entire feast without having to talk to anyone, which didn't seem unlikely. Everyone was flocking around Inza and looking at her, smiling and bowing and dancing.

"It seems I'm not the only one who enjoys the shadows." Aergo's honeyed voice sounded behind him.

"Apparently not," Kaell sighed as he turned around.

Aergo was dressed in a long suit of pure black fabric, patterns like a tree's roots made from small emeralds embroidered on top of it. He wore a headband of silver, lined with emeralds, his eyes shining bright underneath it.

"I must say, Kaell, you look quite breathtaking tonight," Aergo said as he let his eyes roam up and down Kaell.

"I…euhm… Well, thank you. I guess," he muttered back. His cheeks burning hot he turned away so Aergo wouldn't see it.

"I think I will go and dance," the Kir'in said as he walked away, his own red cheeks and soft smile hidden from Kaell. Kaell just nodded and watched him walk away, losing him in the crowd and doubting if he should follow him. It was strange being around Aergo, he didn't feel nervous, quite the opposite actually, something about him made him feel at ease yet his body always froze up like it wasn't his to control anymore.

Someone shouted his name from across the field, it was Etaín who had stuffed her mouth and held even more food in her arms and now came walking toward him, Raven not far behind her. People actually had to jump aside not to be walked over by Etaín, the Surr'um were tall but Etaín still towered above them. Etaín wore a dress with the color of thistle and had body paint in the same color, her ashen hair intricately braided. Raven wore a dress like the twilight sky, a deep purple fading into a dark black, her black hair loose on her back and an onyx crown adorned her head. Her spear hung on her back, the dress woven around it.

She really doesn't go anywhere without that thing, Kaell thought.

"Kaell, you should really try the food, it is delicious. I could eat this forever and be the fattest Laretu this world has ever seen but I will be the happiest one as well." Her words were barely understandable as she talked with her mouth full. She stuffed some kind of pastry in her mouth and groaned loudly before she ran back to the table to grab some more, knocking over a few people on her way there. Raven sighed but her face was emotionless and stiff and Kaell couldn't read it, he never could.

"Raven, I haven't thanked you for…" Kaell started but was cut off by Raven.

"Don't, please don't," she said, her eyes were distant. "It's getting late, I'm going back. Enjoy your evening, Kaell." Her voice was soft and her words quick. After she nodded at him and looked around, she left and Kaell was alone with the shadows again.

Most of the night he stood there, sometimes grabbing some food. He spotted Ara and Rynn across the field. The Nuan dressed in a translucent white dress that flowed in the wind like pale smoke and Rynn dressed in robes from the waist down, the crystal scars running through his dark skin visible to the world, the fire in his eyes burning soft like embers. Rynn talked to Ara in hushed whispers, both of them looking around with wary eyes. Kaell didn't understand the Nuan, she always seemed to be on her guard, never trusting anyone. He probably never would understand her and didn't know what else to expect from someone whose entire people had been murdered. She must have suffered more than he could ever know, more than he wanted to know so he pushed it out of his mind.

He looked for Inza and saw her dancing with Etaín and some Surr'um, she caught his eyes and he gestured he was going back to which she nodded and immediately came to him.

She was breathing heavily and Kaell smiled, she could always lose herself in music, lose all control, just be joyful. It was her greatest strength and he adored her for it.

As soon as they left the field the Surr'um that had brought them there accompanied them back to their building.

When they arrived Inza hugged Kaell tight. "I love you, old man," she mumbled into his chest and he kissed her on her forehead before she went into her room.

With the help of the Surr'um he undressed and laid down in bed, his eyes heavy with sleep.

Darkness surrounded him, the air hot and scorching in his throat. The heavy silence pressed against his ears. There was no light, no sound. Kaell waved his arms around him but couldn't find anything in the solid black around him. Soft whispers broke the silence, even his Kurr ears had trouble hearing them but that didn't last long. Like a howling wind the whispers turned into screams. Inza's screams.

"KAELL," she wailed time and time again. Her agonizing screams filling the darkness around him.

"INZA," he yelled back, again and again, running around trying to find his sister. Soon his throat was too dry to yell and his lungs burned in his chest as if the air itself was made of fire. The screaming stopped, the last one echoing through the dark.

Dark thoughts immediately filled Kaell's mind and he started running frantically through the black abyss around him, still blind and again cloaked in silence. Something hit his feet and he crashed into the floor. His hands landed in a thick, warm liquid and he slipped, falling in it with his entire body. Soft light broke the darkness and he saw the pool of blood around him, sticking to his face and fingers. He shivered, and with fear in his eyes he turned around. There laid a body, lifeless and limp, amidst the pool of blood. He turned it around so he could see the face. It was Inza. Cuts and burns all over her skin. Kaell's eyes stung with tears as they fell upon her pale face, pulling trails in the blood.

She was still breathing, very shallow and ragged.

"Why? Why didn't you protect me, brother? I trusted you," she breathed to him, just loud enough for him to hear.

"I'm sorry, I am so, so sorry. I tried, I truly did." He wept over her, but her eyes were already empty, her breath gone. Her dull eyes staring into the dark abyss around them, forever lost. And Kaell screamed.

Bathed in sweat he shot upright, his bed soaked and his hair sticking to his forehead. He was panting through his dry throat and it took him a moment to realize where he was. As soon as he did, he noticed Inza standing in the doorway, blankets wrapped around her and her long hair a waterfall of messy curls with a concerned look on her face.

"Are you okay? I heard you scream."

He smiled at her, a genuine smile, he was happy it was just a nightmare and she was still here.

"It was just a bad dream, my *Menare*. Just a bad dream, that's all," he said in his sweetest voice, hoping to ease her concern. She handed him a towel.

"You always wake up in sweat when you have a nightmare, so I thought you could use this."

"Thank you, sis," Kaell said as he took the towel and started drying the sweat.

"What was it about, your nightmare?" Inza sat down beside him on the bed.

Kaell smiled. "It doesn't matter anymore, it was just a dream. You should get some sleep if you can, I have a feeling you will have to deal with a lot more admirers tomorrow."

"Can I sleep here, though? I don't want to be alone right now," she asked with a soft voice, as if he could ever say no to her. Kaell opened his arms to hug her but Inza pushed him away. "Ew, no idiot," she laughed. "You're all sweaty. After you have taken a bath tomorrow you can get a hug."

She curled up on the floor, her blankets as a nest around her. It had always been her favorite way of sleeping and Kaell expected it would never change, or at least he hoped so. For a moment he looked at her in silence, thanking every High Immortal he knew that it was just a dream.

"You haven't called me Menare ever since we left home." Inza fell silent for a moment, "I miss home, Kaell." She paused again, she knew he missed home just as much. "Could you maybe tell the story again of how we discovered the menares? I love that story."

"Of course I can, you just close your eyes and have some sweet dreams, okay?" Kaell answered with a big smile on his face, he too loved to tell that story.

"It was a warm, autumn morning and the sun was just peeking over the mountaintops when you woke us up to come explore the forest with you. So, mother packed enough food for a day and we went into the forest, following you as you danced between the trees. You had just learned how to talk to the trees in our forests and you told us they gave you clues as to where we were going. You ran through the forest, kicking up leaves and singing your self-written songs until we finally reached a clearing that lay lower than the other parts of the forest. The clearing was a bright green and filled with birds and other animals, as if it was untouched by the seasons. There was a tiny waterfall on the other side that fell into a large pond, the water reflected the golden light of the morning sun like a golden mirror.

"But our eyes were most amazed by the large flowers that grew there. Thousand-leafed with a center of bright red that became more golden orange than dawn toward the edges. They were so big you had to hold them with both hands. None of us had ever seen a flower like that so we had to give it a name, mother told us you should have the honor of naming it for you were the one who found them. You decided to call them Dawnflowers because of their uncanny resemblance to the morning sun that day. Mother told us the Kurr word for dawn was *mena*, and the word for flower was *re*, and your eyes went wide with awe, the biggest smile you could make on your face because you thought it was the most beautiful word ever. We spent the entire day in that clearing, swimming in the cool waters and ate all the food we had with us. Mother drew all the flowers she could find while we played with the many animals that were there. You even shifted into a deer so you could race with the other deer that were there. I'm still certain they let you win because of the joy in your eyes."

Kaell actually laughed out loud, his heart warmed by that fond memory. He took a breath to go on when he heard a soft snoring from somewhere underneath the nest of blankets. Kaell figured he too should try to get some sleep but was certain he wouldn't be able to close his eyes again after that nightmare. So, he quietly grabbed some pants and a shirt out of the wardrobe and after he took a quick bath he went outside. The nightly sky here was darker than it was at home, there were not as many stars and those that were there had trouble piercing the canopy of these enormous trees.

At night however, the forest was different. Small flowers had opened up all around the city. Like glowing pearls, scattered through the high grass, their light was soft and either white or a pale green, the paths were like black rivers flowing through the sea of light. Kaell's feet followed the paths while he cleared his mind of all thought, wandering the old forest. The paths took him to the riverside, it glistened in the little starlight that was there. Many flowers were stuck against the banks of the river, probably from this morning when the Surr'um had put so many in the river.

Among them was Aergo, the water reaching all the way up to his chin as he sat in the river with his eyes closed. The faint light of the flowers painted his skin as silver as the water that framed his face, and Kaell felt warm inside as he stood there, looking at Aergo, his heart racing and his cheeks flushed red. He quietly sat down, not wanting to alert Aergo and ruin the moment. Hours could have passed and Kaell would never have noticed, he could look at Aergo forever and not get bored. A twig snapped as he sat down, startling both Aergo and himself. Aergo rose out of the water wearing nothing but his trousers and holding a dagger out in front of him.

As soon as he saw Kaell he relaxed. "If you wanted to see me shirtless you should have just asked, handsome," he said with a sly smile. Kaell didn't know what to say, he couldn't stop staring at Aergo's smooth, muscular body until Aergo came out of the water and put his shirt back on.

"So, what made you come look at me?" Aergo asked.

Still a bit speechless, Kaell searched for words. "I couldn't sleep." he eventually got out.

"Nightmares?" Aergo asked. "Or just troubles with sleeping alone?" he asked as he winked.

"The… the first one," Kaell whispered as his heart started pounding in his chest.

"Tell me about it." Aergo paused for a moment, savoring the silence of the forest. "You know, they say these waters can heal anything, if you know how to use it. The whole healing of your sister today was proof of that I suppose. You wouldn't happen to know how to use the water?"

"I don't. Why? What do you need healed?"

Aergo pulled away his hand and fixed his sleeves while avoiding Kaell's eyes for a moment. "Nothing right now, I'm just asking in case you ever break my heart, handsome." He then smiled with his biggest smile.

"You can't break what you don't have," Kaell said but still felt his cheeks burning and butterflies fluttering in his stomach, still trying to deny the feeling meant anything.

"Ouch. I'm not *that* cruel." Aergo teased Kaell, placing a hand over his heart. "Well, I guess that means there is enough space if you ever give me yours," Aergo teased before he disappeared into the nightly shadows of the forest.

Kaell needed a few moments to catch his breath and get his heart to slow down, but he couldn't get the feeling out of his stomach. He thought about what Aergo had said about the water, about how it could heal anything and hoped, maybe he could heal his Bond, maybe the water would give him what he missed.

Kaell reached into the water with his hand, which felt more like silk than water, his hand wasn't wet when he pulled it out it just tingled with warmth. He looked up the stream and noticed stairs going into the water at several points. Kaell made his way to the nearest one and took off his shirt. He was waist deep into the water when he heard a soft singing echo through the forest. Standing still in the water he listened for a moment, his body tingling. The song was very beautiful and brought tears to his eyes, his heart filled with warmth and love and joy.

"They are praising dawn," a soft voice sounded from behind him. He turned around, sinking into the waters to hide his bare chest. There was nobody he could see.

"Up here, my child." Up in the tree sat a woman cloaked in vines and leaves and flowers. Her skin was a golden brown and her eyes like those of a deer. Fireflies floated around her head and made it looks like she wore a crown of light. She jumped down and landed on a root close to the stairs.

"They greet her every day, right as her very first light peeks over the horizon, although not everyone can hear them.

"So, are you having a nice swim?" she asked him as she tried to balance on the roots around her. Kaell was paralyzed and he wasn't certain if he should get out as fast as he could or if he was allowed to stay in the water.

"It does feel nice," he answered with the softest voice. The woman laughed and the leaves around them rustled, seemingly sharing the joy.

"I'm glad you're enjoying the most sacred river of the world. You would look better if you didn't try to hide yourself in the water. The fact that you have no Marks doesn't make me think any different of you."

Kaell lowered his eyes in shame and slowly rose from the water, the woman didn't even glance at him as he did and he wasn't sure if that was better than the judgement others gave him. As soon as the woman turned her back to him, he looked down to inspect his chest, nothing had changed.

"It won't give you what you seek, that Mark is not yours to have," she said to him, softly singing along to the song in the distance, "Your Mark can only be given by few, if they are not too blind to see it."

"What do you mean?" Kaell eagerly asked. "Can you give it?"

"Easy there, buddy," she chuckled while she climbed the tree again, "You won't get what you're looking for here, that knowledge lies deeper into the forest. The Dan'um will take you there today, it is there we meet again. Enjoy the journey, you're coming past one of my favorite spots." Before Kaell could say anything else the woman had already climbed the tree and he lost her between the leaves and branches. The song ended and the silence returned to the forest.

"Oh wait, I forgot something," the woman shouted out of the tree before she poked her head through the leaves. "Take the Ilunari with you, if anyone questions it, show them this." She threw down a necklace for Kaell to catch but when he looked up again, she was gone.

He inspected the necklace, it was a pendant made from wood, amber and silver all twisted into a flat circle. It was very pretty and felt warm in his hand. He hung it around his neck so as not to lose it and got out of the water. He wasn't wet and could immediately put on his shirt and go back now that the first light had indeed chased the stars away. Kaell was far too busy with the encounter to pay attention to his surroundings and he didn't notice the Surr'um around him gazing at the necklace and some even bowing as he passed them on his way back.

Chapter 18
Ara-Ashin

Light seeped through the window as morning came, Ara could even hear a bird in the distance. She walked over to Rynn and shook him awake, she didn't understand sleep, Nuan didn't need it and it was so much better if she compared herself to humans.

Ara got into a dress the Surr'um had left for her, it was made from a very light and soft fabric that was almost like a second skin, it was much better than the dress from the night before, this at least didn't feel like clothing. In the living room she found the table filled with food but just the thought of eating already disgusted her.

Rynn stumbled in, dressed in some deep red robe of sorts and started eating as soon as he saw the food. Bread, chicken and fruit went into his mouth and Ara couldn't bear to watch it another second or she would actually throw up her guts. Someone knocked on the door and Ara sighed so loud that the person outside could easily hear it. She was absolutely not in the mood to deal with any of those blasted Surr'um, let alone the others who they travelled with. As soon as she opened the door, she tried to enter the mind of whoever was there to send them away but when she tried, she was knocked back so violently that her nose started bleeding.

"My mind is not yours to enter, and it never will be *Nuan*." It was Yira, her face hard and cold.

"Great, it's you. You're the last person I wanted to see this morning," Ara replied, putting as much hatred in her voice as she could as she wiped the blood off her face. "What do you want?"

"We're gathering on the crossroads, and I am here to take you there."

"Why do we have to gather now? If it has anything to do with that damned Kurr girl we won't be there." Ara was so sick that everything had to be about her. So she got a mark after she was dropped in a river and her hair grew long. Who cared? She was the reason they almost died in Arga in the first place, she was basically a corpse already and it had slowed them down. She was nothing special, just a shifter, there are plenty of those, but there was only one Nuan in this realm left, only one who could take the Throne of Light and restore this broken world.

"You're a loud thinker, you should really work on that." Yira interrupted her thoughts, "And to be Nuan is one thing, to take the Throne of Light is a whole different thing. Being a creation of Nuana doesn't give you the right, your actions do." There was no way one could miss the hatred between the two, it hung thick in the air, like smoke.

"I can think as loud as I want to, if you don't like it then don't listen." Ara paused, lifting her chin. "Who are you anyway to tell me whether I deserve to sit on the throne that is rightfully mine? You had one job and you failed it, quite miserably, and now you try to act like you are more important than you truly are. I see you for what you are and in time, so will the others." Ara wiped the remaining blood off of her face and checked if any fell on her dress but it was clean.

"Lead the way then, misty eyes. It's about time they gave me what I came here for," Ara said as she gestured to the path behind Yira. But Yira didn't move, instead she looked at Rynn who was still enjoying the food inside, unaware of their conversation. Ara sighed loudly and called for Rynn in her mind, he immediately stood up and came to her side.

"What are you doing to him, Ara? He is not your puppet and it will not go unpunished if you keep your grasp on him," Yira whispered, her hatred even more vibrant.

Ara said nothing nor did Rynn, he would not do anything unless she told him so, she was in his soul and nothing could get her out and Yira knew it. Ara had never intended to keep him for so long, the human mind was a weak and filthy thing and she did not enjoy being in it. The only reason that she kept him was that he could keep her alive, or well, his power could. She had seen his soul, his potential, and even though she could not awaken his inner strength, he was still a very powerful mage.

Perhaps that was the reason Yira was so mad that Ara had the mortal's mind in her grasp, now she couldn't do anything to her, wipe out her failures. The silence between them lasted longer than Ara wanted so she stepped out on the path and Rynn followed, ignoring Yira in every possible way.

Yira paced toward the crossroad where the others were already waiting for them. *Good*, Ara thought, now they could all take a good look at the real important person.

In the middle of the group stood four girls who looked exactly like Yira, one with moonstone rings through her lips, another with crystal spun over her ears, the other two were unfamiliar to Ara but were undoubtedly other sisters of Yira. One had crystal spun all over her skin as if she was made out of cracked porcelain, the other one had a large moonstone pin that went into her face right under her nose and came out underneath her chin, there was a constant stream of blood that dripped off of the bottom of the pin.

"I see the family is together again?" Ara asked teasingly, Yira was wise enough not to react but a grin still appeared on Ara's face.

As soon as they reached the group, the Dan'um started walking. Ara stayed in the back with Rynn, keeping an eye on everyone in front of her.

"Where are we going, exactly?" Etaín asked Raven.

"The deep forests, home of the Dan'um. They want to present the Child of the Forest to the Queen and the knowledge I seek I will probably find there."

"You don't seem too excited to go there, Ilunari," Ara mixed herself into the conversation.

She could see Raven's hand grab her spear tighter and even the Dan'um paused in his tracks for a short moment.

"I admire your observational skills, Nuan," she responded after the silence.

"And may I ask why it is that you don't want to go?" Ara said with her sweetest voice. She could guess the answer, there was probably no place that Raven didn't have enemies, even though they might know her by another name. She wanted to hear it from the Ilunari herself though, push her far enough that she would reveal who she truly was, what she truly was. Ara couldn't read her mind, it was covered with shadows and darkness that no light seemed to pierce.

"No," Raven said back, her voice cold and empty like always.

Ara chuckled, it didn't matter, they would probably find out soon enough.

Nobody stood on the side of the roads as they walked out of the city, nor were there any outside of the city. Ara had expected them to bid them farewell or at least bid Inza farewell. Inza walked besides the Dan'um with her brother. Her hair was braided and filled with flowers and leaves of all kinds, it was quite beautiful, she fit right into the forest around them. The forest grew denser as they went deeper and the road turned into a path and the path disappeared, they relied on the Dan'um to lead them to where they needed to go. Etaín fell back to walk beside Ara after a while.

"Bored of the forest?" Ara asked her teasingly. She hadn't made her mind up yet about the Laretu, she knew they were honorable people and that they fought valiantly against the enemies of the Light, so Ara was quite grateful for them.

"I'm not really a forest person, give me mountains or fields and I'm happy," Etaín responded, "I was wondering, did you know Nuana personally? Being one of her creations and all."

Ara smiled, finally, a respectable person in this world.

"Yes, I did. Why do you ask?"

Etaín's jaw slightly dropped, "Well, she has been gone for a very long time yet everyone seems to talk about her and even honor her." She paused before she looked at Ara in awe. "Wait, if you knew her you would have to be incredibly old."

Ara laughed at that last remark.

"Yes, to your standards I am old, however there are plenty of people who are older. That aside, the world is right to remember her. Lady Nuana was the greatest blessing this realm had ever seen, together with her sister, she smote down the wretched creatures that destroyed world after world. They brought balance to this realm when no one else could.

"It was Nuana who took in the humans when they landed on our shores and found nothing but war and destruction, she showed everyone kindness and the beauty of life and so many followed her ways. She made life good, until one day, shadows slew her in her own home and tried to erase everything about Nuana, killing all of my kind and leaving her throne empty. But they couldn't erase her, Nuana had touched too many souls with her kindness, Egìl took up his blade and avenged her, he took the throne of humankind and led them into battle against the darkness itself and still does to this day." Ara felt a tear rolling on her cheek, a tear of pride but also loss.

"My people have always fought against the darkness of the south, Megana must pay for what she did, when I get the chance, I too will join the army so we may someday avenge her." Etaín spoke with such determination that even Ara suddenly got a lust for battle, for the defeat of Megana, she envisioned herself slaying the

Guardian of Darkness herself, so the world could see her power and Ara would become the next Guardian of Light.

To be chosen you would need to die first. A voice echoed in her mind. Ara looked to the side and met the eyes of one of Yira's sisters, the one with the spike through her jaw.

Only the Abarriim can make a mortal into a High Immortal, and they only choose those who are no longer bound to their bodies. The voice made Ara feel sick in her stomach for some reason and when she looked away, she found all the other sisters looking at her. Ara drew out Rynn's fire a bit with her mind, his eyes blazing as a warning to all of them, for they too knew what he could do to them.

Aergo looked over his shoulder. "How do we know it was Megana who killed her, though? I mean, it was her sister and they are always together in the stories."

"Nuana was killed by shadows, shadows are a spawn of darkness. So, unless you know another Guardian of Darkness then I would gladly hear it." Ara's voice turned cold and hard as she spoke.

"No, I mean, it's quite obvious that it came from the Shadow Lands but what I was wondering about was: What if it was not Megana but someone else from the south entirely?" Aergo continued, his honeyed voice soft as always.

Ara sighed loudly. "Have you not been told the tales of old?" She looked at Aergo but he responded with nothing but silence. "I guess not. A High Immortal cannot be killed by those of mortal blood. Mortals can hurt them with Bleeding Steel but never kill them. It takes High Immortal blood to end High Immortal life. Besides that, Megana did not even attend the ceremony for Nuana and invaded the day after." It made perfect sense so she didn't understand why anyone could doubt it.

Aergo nodded. "That makes it quite obvious indeed. Perhaps Lady Megana should have thought it through a bit more."

Ara felt a soft rage grow in her stomach. "What do you mean she should have thought it out better? Would you rather have your queen murdered and have no clue as to who did it? You are no better than that bitch if you think that way."

A heavy silence fell over the group and the Dan'um leading them even stopped walking and turned around. His gaze went from Ara to Aergo to all the others of the group.

"You are as careless with your words as you are with your thoughts, Ara-Ashin," he spoke with a heavy accent that made it sound like High Speech more than common tongue. Ara was speechless, she didn't think he could understand her and by the looks of it the others had thought the same.

"You are free to speak and think whatever you want, Nuan, but I warn you that your words are heard, and you speak of matters you do not understand." The forest around them was silent, Ara would even say it was listening.

"How… how do you know my name?" Ara asked quietly, trying to keep her thoughts from running wild.

"We know more than just your name, Nuan. We know more about you than you know about yourself," he responded and turned around, moving further into the forest. As they all started walking again Ara caught Raven's eyes, cold and hard but somehow knowing. Ara was done waiting and tried to enter Raven's mind, hoping to find everything she needed.

A cold wall of darkness and shadows raged around her mind, like a black storm on a winter's day and as soon as she touched it, she felt a cold blade press against her throat. It was strange, but it almost felt like the blade was calling out to her, not in a welcoming sense, more with a sense of disapproval and disgust. A feeling not unfamiliar to her.

"This is my final warning to you, Nuan. I suggest you keep to yourself unless you wish to enter the Whispering Halls early." Raven noticed the fire in Rynn being drawn out and now whispered so soft only Ara could hear it.

"His fire will not kill me, Ashin, yet my blade will deliver you a slow and painful death so you can fail your people one last time."

Raven's kept Ara's gaze for a moment and Ara made Rynn take back his fire. After a long silence the spear was pulled back and Raven moved past the Dan'um, who started to lead them further and further into the forest.

They walked for hours on end without stopping and in complete silence until twilight crept over their heads. Ara's legs were starting to hurt but before she got a chance to complain they had stopped in some sort of a clearing. Ara was catching her breath when she saw Inza stare at something with her mouth wide open, Ara followed the Kurr's eyes and her jaw dropped as well.

They stood at the feet of a massive statue. It was actually more like a tree that grew in the shape of a hooded woman holding a large, blue, crystal flower. Moss and vines hung down from her arms and shoulders, and her body was cut in numerous places from which small streams of silver water flowed down to the roots where it pooled and flowed toward the river. Fireflies lit up in the soft twilight and deer gently moved between the surrounding trees. The Dan'um had dropped his robes so he wore nothing more but his trousers, he was lean and Ara could see his muscles move underneath his skin. Across his back and chest there was a band of dark green markings of the same symbols that were in the Temple of Light. Ara knew they were letters of High Speech, she had never learned the language, it was taught in their training but she didn't receive much of it. The Dan'um was washing himself while humming some song Ara didn't know.

"I could use a wash too," she mumbled to herself while she was already pushing her dress off her shoulders but Yira stopped her.

"If you want to wash yourself you can use some of the water we brought. These waters are very sacred and if any of you touch it you will either die a quick death or be cast out of these forests for good." Inza was already stepping back. "Don't worry, all descendants of the forests are free to enter the water, Kurr can enter just as I do." Yira's voice went from harsh to gentle when she spoke to Inza and Kaell.

"Can we at least get a fire going, safely of course, I am starving and need something warm in my belly," Etaín said, her hand on her growling stomach.

Yira shouted at the Dan'um in High Speech, who responded with few words and nodded to the side.

"There is a large stone upon which we can make a fire if we are careful," Yira said and Etaín was already moving there and gathering sticks she found on the way.

"All we need now is fire and something to roast," she said as she was piling the sticks.

"We got the mage for fire and I'll get some good meat, there seems to be plenty around here anyway," Aergo answered as he pulled out his knives.

"Rynn, if you would be so kind?" Etaín asked and pointed toward the pile of sticks.

Yira and her sisters looked at Ara, who let out a small sigh before she commanded Rynn to do what was asked of him. He breathed into the wood and it caught fire right away, its warmth soothing the pain from the long walk. The Dan'um now joined them as well and held some bread in his hands, which he seemingly pulled from nowhere. All of them were handed their bread, except for Raven, who it was thrown to as if she was a dog.

The Dan'um said something in High Speech which lead to them arguing for a moment until Yira interrupted them.

"What do you mean summoned?" she asked with a face full of confusion, "Why would the Dan'um summon you when you're banished from their lands, you haven't exactly deserved redemption yet? Unless the Queen has summoned you, you are not allowed to cross the borders of Dan'um. I fear you have to stay here or turn back, *Indimaronth*."

Raven sighed, "As I said, I do not know who it was, if it even was a 'who.' I just explained it to him and you heard it as well. It came to me in Elebok and told me to find it here. So yes, I was summoned to come to this forsaken forest, again." The annoyance in her voice was obvious to anyone. Kaell scuffled around for a little bit before he stood up and held out an amulet to the Dan'um.

"I, eh, was given this and told to, well, make sure, that, eh, Raven would come with us." His voice was trembling but all of their attention went to the amulet.

"*Mirhan*," whispered the Dan'um softly. "I will take you to the queen, she will judge your words to see if they are true, *Indimaronth*," he continued before sitting down. The entire group fell silent and stared into the fire. From the edge of the forest they heard a soft panting as Aergo was pulling a young deer toward the fire, nobody stood up to help him and when he finally got to the fire, he dropped the deer and pulled out his knife from its throat before he put his hands in his side and sighed.

"Why did I go hunting? Now I missed all the drama."

Chapter 19
Aergo

"You truly have a way with food, my friend," Aergo said as he took another bite of the meat. He hadn't eaten anything this delicious since he left Xisq. Now all of them were filling themselves with bread and meat, well, all except Ara, who didn't seem to have any interest in the food or the fire but kept staring at the large statue beside them.

"I love eating too much to not know how to cook, Kir'in," Etaín chuckled.

"I have to admit, Laretu cooking is one of the best things in the Shining Lands and probably outside of it as well. Your feasts must be a true pleasure, aren't they?" He could only imagine the amount of food a group of Laretu could eat in one evening, Aergo had seen Etaín raiding the Surr'um buffet the evening before.

"Hmmm, Raven can confirm that." A short silence fell and Etaín and Raven exchanged looks, "Never mind actually, that was anything but a pleasure." Etaín stood up and walked into the forest, disappearing from their sight.

Raven answered the question before it could be asked.

"We were attacked that night. Etaín's father sacrificed himself to defend his daughter, without him, she would have died that night." Her eyes were distant, probably in the memory of that day.

"Who is stupid enough to attack a gathering of Laretu? Everyone knows not to fight a Laretu if they have the choice, let alone fight a group of them," Aergo said as he flipped out a small knife. His belly was full and he was now carving one of the bones into a pendant, maybe he would wear it as a necklace.

"Shyvna was stupid enough." The whisper was barely heard over the crackling of the fire. Now the Dan'um was also interested. "Shyvna, Lady of Blades, the Mistress of Battle?" he asked Raven, who simply nodded in return.

"She used to be the protector of the Laretu, why would she attack… Oh, I see," he said as Raven glared at him. "Seems the wrong one sacrificed themselves that night." His voice went darker as he said that and Aergo couldn't help thinking about all the reasons they had this hatred between them. He would figure it out another time, knowing the Dan'um spoke common tongue he could pry some answers out of him. Tongues always loosened when they got to speak about annoyances and hatred, and he would simply be the ear that listened.

The silence got a little too heavy for Aergo so he turned the attention away from this drama.

"Ara, tell me, your eyes have been glued to this statue all evening. Would you be so kind as to tell us why?"

She sighed and waited a little before she answered his question. "Once, before the war came, before High Immortals started slaughtering their own kin and brought war to this world, there were statues like this everywhere. Anndar was filled with glorious statues of Nuana, and Nuana herself would walk the streets. High Immortals walked among the people like friends, not rulers. Houses of Silence were everywhere and they were full. But I learn from Rynn's mind that this was ages ago, that all of this changed when this land was forced to war by…" She glanced over to the Dan'um, whose eyes told her to choose her next words carefully. "By unexpected events, to call it that."

Etaín sat down again, silent and her eyes red. They chose to pay no mind to her and give her the time she needed.

"Houses of Silence? What are you talking about, Nuan?" Kaell dropped into the conversation.

Ara rolled her eyes and looked around, expecting the others to know, but in all honesty Aergo didn't have a clue either. It didn't sound as glorious of a place as Ara described it.

"Well, from now on I will just expect that you know nothing of the past. I have to give it to you, it has been long and you are only young. A House of Silence is a place of worship, a place where mortals come and ask for a High Immortal's help or guidance in a more serious way. It showed the High Immortal that you cared about it, that it was not just a random wish one had, that you were willing to put in extra time and effort, asking them to do the same."

"Oooooh, you mean those temple things? Yeah, they are a rare sight these days, sweetheart. There is only one left in Xisq, if that one is still active that is. The others are now either storages, homes or bathing houses, although one is a, well, let's call it a place where a lonely man or woman can, satisfy, their certain needs." His face went wide with a smile while Ara's face quickly filled with disgust.

Raven chuckled. "You have a lot of catching up to do, Nuan."

"Well, if you need someone to teach you, here I am." Aergo opened his arms wide as he said it. He had a habit of making himself useful to anyone around him, that way everyone around him was willing to help him when he needed something done himself.

"The human has already opened his mind to me so I doubt you could tell me more than the contents of the library of the Academy," she snarled back at him.

"You mean to tell me that this human boy, at the age of what, twenty, has read all the books in the Academy? From what I know that's a lot of books. Nevertheless, an eternity of reading books could not tell you what I can." His voice sounded so sweet it was almost like his words were literal honey.

"How so?" He had piqued her interest.

"Well, because whispers in the streets never end up in books, and I happen to have heard them for a beautiful 217 years now. But if you are content with your human's mind then I will hold my tongue." Inza's eyes grew wide in surprise and he noticed Kaell seemed confused as well.

"I seriously doubt you are physically capable of shutting up, Kir'in," Etaín scoffed across the fire. Aergo placed his hand over his heart, pretending to be hurt and Etaín rolled her eyes.

"Wait, how can you be so old?" Inza burst out. Aergo laughed and shook his head.

"Old? I am only 217, my life has barely begun, sweetheart."

"He's Kir'in, they live much longer than Kurr, or Laretu and Humans for that matter. To Kir'in he is about the same age your brother is to you, although he will probably live much longer if he doesn't annoy the wrong people too much," Raven said as she twisted her spear around, casting dancing reflections around her.

"Well, how old can you get then?" Inza asked Aergo, her eyes sparkling and bright.

"You're a curious one, aren't you?" Inza nodded back at him. "Well then, most of my kin grow to be around eight hundred although 820 isn't uncommon anymore these days. It may seem old to you but I overheard Ara mentioning that she lived in the days when Nuana was still alive which makes her, what, over four thousand years now? And I won't even begin to guess the age of an Ilunari, or these forest dwellers for that matter, they have eternal youth and I never heard of one dying of old age" Aergo said as he nodded at Raven and the Dan'um.

"That's because none of us have died of old age, and you shouldn't call us forest dwellers, it's disrespectful," the Dan'um said.

"Apologies, sir. What should we call you and your kin then, especially when referring to both Surr'um and Dan'um?" Inza quickly asked.

The Dan'um grunted, "Preferably just Dan'um and Surr'um, we are not the same, not anymore, but if you must refer to us both just use U'um, that covers all of our races. To me you can refer as Ynohan, Ynohan Kuslae-Hern, to be exact."

"If you must know Kir'in, I turned 3999 last winter, according to the mage here," Ara said with her head held up high. Aergo never saw Rynn talking to Ara yet somehow, she knew everything, the Nuan was probably all over his mind and he felt sorry for the boy, to never have a thought for yourself would be a horrible way to live, it would be for Aergo for sure.

"Now tell me, Ynohan, as a Dan'um you too must have lived quite some years, and in all honesty, I am more curious about your tales than those of the Nuan." Aergo turned to Ara. "No offence, sweetheart, I just heard a rumor that you were locked in a temple ever since the death of our beloved Lady Nuana."

Ara looked him straight in the eyes, no clear expression on her face. Not one for jokes, Aergo noted.

"I am, by far, not the oldest here. I am about the same age as Ara-Ashin, and I spent all my years in these forests so my stories are limited as well, Kir'in," Ynohan said to him. They heard a loud snoring from across the fire and saw Etaín sleeping behind Raven. Aergo himself had to admit that he too felt quite weary, he hadn't slept since they entered Arga and honestly, he didn't want to, that city had opened wounds that had taken years to heal.

The others laid down as well now, as if Etaín's snoring was the signal for sleeping. Raven, Kaell and Ynohan didn't lay down and Aergo sat closer to the Dan'um, giving him the freedom to talk with him unheard.

"Ynohan, I have a problem and you may have a solution. I…" Aergo started but the Dan'um interrupted him.

"Yes, I can help you sleep," he started, Aergo frowned, could the Dan'um read his mind or something?

"Your eyes show your lack of sleep and Arga is a place not many leave alive and those who do leave it alive often have a troubled mind. Wait right here, I will be back in a second."

Ynohan stood up and walked toward the statue, scooped some of the water in a leaf and walked back to Aergo.

"Take your robe off, Aergo," Ynohan said quietly. Aergo's robe dropped to the ground and the air stung in the dozens of cuts across his chest and wrists. Even though he stood right next to the fire the air was cold, at least, for someone in just pants. The Dan'um dipped his hand in the silver water and traced over his every cut and bruise. It didn't hurt, it was more of a warm, tingling feeling and Aergo relaxed as the water found its way into his wounds, closing his eyes until he was told to put on his robe again. He looked down at his wrist and found his skin closed again, only a few new scars marked his body now, the others gone without a trace.

"Lay down now, child. Let the blood of Mirhan ease your mind and grant you sleep." And so Aergo closed his eyes and quickly fell deep into a dreamless sleep.

The soft sunlight tickled his face, a feeling he wasn't used to anymore after living all these years in an underground city. He smiled, enjoying the warmth on his face, before he stretched the sleep out of his limbs. As he stretched his arms, he felt himself pushing against a body. Aergo opened his eyes and saw he lay against Kaell, who looked him right in the eyes.

"Good morning." Kaell's voice was a little rough and shaky, his cheeks flushed red.

"It's a good morning indeed," Aergo said and pushed a little more against Kaell's chest. Kaell looked down at his chest.

"Do you mind?" he asked Aergo, who smiled.

"Most certainly not." He made his voice as sweet and warm as he could and laughed when Kaell's cheeks burned red. Aergo stood up and stretched a little more, feeling Kaell's eyes on him. The others were still asleep and Raven and the Dan'um were missing so Aergo looked around the clearing but they were nowhere to be seen.

"They are training near the river or something, they were talking in that strange language of theirs," Kaell mentioned when he saw Aergo's searching eyes.

"Time for a little stroll then, don't you think?" Aergo was already walking toward the river and saw Kaell scrambling to his feet after checking if Inza was still asleep. When they got closer to the river, they heard the sound of weapons clashing, wood on steel and steel on steel. It echoed between the trees like a melody. As soon as they stepped out from between the trees, they saw Raven and Ynohan dueling. They moved across roots and branches that entwined above the river and over the rocks that stood in the river. The Dan'um was bare chested and sweaty, bleeding wounds all over him, Raven only wore a band across her chest and her leather pants, revealing her pale skin crossed with scars and a large intricate tattoo along her spine. She and her spear were as one, moving with such ease and grace that it almost seemed like a dance, a very deadly dance.

Ynohan wielded a single sword, beautifully crafted from a pale steel. Aergo could see the finesse of the blade from this distance. They both moved with grace but it was clear that the Dan'um was of no match for Raven. Ynohan grunted as he dodged another attack, breathing heavily. Aergo could barely see Raven breathing, that was how relaxed she was.

"That doesn't look like a friendly training, Aergo," Kaell started and Aergo completely agreed with him but had no clue how to stop it or if they should even interfere at all. He had seen the cold look in Raven's eyes when she held her spear against Ara's throat and he had no desire to see that look again, Raven was best kept as a friend.

"That's because it isn't friendly, and most definitely not a training." One of Yira's sisters, the one with the crystal covering her skin, was sitting on the side of the river, eating an apple.

"Oh, hi, we hadn't seen you yet. You're one of Yira's sisters, right?" Kaell said to her. She laughed.

"You wouldn't have seen me unless I said something. But yeah, I'm one of Yira's sisters, my name is Sera. Yira never introduces us, so don't worry that you don't know my name." She took another bite of her apple.

“What did you mean when you said they weren’t training?” Aergo asked her, he had noticed the tension between Ynohan and Raven, it was hard to miss, but to fight over it? That seemed a bit dramatic to him.

“They are dueling, if you can call it that. She could do this in her sleep if she wanted to. She has to draw blood to win and he just wants to push her into the river, or make her bleed into the water. But he knows he won’t succeed in either of those.” Sera took another bite of her apple, cheering when Raven’s spear cut into Ynohan’s arm.

“Why would he want to push her into the river, or make her bleed into it? What does that bring him?” Aergo didn’t understand a single thing about it.

“Well, Kir’in, she was banished from these forests a very long time ago, now your friend here carries the Heart of Mirhan and says that she needs to be taken inside. Usually, she would have been killed on the spot if she even set foot in the forest, well if they could kill her that is, but now she has received the highest form of protection.

“Ynohan has a deep-rooted hatred for her even though he only knows her from stories, as do most. So now, Ynohan is trying to break her protection by making her commit a new crime against his people. If she is to ever touch or defile the waters of the forest, she will be punished as if she broke her banishment. But Ynohan is a fool, a stubborn one too, only the queen has the power to defeat this Ilunari but Ynohan will try anyway. They will stop soon, I believe Raven has little time to waste.” Sera cheered again when Raven drew blood once more from the Dan’um. Sera stood up and walked back to the camp but Aergo lingered long enough to see the Dan’um letting himself fall into the silver waters below. As Aergo passed Kaell he brushed his hand against the Kurr’s for a moment, enjoying the sudden red in Kaell’s cheeks.

“Why do you cheer for Raven and not your own kin, Sera?” Aergo asked.

“What do you mean?”

“Well, you cheered for Raven and not Ynohan, shouldn’t it be the other way around?”

“Oh Kir’in, I am no Dan’um anymore, that time is long, long gone.”

Aergo frowned and he could see Kaell do the same.

"Anymore? What do you mean, did you change races or something?" There was obvious confusion in Kaell's voice.

"Right, nobody told you about us. Me and my sisters were once Dan'um, then we died, were chosen by the Abariimm, made High Immortals and given tasks which we then complete as well as we can. It's not that special really."

"The Abariimm are just a myth, right?" Kaell asked, still confused.

"They most certainly are not, they are very real but you don't get to see them when you're alive and most don't see them when they die either. It's a shame nobody teaches this stuff anymore in the Shining Lands, but it's not my business."

They walked into the clearing and found that everything was already packed and ready to go. Etaín was sitting behind Inza and braided her hair, sticking flowers into it that Yira was plucking around them, while Inza was braiding a flower crown out of white flowers that bloomed all across the clearing. They were chatting excitedly about the Kurr forests and Laretu lands and Aergo enjoyed hearing their happy laughter and memories of home.

Ara was sitting with her eyes closed, Rynn besides her, looking into the distance with empty eyes. Aergo hadn't gotten a good look at Rynn's eyes when they weren't burning bright, they were actually a beautiful brown, he knew humans found brown eyes plain and boring but only humans and U'um could have brown eyes, so where humans found the violet Ilunari eyes special all the other races admired the brown eyes of humans.

Overall the boy looked quite plain, if it wasn't for the carnelian crystal that webbed over his skin. Aergo found the boy very familiar, but couldn't quite figure out why, if he ever got the chance to talk to Rynn when he wasn't some puppet, he would try to find out why.

It didn't take long for Raven to appear, dressed in her leather again. Ynohan appearing shortly after that, as he was putting on his robes Aergo noticed that all of his wounds were gone. The water had done the same to the Dan'um as it had done to Aergo's wounds the night before.

"We will leave now, I want to reach Irs Ia before the sun sets so I can present you to the queen," Ynohan said and was already moving into the forest, following a path Aergo could not see. Everyone got to their feet and went after the Dan'um quickly, except for Ara and Rynn. She didn't seem to have noticed that they were leaving and for a moment Aergo was tempted to leave her behind as well but he wanted the key to the Vault and he had a feeling they would only give it to the Nuan. So, he walked over and tapped her on the shoulder, Rynn's eyes following his every move.

"Nuan, we're leaving, so you might want to come along," Aergo said to her, smiling kindly. Ara simply opened her eyes and stood up, moving past Aergo without saying a word. He sighed and shrugged his shoulders. Sera noticed him from the edge of the forest and gave him an understanding look, clearly sharing his annoyance toward the Nuan. Sera walked beside him as they followed the Dan'um. They walked in silence for a moment but questions burned on Aergo's tongue.

"Ask your questions, Kir'in," Sera laughed.

"It's not nice to read someone's mind uninvited," Aergo laughed.

"It's hard not to listen when someone is shouting," she responded, Aergo had to give her that, his thoughts could be loud from time to time.

"I suppose that's true. I was wondering about the Ilunari, everyone seems to know her yet nobody seems to be fond of her. An old friend of mine was particularly interested in her and her spear yet was afraid to come too close to her, and I haven't seen him afraid of anything besides Arga."

"Spare me your sweet words Kir'in, speak clearly and ask your questions." Sera knew his questions but seemed to enjoy the little banter.

"Who is she, and what is she? I saw her in Arga, she wasn't Ilunari there."

Sera kept quiet for a moment, her sisters glancing at them.

"Who she truly is, is not for me to say, she should tell you herself. You are right about what she is, she isn't a standard Ilunari. She is *Indimaronth*, a Mistwatcher as they call it. They were ancient warriors who were trained in the ways of the Mists, only their own order knows what that way is but it is said to hold great powers. Among many it means they can travel to Elebok and the Whispering Halls whenever she wants.

"Yira was taught some of their secrets by the Abariimm so she could see without her eyes and use her mind to fight as well. Raven is one of the last *Indimaronth*. She holds more secrets but we don't know all of them, my sisters and I know why so many dislike her, it is the same reason she was banished from the Dan'um forests but I am not allowed to say why because we are obligated to remain neutral to anyone for we do not know what our next task will be. Does this answer your questions, Kir'in?" Sera asked him.

Aergo simply nodded, it did answer some of his questions but he feared he now had more than he had at first.

"Who is this friend you spoke of, the one who had an interest in Raven's spear?"

"His name is Tuales," Aergo started, only to be interrupted by Sera.

"Tuales? The blood mage?"

Aergo nodded again, surprised that she knew Tuales.

"Then I know who you are, Aergo Blackfang, son of Maren Blackfang. And I see why you survived Arga, and I am very glad that he did not get his hands on Raven's spear."

Aergo was speechless, his father's name hadn't been mentioned in centuries.

"You knew my father?" Aergo asked her.

Sera nodded, "Your father was a ruthless man, did everything for power but did give many people a home. It was no surprise he became friends with Tuales, that blood mage makes promises of power he cannot yet fulfill, not unless he gets his hands on his book."

Aergo didn't like being reminded of his father, Aergo had respected his father's goals but had never approved of his means. Maren Blackfang was known as a murderer and a cruel man, Aergo had learned his ways from his mother, she taught him how to influence someone's mind, trick them and use their secrets to get what you want, to make them believe that they had to work for you, that it was the right thing. He would not get the same fame as his father but would stay in the shadows, unseen, because they cannot catch what they cannot see.

"This book you speak of, is it the Scarlet River?" Aergo asked Sera, trying to lead the conversation away from his father. Sera nodded but seemed distracted, Aergo could see her sisters being more restless as well as Ynohan. Raven appeared to be more nervous as well and held her spear tight.

"What is happening?" Aergo asked Sera.

"We have reached the Gates of Irs Ia, soon, we'll be home again," Sera sighed in relief.

Would they have reached Irs Ia already, the capital of the Dan'um? They had only been walking for a short time, or at least that was how it felt to Aergo. However, his legs were weak after the journey and his stomach twisted from the lack of food now that he thought about it.

It was a matter of minutes before the gates came into vision. Trees twisted into each other, reaching for the sky, ancient and gnarled, forming a wall that would make anyone feel small. There was no path through the wall of trees, at least none that Aergo could see.

"It looks pretty closed for a gate," Aergo whispered to himself.

Ynohan walked up to the wall and started speaking in High speech, Yira and her sisters softly echoing the words. After he was done the forest around them moaned loudly and the trees around them started moving, the roots slithering like snakes toward Raven, they twisted around her ankles and grabbed her arms and neck, rooting her in place. Raven didn't even flinch but did snarl at Kaell.

"Perhaps now would be a good time to show the damned amulet to these murderous trees, before I come and cut if from your neck myself."

Kaell's eyes went wide and he hurriedly took the amulet from his neck and held it up high toward the wall. Immediately the trees stopped moving and a loud voice echoed between them. Shivers went down Aergo's spine, the voice was as if the wind itself shouted through the trees, rustling the leaves like a storm.

Ynohan pointed at Raven and the roots slowly loosened around her, leaving red marks where they had been. Raven shook the last roots off of her and walked toward the wall while she shouted something in High Speech to it and the trees moved out of her way, creating a tunnel through the massive wall. Aergo could see Ynohan clench his fist and grinding his filed teeth before he turned around and forced a smile, gesturing the others to follow.

The trees had formed a long tunnel with a roof that reached above the canopy, light cascaded down through the many windows between the branches. On the sides stood tall trees that wove into each other, making a solid wall. There was no end to be seen because the path only formed right in front of Raven, who walked in front, and behind Aergo the trees moved back, closing the tunnel right behind them.

Yira started singing softly and her sisters joined her within a second, their voices forming one single harmony. It was a strangely beautiful song, it didn't sound happy, it was more a song of longing. Aergo didn't understand the words as they sang in High Speech but he felt it, the hairs on his arms rose up and his eyes filled with tears. Ynohan had joined the song, his low voice mixing with the soft singing of the sisters. Aergo fought back the tears in an attempt to stay sharp. This was the first time he visited Irs Ia and he had learned to be wary of new places, he couldn't let tears blur his vision, he wanted to see everything clearly as soon as they finally left this tunnel.

The song ended and not a second later the last trees parted and they stood on the bank of a large, silver lake.

In the middle stood a gigantic tree with roots large enough to build houses on, they reached to the side of the lakes forming massive bridges to the center. They were of a dark wood that Aergo had never seen before, the leaves of the tree were a greyish green as if someone had mixed silver and green paint, drawn leaves and placed them on the tree. Along the sides of the lake were countless buildings of stone and crystal, others were grown into the trees, both in the branches and the roots. They could see crowds of Dan'um walking around, large roads leading deep into the forest, one river flowing into the lake and many rivers flowing outwards.

"Welcome to Irs Ia," Ynohan said before he crossed the nearest root-bridge toward the center, "The queen will see you now."

The wood groaned as the roots parted for them, opening a way into the massive throne room. A dark, golden light fell through the cracks between the wood around them, casting its faint light upon the four thrones that stood at the end of the room. All four were made of wood, although every one was made of a different type of wood. Three of the thrones stood on a small platform. The left one was blackened and dead, the right one pale and engraved in High Speech, the middle one was made out of a warm oak, upon it sat Edhro, King of the Surr'um. He was dressed in gold and green, his brown hair falling down over his shoulders, his amber eyes burning with hatred as soon as he saw Naka enter.

On his head his oaken crown was filled with young, golden leaves, a sign spring had arrived. The fourth throne was placed higher on the wall behind the other thrones, looming above them, it was made from the same dark wood as the tree they stood in and upon it sat Queen Serielye. Her skin was blacker than a raven's feathers and marked with silver, her hair was grey and green like the leaves of the tree, she wore a dress made from roots and branches that seemed to still be alive. Her eyes were covered by a band of dark metal with spikes that rose above her head, a macabre crown for the queen of the forest. She was hauntingly beautiful and managed to send shivers through Naka's spine by simply sitting there. They had barely entered when King Edhro rose from his chair and pointed at Naka.

"You were banished from these lands, murderer! Now, we shall have your head," he thundered in High Speech. Immediately, armed Dan'um came from the shadows and Naka grabbed Nárymm, ready to fight her way out. She had been summoned here by that strange voice in Elebok and she would not let anybody stop her from finding it now. The first Dan'um threw a swing at her but stopped right before she could block it.

"Hold," the queen's voice echoed through the room, she spoke in High Speech too but her voice was dangerously calm and cold and sounded like a forest in the wind, the wood around them moaned, echoing her voice. Slowly, the Dan'um moved back into the shadows, merging with them until they seemed to disappear.

"You hold no power in my forest, Edhro, and you most certainly do not command my people. Now sit down and hold your tongue unless I ask you something," the queen said, still not having moved at all. King Edhro's eyes spit fire at Naka but he turned around and sat down on his throne again, his fear of Queen Serielye was bigger than his hatred for Naka.

"We shall speak alone after the others are gone, Mistwatcher," the queen continued in High Speech to Naka, who bowed her head in return.

"I don't think I have ever seen a more unique group of people in my throne room, and we had many here. Tell me, do you have a reason to be here or are you all travelling with the Ilunari?" The queen now spoke in the common tongue, her voice still held the sound of a forest in the wind. The others remained silent for a moment until Ara stepped forward.

"I am Ara-Ashin, I have come to take the key to the Vault in Xisq so I can take the Heart of Light and bring Nuana back." Even now the Nuan held the arrogant tone in her voice and Naka could see Edhro's eyes burn brighter with every word.

"Of course you are, Ara-Ashin, but it is not ours to give. However, the one who can give it is within our midst but must come to you freely," the queen spoke with the same calmness. "What of the human? Did he surrender himself freely to you or did you take him?"

Ara looked at Rynn nervously. "His name is Rynn, he surrendered himself freely when he freed me."

The queen didn't respond to it but instead pointed at Kaell and Inza. "It has been many, many ages since we saw a Child of the Forest and we are glad to have you, but for you the question is the same."

"Your majesty," Kaell stepped forward, "we came here so my sister could learn more about her powers and what she truly is since our Kelsul have nothing left to teach her." He kept his eyes on the floor the whole time and his voice was trembling softly.

"Your Kelsul never had much to teach but fortunately we possess all the knowledge you need. We shall take you to our best teacher, and I believe you are still Markless. Am I right?" The queen said and Kaell's cheeks went red in shame, he nodded.

"Such a disgrace." Her voice was as cold as ice, and Kaell looked as if he wanted to die right on the spot. "Your Kelsul are blind, luckily we are not so you shall get your Mark soon."

Kaell's eyes filled with tears, Naka knew he must have been treated horribly if he didn't have a Mark, so it must be such a relief to hear he would finally get one.

"Kir'in, we have traded with your kin for many years, what is it you seek here?" The queen turned to Aergo.

Aergo bowed with extravagance, "Your magnificent highness, I am Aergo Blackfang and I have come to receive the key to the Vault as well, the Nuan and human are my prisoners until then."

Naka smiled a little, it was of no use to sweet talk Queen Serielye, it was better to be blunt for she already knew everything there was to know about everyone. The only reason she asked was out of courtesy and because Edhro didn't possess the same knowledge and had the right to hear so.

"Spare me your words, Aergo Blackfang. We know you simply seek its riches and its power. Your father and many others came here to ask for the same, for them applied the same that I have already told the Nuan. I simply warn you, Kir'in, do not go searching for riches here for you will not like what you find." The queen's voice had become even harsher.

"That brings me to you, Laretu. You are the first of your kin to ever set foot in my forest, however, I have fought alongside your ancestors when the humans sought to conquer the world. So, we value your kind even though it has been ages since we last saw one."

Etaín kneeled and bowed her head. "I am Etaín of house Mirdar, I travel with Raven since she helped me defend my hometown against Shyvna, the High Immortal of Battle."

Queen Serielye kept silent for a moment and King Edhro frowned and sat upright when Etaín dropped Shyvna's name.

"You mean to tell me that Lady Shyvna came to fight the people she once swore to protect?" Edhro exclaimed. Etaín simply nodded, her head still low.

"Well then, Ynohan, take our guests somewhere else, make sure they have the necessities," the queen continued as if she had heard nothing unusual. The others were escorted outside and the tree closed behind them, leaving Naka in the eerie silence with the king and queen.

"You have brought some unique people to my forest, Naka," Queen Serielye said in High Speech, slowly rising from her throne. The roots of her dress moved and twisted with her every movement and from the walls branches reached out, forming a path down for the queen. Her bare feet seemed unbothered by the unevenness and rough surface of the wood.

"You claim you were summoned here by someone you met in Elebok, a silver wisp of sorts."

Naka nodded. Queen Serielye heard every word that was spoken in her forest so she knew what Naka wanted to know.

"Then your banishment is lifted, you are still no friend to us but we have more important things to do than waste our time on punishing you for breaking your banishment." She had reached the floor and stood in front of Naka, bowing down until she stood face to face with Naka.

"You have released your powers again, yet you still try to deny who you truly are," the queen said softly almost whispering, her warm breath brushing past Naka's face.

"It's hard to hide your fears in Arga, so it wasn't really a choice," Naka said.

"What business did you have in Arga? And how did you manage to get out alive?" King Edhro's voice echoed, the rage had faded from his voice, instead there was interest now.

"Tuales is one of Aergo's allies it seems, he sent us there with a shadow gate. I didn't know where he would send us, otherwise I would have stopped him. I guess his greed made him forget that we are not invincible. Luckily, the King of Embers went easy on us for some reason so we had the opportunity to escape," Naka scoffed. Queen Serielye was now pacing through the room. "He never goes easy on anyone, I suppose you remember you first visit to Arga," the queen said and Naka nodded, the memory made her skin crawl. "But I thought you would have figured it out by now."

Naka frowned, she could see a spark of fear in Edhro's eyes but she didn't know what the queen meant.

"Fire, forged by nightmares
will turn life into ashes from which it may never rise
wood will scorch and stone will melt
in the fire that will break the Watchers."

Her words echoed through the room, wood moaning, roaring almost as she spoke the ancient words. It seemed to know what kind of pain and destruction it would bring even though it had never even felt the touch of fire before.

"Rynn," Naka whispered, finally understanding.

"Yes, the mage. They poured fire into him, as much as they could, and you brought him to our doorstep, ready to fulfill the prophecy." Queen Serielye's voice didn't show any fear, even though the one thing that could destroy them walked amongst them.

"You saw the fire in him long before we entered your forests, if you didn't want him here you should have kept him out. If the prophecy fulfills itself it is your own doing. Now, everyone seems to know this 'silver wisp' that summoned me except me, so perhaps you could enlighten me." Naka had enough of being blamed for everyone's misfortune. Queen Serielye walked back up to her throne, keeping silent.

"I will enlighten you," a voice echoed through the room. Naka shot around, suddenly standing face to face with a Dan'um. Its skin was a pale silver, glowing softly in the shadows. Its eyes were like pearls, changing color as the light hit them, Naka couldn't look in them for more than a second before a stinging pain filled her head.

"We have been expecting you, Naka. We are glad you are here at last, and we must move quickly. Your friends have already been gathered." It barely moved its lips as it spoke and turned around after its last words, nodding at the king and queen and walked out of the throne room, Naka following it closely. She couldn't figure out whether it was a man or a woman, she had never seen this person or anyone like it, the eyes looked like the silver wisp she had seen but not quite.

They walked across the bridge to the other side of the lake, toward the city and Naka regretted not having a cloak of sorts but they took a road along the waterside, avoiding the city. The Dan'um took her to a small field on the side of the road where the others waited, surrounded by large white stags who had antlers of silver from which flowered vines hung down, white stags from Kadhren. Most of them were gathered around Inza, who petted them all and whispered in their ears, smiling in awe as the animals nudged her with their noses.

Naka grabbed the arm of the Dan'um, "Tell me, before we join them, who is so important that the white stags of Kadhren have come to take us to them? I may not know a lot about your kin, but I know that when the white stags of Kadhren are there, it's important."

The Dan' um remained silent for a long time before it turned away and stood beside the stags, ready to leave. Naka took a good look around and noticed a familiar face she didn't expect, he saw her too and Naka smiled.

"There she is, my favorite Ilunari in this realm!" the man shouted in High Speech throwing his arms wide open in a welcoming gesture. Tarm, he looked exactly as Naka remembered, brown, messy hair, tanned skin and his same piercing brown eyes, but most importantly, his eternal, big smile. Naka almost fell into his arms when he got close enough, hugging him as tight as she could, it had been a very long time since she had seen a friend. Tarm returned the hug and whispered in her ear.

"I believe I should congratulate you, now that King Varne finally got what he deserved."

"Yes," Naka simply answered.

"I was there when it happened, I saw it all." His words were soft yet she could hear the joy in his voice, "He got exactly what he deserved, my dear, exactly what he deserved."

Naka closed her eyes, not allowing those memories to enter her mind again, before she let go of the hug and smiled.

"Good. So, tell me, what's going on Tarm, because these Dan'um won't tell me a thing."

Tarm laughed loudly, startling the others in the field.

"When do the Dan'um ever tell you anything? They're mysterious creatures, remember?" He made mocking gestures, trying to imitate the silver Dan'um on the stags. Naka chuckled, she had missed her only friend quite a lot during her hiding.

"Ah well, I'd be just as secretive if I knew all this forest hides," Tarm sighed, his eyes looking into the empty spaces between the trees. "But to answer your question, yes, I can tell you what's going on. Just get on the stags and I'll tell you on the road, time is not our friend today."

“He never seems to be,” Naka sighed deeply and Tarm smiled at her. They were about to get on the stags when one of the Dan’um stopped their stag besides Naka and pointed at Etaín.

“The Laretu cannot ride the stags, she’ll break them,” they told her in High Speech. So, Naka quickly rode to Etaín.

“They don’t want you riding the stags, they fear you’ll break them.”

“Thank the good Lord Merrtu, I completely agree with them.”

Naka laughed, “Isn’t Merrtu a Guardian of Battle? The one with the white horns and a breath so foul that it could kill a wolf or something?”

Etaín nodded fiercely. “Yeah, that’s the one. He is a Guardian of Battle, of the charge to be specific, and it was a *pack* of wolves. I liked his stories the best when I was a kid, painted my horns white and ran around the town all day. And I still thank him every time I don’t have to ride anything, like now.”

“Well, then you better put your running shoes on because I have a feeling that we won’t stop for you until we reach wherever we’re going.” Naka turned around, signaling the Dan’um that they were ready to go. The Dan’um nodded and shouted, the stags running into the forest right away. Etaín shot away only seconds later, slowly catching up to the stags with pride on her face. The wind blew through Naka’s hair and she closed her eyes, it was the best feeling known to any Ilunari when the air brushed their skin, the stronger the better.

An Ilunari couldn’t live without the feeling for too long, it was actually possible to die from a lack of wind for them. Perhaps it was because their home floated so high in the skies, or maybe it was because they were made from wind itself according to the old tales, nevertheless, it was true. Even in death they couldn’t miss it, so Ilunari always placed the bones on the high peaks of Oured, the Howling Isle, so that the wind could brush against them even in death. Years could pass and Naka could spend every day facing the wind, enjoying the strength of the air around her.

Eyes closed she let the moments go by, not caring where the stags would take her, knowing she couldn’t do anything about it anyway. That was until a loud crash suddenly echoed through the forest, wood breaking in a thundering explosion followed by a loud cheer from Etaín. Naka looked behind her and saw the Laretu shake off splinters from her head, behind her was a fallen tree that was now broken in two. Etaín gave Naka a proud look and she just smiled in return. Inza and Aergo cheered as well, seeing what had happened, encouraged by their cheers Etaín roared loudly and picked up her pace even more, slowly edging her way to the front of the group.

"They never cease to amaze me, those Laretu," Tarm chuckled at Naka.

"They keep surprising me as well, even after all those years. I like them better than the Arkul, all they do is fight everything, at least Laretu have some culture still," Naka sighed, already annoyed by the thought she would have to go to the Arkul again.

"Hmmm, true," Tarm agreed with her. "The Arkul are quite often nothing but a bloodthirsty army, trying to conquer the world. I'm glad the Laretu are nothing like their ancestors from the Red Mountains."

"Let's not speak of the Shadow Lands anymore, rather tell me where we are going."

Tarm nodded, knowing her reasons behind it.

"Very well then, not a word about it. As to where we're going, first, to Mir Mirhan, the Lady of Trees herself has summoned us all there. Probably because of the unique members of your travelling party," he said, nodding at Ara, Inza, Rynn and eventually at Naka as well.

"Great, so I'll have to face another angry High Immortal. As if I have not faced enough yet," Naka was seriously considering throwing herself off of the stag right here and now and just running into the forest. However, Tarm gave her a comforting smile.

"My old friend, not all High Immortals are angry with you. Mirhan knows that you did what had to be done and has forgiven you a long time ago. Her people have a little more, well, trouble with the forgiving part. Serielye too knows why you did it, she just chooses to hold a grudge against you."

Naka was confused and couldn't find words to express her thoughts.

"What do you mean, not all High Immortals are angry? They made their feelings very clear back then," she eventually blurted out.

"It's been a while though, hasn't it? Things have changed, and although it doesn't really show, the world has moved on." It was comforting for Naka to hear those words. She had been running, hiding and fighting for all those years, constantly looking over her shoulder, never seeing the world, only the danger that it held for her.

"Fair point. You said first, does that mean that Mir Mirhan isn't our final destination? What lies beyond there because I thought the Watched Seas started there?" Naka asked.

Tarm shook his head and pursed his lips, he always pursed his lips when he was about to reveal a secret of the world.

"The Watched Seas don't exactly start there. Beyond Mir Mirhan lays a strip of land, surrounded by wave where one cannot enter except when brought there by Kadhren creatures."

"No map shows that strip of land, no book speaks of it. I have never heard of anything that lays beyond Mir Mirhan other than the Watched Seas," Naka interrupted Tarm, but he just continued after she was done.

"On this strip of land there is a temple, made from starlight, woven around a foundation of white stone unfamiliar to this realm. It is in this temple that they live. They bear the title of Silver Eyed, their names abandoned when they were chosen. The Silver Eyed is a soul, banned from the Whispering Halls for all eternity, reincarnated if their current body dies. Nobody truly knows why the soul was banned, some say that in its first life it has done something unspeakably wrong, others say it was blessed because of its purity. All it ever says is that it must guide, we don't know who it must guide, we don't know where it guides us to. They can see across every realm, across every time, it is said to know everything, truly everything. And it has summoned you."

Naka was stunned. She had never heard a single word about this Silver Eyed but when Tarm spoke of them she could see his unease. Reincarnation was only possible when the Abariimm chose a mortal to become a High Immortal, no soul came back from the dead more than once, and that was rare on its own. Naka understood why this person hid itself from the world, the power to never die on its own was incredible, but then they also had the power to see into every realm, to see across every time, to know absolutely everything, if someone ever got control of them, they could rule every realm for all eternity. The idea sent shivers down her spine, she had seen much power in her life, but this was a power she could barely wrap her mind around, a power that could decide the fate of everything, including her own, and she was going straight for it.

Chapter 21
Inza

They arrived at Mir Mirhan right when the golden light of the setting sun cascaded over the horizon, bathing the forest in its warm light. The forest was much more open here, the air much lighter and quite a bit warmer. Sweet scents of nectar greeted them as they crossed the last river into Mir Mirhan, and Inza's breath was stolen. Before them lay a sight more beautiful than Inza could have ever dreamt of.

They stood on a slope covered with small streams and pools of silver water, ancient roots weaving around them, creating paths that lead up to the magnificent tree on top of the hill. The tree itself rose high above the surrounding trees, its trunk was big enough to house a small village, across its bark were several deep cuts from which the silver water sprang that flowed down the hill, feeding into streams that became rivers the further they got from the tree. Fireflies floated everywhere, ready to provide the light when the sun would finally sink behind the horizon, they swirled around the blue and purple flowers that stood high on their stems in the water.

Inza dismounted her stag and petted it for a moment, whispering thanks to it for carrying her. Step by step she slowly wandered onto the roots, feeling them come alive as her feet touched the crooked bark. When she took her feet off of the wood, she noticed that soft hairs of moss grew there, softly glowing in the coming darkness of twilight. As soon as Inza noticed that she started dancing and running across the roots, touching every bare piece of wood, leaving it green and glowing. It didn't take long for the fireflies to join her in her dance, twirling around her, as careless and free as Inza felt.

The feeling of home, of freedom and peace echoed through her body, filling her with laughter and joy as she ran further up the hill, searching for more bare roots to walk across. The others followed slowly, amazed by the serenity and beauty of this oasis of peace. Inza didn't stop for them, knowing they would follow after all and too busy enjoying the moment. She had almost reached the top of the hill when she heard a happy squeak from behind a thick root so she climbed up on it to glance at its other side. There was a large, green ball that looked like a huge and fat bumblebee that looked at her with its large, black, beaded eyes that sparked with joy. It softly glowed as it started buzzing around Inza, dancing with her and the fireflies, nudging her every few seconds to be petted, glowing brightly when Inza did. Together they danced further up the roots, all the way to the tree's trunk where the ground was covered with silver water and countless blue flowers that glowed when Inza moved past them.

"It is an honor to have you here, *Eobatr*," a soft voice danced in the wind. From behind the tree a woman as beautiful as the oasis stepped into sight. Her skin was like polished oak, covered in cuts just like the tree, and her dark hair fell down her shoulders in soft curls. Eyes of gold that faded into silver toward the edges of her irises, shimmered like gems in the light of the fireflies. She wore a dress made from flower petals and spun silver and gold, it barely touched the floor and her feet were visible whenever she moved. Inza's jaw dropped a little and the woman giggled softly, making Inza blush and close her mouth immediately. The woman laughed even harder when Inza dropped to her knee, bowing before the woman.

"You, you're Mirhan," Inza mumbled, and the woman raised her eyebrows. "The trees, they whisper your name, and, well, everything that lives here whispered your name when you appeared so I figured…"

"Don't worry my child, you were right. I am Mirhan indeed, but not many need to bow before me, especially not you," Mirhan said as she reached her hand out to Inza to help her up again. Her hand was soft and warm and left Inza's skin tingling where they had touched, Inza saw that moss had grown on Mirhan's skin where they had touched, miniscule blue flowers bloomed in it.

"I see you have already made a friend?" Mirhan asked as the green ball nudged at Inza's shoulder. Nerves and excitement had made her forget the words to answer so Inza simply nodded.

"They don't often show themselves to strangers, they are shy beings, but this one seems to be very fond of you, *Eobatr*." Mirhan's voice calmed Inza's nerves down, it was soft and warm and danced through the air like a song.

"I have never seen anything like it before, but it's very adorable and happy," Inza said, the green ball immediately glowing and squeaking happily as it started dancing around her again.

"Perhaps you should give it a name, it doesn't have one yet." Mirhan had barely spoken the words and the fuzzy ball hung before Inza's face, looking into her eyes, eagerly waiting for its name.

"I will name you Yaë," Inza said confidently. "It means happy in Kurr, my mother called me that when I was younger and now, I will call you that." Inza didn't even need to ask if it was happy with its new name because it started glowing brightly and squeaked with enthusiasm as it wiggled itself into Inza's arm until she held it like a cat.

"Good choice. I'm surprised you know some of your native tongue after it was forbidden at the start of the war," Mirhan said as her eyes looked past Inza to the rest of the group that had finally reached the top of the hill as well. Inza dashed to Kaell right away to show him Yaë.

"Kaell look! This is Yaë," she said as she carefully showed the green, fuzzy ball in her arms that was glowing softly and made a soft sound that resembled purring. Kaell smiled and gave Yaë some pets, which it seemed to enjoy quite a bit as it started purring louder.

"Tarm, welcome back. I hope your travels were full of stories to tell?" Mirhan greeted Tarm who slightly bowed to her and smiled.

"They always are, my lady," he responded. Mirhan already looked past him and met eyes with Raven, whom she greeted in High Speech before they spoke the common tongue again.

"Welcome, *Indimaronth*, I am aware that last we spoke I was unrightfully cruel and I need to give you my apologies for that. This time you are a guest and not a prisoner and you shall be treated as one, however I do wish to exchange words with you, Tarm and the sisters about some important matters.

"First, I will make sure the others have a place to sleep for the night for the sun is almost beyond the horizon and tomorrow will be a day filled with all kinds of activities."

Mirhan moved around the tree, humming a song Inza didn't know. Slowly the tree awakened, curling its roots into nest-like shapes, moss growing on the inside to provide what appeared to be a soft bed.

Inza curled up inside the mossy nest, Yaë against her chest, and found herself comfortable right away. She was used to sleeping like this and actually preferred it over a bed, the air here was just warm enough to not need a blanket although she did like the weight of it.

In the nests around her the others tried to settle themselves as well, except for those who joined Mirhan in a larger circle of roots, just out of hearing range for most people, but Inza was Kurr so she heard them quite clearly. Not that it was of any use, they spoke in High Speech so she didn't understand a word of it, probably the reason they used that tongue after all, Inza figured.

"Why don't we get one night with a proper bed, this isn't even inside," Ara complained, hissing to no one in particular it seemed, but Inza could obviously hear it and she knew her brother heard it as well. She looked over the edge of her nest, attempting to see Ara who was trying to sit comfortably in the middle of the nest. It took her a little while but finally she did manage to be satisfied and closed her eyes, she completely stopped moving right away. Inza couldn't see her breathing nor did she hear it anymore, she observed Ara for a while, but it was like looking at a statue so she sank back into her nest, curling around Yaë. Sleep didn't come quickly because she wasn't tired at all so she lay awake, listening to the forest around her. Much of it she couldn't understand but she liked the calming voices, the slow, swaying of the trees and the soft singing of the fireflies made for a melody that soothed her into sleep after all.

It wasn't until something warm tickled her face that she awoke. Her sleep had been dreamless but deep so she stretched her stiff muscles and yawned loudly, not realising the others were still asleep. Yaë nudged at her face, tickling her until she petted it to which it purred in response. Peeking over the nest she saw Kaell was still asleep, he didn't sleep that much so she decided to let him sleep, and the others were fast asleep as well. Time to explore, Inza figured.

Dawn had just passed and the hill bathed in light and life. There were many more flowers than last night, the rainbows of color greeting the sun, butterflies, squirrels, rabbits, deer and many more animals now wandered the surrounding areas, carefully drinking from the pools and grazing on the grass. Further down Inza saw Mirhan moving gracefully across the roots, leaving behind a trail of moss and flowers, butterflies and bees dancing around her head on which she wore a crown of flowers and moss. She wore a dress made from hundreds of small, pink flowers woven together with silver leaves and vines. Inza quickly went down the roots to greet her and when she did Mirhan smiled wide.

"Good morning, *Eobatr*. Did you sleep well?" she asked her to which Inza nodded in response.

"I'm glad to hear that. Today will be a big day for you and your brother. I was going to wait until your brother was awake but I heard he needs his sleep so why don't we start already?"

"Start with what?" Inza wasn't sure what she was talking about.

Mirhan took Inza's hand. "You came here to learn about your gifts, didn't you? Well it's about time you did." Inza's eyes went wide, she enjoyed this place so much that she had forgotten why she had come here. There was absolutely no attempt to hide her excitement.

"Will you teach me how to shift into anything I want? Can you teach me how to control my healing? I mean, of course I can heal some things but I mainly just hope for the best. Oh, and can you teach me how to talk to all the trees and animals?"

Mirhan laughed aloud, a deep, warm, welcome sound. "Yes, I can teach you all of that, however, I can teach you so much more. You are a Lifeheart, your powers extend much further than the ones you know already. Come, I will show you." Mirhan led Inza to a patch of grass near the bottom of the hill and handed her a seed. Inza took it and gave Mirhan a questioning look. "Plant it and I will teach you how to grow it," she said. So Inza carefully dug a hole and put the seed in and covered it with soil again.

"Now, try to find the seed. Everything has a unique energy, it is possible to find that energy and connect to it. After that you can shape the energy, give it some of your own, guide it and help it grow," Mirhan said as she knelt beside Inza, who was staring at the patch of soil. Inza closed her eyes and tried to focus, she could hear the trees and the grass, the birds and the flowers. It didn't take her long to find the seed amongst all of them, she actually felt its energy, small but eager to grow.

"I found the seed, what do I do now?" she asked the High Immortal.

"Now you imagine your own energy flowing into the seed, as if you are watering it. You don't need to worry about losing your energy for you are a Lifeheart, you create pure energy in your essence, making you an undepletable source. Just imagine your energy raining down on it so it can grow roots and branches and leaves," Mirhan answered.

As soon as Inza imagined this she opened her eyes, seeing the small stem peek above the soil, grow its first leaves and quickly reaching for the sun and skies, roots wiggled beneath their feet. In a matter of seconds, the seed had become a tree, its branches filled with leaves and blossoms, and the bees were already buzzing to collect its sweet nectar. Inza was speechless, the tree looked as if it had been there for decades and she couldn't believe she had just grown an entire tree with her powers.

"That is so epic," was all she could say about it and Mirhan giggled.

"I know, and this is only the beginning. I must say that it is better to let things grow in their own time, it is more natural. It won't hurt if things grow through your power but it might take the world time to get used to a sudden change if you ever happen to do this on a larger scale."

Inza made a mental note of the words, still filled with excitement and amazed by the idea that she could do this on a larger scale. This is also a way to heal wounds, simply imagine your energy flowing into the person and their body will guide the healing.

"Come," Mirhan continued, "your brother is awake and I think it is about time that he got his Mark, don't you?"

Inza's eyes went even wider in surprise, "Kaell is getting his Mark today? And how do you know he is awake?" she fired the questions at Mirhan, who laughed again, amused by the eagerness of Inza.

"Oh *Eobatr*, Kaell is getting a Mark today, and a very special one too. Your Kelsul have forgotten much, too much. I suppose that makes sense when you have a short lifespan and don't write things down, then it is just a matter of time before things are forgotten. How do I know that he is awake? I am the forest, I am life. Every tree, every flower, every blade of grass is connected to me, my siblings and our father, *Sulvimaronth*. So, we know everything that happens near them, especially in these woods." Mirhan gestured at everything around them.

Inza had noticed how the plants and animals danced to the melody of the High Immortal's voice but thought she had just imagined it. Mirhan stopped all of the sudden, twirling around with grace and a big smile on her face.

"Before we go and get your brother, we should make sure you look your absolute best for the ceremony, since you will be a big part of it." Mirhan was right, Inza did look a bit messy with her long hair all tangled and frizzy and her dress scrunched up.

"I'm a big part of the ceremony?" Her voice became smaller than she wanted, Kaell deserved this ceremony, he had been teased all his life for being Markless at home, as if he could do anything about it.

"Oh yes, my child, but worry not, it will be exactly as it should be. But first, pick a flower you like, any flower."

Inza looked around, searching for a flower she liked more than the others. Her eyes fell on a lily-like flower, white, speckled with gold as if someone had splattered paint on it with great care, and she pointed at it.

"I really like that one," she said.

"Oh, what an excellent choice. Okay, close your eyes for a moment and try not to move too much."

Inza closed her eyes and Mirhan started humming a song, but Inza couldn't help but look anyway. Petals of white and gold appeared over the dress she was wearing, the old one slowly falling away as the petals formed a new dress. Even her hair untangled and braided itself into an intricate braid in which flowers wove themselves. She admired the new dress, it didn't reach past her knees and flowed beautifully whenever Inza spun around. It didn't feel like it was made from flowers, it felt more like silk but much, much softer. There was a part missing in the side where her skin showed.

When she looked back at Mirhan the High Immortal was holding a band of woven gold, laid with white gems that sparkled in the sunlight, it looked quite similar to Inza's necklace. She placed it onto Inza's head as if she were crowning her, it was a perfect fit and felt slightly warm.

"Now you're ready, let's get your brother so we can do the ceremony with a little more privacy. Unless you want to involve the entire group but I doubt that. Tarm will be there no doubt, they never miss an opportunity to witness something important like this," Mirhan said as she took Inza's hand again and lead her up the path of roots again, the roots put themselves in such manner that they formed a direct line up the hill instead of crawling wherever they grew.

When they reached the nests Kaell was indeed awake, the others were still sleeping except for Raven who was nowhere to be found. Inza ran to Kaell right away.

"Kaell, you're getting a Mark today! Mirhan said that she is going to give you a Mark right now! Today is the day we finally prove the Kelsul wrong!" Inza was whispering so the others wouldn't wake but she knew her brother would hear her loud and clear.

Kaell opened and closed his mouth a few times, not being able to speak a word before his eyes filled with happy tears. Inza hugged him tightly, knowing how much it meant to him. Mirhan gestured to follow after they let go of each other, leading them down the other side of the hill where a small waterfall cascaded into a larger pool. Inza didn't see Tarm but she did see a woman, dressed in a white, silken dress, who bathed her feet in the silver waters.

"Didn't you say Tarm was going to be here?" Inza asked Mirhan quietly. Mirhan simply laughed and nodded at the woman. "Tarm is here, except right now, Tarm is called Tess." Inza didn't understand and her confusion showed in her eyes.

"Tarm and Tess are the same person, sometimes they are a man and call themselves Tarm, other times they are a woman and call themselves Tess. They were born that way, it's nothing rare, just often misunderstood." Mirhan paused for a moment as she stopped to enjoy the sunlight on her face before she continued, "When they first came here on their travels, I felt sorry for them, struggling to keep up their appearance with their current gender. So, I gifted them the ability of shifting, or well, a form of it. Now they can shift their appearance into the one that matches their gender at every moment, needing nothing but a few moments to change clothes." Mirhan kissed Tess on the cheek when they reached the pool and walked into the shallow waters. Inza too, walked up to Tess to kiss her on the cheek.

"You look beautiful, Tess," she said, making Tess's cheeks flash red, before she too walked into the water with Kaell.

"Kaell, please take your shirt off," Mirhan said and waited for Kaell to do so before she hummed the same song as when Inza got the dress she wore now. The same white and gold petals appeared on Kaell's legs and waist, giving him pants of the same colors as Inza's dress. He too received a woven band of gold with white gems from Mirhan to crown his brown curls.

"The Mark you are about to receive is a very rare Mark. One that hasn't been seen in thousands of years," Mirhan started, softly moving her hands to which the water seemed to respond, slowly flowing upward around both Kaell's and Inza's body. "It is a Mark of a Bond, meaning you are Bonded, just in a very unique way. You did forge it that night in the forest, your Kelsul were simply too blind to see what it connected to. This bond you made was not with an animal, it was with your sister." Kaell and Inza looked at each other, surprise in both their eyes, not knowing that it was possible.

"This Mark will do more than show the Bond, it will complete it. Meaning your bodies will share the wounds you suffer, share death when it comes, but you also share your healing and your strongest emotions. Once the Bond is made it cannot be broken, not even in death or beyond it." The water started burning into Inza's skin on her side and she could see the same thing happening on Kaell's chest. She refused to cry, no matter how much it hurt, this was the moment Kaell had been dreaming of all his life and there was no way she would ruin it.

"You will be able to speak through your thoughts no matter the distance between you, if you choose to. Kaell you will notice your senses will be heightened and your body stronger, you will be faster and stronger than you were before and will be able to hear the whispers of the world around you if you care to listen, animals will come to your aid if you ask them to.

"Inza you have already unlocked most of your powers so you won't notice much of a shift. However, you won't turn nature violent anymore whenever you experience fear in any way," Mirhan continued.

Inza saw Kaell fidget with his hands and clench his jaw, his eyes locked on the water. What did Mirhan mean that she wouldn't turn nature violent anymore? She truly didn't know what the High Immortal meant, nature had always been exceptionally kind to her.

The burning feeling stopped and Inza looked down to see a silver Mark on her side, two identical shapes woven into each other forming a circle in the middle. Kaell had the same Mark on his chest, right above his heart. Inza was filled with an extreme gratitude and joy, her eyes tearing up as well, blurring her sight. She was certain that it came from Kaell, remembering Mirhan's words.

"The Bond is complete. You are no longer Markless, Kaell, you are Bonded now," Mirhan finished and smiled lovingly and Tess cheered. Inza hugged Kaell tightly and he returned the hug with equal passion before he suddenly let go and started sniffing the air like a wolf looking for prey.

"What are you doing?" Inza giggled, he looked quite ridiculous sniffing harder and harder.

"The air is so sweet, I can smell every flower, I can… I can hear them." He paused, listening to the world around him. Inza imagined it was quite confusing to suddenly hear the world, she was born with that ability and had gotten used to the constant noise but to her brother it was completely new.

"You heard this all along?" Kaell asked Inza, his mind elsewhere.

Mirhan moved out of the water. "Breakfast will be served in a few moments on the hill, I myself am quite hungry," she said, Tess joining her as she walked away, leaving them alone in the pond.

"Kaell?" Inza asked carefully, knowing that her brother felt her nerves. His eyes locked with hers, already knowing the question that was going to follow.

"What did she mean?" There was no need to speak every word, even less than before the Bond. Kaell took Inza's hands in his own and Inza could feel him searching for words, unaware that his thoughts lay bare to her.

"Inza, it… It was never your fault. I just wanted to protect you from… them." His words diminished into whispers, undetectable to anyone else.

"Protect me from what, Kaell? Myself?" Fear that her suspicions were true rose in her.

"From guilt, from those who didn't understand that you had no choice."

Fear nearly choked her. "Did I hurt people?" Kaell shook his head, but Inza felt a different answer through his mind but she couldn't bear to confront him.

"Did I kill…" she began but was immediately cut off by Kaell.

"No. Nobody died because of your curse. Always remember that, none of this was ever your doing or responsibility. It's gone now and we're not home anymore so there is no reason for us to worry about any of this."

Inza felt his surge of relief when he said that they weren't home anymore while she missed home from time to time.

"I suppose you're right," Inza sighed, even though she was angry she thought it better to leave it for another time. She understood why he hadn't told her, though she disagreed. A lot of people could have been spared the trouble she caused by telling her and having a house built somewhere away from Rindun. But then again, it would have made her feel terrible to know she was a danger to others. "We should get to the top of the hill, I'm actually quite hungry now that I think of it."

Kaell laughed awkwardly, trying to hide his feelings without success. "Yeah, me too. I love you *Menare*," he said as he hugged her gently.

The breakfast was a collection of colorful fruits that tasted like pure sunlight, breads filled with spices and nuts coated with honey. There was water, sweet summer wine that tasted like strawberries and honey, and nectar that tasted like it came right from a flower.

Afterward, Mirhan took Inza down the roots again and made her forget the serious conversation she had with her brother. She learned how to use her healing on both the earth and any living creatures, she learned how to sing the plants around her to move and grow as she desired. Mirhan also taught her to shift into some new forms and how to teach herself how to change into a new form. They didn't go back until the cloak of night had driven the sun past the horizon and the fireflies clouded the hill like a mist of stars. When they had almost reached the top Mirhan stopped Inza.

"My child, I have taught you much today and I will teach you more tomorrow before you leave, but I must warn you. You have great power, greater than most, however this power also comes with great risk. Your body can only take so much because you are still a mortal. I must be honest and tell you that I don't know where your limits are and I think you will never use power of that extent to ever find them, but I did feel the need to warn you. Healing, shifting or any other form of magic you possess might be your end if you use them carelessly so please take great care, *Eobatr*, I'd hate to see you fall prey to what might be the thing to save this world." Mirhan's words echoed deep within her soul and she felt a sudden fear. This great of a power, she wasn't sure she was ready.

Chapter 22
Rynn

Morning had come too soon for Rynn. For the first time since he met Ara, he had dreamed again. He couldn't remember much of it, mainly just a feeling of freedom as if he had been released in a way. Around him the others were already readying themselves for their departure. Last night, Ara had urged the importance of their trip since most had forgotten their goals, but not Ara. She had remembered that it was urgent that the Heart of Light would be retrieved so the Throne of Light could be restored and perhaps then could they bring an end to the war of Shattered Light. There had been an awkward silence that was only broken when Mirhan suggested that they would leave the next morning. So, they would. Ara was pacing around the tree but came to Rynn as soon as she saw he was awake.

"Good morning Rynn, how do you feel today?" Her tone was different, more careful and warm. Rynn felt all fuzzy inside as she looked him deep in the eyes, trying to find the answer there.

"I, euhm, I feel good, thank you," he muttered. "How do you feel today? Are you ready to get the key to the Vault?"

"Good, I'm glad you're feeling good. I am always ready, so I suggest you are as well. Tess has told me we will arrive at our destination this afternoon if we leave soon, so I suggest that Mirhan hurries with her lessons or that the Kurr stay behind. They don't seem to understand the importance yet, but they will." Ara walked down the roots, toward Mirhan and Inza to make sure they left on time when Rynn felt the familiar mists of Yira behind him.

"Hey," she said. "My sisters and I won't come with you today. We have some pressing matters we need to attend to. So, I came to see if you were okay and to say goodbye." Yira too spoke with more care and warmth, and he could feel her mists wrap around his mind.

"I'm sure you'll have important matters as a High Immortal, but don't worry about us, we'll be fine. We will simply get the Heart and open the Vault and from there Ara knows what she is doing. I just hope we can bring back her people as well, then she won't be so lonely anymore." Rynn paused a moment before he continued. "Yira, could you please stop trying to enter my mind? I can take care of myself, you don't have to worry about me so much." He had barely said the words as the mists withdrew without hesitation.

"Very well," Yira sighed. "But I will keep an eye on you nevertheless, Rynn Firevein."

Rynn had never heard that title before, but he liked the sound of it.

"Did you just make up that title? Because I control more than just fire, you know?" he asked her.

"It's what they call you at the Academy nowadays, you are a living legend there. Although some aren't as fond of you and tend to blame you for the destruction at the Academy. Speaking of your powers, the person you are visiting, the Silver Eyed, can teach you how to use your full potential, so I'm happy for you," Yira said, turning away from him. "I'm glad you seem more like your own now. Goodbye for now, Rynn," she whispered before she descended the hill toward her sisters.

Teach him to use his full potential, Rynn was even more excited to see this Silver Eyed than he was before. Ever since Arga he hadn't been able to summon anything but fire. He had tried, secretly at night, when everyone else was asleep. He had felt so useless during their escape from Arga, except for when he absorbed the fire outside of the gates. It could just have been so much easier for them had he been able to use his magic. Just the thought of it made his veins glow with fire until a cold hand pressed against his shoulder, Ara.

"There is no need for your fire here, mage. The stags are ready to leave so let's go, we have no time to waste." The warmth had faded from her voice again, perhaps she was disappointed to see that Rynn still held little control of his magic. He admired Ara quite a bit for always containing her emotions and powers. Nuans were gifted with a large array of powers and never in any of the stories Rynn had read, did one of them lose control of their powers, not once. Perhaps she would teach him about it when they had ended the war and left it all behind. The stags were indeed waiting on them, the rest of the group already mounted and Etaín was jogging in place, ready to run along with the stags.

Riding the stags was quite a pleasant experience, they ran with such finesse that one could barely feel that they were travelling at such great speed. It didn't take long before they could smell the salt in the air. Kaell and Inza were the first to hear the waves and got excited. Inza decided to shift into a hawk and now flew high above them. Her brother explained that she could see the sea from there, that she had never seen it before in her life and that she hadn't shifted since they left their own forests.

Rynn couldn't help but look up every once in a while, he had never seen a shifter before he met Inza, he had only read about them in the books of the Academy and heard the stories in his youth. Moments later Rynn could hear the waves as well, he could even spot the waters through the trees every now and then.

The Dan'um told them that they were about to cross the Veil but when they left the last tree behind all that lay in front of them were beaches with golden sands on which turquoise waves crashed down, leaving behind all kinds of treasures from the deeper seas. There were shells as big as Rynn's hand, with all kinds of pearlescent colors. None of the stags seemed to care as they got closer and closer to the waters and Inza swooped down to shift back and sit on the back of her mount again.

Rynn noticed that everyone except the Dan'um and Tess became uneasy as they galloped toward the turquoise depths. The first stag reached the waves, its hooves hitting the water, and the stag and its rider vanished completely. It was as if they had never actually been there, not a single trace of it left, not even the faintest hint of magic hung in the air. One by one the others disappeared and when Rynn did, he could barely believe his eyes. They rode across a bridge of rock and wood woven together. Plants grew in the curves and cracks, trees with dry, weathered barks rose above them, casting thin shadows on their heads. A clear path lay ahead of them, at the end lay a bay, in the middle a large temple-like building surrounded by pale trees and white grass. The temple itself was built from a stone that glowed like starlight, crystal patterns woven into the sides of the towering walls. It was beautiful unlike anything Rynn had ever seen. Arms of stone and wood wrapped around it, protecting the bay from the roughness of the seas around them, forming a shape that looked like a crescent moon with tall pillars closing the circle.

"Welcome, to the Silver Temple," said Tess with a big smile on her face. They seemed exceptionally excited to be here and, in all honesty, Rynn understood it completely.

The stags lead them all the way to a bridge that connected the island with the temple in the middle. Lead by the Dan'um, they crossed the bridge, passing through the massive doors of spun silver and crystal. Inside, there was a large open room with a floor of glass, allowing the light to dive deep into the ocean. There weren't many decorations, which allowed their voices to echo through the room, even the sound of wind and waves echoed with their voices, almost as if they spoke to them and all they had to do was listen. Light fell down from the ceiling in wide beams, hitting the dust and salt in the air to create a mist of silver clouds above them.

"Welcome, to all of you." It was as if a thousand voices spoke in perfect harmony, ancient and wise. Eyes of silver light pierced Rynn's soul as he looked up, he had never felt this exposed in his life and he knew that those eyes knew everything there was to know about him. The eyes belonged to a face that glistened with silver light, framed by hair that was nearly white but still held hints of green when it caught the light. They wore a robe of what appeared to be liquid starlight, flowing gently with their every movement. Where their skin showed, one could see white markings that were barely distinguishable in the silver glow. Overall the man was tall and muscular with broad shoulders and arms like logs, the body of a smith, not at all what Rynn expected to see. He had expected to see another scrawny man, perhaps lean at best. That was what he was used to seeing when it was someone involved with magic, almost everyone at the Academy looked like that.

"You didn't expect this body. Well you are not alone; the others seem to agree with you. Even you, Wanderer, seem surprised." The Silver Eyed nodded at Tess, who just returned a gesture to admit they were right. Ara stepped forward, ready to speak but the Silver Eyed stopped her before she could begin.

"I know why you're here, Ara-Ashin. In fact, I know why each of you is here so please, do not attempt to hide your intentions, your every move has been clear to me even before you were born. And yes, I have everything you are looking for. Follow me, then I will take you to what most of you seek."

He led them up a set of stairs, twisting around a tower until they reached a room, empty except for a single, white gem that floated in the middle of the room. It shone with such force one had to shield their eyes to avoid going blind. Ara however, looked straight at it, entranced by its brightness.

"It feels… familiar," she whispered.

"It has been near your kin for many ages, you were tasked to protect it with your lives, and you did. You protected it until there were no lives left, so it came here. This will open the Vault in Xisq for you." He carefully took it out of the air and placed it in a box of white metal, the room going dark when the lid closed. The box was handed to Ara and tears filled her eyes but the Silver Eyed had already turned himself to Rynn.

"Your magic is powerful and will decide the fate of many, so choose wisely how you use it," he said to Rynn as he pressed his silver hand against Rynn's chest, sending a surge through Rynn's veins that made them glow, not red like fire but with a more bright and pure light.

"Do not fear the fire within you, fear feeds it, makes you lose control. But remember that fire needs fuel to burn, so if you choose to work with that energy, make sure there is enough for you to survive. However, you can draw from this fire, turn it into something else. This way it doesn't need to feed on something and you can use it without the same dangers." He paused for a moment, allowing the words to sink into Rynn's mind. "Go downstairs, on the other side of the bridge there will be a woman waiting for you, her name is Diranthaín, she will spar with you, teach you how to use your energy correctly."

Rynn didn't need to hear those words again, he felt his magic again, deep in his heart, deep within the fire. He almost ran down the stairs, nearly tripping over his own feet more than once. With heavy breaths he ran across the bridge, already seeing the woman standing on the other side of it.

She was Arkul, Rynn had seen them in a number of books in the Academy. They were a bloodthirsty warrior people from the Red Mountains that lay deep in the Shadow Lands. Her eyes were silver like the Dan'um that had brought them here but everything else seemed to be like the books. A thundercloud grey skin, crossed with scars, four massive horns with white hair falling down from between them. At the end of her spine grew a large, bony tail that softly swept across the ground as she moved. She was almost as tall as Etaín and slightly resembled her as well. Arkul were said to be the ancestors of the Laretu, Laretu splitting off after some old war when Nuana and Megana had just settled in Allaea.

"Hi, I Diranthaín. You Rynn?" she said, slapping her chest with her fist as a way of greeting. Her accent was heavy and Rynn had trouble understanding it properly so he simply smiled and nodded. Diranthaín smiled as well and gestured Rynn to follow her to a more open spot a little further on the island.

"Sorry for speech, I know not language," she said to Rynn, smiling brightly. Her voice was kind and her face didn't bear any harm in it as far as he could see so he just smiled back and nodded to make her feel a little less uneasy about the language barrier.

"Do same," she said, forming a ball of fire between her hands. It came easily to Rynn, he couldn't stop the fire from filling his veins and eyes and he hesitated with his fire, afraid to harm anybody, she noticed his fear and stopped him.

"No fear. Magic do no harm in circle." She pointed at the engravings in the ground around them. Rynn recognized the symbols, it was a more advanced version of the training circle they used at the Academy. It used to contain any magic used inside it and if magic was fatal to someone it simply teleported the person outside, preventing them from death but leaving some serious injuries nevertheless. Rynn nodded and began forming the fire with new found confidence.

"Now change." She nodded at the fire in her hands and Rynn saw the fire in her hands changing into an orb of pure energy. He focused, at the Academy they had taught him basic energy transformation but he had never bothered to take any advanced classes in it, a decision he regretted dearly now. The key was to strip any specifications from the energy, leaving nothing but its essence behind. After that, energy could be shaped into anything, although some things had a higher energy level than others, causing the volume of the creation to differ according to how much energy you use.

It took him a few tries but Diranthaín was patient and started over every time he did, showing it to him in slower steps every time. She was extremely kind and gentle with her teachings even though she didn't use that many words. Eventually he got it, turning the fire into the same ball of pure energy that Diranthaín held between her hands.

"Now shape," she urged him, shaping her own energy into a ball of ice. "Pure can become everything, you choose." She changed the ball back into pure and into a series of other energies within a matter of moments. Lightning, air, water and many others as well before she turned it into a butterfly made from fire that fluttered happily toward the sun until they couldn't see it anymore. Rynn tried it for himself, feeling his own magic grow stronger besides the fire, it was good to feel something else course through his veins after the fire.

"Can you change everything into energy?" Rynn asked. He knew that the energy inside of him could be directed as he liked, could be turned into all kinds of magic without transmutation. It just became.

"Everything have energy, everything can transmute. Just not everything into everything. Elemental transmute into elemental, earthly into earthly, organic into organic, light into dark. Those are cores of magic. All cores can become their own pure, all pure can be stored in object, like ring, to use later.

"Maybe we spar? You have asked enough questions. Experience best lesson."

Rynn never was a fan of sparring with magic, but this training had given him a little confidence so why not?

"Sure, I'll spar with you. Rules?" Rynn asked, a large grin on his face.

"Don't lose!" Diranthaín shouted before she shifted the ground underneath Rynn, making him fall on his back.

"Okay, okay, then prepare to break the rules, Arkul," Rynn laughed, getting a thundering laugh in response. The circle around them would prevent either of them from dying from magic as long as they stayed inside of it.

Diranthaín threw a ball of fire at Rynn but he jumped aside before it hit him, sending a wind of frost back at her. She was fast and blocked it with a ward before returning fire with a whip made from lightning. And so, they fought, magic against magic. Rynn was surprised by the Arkul's strength and skill in magic, they weren't exactly known to possess any powers, but Diranthaín completely broke that stereotype, throwing spell after spell at him, while he returned the favor.

Rynn had powerful magic, but her physical strength and endurance managed to keep her up and going, making the fight quite a challenge for Rynn. He decided to use his fire after all, trusting in his ability to transform the energy when it became too much for him, sending a wave of flames toward Diranthaín. She just smiled and took control of the flames, shaping them as they flew through the air, turning them into a flaming fox that had a life of his own, absolutely baffling Rynn. He realized she had done the same with the butterfly earlier, although he had thought that she controlled the butterfly. This fox had as much as a life of its own as Rynn did. He lowered his hands as a sign of a break, breathing heavily as he admired the fox.

"She can weave temporary life into anything she desires." It was the Silver Eyed. He stood at the edge of the circle, the others beside him. Apparently, they had been watching their fight, Rynn hadn't seen anything beside his opponent until now. Only now did he notice the ground beneath their feet, scorched, frozen, shifted and crumbled everywhere as a result of their magic.

"How long is temporary?" Rynn's curiosity took over.

"Depends on the size of the creation. The bigger it is, the shorter she can keep it alive. This fox can live for roughly a day, the butterfly from earlier might live weeks unless she chooses to undo her creation." Diranthaín smiled with pride and nodded at Etaín when she saw her. Etaín's jaw dropped open wide and she couldn't take her eyes off of the Arkul. Diranthaín waved her hand at the fox and it fell apart in soft flames that quickly died on the stone.

"Diranthaín, please lead our guests to their chambers, make sure they have something to eat and have everything else they might need. Afterward come see me, we have some business to attend to before night falls," the Silver Eyed said before he walked back toward the temple.

The sunset had already begun and the idea of food in his belly made Rynn very happy after all this sparring. On the way to their chambers he walked aside Ara and talked about how happy he was that he could use all of his magic again but Ara didn't respond, she didn't seem fully there, her mind wandering another realm while her body remained here.

Their chambers weren't too far away, there were a handful of houses dotted between the pale trees and on a small field there was an array of food, from fruits to meats to pastries. As they were stuffing their bellies with food, they were silent. Rynn didn't know what the others had done with the Silver Eyed but he could imagine why they were silent, if he could awaken Rynn's magic, who knew what he helped the others with. Inza showed Kaell and Aergo her newly learned tricks, growing small flowers whenever she touched the ground. Etaín was trying to have a conversation with Diranthaín, but the language barrier seemed to be quite a problem for both of them. Raven had disappeared into one of the houses after she had taken a few bites of food. Rynn had only just eaten a few things when Ara stood up and went to their house, telling Rynn to follow her with her mind.

"I need to meditate, things are now set in motion. You can sleep now, I will wake you when I need you," she said before she sat down in the middle of the room and closed her eyes. Rynn took a few moments to fall asleep, the feeling of his magic still coursing through his veins quite vigorously.

His sleep didn't last long. Ara woke him in the darkest part of the night. *'Follow me, quickly,'* she echoed through his mind. His body seemed to act on its own as he gave his mind to her. He trusted her, she had a higher calling and he was glad he could help her achieve it. Outside, the world was quiet, only the stars and a red sliver of the moon in the sky, the scent of food still hung in the air.

"Are you certain of this?" It was Aergo, he appeared beside them as if he stepped out of the darkness itself. He wore a necklace Rynn hadn't seen on him before, a bone tooth on which small hairs of moss glowed in the night.

"Yes, he can take us there," Ara said as she nodded at Rynn. "All we need is to leave a message to that wretched Raven." Rynn felt Ara pull the fire into his veins.

"Why do we need to leave a message? We can just leave and do what must be done," Aergo argued in harsh whispers.

"This *must* be done, Blackfang. You haven't seen the shadows that cloud her mind, she is a child of darkness itself." Ara turned to Rynn. "Burn the island. Burn it all. Let them know what happens to those who oppose the Light."

"Why?" Rynn managed to ask as the fire burned in his veins, Ara pulled every single bit of it out of his heart.

"You saw her in Arga, you saw the darkness she holds within. She hates me deeply, and she will do anything within her power to kill me, to kill Light itself if she must. These others have placed their trust in that bitch because she saved them once, but I see right through her. I hope I do not need to remind you of what the darkness has done to those who follow the Light."

Her words stung like hot knives, she wouldn't lie, he trusted her. He felt her rampaging through his mind, uncovering the memories of the day when his mother died, of her cold corpse in the streets, left to rot. He remembered how King Egìl had told them that shadows had come and murdered sixty-one humans that followed the Light. His fire raged through his veins as he remembered it all, he would show Raven, that abomination of darkness, that he was not to be messed with, that this time the light would prevail.

"Now burn it all, Rynn. Show them what happens when they cross me." Her voice echoed through his mind and the memory burned in his eyes. Anger overtook him, the fire flowing from his veins like red rivers of death, Ara pulling out more of his power. Tears fell to the ground, hot enough to burn the stone. And he screamed. He screamed with agony and grief. He had travelled with a servant of darkness, a servant that might have murdered his mother, a servant that he had sought for so long, to deliver to it the pain that he had felt for all those years. He let go of every bit of fire that he could until he felt his skin burn to feed his magic.

"Well done, my dear Rynn. Save some magic because we need to leave this place, teleport us to Xisq, use Aergo's mind to find the place. After that, we will save this world from the darkness," Ara whispered, her lips touching his ear as she spoke to him. Aergo and Ara took his hands and he found the place in Aergo's mind but before he teleported, he took a good look at the raging flames around them and found pride and a little satisfaction.

Serves them right, he thought, and they disappeared.

Chapter 23
Kaell

Kaell's coughs echoed through the temple as the smoke refused to leave his lungs. He could still feel the heat upon his skin and saw the fire burn before his eyes even though the temple was completely serene, oblivious to the fire that raged outside. They had woken to Rynn's screaming and the fire that followed shortly after. Etaín had already been busy breaking down the door of Raven's building, burning her flesh and skin every time she touched the hot metal door.

Inza was attempting to heal the burns, but Kaell felt her guilt rising as the burn slowly became a massive scar that twisted and turned across Etaín's arm and side, even Yaë brushed against the flesh in an attempt to help. Kaell thanked every High Immortal he could think of that they escaped the burning hell and found safety within the temple. The Silver Eyed had been waiting for them on the bridge, telling them to go inside.

Raven was hissing words at the Silver Eyed in High Speech, the man responding in common tongue, saying it was not their right to change the events, no matter how disastrous they were going to be. Kaell agreed with Raven's anger but also suspected that the Silver Eyed spoke the truth, to know everything meant one could shape the entire world to their desires so he figured that the High Immortals had denied them the ability to interfere, Kaell would have done the same if he was a High Immortal. Raven only held her tongue when they heard a loud crashing, the bridge had been engulfed by flames and broke down, fragments falling down into the calm seas below.

"Where is Aergo?" Kaell asked the Silver Eyed, Kaell wouldn't believe that he would leave freely with Ara and Rynn, that he would approve of this destruction.

"He probably just left because he has the key now, he just wants to open that Vault, get its riches. Queen Serielye saw it right away, we should have listened to her," Etaín said through her teeth as Inza was still trying to heal the burned flesh.

"Aergo left because he needed to protect his people," the Silver Eyed said. "His people would refuse Ara-Ashin access if Aergo wasn't there, and if you look outside you see what would have happened to his people, had they refused her. It will settle your mind to know he wanted to warn you, but the Nuan did not allow it. She thinks all of you serve the Darkness." Their words were calm and patient, almost as if they were waiting for something else.

"Follow me, the time is here," the Silver Eyed whispered.

They led them down a flight of stairs, descending far below the surface of the sea. Water swirled around them as they walked through halls of crystal, looking into the calm, turquoise depths. At the end of the last hall there was a wall of perfectly smooth stone, lines of silver and blue ran through it, pulsating with life. Perfect circles and straight lines formed an intricate pattern within the grey stone. The Silver Eyed stood before it, the silver and blue liquid reaching out to their hand, frantically trying to connect with them. When it did, a wave went through the walls, through the lines, the liquid crawling out of its ridges and flowing toward the hand where they pooled and shivered until all of it had collected itself there and then it stopped moving. What remained was a perfectly smooth mirror, reflecting the Silver Eyed and themselves behind him.

"Behind this mirror lays a secret kept even better than my existence." their words were soft yet the echoes made sure they resonated deep within their bones. "Behind this mirror lays another vault. It contains artifacts of immense power, things that are more dangerous and powerful than anything in Xisq. Before you reach that vault there is a challenge that every mortal who wishes to enter must face, and so you must face this as well. However, you are not mere mortals so you should be able to succeed.

"Before you ask, I do not know this outcome for certain, futures can change and I do not know which one this will become. Nevertheless, when you enter the vault you must collect two items for me, do not take anything else once you have entered the vault. Those artifacts are there for a reason and they are there to stay until they are needed. What I need you to collect is an egg, found on top of the monolith, and a seed, found in the crystal tree. You will know when you see it. Under no circumstances let any form of magic touch the egg, nor place the seed in anyone else's hands but the shifter's, magic is fine near the tree, just not near the egg, it will kill you if magic touches the egg. Now go through and hurry, these flames do not wait."

"Why is it that I get the feeling you're not coming?" Raven asked, clearly done with the Silver Eyed.

"I cannot move through the mirror, besides it being solid to me it would mean the portal would close behind me, never to open again since the door can only be opened from the outside. Meaning that I would have to patiently await death so I will gain a new form." Though the Silver Eyed remained calm and their words soft, somewhere deep inside Kaell it caused fear, this person already knew everything and couldn't die, so why would they care about anything in this realm? Raven rolled her eyes and poked the mirror with her spear, it tapped against the surface but didn't go through.

"You know why it cannot enter this vault," the Silver Eye said, to which Raven responded by rolling her eyes again and carefully handing over Nárymm to the Silver Eyed.

"If you truly know all, then you know the importance of it, and you will know what I will do to you if anything happens to it, reincarnation or not." She looked into their eyes, immune to their peering gaze until the point it filled the entire hall with tension.

"I am aware," was all they said. "Inside there will be weapons, find them. You will need them to survive."

Kaell sighed in relief, all of their weapons were probably being destroyed by the fire right now. Raven went through the mirror first, disappearing without causing a single ripple on its surface. Etaín followed, then it was Kaell's turn. He didn't feel himself going through the mirror although as soon as he had stepped through it, he felt uneasy in his stomach, like a deep hunger or something, he couldn't quite place the feeling. Inza stepped out behind him, without Yaë, as he took a good look around him. They stood in a field surrounded by rocky walls that rose above them like mountainsides, pillars of stone dotted the field like claws. Beyond all of that was a set of stairs that wound up a high peak upon which stood a circle of stone, the air within it softly trembling. Above them was a sky, filled with dark clouds that didn't move with the wind.

"Where are we?" Etaín asked, a good question.

"Don't care, but I think we need to go there." Raven pointed at the top of the peak. They slowly advanced into the field, not sure what to expect when Kaell saw something shiny across the field. He focused, which was much easier since the Mark, and noticed there were two swords, stabbed into the rock.

"Raven," he whispered, pointing at the swords. She followed his eyes, nodding that she had seen them and they made their way toward them. A soft hum went through the stone, vibrating the rock itself, and small stones rained down upon them from the stone pillars and mountainsides. They stood still for a moment, holding their breath, but then Raven dashed toward the swords with immense speed, barely touching the ground. It almost looked like she teleported to them.

In agonizing silence, they waited until the world went quiet again, the feeling in Kaell's stomach grew with each passing second. Inza spotted a large battleaxe a little above where Raven stood and pointed it out, Raven followed her finger and started to climb. She moved surprisingly fast, it didn't seem to bother her that the rock was practically vertical. As she was pulling out the battle-axe, another hum trembled the world, much louder this time. More rocks fell and Raven held up her arms in an attempt to protect herself but the rocks were sharp and cut her skin nevertheless. She had pulled out the battle-axe and threw it down, the blade slammed into the ground right before Etaín's feet, who gave Raven an angry stare for almost cutting her feet off. It was at that moment that the rock behind Raven split open, several large, gaping holes had opened behind her but before she could turn around masses of rat-like creatures were already bursting out of the holes. They were the size of small dogs with sharp fangs that twisted around their jaw, their claws were long and rattled across the stone as they ran toward the group. Raven was already cutting down everything that came within the range of her swords but eventually had to jump down from the ledge, upon landing she drove her two swords into the ground which created a harsh, almost screaming sound.

Etaín put herself between the rats and Inza and Kaell. Inza had already shifted into a massive fox and was jumping from one rat to another, ripping their throats and leaving her fair share of corpses behind. Kaell decided to lock out Inza's thoughts as much as he could because he had no interest in hearing her primal thoughts. In the meantime, Etaín too, was going wild, fighting the rats with a face that showed how much she enjoyed battle.

With no weapons on him Kaell was running toward the other side of the field, trying to escape the seemingly endless waves of rats or whatever they were. One of them had followed him and he could hear its ragged breath closing in on him. Kaell was fast but the creature was faster and jumped on his back, driving Kaell to the ground. He was barely on time to wrap his hands around its head, keeping its fangs out of range of his face. Through his mind he called out to Inza but he had no idea if she heard him since she was busy herself.

The rat wriggled in his hands, trying to claw out of Kaell's grip. Its eyes were blooded and red, filled with hatred but behind that there was nothing, just a soulless void. Drool was slowly dripping onto Kaell's face, the rat flashed its teeth in another attempt to bite his throat, nearly succeeding when suddenly, it was ripped away from Kaell by a large fox. Inza. Kaell sighed, letting his arms fall down and closed his eyes for a moment before he laughed quickly. There wasn't much left of the rat after Inza was done with it and after she checked if Kaell was okay she ran back into the fray, ready to take on some more rats.

"Kaell, above you!" It was Raven, she was standing on a pile of dead rats and somehow had found the time to spot something on the ledge above him, it was far but he figured he could make it. His arms were weary from the struggle with the rat yet he found strength in his muscles that wasn't there before, he figured it came from the Mark so he smiled and glanced at it for a moment, satisfied with his new powers.

Determined, he got to the ledge Raven had pointed out and when he peeked across the edge, he saw what she had meant. Before him, a bow stuck out of the rock, it was made from some material Kaell didn't recognize, engraved with strange symbols and lines. Kaell took it in his hand and immediately felt comfortable with it, however, there were no arrows.

The bowstring glistened in the faint light that shone across the field. With care he pulled back the string, feeling its resistance against his fingers, as he pulled it an arrow appeared on the rest. It was of a pale wood, just like the bow itself, and had similar inscriptions on the shaft. He looked past the arrow, toward the waves of rats where the others were fighting frantically. Kaell took a long breath while he pulled the arrow back, he enjoyed the feeling of a bow in his hand, it had been days since he held one. The first arrow flew through the air, singing for a short moment before it planted itself deep within a rat that had made its way onto Etaín.

She turned around, alarmed by the sudden impact. When she noticed the arrow in the rat, she looked up at Kaell and raised a thumb before she started swinging her battle-axe around again.

Arrow after arrow he sent flying through the air, planting each of them in a rat. Inza had taken herself a little more to the side and was catching her breath so Kaell decided to focus more on the rats around her, giving her some hard-earned rest.

The stone beneath their feet rumbled again, this time without any sound, at least for a moment. Not long after, the rock beside the staircase splintered, revealing a serpent-like creature of enormous size. It had legs as big as tree trunks, teeth like swords and claws like spears stained with blood. Its scales were a dark purple and full of scratches, on the end of its tail was a large hammer-like piece of bone. Three burning, yellow eyes lay deep within its skull and looked at them with rage, but behind them wasn't an empty void, there was intelligence there, and Kaell didn't know what frightened him more, no soul or a consciousness set on killing them.

When the serpent moved, its scales shrieked a bone-chilling song that bounced off of the stone around them. Kaell could hear Raven curse under her breath, with which he completely agreed. Etaín however seemed to be happier and happier as it moved closer to them, charging at them with immense speed. She grounded her feet, twisting her body to take the blow and lowering her head. Lightning flashed above their heads, thunder rolling across the sky before the clouds started to empty themselves, soaking them all within a matter of seconds. *Great,* Kaell thought, as if they didn't have enough trouble already. Kaell fired his first arrow, which bounced off of the scales leaving nothing but a scratch.

"Aim for the eyes, Etaín and I will keep it busy for as long as we can," Raven whispered, knowing Kaell's Kurr ears would be able to hear her anyway. "We best kill it quickly because I don't think we could sneak into the portal with this thing alive."

Kaell smiled at Raven and nodded, letting her know that he heard her. The serpent and Etaín clashed, pushing Etaín back and crumbling the stone beneath her feet. Underneath their feet they could feel the impact as well, the shockwave rippling through the stone, breaking the walls around them even further. Blood dripped from Etaín's head, dripping past the massive grin on her face. She had brought the serpent to a halt, and had earned Kaell's respect as well. Now she swung her battleaxe at its neck, knocking it to the side a little but only scratching the scales. An arrow flew from Kaell's bow, hitting the serpent in one of its eyes, making its entire body shiver. It screeched, the blood-curdling sound mixing with the thunder from the sky and shaking the stone pillars, one collapsed and Kaell could barely get away in time.

The serpent had knocked down Etaín and raised its claws, ready to end her. Kaell was scrambling to his feet but knew his arrows wouldn't cause much damage unless he hit one of the other eyes. Suddenly, a massive root grew from under the serpent, pushing it over and saving Etaín. Inza stood behind the root, her long hair dragging across the ground, her eyes burning bright.

The serpent noticed her and swooped its tail at her. Kaell screamed at her, both with his mind and his voice but he was too late. When Inza turned around to see what he meant, the bone tail hit her in the stomach, launching her with incredible speed into the wall behind her. The stone itself gave away, denting the wall where Inza hit it. Kaell felt every bone in his body break and fell to the ground, coughing up blood and clenching his teeth as his skin ripped open across his stomach. The world went black before his eyes and his breath came with incredible difficulty. Inza fell down from the wall, hitting the ground like a lifeless doll, and Kaell felt how she landed upon the sharp rocks, his skin being pierced on multiple places. He could faintly hear Etaín and Raven fighting the serpent, the sound of its scales piercing through the pain. Very slowly, his healing kicked in, he still felt Inza's energy nearby and he decided to allow her body to take whatever energy she needed from him. He just hoped she would make it. Immediately he felt his body draining, Inza taking in every bit of energy he could miss. His body suddenly burned with pain and he felt his bones and muscles move to their original positions, even his skin wove into itself, closing his every wound. When his vision returned, he saw Inza crawling out of the stone, her wet hair weighing her down. She grabbed a rock from the rubble and her hair with her other hand and sliced it all off at shoulder length, dropping the long hair on the ground beside her. The cuts on her face and arms were healing as Kaell looked at her while she walked toward the serpent with determination in her eyes, the rock around her cracking open to reveal roots twisting and turning as she moved her hands.

Raven sat upon the neck of the serpent, trying to push her swords between his scales. She saw Inza as well and immediately rolled off of the beast, gesturing for Etaín to move out of the way. Inza screamed as she threw her hands forward, roots wrecking the stone as they sped toward the serpent, wrapping around it wherever they could take hold. Scales shattered as the roots gripped it tighter and tighter around its neck and body.

Inza moved her hands, weaving the roots around the creature, and slowly made a fist. The roots wrapped tighter and the serpent let out another blood-curdling shriek that died into a gurgle until the sound of thunder and rain was the only thing left.

Water had turned the field into a shallow lake and filled it up more and more. Raven nodded at Inza as a way to thank her and Etaín gripped Inza's shoulders and laughed loudly.

"Now that was a fight. Well done, Inza, well done," she exclaimed, clearly satisfied with the defeat of the serpent, although Kaell thought that it might also have been the result of the serpent hitting her in the head so hard.

Raven was pulling out claws, scales and teeth and even cut out the two remaining eyes and bound them all in a piece of cloth that she pulled out of nowhere. She noticed everyone's questioning looks as she wiped the creature's green blood from her blades.

"This serpent is one of the Qarn. It's sad I don't have a phial as well; its blood holds powerful properties. Nevertheless, these things," she held up the piece of cloth, "are still very useful. They are worth a lot, and I mean a lot, so you can imagine they have a few uses here and there."

"The Qarn are things of legend," Etaín said. "People whisper their names in stories of ancient battles to make it all a little more epic."

"You both seem to know about the Qarn, yet we have no clue what you are talking about," Kaell said, starting to make his way toward the stairs. He wasn't fond of the serpent and even the look of its twisted corpse made him feel uneasy, so he would like to get out of there as soon as he could. The others followed him as well but he held Inza by her hand, she seemed in shock and Kaell could feel her weariness on him as well.

"The Qarn are creatures of legend, yes, but they are real as well. Essentially, they are a High Immortal race of serpentine spirits, empty shells that attune to their surrounding energies to take a form," Raven explained. "They are said to have come into existence during the first wave of creation, making them older than the Masters. Because they are High Immortals, their spirits don't die, their physical form can be killed but as you noticed it is quite difficult. Once it dies it becomes a spirit again, waiting until it has collected enough energy to manifest itself again. They are extremely rare since they can't create any full blood offspring, only half breeds which are far less impressive. The Ilunari wyverns are offspring for example, they're cool, sure, but nothing like their ancestors. This one was still relatively young, luckily, we would have never survived against an older one."

It was almost as if she was annoyed by the creatures, like they were a pest of sorts. Kaell just wished with all of his heart that he would never have to fight one of them again, old or young.

The stairs seemed eternal as they climbed step after step. All of them were tired from the fight and every step was like climbing a mountain. It seemed like an eternity had passed when they finally reached the top, the wind was so strong that they actually had to struggle not to get blown off of the peak so they quickly stepped through the stone circle. Kaell looked down at the Qarn's corpse down below but shivered when there wasn't a corpse anymore, just broken stone and his arrows laying in the middle of the field.

They were in the vault now, and Kaell had never felt so tiny and unimportant. Pillars reached so far above them that they couldn't see their ends, clouded glass, layering in between them to create floors, at least, that's what it looked like. Gold wove through the grey stone and appeared to be the only warm color there. Everything was blue and grey and white, pale light filling the halls, leaving no room for shadows to hide in. They stood in the middle of a circular hall, a different path leading deep into the clouded light. There was complete silence surrounding them, only faint whispers entered Kaell's mind, but he could barely discern them among his own thoughts.

"How will we ever find what we need?" he whispered, afraid to break the silence.

"Who is the luckiest person of this group?" Raven asked, her face radiating annoyance of the highest order. Etaín scoffed and twisted the battle-axe around in her hands and pointed at one of the hallways.

"We should probably get started with that one," she said, already walking toward it.

"Why that one?" Kaell asked, not seeing any difference between any of the choices.

"Because it's better than standing around waiting for some special sign to tell us where to go." She shrugged and Kaell was a little flustered by the simplicity of her answer, although he had to agree with her. They followed Etaín into the hallway, finding nothing but empty walls no matter how far they went until at one point they saw an open space at the end. As they walked in, Kaell noticed it looked exactly like the one they arrived in.

"This looks awfully similar to where we came in," Etaín said, but Inza pointed across the room.

"It is the one where we came in. Look, the floor is wet on exactly the opposite side," she pointed out. There was indeed a wet trail leading into the opposite hallway, a wet trail just like the one behind them.

"Did I manage to pick the one hallway that magically brings you to where you started? Because if that's the case I'm not picking anything anymore." Etaín held her hands up in a defending manner and awkwardly smiled. Raven put her hand on Etaín's arm as a way of comfort.

"I don't think any of those hallways lead to anywhere but their beginning. There must be a solution that I'm not thinking of." She sounded distant, lost in thought, and she started pacing through the room, looking into every hallway.

"Inza, do you think you could shift into something fast and check out some of the other hallways? If you're too tired don't do it, then I'll figure it out in a different way."

Inza just nodded and shifted into a falcon, flying into another hallway.

"I can run down a few as well. You're checking if they all lead to this place, right?" Kaell asked, he was tired but if they split the work all of them would save some energy.

"Yeah," Raven answered. "I'll run down a few as well. Etaín, please wait here, then we know we end up here every time." Etaín nodded and sat down in the middle, happy to get some rest.

Every hallway Kaell entered was empty, some seemed longer than others but after a while he really didn't know anymore, it just went on and on, only to lead him to the start every time. He reached out to Inza, who managed to show him the same empty hallways through her mind. It didn't take them long to check all the hallways, so they came together in the middle, catching their breath from the endless running and flying.

"Maybe this is another challenge for us," Etaín started. "It's a vault right, containing incredibly powerful things?"

"Yeah, it is. Why?" Raven asked.

"The best kept secret in this realm, that's what that silver guy said, right?" Etaín slowly stood up, somehow appearing to understand this place. Kaell was completely lost still and was happy someone else had figured it out. Raven nodded as a response to Etaín's question.

"What if the secret *is* its protection?"

"I don't follow you. Secrecy is always a protection, people can't do anything if they don't know it exists," Raven said, just as confused as Kaell and Inza.

"Yes, exactly. What if you could only find something when you know it's here? What if the hallways lead to their beginning because we are searching, instead of finding?" A large grin appeared on Etaín's face, clearly proud of her solution. Raven fell silent for a moment, her brain trying to process what Etaín just said, to Kaell it sounded like she might have been hit in the head too hard by the serpent but then again, he didn't have a more logical solution.

"You might actually be right," Raven said, still frowning. "All we have to do is focus on the thing we want to find. Like the egg."

"Well let's go then, there is an island burning while we are here," Etaín said, already moving toward one of the hallways. They walked through the hallway, appearing to lead them nowhere when slowly the walls changed the further they got. It turned from grey and gold into a darker grey with less and less gold until they reached the end of the hallway. They stood in the open air it seemed, no walls, no roof, no pillars anymore. A small distance from them stood a monolith, flawlessly smooth and perfectly black. No stairs or anything, just a solid pillar of black, smooth stone, pointing up to the empty sky. On its top a floating orb of black and purple, the egg. Now they had to figure out how to get it.

"Can't you turn into a bird or something and grab the egg from up there?" Etaín asked Inza while looking up at the monolith. They had just walked around the entire thing, no sign of stairs or anything else to get to the top.

"Doesn't shifting count as magic? The Silver Eyed made it pretty clear that no magic should touch the egg," Inza responded. Everyone sighed and looked up at the monolith now.

"If anyone has a hidden talent, now would probably be the time to share it," Raven sighed, poking the monolith with her swords, not even leaving a scratch.

"I don't see how my ability to outdrink my village would help here, but at least you know now," Etaín said, grinning as she was satisfied with her own joke.

"I was more hoping for a talent of climbing perfectly smooth walls but if I ever need to win a drinking competition, you'll be the first to know." Raven gave Etaín a smile, the serious tension breaking a little.

"I don't know how strong you are, but I suppose not strong enough to throw Raven up there so she can grab it?" Kaell asked. "It's just that I saw how far Raven could jump up the wall back with the serpent so I figured that maybe if you gave her a boost, she might be able to reach the egg."

Etaín flexed her arms to show her muscles to Kaell. "I think I'm pretty strong. Why don't we give it a shot?" she said, looking at Raven.

Raven shrugged and put down her swords. "We don't really have any other options anyway. You ready?"

Etaín just nodded and picked her up, placing Raven's feet in her hands as she squatted down.

"Three, two, one." They counted down and Etaín threw in all the power she could, feeling Raven push herself off of her as well. Raven shot through the air, the others holding their breath as they saw her slowing down before she reached the top. She tried to grip the edge but only a few fingers managed to get a hold of the monolith. Completely still she hung in the air, Etaín praying to all the High Immortals she could think of, knowing none of them could help them here.

Raven struggled trying to get her other hand on the edge as well, pulling herself up on just three fingers. She swung herself a little bit, hoping to make it easier for herself. Eventually she managed to get hold of the edge with both hands. Etaín sighed, realizing she had held her breath all the time. Inza shifted into an eagle, quickly flying up to Raven.

"She can't pull herself up, the monolith is smooth on top as well," Kaell explained. Etaín forgot that they could hear so well, but at the same time was thankful for it.

"But wasn't she not supposed to shift near the egg, because it's magic and stuff?" Etaín asked and Kaell frowned.

"Raven said that Inza could give her a push. I just hope she knows what she is doing," he responded. Inza had reached Raven and pushed against her legs with one hard motion, allowing Raven to get herself on top of the monolith. Kaell rubbed his shoulder blades with an uncomfortable look on his face. Raven disappeared over the edge and Inza came flying down, shifting before she hit the ground and landing gently on the stone with her bare feet. Nothing seemed to happen on top of the monolith for a while and Etaín's neck started to hurt from looking up for so long.

"She says we should move, she's coming down again," Inza said out of the blue, hearing Raven's whispers from the top of the monolith. They had barely moved aside when Raven jumped off the edge, holding the egg in one hand, her hair flowing behind her like a trail of shadows.

Etaín worried, it was a long way down to just jump, perhaps she could still catch Raven, but she had specifically told them to move aside and Etaín trusted Raven to know what was best for herself. Raven hit the ground at immense speed, landing on her feet and one hand with incredible lightness, as her hair came down beside her. Dust blew away in a wave yet both the ground and Raven remained unharmed in any way. She stood up, holding out the egg toward Etaín, who hesitated to take it. That was an artifact of the High Immortals, who knew what kind of powers it held and if it truly was an egg, who knew what could be inside of it.

"It's best if you hold it, you possess no magical powers whatsoever. It will be safest in your hands," Raven said, instilling both pride and sorrow in Etaín. She was proud that she was the one to keep the egg safe, however she did feel so incredibly average to have absolutely no powers whatsoever. The sadness didn't last long, she might not have any magic but she did realize that nobody else could have thrown Raven to the top of the monolith, so without her they would never have laid their hands on the egg.

"Next up, a seed in a crystal tree. Let's hope it doesn't grow on top of some wonderful monolith," Raven sighed as she walked past them, back into the hallway. She kept on muttering things in High Speech under her breath.

Etaín carefully carried the egg, it was quite beautiful. She could see now that the shell was mainly black and purple but all kinds of colors wove through the shell, gold, yellow and green spots, a marbled red and blue. It was like the colors of the world had all left their mark on this one egg, from seas to forests to the mountaintops touching the sky. All of them could be found on the shell of this egg. Etaín could stare at it for hours, and perhaps she had because when she looked up, they had already arrived at the crystal tree.

It was made from a clear crystal, pulsing with light, its leafless branches reached high and wide, taking up the entire cave. The floor here consisted out of several pieces of stone, connected by clear crystal roots, that led toward the trunk of the tree. Through the wide cracks in the stone Etaín could see the bottom. Underneath them lay piles upon piles of bones. Skulls of every race she knew and many more she didn't recognize, bones as big as Etaín herself. The hairs on her body rose when she saw roots of the tree had taken hold of every bone down there, as if they were feeding on them. She decided not to look down again, trying not to imagine how all those bones got there. Even on the roof there were skulls and bones, embedded in the dark rock.

Inza was walking across the roots and stone toward the tree, she had spotted the seed in its very core, glowing vibrantly green. Kaell tried to follow her, but as soon as he set foot on the crystal it shattered beneath his feet, he was just quick enough to step back on the rock. The tree emitted a soft hum, twisting into itself a little more.

Although Etaín tried not to look down she couldn't help it, she cast a quick glance at the bones, the piles seemed to have moved and lay against the rock now, fingers and teeth reaching upwards.

Etaín shivered, stepping back a bit, accidentally touching the crystal herself, shattering it upon touch as well. She followed the falling shards with her eyes, seeing the bones move, seeing them crawl up the stone. At first it had seemed that they were far down, but now they had reached quite high already and Etaín expected that they needed just one or two more shattered roots before those weird bones would be able to get her.

"Euhm, Raven?" she whispered, trying not to alarm Inza.

"What?" was her response.

"Well, it looks like those bones are coming toward us every time the crystal shatters."

Raven looked down at the bones and then back at the tree.

"Then let's hope the tree doesn't need to break for Inza to get the seed," she whispered, clearly unsettled. Inza had reached the trunk of the tree in the meantime and laid her hands upon the crystal. A wave of energy pulsed through the tree, flowing down into its roots and down into the bones, which started moving again. Flesh and skin started to grow back on them as life pulsated into them. Etaín looked around at Inza, the tree slowly twisting open, sending cracks through the crystal roots that surrounded it.

"Get away from the roots. Come on, get into the hallway, quickly," Raven urged. Etaín quickly came but Kaell kept standing where he was, waiting for his sister to make it back.

"Inza, get the seed and get back here," Raven shouted. "Just break the crystal. It's breaking anyway and we need both the seed and you here, right now." Her tone became more hurried with every word. She sliced a hand that had just reached the edge of the stone, Etaín looked down and saw the hordes of flesh-covered bones were already reaching the edge of the stone. Inza was pushing her hand through the tree, her fingers reaching for the seed but not succeeding. The tree was still twisting itself to open up, sending larger and larger cracks through its roots, shattering more connections between the stones. What was left of an Ilunari body had crept up to Etaín's feet, one violet eye in its broken skull, and Etaín raised her battle-axe high, holding the egg far behind her, and sent it crashing down upon the corpse, cutting it in half and kicked the remains back into the cavern where it simply tried to crawl back up again.

"Stand as far back as you can Etaín, keep the egg safe," Raven said to her. Etaín nodded and moved further into the hall, she was not afraid of battle, never had been, but this was no battle, this was just creeping her out. Inza was still pushing herself into the tree and managed to grab the seed. The tree exploded in thousands of shards, sending Inza flying through the air, Kaell's skin opened up just like Inza's and Etaín could see him bare his teeth in agony. Inza had landed on a rock a little away from Kaell and was filled with shards of crystal, and unconscious. Her wounds couldn't heal with the shards still in them and she was losing blood as long as she couldn't heal. Kaell had thrown the bow on his back and was jumping from rock to rock, trying to get to his sister. Blood pouring out of his wounds, not being able to heal either.

"Don't touch the seed, Kaell," Raven whispered, she was cutting through the hordes of corpses that managed to crawl across the edge. Kaell seemed to ignore her, focusing on his next jump. He was getting visibly weaker with every second that passed but he made it to Inza after all. With panic he started pulling out every shard, the skin healing as soon as the shard was gone. It took him effort not to touch the seed that was laying on Inza's stomach, which was the size of her fist and pulsed with light.

Inza coughed up blood as she slowly came back to consciousness, almost all the shards were out of her and her wounds were almost completely healed already, thus Kaell's wounds as well. The corpses were creeping toward Inza and Kaell but Inza shifted her hand into a claw and managed to slash through the closest ones. She clenched her teeth as Kaell pulled out the last few shards of crystal, allowing them to fully heal themselves. With help of her brother she got to her feet again and she shifted into a wolf, holding the seed between her teeth as Kaell sat on her back.

Within a matter of seconds, they had reached Raven and Etaín, running into the hall. As soon as Inza stepped into the hallway the corpses turned lifeless again, falling down into the cavern to rot again.

In the middle of the broken tree sprouted a small stem with one leaf from the same crystal as the shards around it.

They had reached the room where they had come in again, Inza had shifted back again and was visibly tired, her eyes had gone dull and she dragged herself forward, leaning on her brother and holding the seed tightly.

"How do we get out again?" Kaell asked. Etaín wanted to know as well. She was completely done with this damned place and seriously hoped she would never have to come here again. He had barely spoken the words or a silver mirror appeared in the middle of the room. None of them asked a question but just walked through it, recognizing it as the mirror they came through in the first place. Luckily it was.

They stepped out of it, into the crystal hall under the sea, the Silver Eyed waiting patiently for them. The seabed was filled with remnants of the bridge and even parts of the temple, the orange light of the fire was shining down into the waters. Etaín held out the egg for the Silver Eyed to take it but they simply handed Raven her spear and turned away, leading them back up the winding stairs into the temple. Parts of the walls and even a piece of the roof had crumbled, leaving gaping holes that showed them an entire island engulfed in flames and lava.

The heat was unbearable and Etaín immediately broke a sweat, she couldn't help but touch the twisted scar on her arm where the fire had burned her when she had tried to free Raven from her house. Inza had tried her best to heal it but this scar she couldn't heal.

"Take the egg to the flames, throw it in there," the Silver Eye said, pointing at the fire across the water.

"How do you expect me to get to the flames? I don't have wings to fly across this gap, in case you hadn't noticed." Etaín began to feel anger rising within her, first they had allowed Rynn to burn the island, then they had sent them into that damned vault, risking their lives, and now they wanted her to somehow get to the flames?

"You can throw the egg across, into the fire," he calmly responded. Of course she could throw it across, perhaps she would send him flying as well. They would reincarnate anyway. Etaín scoffed, making it clear that she was done with them, before she hurled the egg she had been so careful with until now. The flames engulfed the egg and for a moment nothing happened, but then the flames roared and twisted into themselves, they drew from every corner of the island, flowing toward where the egg had landed. A few minutes later all the fire had gone, nothing but smoke and ashes remained among that what hadn't been consumed by the fire. In the middle lay the egg, its shell had shifted from mainly purple into a sunset kind of color scheme, red and orange were now the dominant colors.

The fire had truly wrecked the island, nothing, absolutely nothing, had survived the flames. Even the rock had molten and shaped into a completely new island.

"It was time for something new anyway, new body and everything," the Silver Eye said before they took the seed from Inza and walked toward the middle of the temple. There, they dug in the stone, the rock crumbling at their hands like it was dirt, and placed the seed in the hole. Immediately a tree sprouted from the seed, grass, moss, flowers and plants of all kinds rose from the rock, taking over the temple and changing the silver and white into emerald and gold.

Only minutes later they stood in what could have been the heart of a forest, silver flowers sprouted under their feet and the trees grew silver leaves. Inza fell to the ground, and embraced the green all around her as Yaë nudged itself between her arms, she fell asleep seconds later. Kaell was already asleep against the trunk of the tree. Roots of the tree were reaching out across the gap toward the island, forming new bridges for them to walk across. Etaín however, had no interest in going across them, instead she joined Kaell against the tree, letting out a long sigh as she sat down. She had never before been so glad with the blessing of rest and she was asleep before she had closed her eyes. Until she woke up again, they would have to find another to collect eggs and seeds or whatever it was the world needed. For now, she would enjoy her dreams of massive feasts and joyful battles.

Chapter 25

Aergo

"You twist and turn his mind, force his traumas on him, and for what? To burn down an island so they wouldn't follow us! How in the name of Nuana would they have followed us? In case you have missed it, the mage, the only person who can teleport across the land, is with us!" Fury was an understatement for what Aergo felt coursing through his veins, and Ara couldn't wipe the judgmental look off of her face, but now she broke.

"Do not use her name, Kir'in. I do not expect you to understand my actions nor my reasons," she hissed back at him.

"I do not care if I understand your reasons or not! You cause harm to people who do not deserve it, people who have helped you even. I don't trust the Ilunari either, but all the others do not need to die because of that! Yet you want to enter my home, want my help. I should just lock you up again, I'm sure I can find someone to pay a pretty price for the last Nuan." Aergo turned away, scanning the area around them as they approached one of the entrances to the underground ruins of Xisq. It was a simple latch, hidden underneath rocks and dirt, located between the roots of some old tree a little away from the main road. They were lucky that not many travelled the road at night so they could slip into the tunnel unseen.

As they moved closer to the ruins Aergo's mind started to calm down, he still seriously disagreed with Ara's actions but he too would like to see Nuana return, and she had promised she could arrange that. Aergo had even asked the Silver Eyed for advice, since he said he knew everything. He had told Aergo to go with them, for if he did not Ara would have created a way to the Vault by force, not caring about Aergo's people. So logically, Aergo had made himself valuable to Ara and acquired a position of trust with her, she might have the ability to read minds but Aergo had a way with words so he always got exactly what he wanted.

He was glad to be home again, among his family, although he would miss the presence of the others. It wasn't exactly like he had made any friends, yet he had grown quite fond of especially Kaell and Inza. Those two brought a certain warmth to the world that he didn't see a lot anymore. He would go back to the group after business here was done. The Silver Eyed had taught him how to use the shadows as a means of transportation, he had said there was much more to learn about the shadows for Aergo, all he had to do was come back. They were reaching the underground city now, Aergo could already hear the first sounds coming from them. Night didn't mean sleep here, night meant secrets and treasures. So many secrets were never to see the light of day, so the night was perfect for them.

"For a leader of a group of thieves and assassins you don't exactly seem to do a great job at hiding your prisoners." It was Lily, she stepped from the shadows only a few steps into the ruins. She was playing with a dagger, her fingers too quick to follow.

"That's because they are not prisoners anymore, my dear. We discovered we would benefit more from working together. Besides, it's not like we could contain the mage anymore, you've seen the chains he ruined," Aergo said, happy to see her again, and rubbed her bald head. She punched his arm and gave him her tough look.

"Yeah, I did. They couldn't repair them so I already sent Thom to get new ones from the Seat, down south," she said, showing she had taken care of things around here. "Tuales has been bothering me and Rysa until even Rysa lost her temper. He has gone mad waiting for your return, he keeps on telling us how important it is that he gets his hands on that book."

"I will speak with him, we can give him what he wants." Aergo hoped it would be the last thing Tuales needed, that perhaps he would leave them. Sure, it was a useful ally to have, he just wasn't sure that Tuales was an ally.

"Well here's your chance. I will get Rysa and a few others to accompany us. Do you need anything else, my lord?" Lily asked, nodding when Aergo shook his head.

Up ahead Aergo could see Tuales waiting. He looked more unsettling than he did before, his eyes moved quickly and looked heavy, cracks had appeared in his skin and his hair could just as much have been made from blood-stained straw. Tuales noticed Aergo as well and nearly ran toward him.

"Tell me you have the key, I need to open the Vault," a thousand voices snarled at Aergo.

"I'm doing great, still very much alive as you can see, even after Arga. Thanks for asking," Aergo said, mockingly smiling at the man whose face tightened and his eyes shot fire but he held his tongue. Eventually Aergo sighed, he didn't expect a reaction he just really wanted to mock the sorcerer now that he had something he needed.

"Yes, we have the key. Let's get to the door and you can get your precious book. I take it the lack of distraction won't stop us from going through the Keeper's guard?" Aergo's annoyance was clear in his every word. He was excited to open the Vault, yes, he too had dreamt of it ever since he learned about it. But he was never desperate like Tuales.

"My lord," Rysa said. "We had to strike a deal with the empress."

"Excuse me?" Aergo couldn't believe his ears, for so long he had kept these ruins a safe place for his people and now they had made a deal with the empress?

"They busted one of our taverns after we created our little… distraction. So, we struck a deal to satisfy them. They did not find entrances to our city, but we wanted to prevent them from searching." Her words were soft, she knew what she had done, but Aergo trusted that this had been the best option for them all, this was her home too after all.

"And what did we have to provide in return?" Aergo asked.

"In return you will allow me to join you when you enter the Vault," a soft, yet cold voice said from behind Tuales. Aergo's eyes shot toward it, and was utterly surprised to see what they found. It was another Nuan, a woman too, clearly older than Ara but not as purely white as her. Every shadow on her body seemed darker, her eyes lay deep within the shadows, dark and wary of everything. Something seemed off about her, but Aergo couldn't place it, his gut told him to keep an eye open for her and he noticed Rysa and Lily being wary of the lady.

"I thought I was the last of us," Ara whispered, hardly believing her eyes as well.

"In a way you still are. I was Nuan once, but the shadows have grown heavy on me. Now, I am no longer pure, no longer Light. I am but a shadow of what a Nuan is supposed to be, but I thought I was all that was left of our kind, so I have been advising King Egìl to my best ability in an attempt to end this eternal war." As she spoke, she seemed to search for words, as if she never spoke aloud in her life.

"I will explain everything later, as you must know this Vault has something to do with the return of the Lady of Light. So, it's about time we open it," she answered Ara's questioning looks. Tuales had broken down the wall already and the Keeper's Guard stepped aside as they passed through.

Aergo could still see their empty eyes in his mind from the last time when they had tried to open the Vault. Once again, they stood before the red and gold door, the golden eye motionless in its center. Ara revealed the key, its white light filling the hall, reflecting itself on the mirror-like floor, nearly blinding everyone but the Nuan. She walked up to the door, holding the eye out in front of her and the liquids in the door were reaching for it, lifting themselves up and stretching out toward the bright orb of light. They wrapped around it, pulling it from Ara's hand and started to swirl around it before they pulled away to the sides, disappearing into a small, carved out space within the wall.

The gold gathered around the eye, forming a disc that then widened as well, taking up the entire hole where the door had been at first, then it just stopped moving. Tuales was the first to step through it, seemingly knowing exactly what it was and taking the key with him as he entered. Aergo made sure he and Rysa remained in the hall as the last ones.

"Rysa, I need you to stay here and defend this doorway. Deal or not, I don't trust those guards at all. If they make a move you don't like, kill them. I will deal with the empress if she gets mad," Aergo whispered, soft enough not to echo his words. Rysa, nodded and loosened her knives on her back, ready to kill whenever she needed to. Then Aergo stepped through the golden portal as well.

The inside was massive, and absolutely breathtaking. Pillars made from a deep red stone rose high, carrying a curved roof of the same stone. Golden lines wove up and around the pillars, marbling the stone in a most elegant manner. It was like they had stepped into a temple the size of a city, Aergo had never seen anything like it and doubted he ever would again. Countless altar-like pedestals stood in the hall, rows upon rows of artefacts, Aergo recognized some from the myths and legends but most of them were completely new to him.

On every side there were more halls, leading toward doors or rooms filled with all kinds of things. In one he saw books and scrolls, Tuales was rampaging through them. Another held a statue made from a stone so pale it could have been snow. Around him lay weapons, armor, books, crystals, plants, stones and so much more.

One gem in particular caught his eye, a star-shaped diamond, black as night but when he held it against the light thousands of small dots appeared in the blackness. He quickly put it in his pocket because somehow, he felt like he was the one to take it. Lily had pulled out a bag and put everything in there that Aergo pointed at. He wasn't sure how many times he would be able to return to this place so he took this opportunity to take anything that he thought to be useful for them. Ara and the other Nuan were standing in the middle, Ara's eyes closed while the other whispered into her ear. Several images of Ara stepped out of her body, exact copies that looked like ghosts, and started walking around the Vault, touching every artifact and entering every room. It took her ages to explore the Vault and every once in a while, one of her copies brought back an artifact but the other Nuan simply shook her head. The last copy returned, holding a small pearl that glowed softly and the other Nuan shook her head again.

"Where is this damned heart?" Ara yelled, startling Aergo a little. "Those forsaken sisters told me the Heart of Light would be here, that this was the place where I would find the thing to make me the Lady of Light!" As she was shouting, she threw artifact after artifact across the hall. "I curse those sisters, that *bitch* Yira is nothing but a failure, a desperate, little wench!"

"So, is that what you're looking for here, the Heart of Light?" Aergo asked, but Ara shook her head, clearly confused.

"It should be here, at least, it's supposed to be," Ara said.

"Why," the other Nuan started, "would we need an artefact to make you Lady of Light?"

"I'm not sure I follow you," Ara mumbled, confusion dripping from her every word.

"It seems wrong to me to need an artefact to make you Lady of Light, when you so clearly are meant to be that." She paused, stepping back from Ara and bowing before her. "You are the last child of Nuana, the last remnant of Light we have left. Only you can become our light in this world of darkness. I heard rumors that you have died and came to life again to show this world your light. I do not care that you are mortal, if all, it makes you better suited to be queen. High Immortals don't care about us, to them we are worthless, pawns in their eternal wars. You are not like them, you will fight for the mortal cause, you can end this war, you can save us all."

Ara straightened her back and teared up, Rynn fell to his knees right away. Aergo and Lily hesitated for a moment but when Ara noticed she gave them a look that Aergo recognized, a look of a person going mad, and Aergo saw fire seeping into Rynn's veins so he quickly bowed before Ara, Lily following his example.

Ara seriously expected them to immediately praise her because some Nuan thought Ara was a savior. It wasn't even a question, she actually did expect that. Well, let her believe he would serve her just like that, he feared it would be the only way to keep his people safe from her wrath. She wasn't Nuana, and never would be, not to Aergo or his people. He wouldn't call her Lady of Light until she had proven herself to be that, and the only way to do so was to end the War of Shattered Light. If she did that, Aergo could follow her, but he wouldn't follow her blindly.

"Do we seriously abandon the rules of the Abariimm because this woman says so? If the Nuan isn't chosen by the Abariimm she will not be Lady of Light, whether she wants it or not," Lily whispered to Aergo.

"We do not abandon those rules, sweetheart. She isn't the Lady of Light, probably never will be, but if she becomes queen I'd rather be at her side, pretending to be loyal, than die because I oppose her. When the time is right, and it will be, we will take her crown for ourselves."

His whispers were soft, unheard by Ara. Lily smiled and nodded, understanding Aergo's plan.

Tuales' screams came from the room in which he was rampaging. Joyous words in all kind of tongues echoed through the Vault and he came walking toward them, holding a very thick book, bound in what Aergo could only identify as skin, old and cracked, seemingly from all kind of races and stained with blood. All weariness had faded from his face, the cracks in his skin had disappeared as well and his hair was shiny again. His eyes flicked between Ara and the others, noticing how they bowed before her, but Ara let her hand slide across her throat, feeling where Tuales had cut her skin open so effortlessly to draw out her blood and he flashed his filed teeth at her.

"So, you're the new Lady of Light then?" he asked in his thousand voices, excitement still seeping through his words.

"Yes, I am," Ara responded, uneasy at the sight of him yet not averting her eyes.

"Then I suppose we will meet again," Tuales said, mocking a bow and pacing through the golden portal back into Xisq. A moment of silence followed, although it wasn't truly quiet in here. Aergo could barely hear it, and perhaps it was just his imagination but he could swear he heard the sound of a beating heart.

"What is next?" Ara broke the silence with her question. Aergo and Lily stood straight again and carefully went through some of the last artefacts, picking small items to add into the bag, while Aergo kept a close eye on Rynn's veins.

"Next, I take you to Anndar, present you to King Egìl and the people, and, if you are revealed to be the next Lady of Light, you will be crowned. After that, you decide what is next, my lady," the Nuan answered.

"Then I suggest we hurry up," Ara said with determination. "It is time to kill the High Immortal of Darkness and give me my crown."

Epilogue

The walls around them were dark and old, they had heard many secrets and had kept them well. Their purpose had been forgotten by many long ago, just as the purpose of the sisters had been forgotten by many. But they remembered. The sisters always remembered. They spoke through their minds, keeping the sacred silence that surrounded them, preventing the walls from listening in on their secrets. They heard the things that moved in the shadows, they knew that death lurked there, but some things needed to be discussed, regardless of what lurked in the darkness.

"Tell us what you have seen, sister," Sera told Yira.

"The bird will bring back the Light, and the Light will side with the Dark. They will tear open the wound we have been trying to heal. Then fire will break the Watchers, break the line. Blood, sick and twisted, will give life to something that should stay dead. The Corruptor, Galmorn will rise again and he will consume the world and leave nothing but death and corruption." Even though her words were only spoken in their minds the temple around them shivered when the memory of Galmorn surfaced after all this time.

Breaths now came from the shadows, too many to count, but never too many to fight.

"Then I suggest we kill the fire," Mera said, the blood dripping from the spike through her chin was the only sound besides the breaths in the shadows.

"We cannot kill it, if we do it would only make it burn brighter. No, this fire needs to burn out," Yira sighed, the thought of his death already saddened her. Those hiding in the shadows stepped out now, rows and rows of people of all races, their faces covered, only revealing their eyes, all of them holding a blade. The sisters attacked first, their hands swift and deadly as they found the weak spots of their enemies, shattering bones where they touched them. They did not have weapons, they were forbidden in this forgotten temple, but they had never needed weapons to be deadly. Yira clouded the minds of those foolish enough to look in her eyes, Mera made her enemies vomit blood until they died, Sera turned their skin into a field of blisters that burst with blood and gore, Cara stripped the others from their voice while Kira stripped them from hearing, making their ears bleed. The combat lasted only a few moments and corpses laid scattered across the floor while blood pooled around them. The white cloth of the sister's robes was painted with red.

"Our time has come, sisters," Yira whispered, determination in her voice. "A new Era is about to begin, and it will start with death."

Glossary

Humans
Height: 1.60-2.00m
Lifespan: 70-90 years
Skin color: fair - dark brown
Hair color: shades of blond, brown, red, black
Eye color: shades of brown, blue, green
Homeland: northern and western Plains, original homeland unknown
Capital: Anndar
Leader: King Egìl
Humans landed on the shores of Allaea near the end of the Third Age. They weren't welcomed and fell into war with the U'um and the Laretu right away. This war nearly drove the human race to extinction but Lady Nuana took the humans under her protection and allowed them to settle in what is now Anndar. The other races still look down upon humans for their lack of powers, strength, wisdom and their short lifespan however, humans have managed to survive and make themselves valuable because of their knowledge of farming, thus providing food for the Shining Lands and helping them thrive.

U'um
Height: 2.00-2.30m
Lifespan: can't die of age
Skin color: all the colors of wood
Hair color: shades of silver, green, brown and gold
Eye color: shades of brown, green and gold. Dan'um often have a shade of purple in their center
Homeland: the eastern forests
Capital: Irs Ia
Leader: Queen Serielye (Dan'um), King Edhro (Surr'um)

They have pointed ears, extreme speed, affinity for healing magic and anything nature related.

The U'um are descendants of Ilunari. Some Ilunari swore a vow to Lady Mirhan to protect her forests and in return Lady Mirhan turned them into U'um. Later the U'um split into groups, one being the Surr'um, those that lived on the forest edges, the other one the Dan'um, those that stayed in the deeper parts of the forests.

Ilunari

Height: 2.00-2.30m

Lifespan: can't die of age

Skin color: very pale

Hair color: black, sometimes silver

Eye color: shades of violet and green

Homeland: Iri'iun

Capital: Cysta Imen

Leader: Brim Caliannae

They have pointed ears, are extremely fast, strong and light-footed. They are also often gifted with some form of magic, mainly magic connected to air as they were created by the Lord of Air. Ilunari are considered the wisest of races because of their past endeavors to collect as much knowledge of the world as possible. Not many see them outside of their homeland.

Laretu

Height: 2.30-3.10m

Lifespan: 90-120 years

Skin color: shades of grey

Hair color: shades of ashen blond, brown and black

Eye color: shades of grey, green and blue

Homeland:

Capital: Murra

Leader: Warchief Kanu

They have ram-like horns that are often adorned with rings. Laretu are known for their incredible strength and resistance to pain. They are formidable warriors and skilled crafters of weapons and jewelry, their cuisine is admired all across the world just like their skills in battle.

Kurr

Height: 1.70-2.00m

Lifespan: 80-130 years

Skin color: lightly tanned to sunkissed

Hair color: shades of brown and red

Eye color: shades of yellow, orange and red

Homeland: High Forests

Capital: Rindun

Leader: Ebur of the Wolves

Kurr have slightly pointed ears. Nearly every Kurr was born with powers that fully develop after they have been given their Mark, a sacred tattoo. All Kurr possess the gift of regeneration allowing them to heal even the most severe wounds within a matter of days. Kurr also possess incredible sight and hearing.

Kir'in

Height: 1-70-2.00m

Lifespan: 800-820 years

Skin color: pale skin

Hair color: shades of black, green and white

Eye color: shades of blue and green

Homeland: Fanglake and surrounding lands

Capital: Xisq

Leader: Empress Lyana

Kir'in have fangs and are considered the most attractive race, their beauty and voice naturally have a charm to them. Kir'in are known to be the traders of the world but also as assassins and thieves.

Arkul

Height: 2.50-3.10m

Lifespan: 80-110

Skin color: reddish brown to black

Hair color: white or grey although they dye it red quite often

Eye color: shades of brown and grey

Homeland: the Red Mountains

Capital: Shagar

Leader: Arin Bloodborn

Arkul are the ancestors of the Laretu. They can have up to 5 horns and have a bony tail. Their homeland only has red-colored water so their skin and hair is often reddish because of the water they wash it with.

Abariimm

Height: 3.00m

Lifespan: can't die

Skin color: copper, silver and gold

Hair color: white, black, silver, copper or gold (same color as their wings)

Eye color: silver or gold (glowing and without pupils)

They have wings with a wingspan between the 10-15m in the same color as their hair.

The Abariimm are the first creations. They are all-knowing and all-powerful and completely neutral and emotionless. The Abariimm are the judges of everything and it is them who decide who becomes the ruler of an aspect. They also decide to which of the Whispering Halls souls go after their death and who gets chosen to become a High Immortal.

Lady Nuana

The High Immortal guardian of Light and ruler of the Shining Lands who was murdered at the end of the Third Age. She and her sister, Lady Megana, settled in Allaea to keep the balance. Nuana was the one who created the Nuan race and protected the humans when they were on the brink of extinction.

Lady Megana

The High Immortal guardian of Darkness and ruler of the Shadow Lands who is suspected to have murdered her sister, Lady Nuana. Megana settled with her sister in Allaea to keep the balance. Lady Megana sent her troops into the Shining Lands after her sister was murdered, thus starting the War of Shattered Light. Ever since the first invasion Megana hasn't been seen in the world.

Elebok

The Realm of Passage, also known as the Twilight Realm. It serves as a gateway to most other realms, including the one to the Whispering Halls. Only High Immortals, souls of the dead and certain individuals can freely pass through here.

The Academy of Nirs Imak

A school started by Nirs Imak to teach mortals about magic and how to control their powers. Positioned close to Telryn, the mage city, and a valuable asset in the War of Shattered Light. The Academy is also a place of knowledge, history and myth. People with magical abilities from all races come there to learn about magic.

Nirs Imak

High Immortal Elder of magic and teaching. Born a mortal Ilunari with incredible magical abilities he was made a High Immortal after his death. He spent many years trying to control his own powers and was locked away deep in the dungeons under Allaea where he suffered in solitude until he had control over his abilities. After this he decided to teach others control so nobody had to suffer like him.

The Whispering Halls

The Whispering Halls are several neighbouring realms where the souls of the dead go. There are many halls and where you go is decided by the Abariimm who judge your soul and your actions upon entering. Both mortal and Immortal souls go here but can never be retrieved. The worst hall is the Silent Hall and the best ones are the Hall of Eraín, the Fertile Hall and the Singing Hall. Once placed in a hall you are bound there and cannot travel to another hall or realm ever again.

Lady Mirhan

High Immortal Elder of the forest, healing, growth and life. She is a daughter of Sulvimaronth and the protector of the U'um, she is the one who turned willing Ilunari into the U'um who now walk the world. When she was born most of the land was dead or dying, she couldn't bear to see it so she cut herself and let her blood heal the world and give it life. It is her blood that runs underneath the earth and gives the gift of life to everything that grows.

The Silver Eyed

The Silver Eyed is a High Immortal soul that was cursed to live within a mortal body when they stood up to protect mortal people. Their body dies when the lifespan of that body is over, or, in case of immortal races, after 10.000 years. Their soul however, reincarnates into a new body every time, taking their memories with them. The Silver Eyed possesses knowledge about everything, whether it is in the past, present or future, although they know every possible future they do not know which one will happen until it actually happens.

The White Creatures of Kadhren

The White Creatures of Kadhren are a great variety of animals born on the slopes of Kadhren. They are guides that can lead one to hidden or forgotten places that you couldn't get to without them. They are also said to be able to take one to other realms. The Silver Eyed are one of the few people who can summon them because of their ultimate knowledge.

Master Irion

High Immortal of Passing and Lord of Elebok. He makes sure the gates in Elebok are safe and that souls pass on through in peace. Besides that he is also a trainer and mentor to Naka, he is the one that crafted Nárymm and handed it to her.

Nuans

A race crafted by Lady Nuana from the purest Light to protect and serve her. Every part of them is perfectly white except for their pupils and their blood, which is almost black. They were all killed before Lady Nuana's murder, only Ara-Ashin survived.

The Dance of Darkness

The Dance of Darkness is a sacred and powerful form of combat. In this dance the minds of both dancers entwine due to the movements. If both perform the dance perfectly they will both remain unharmed and they are then free to fight however they like. If one makes a misstep their mind is shattered, if one is slower than the other it results in injuries and mental pain. The dance can be done with any weapon, even without. The Dance of Darkness is considered one of the hardest of dances just like the Dance of Light. The most difficult of dances is the Dance of Balance, but only very few know this dance.

The 5 sisters

The 5 High Immortal sisters are guides and warriors who are tasked to protect this world from an ancient enemy and fight any signs of it, they also try and maintain the balance of the world as best as they can. Each of them has a unique power that is locked from its full potential by a mutilation.

Yira - the Mist Eyed, she is the leader of the sisters with her ability to see into the future and receive mental messages from other High Immortals. Her powers are those of the mind and are channeled mainly through her eyes. She can fill up another's mind entirely and then crush it completely, the mist in her eyes was meant as a limitation but Yira managed to take control of it and use it to her advantage.

Kira - the Deaf. She has the power to completely strip an area from sound or a person from hearing, her ears are covered with crystal so she herself cannot hear what she is taking away. This crystal also makes her lose the ability to make someone hear what she wants them to hear.

Cara - the Mute. She has the ability to let out a sound powerful enough to kill. 7 moonstone rings bind her lips together to prevent her from using her ability to make people do anything she tells them to, be it a mortal or High Immortal being.

<u>Sera</u> - the Untouchable. She has the power to inflict lethal burns and blisters to anyone she touches with her skin. She could also choose to inflict incredible pain upon those who touch her. Her entire skin is covered in crystal which is to prevent her from using her ability to drain the lifeforce from her surroundings through her skin.

Mera - the Impaled. She has the power to inflict any illness on people near her. A moonstone spike was pierced through her jaws to keep them together, preventing her from speaking, since her voice instantly kills most living things.